Van Buren District Library

W9-BUS-789

DISCARDED

Not Exactly the
THREE
MUSKETEERS

Not Exactly the
THREE
MUSKETEERS

JOEL ROSENBERG

TOR®

A TOM DOHERTY ASSOCIATES BOOK
NEW YORK

Ros

This is a work of fiction. All the characters and events portrayed in this novel are either fictitious or are used fictitiously.

NOT EXACTLY THE THREE MUSKETEERS

Copyright © 1999 by Joel Rosenberg

All rights reserved, including the right to reproduce this book, or portions thereof, in any form.

This book is printed on acid-free paper.

Edited by Claire Eddy

A Tor Book
Published by Tom Doherty Associates, Inc.
175 Fifth Avenue
New York, NY 10010

Tor Books on the World Wide Web:
http://www.tor.com

Tor® is a registered trademark of Tom Doherty Associates, Inc.

Design by Lisa Pifher

Library of Congress Cataloging-in-Publication Data

Rosenberg, Joel.
     Not exactly the three musketeers / Joel Rosenberg. — 1st. ed.
     p.   cm.
     "A Tom Doherty Associates book."
     ISBN 0-312-85782-9 (alk. paper)
     I. Title.
     PS3568.O786N598   1999
     813'.54—dc21   98-43785
                                                        CIP

First Edition: February 1999

Printed in the United States of America

0   9   8   7   6   5   4   3   2   1

3/99
PHT

This one is for (in order of seniority):
Doran, Judy, Kendra, Rachel, and Zara

Not Exactly the
THREE
MUSKETEERS

1

Their Attention is Arrested

"There will be payment for your crimes, foul deceiver. Justice demands an accounting!"

Enh.

Beneath the flickering of the uncaring stars, the smoking torches, and the slow, crimson-to-orange-to-blue pulse of the distant faerie lights, the handsome young warrior leveled the point of his absurdly too-short spear at where the obese form of the wicked prince cringed in a bed that was too small, although understandably so: a full-sized bed would have taken up too much room.

"Aye," the young warrior said, his voice a stage whisper that could carry as far as need be, his accent foreign although impossible to place, "you may count on it, traitor Prince. You sold out Barony Furnael, and today there'll surely be an accounting."

That had already been said, and not particularly well, either.

"By my fathers and theirs, I swear there'll be an accounting," the ramrod-straight nobleman echoed, clapping his hand to the young warrior's shoulder. "I swear that to you, Pirondael, and to you, Walter Slovotsky."

Again, he repeated himself. Redundantly.

Argh.

Neither the warrior nor the nobleman at his side seemed to notice how the prince's hand fumbled with a blade under his pillow. It wasn't as though it was hidden from them, but their gaze never left the prince's face.

"An accounting," the evil prince said with a snicker, "you'd have an accounting, would you? Of course I sold off your barony, Furnael. It was dead, gone, lost, a rotting corpse, stinking in the sun. Are those words you do not understand, dear Baron? If the corpse could serve Bieme, then how could I not let the Holts consume the body bite by bite? Why should I not have allowed them to feast on the carrion?" He leaned forward, as though about to impart a secret, and the baron leaned forward as though to receive it, pausing dramatically, as no word would have been able to be heard through the gasps.

Pirojil leaned back in his seat as the scene played itself predictably, inexorably, repetitively toward the moment that Pirondael would stab Furnael, and then Walter Slovotsky would kill the prince with the single throw of a knife.

He had seen much better, but what had he expected? *Birth of an Empire* was hardly a classic in the spirit of *Iranys* or *Tea for the Tendentious*. The stage was too small, and the actors were by no means the best in the empire.

It did have some virtues, though: for one thing, of the three playhouses open in Biemestren, the House of Wise Tidings was the only one featuring a production Pirojil had not already seen at all, much less repeatedly. For another thing, the lighting was well done: save for the stage, the room was dark, and in the dark, Pirojil was no more ugly than anybody else; his massive, irregular brows, his huge broken nose and jutting jaw did not offend.

At that thought, his blunt fingers went to the signet ring on his finger, the gem as always turned inwards. Of his birthright, it was all that he had kept, though he didn't know why he kept it; Pirojil had long since given up any nostalgia about his short childhood.

The worst thing about the play, though, was the play. Who was this idiot playwright, and what could be done to stop him before he wrote again?

"Aiee!" Baron Furnael screamed. "I am stabbed."

Enough. That was enough for Pirojil. Some light theater in the dark was one thing; to watch an incompetent pretty boy—the hair at his temples whitened to simulate middle age because he wasn't enough of an actor to simply act middle-aged—prance about the stage awkwardly pretending, well, that was not a way to spend the rest of the evening.

Enough.

Time to go back to the rooms, or maybe stop by the barracks. The small detachment from Barony Cullinane was billeted in the imperial barracks, and perhaps there would be something interesting to do there, or in one of the taverns that sprouted up in the neighborhood like mushrooms on a cow flop.

There would be, at least, a fight to get into. The feel of blood on his knuckles or even in his mouth would distract him, for a while. You did the best you could, after all.

He rose and apologetically worked his way to the aisle—there was no need to interfere with the rapt enjoyment of the audience— then up the stone steps to the exit passageway, just barely conscious of the way he reflexively rerigged his sword to hang properly at his side, hilt forward, not quite projecting from his cloak.

As he walked down the sharp-edged stone steps to the mud of the street, three men silently detached themselves from the shadows outside of the theater and moved quickly across the street toward him.

If Durine and Kethol had been there, he would have braced them without thinking of it, planning on faking at the one on the right, then taking the center one for himself, leaving left-handed Kethol the one on the left; Durine could take the one on the right, and then turn to help him out, if needed. Best to get in close, fast, before he found out whether or not they had pistols. And if there were more waiting in the shadows, best to get these three out of the way.

But he was alone, and they were three, and he was many things, but he was not a fool; without warning, Pirojil broke from a walk into a run and made for the alleyway.

There were cries behind him, which suited him just as well. He added his own: "Fire, I smell fire!" and broke from a trot into a full run, dodging refuse and leaping over a drainpipe, figuring that whoever the three were, they'd not be foolish enough to follow an armed man into a dark alley.

If they were, they'd find him waiting for a moment at the other end of the alley, and have two down before the third one was ready. But he'd only wait for a moment, to see if they were fools.

Four others were waiting for him as he exited the alley at a dead run. One held a naked sword in one hand and a flintlock pistol in the other; the second, a short fighting spear with a brass ferrule at the butt for when he preferred to club rather than stab; the third, just a sword; and the last carried a lantern on a pole.

The larger of the two swordsmen, the one with the pistol, took a step forward, brushing aside his own cloak to reveal the red and silver livery of the Home Guard, with the embroidered cuffs that labeled him an officer, as though the pistol hadn't.

Well, maybe the pistol hadn't—but displaying the pistol had. Pirojil's flintlock pistol was concealed in his cloak; he wasn't an officer.

"You're the one they call Pirojil?" he asked.

The one with the spear snickered. "He's sure ugly enough to be."

In another country, in another time, Pirojil would have had his ears for that. Not out of rank, but in a fair fight, one on one. He entered the face for his very private mental book of accounts; someday, if possible, he would repay the fellow with interest.

But that was for some possible future, and this was here and now, and all he did was say, "I am Pirojil."

The leader nodded. "Very well. The dowager empress wants to see you."

Pirojil could have asked, Which one?

There were, after all, two dowager empresses: one, Andrea Cullinane, the widow of the Old Emperor and the mother of the former heir; the other, Beralyn Furnael, the mother of the reigning emperor, Thomen Furnael. And both dowager empresses were in Biemestren at the moment, along with some others from Castle Cullinane accompanying Walter Slovotsky, who had mysteriously disappeared three nights ago.

But Pirojil knew which of the two widows of dead emperors would send armed men after him, and which one would merely have sent for him, trusting him, as well she could, to come to her side if he had to hack his way through bodies to do so.

"Then I am, of course, at her service," he said, as dryly as he could manage.

He nodded as he unbuckled his sword and handed it over along with his own pistol—that saved them the trouble of searching him. If necessary, he could sell his life dearly with the small dagger strapped to his left forearm.

Or with his bare hands.

It didn't make much difference.

"It doesn't make much difference," Kethol said, adjusting the patch over his right eye before reaching across the table to remove a single bone from the stack and add it to his pile, and it didn't matter much at all: the stack was topped by a triangular bone, point up, and there were exactly two bones below that could possibly be removed without causing the stack to collapse. Granted, things were made no easier for playing on a rough-hewn table, finished only in dirt and soot and dried beer, but it would have been the same on a proper, smoothly polished oak table as well. The only difference would be the sound of the bones as they hit the table.

He tilted up his bowl, draining the last of the beef and barley soup.

He had won again, and it was one of Tyrnael's men who would pay for his food and drink, and not just tonight's, but a good tenday of eating and drinking. There was little to it: just a matter of thinking things through a few more steps than the others could; just a matter of saving the bulk of his drinking until after he was done gambling for the night.

Kethol liked the feel of that. The money might be coming from the pockets of the soldiers, but it had been put there by Tyrnael, and there was a certain pleasure in taking money from the nobility. It wouldn't have been as pleasant, of course, as taking it off Baron Tyrnael's dead body, but this was much safer.

Fister ran unclean fingers through his beer-spattered beard, then turned and spat on the ground. "Agh. No place to play, and only three plays to make."

"Two," Kethol said. "Pull the pinbone like you're thinking, and the round one will give enough to lever the base to one side."

Fister cocked his head to one side. "You think so, do you?"

"Double the stakes, and you win if it works."

Kethol was already stacking his own bones when the sounds of tick, bop, and *rattlerattlerattlerattle* told of the collapse of the stack.

His fingers, moving much more dexterously than such large-knuckled digits ought to have, finished stacking his own bones, then stacked Fister's on top of them. "Twenty-three, I make it," he said. Kethol couldn't read, but he could count just fine.

It was while Fister was reaching below the table that Kethol finally noticed that all the other soldiers in the tavern were in the green livery of Tyrnael, except for one youngster in brown Adahan garb who was already making for the front door. He affected not to notice the way that two Tyrnaelians had taken their beer mugs and edged down the bar toward the front door, neatly blocking his escape.

It was past time to leave.

"Now," Kethol said, "if you'll just be paying up, I'll be on my way." He stood slowly.

That was the wrong thing to say. "You'll be playing again; let a man have a chance for some revenge."

It was suddenly quieter and colder in the room.

"I'll be seeing the money first," Kethol said. No harm in making that move, even though Fister had a counter to it. Fister would bring the money out, and then Kethol would have to play him again, and again, until either Kethol lost—as though he could lose against an idiot like this—or the Tyrnaelian owed more than he possibly could pay, at which point the fists would start flying. That was something that Kethol could only forestall with a blade or pistol, but to draw either without provocation—and surely nobody present would testify that he had been provoked—would bring him into conflict with the laws against informal dueling, and not merely the expected-to-be-violated regulations against an honest fight now and then. The emperor himself had been a judge before assuming the Silver Crown; he took his laws seriously, and offenses personally.

The informal rules had almost the force of law themselves; they were clear, and not often violated: Kethol would be left beaten, though not beyond the easy repair of the nearest Spidersect healer, and in the confusion all his money would have disappeared, and his weapons, too.

So as Fister shrugged and brought his pouch onto the table, Kethol echoed his shrug and started to take his seat. Moving smoothly, neither quickly nor slowly, Kethol drew the knife from the belt of the Tyrnaelian on his left and stabbed downward, hard.

The knife pierced Fister's sleeve, pinning his arm to the table. Kethol grabbed at Fister's purse with one hand, pulling the table—beer mugs, bones, Fister and all—toward himself. He slipped the purse down the front of his own tunic, freeing both hands: his left hand to scoop a beer mug up to slam into the face of the Tyrnaelian who had unwittingly donated the knife, while the back of his right fist snapped up and into Fister's jaw, slamming it shut.

Now all he had to do was escape. The front door was blocked, but the door to the kitchen stood open, waiting, inviting. Kethol plunged through—

—bowling over the fat innkeeper's even fatter wife, who had been standing in front of the man-high hearth, stirring a bubbling vat of the same beef and barley soup that now warmed Kethol's belly. He snatched the blackened, food-encrusted ladle from down over the fireplace and splashed a stream of hot soup toward the door to forestall any pursuit before exiting out the back door and into the night, picking his way carefully through the alley while he switched the patch from his right eye to his left, brightening the night considerably.

Shortly, he would be able to dispense with the patch entirely, and by the time the Tyrnaelians went looking for a dark-haired Cullinane man with an eye patch, Kethol would have the dye washed from his red hair and be looking out at the world with his two good eyes.

All in all, not a bad evening, although it would have been nicer if—

"One moment, if you will," sounded from behind him. Kethol turned to face a large Tyrnaelian, sword drawn.

"Bide a while, if you please," sounded from in front of him. There was another; he was surrounded.

"Very well." He drew his own blade. "As you will." Two against one wasn't Kethol's favorite odds, but if running was impossible, then so be it: let the night end with a spurt of blood. Although it was times like this that he wished he hadn't given up the buskins and hunting knife of a woodsman for a soldier's boots and sword.

But that decision had been made long ago, and now . . .

He took a hesitant step forward. Feint toward the one in front, and then—

"As entertaining as this would be," another voice sounded, as a squad of imperials surrounded Kethol and the Tyrnaelians, stepping out of the darkness as though from behind a curtain, "we have some business with this soldier, if you're Kethol of Barony Cullinane."

Kethol doubted that denial would do him very much good, even if it was believed. None of the imperials looked like the gullible sort. "That I am."

"I know." The imperial, a tall, long-faced man whose clothing and well-tended beard spoke of noble origins, waved his free hand at the Tyrnaelians. "Begone, in the name of the dowager empress." He turned to Kethol as though they had already left. "She has business with you, Kethol," he said.

Just as well, Kethol thought.

❀   ❀   ❀

Just as well, Durine thought, as the two footpads approached him from the rear.

If it had gotten much later, I'd have had to go back to the rooms and get some sleep. It would be a shame to go home empty-handed, but that happened sometimes. Kethol would understand; not every hunt brought game.

The footsteps slowed, sounding tentative. They'd realized how big he was, and were getting nervous. So he huddled deeper into his cloak, and added an extra little weave to his step, then clung to a lamppost for support for a moment before staggering on.

The two behind him separated, one ducking down a side street; off in the distance, his feet made *pittapittapittapitta* sounds as he started to run down three streets, three sides of a square, while Durine staggered down one.

Durine stopped, shook his head as though clearing it, then continued on rapidly, the footpad behind him picking up the pace. He gathered his fox-trimmed cape more tightly about himself for just a moment, using the movement to cover how he untied it from his shoulders. Durine wore the cape for more sensible reasons than the way its formlessness tended to hide his size.

The two of them had fairly good timing: the runner came around the corner, half out of breath, just as the other one closed from behind.

"Please, good sir," the runner said. He was really too young to be doing this: perhaps fifteen, beardless without effort, dressed in a workingman's blousy coarse-woven shirt and cheap wool trousers that had been patched often, if not well. But he had just the right look of desperation as he said, "Please, sir, you must help me. My mother—"

That was the moment when the lead-shot-filled cosh was supposed to come down on Durine's head, knocking him down, dazing him. It might not be enough to knock him out, of course, but a bit of work with their boots would fix that. They might not kill him or even leave him crippled, but they would leave with his valuables in their pouches and his blood on the ground.

It would have worked neatly, but Durine had already ducked to the right, his left arm flinging his cloak back like a fisherman tossing a net; there were several gold coins sewn into the hem of it, both as weights and as part of their collective cache of money.

His left foot came up and caught the robber in the gut, kicking him away, the combination of the cloak and the kick taking him out of action at least for a moment, although Durine wouldn't have minded if the robber smashed his head open on the wall behind him.

Moving swiftly, the boy in front of him brought up a knife, but Durine had been looking for that, too, and his left hand came down, seizing the wrist and squeezing it tight so that he could feel bones grind against each other, while his right hand slapped the boy's head back and forth once, twice, three times.

Durine let the limp body drop to the ground, then stooped to pluck the knife from the boy's fingers. No sense in letting a nice knife go to waste.

The other robber had bounced off the wall and fallen on his too-pretty face. The fool didn't have the presence of mind to lie still and hope Durine wouldn't bother with him—he was starting to struggle under the cloak, trying to get to his hands and knees and get it off him at the same time. Durine didn't want to get it all dirty and bloody, so he simply brought the bottom of his fist down on the hidden head, then snatched his cloak away.

The cosh fell from nerveless fingers, and Durine kicked at the head with his boot, just once.

Once was enough.

Durine neither dawdled nor rushed as he retrieved their weapons, using the boy's knife to slice both of the coshes open, letting a stream of lead shot fall to the street. Durine never believed in carrying a cosh; he had hands, after all.

The older robber's knife was a long rusty blade of cheap steel; Durine bent it double against the wall, and threw it to one side. But the boy's knife was another matter. Not a bad knife, at that. A finger-

long blade of good sharp steel, single-edged, wooden hilt tightly
wound with brass wire, flat steel pommel. The sort of thing a nobleman might carry at his waist. Certainly stolen, and probably worth
keeping. With a little work on a new hilt—perhaps a thicker one that
would fit better in Durine's oversized fingers? he would have to think
about that—it would be unrecognizable, as it would have to be if he
were to keep it.

He wouldn't want to be accused of theft, after all.

Durine sliced off a piece of the boy's shirt, wrapped the knife
tightly, and stashed it in his own pouch before he knelt down next
to the bodies. Sometimes it didn't work. Sometimes, even on a nice
bright night like this, a night made for robbery, a pair would go to
ground after their first score, and if that was so, if Durine was their
first intended victim, that meant that Durine would have to find
another set of robbers or go home none the—

Ah. A fat purse gave up a nice handful of bright coins, and the
hidden coachman's-style belt pouch disgorged a trio of engraved
rings and a small handful of unmounted—well, now unmounted—
jewels, although it was hard to tell what they were in the dark.

No matter. The rings would melt down easily enough. The jewels, along with the money, he pocketed, and walked away, not both-
ering to check to see if by some chance either of the two footpads
had survived. What were they going to do, go to an armsman and
complain?

Durine grinned to himself as he picked up his pace, now without
a trace of weave in his walk.

It was all logical, and Durine prided himself on being logical, if
not particularly clever. He and his friends needed more money than
simple soldiers earned, but Durine was unable to take it by honest
means like gambling, and he was almost as unwilling as he was un-
suited to being a thief.

On the other hand, there was more than one way to graze in the
tall grasses that Biemestren had become with the growth in trade of
the empire, and there was little enough else to do with the family
safely in residence at Biemestren Castle. If he could not or would

not graze in the grasses himself, he could eat of those that did, and sometimes the grazing was good, and when the grazing was good the animals were fat with coin.

He was still silently congratulating himself as he approached the barracks and found himself surrounded by a troop of men in imperial livery.

"And you would be Durine?" the officer asked.

"Well, yes." He shrugged. "Somebody has to be. Why not me?"

2

The Dowager Empress

The wind from the city below changed again, bringing the smell of horse urine and woodsmoke to her nostrils.

Beralyn Furnael, dowager empress of Holtun-Bieme, quickened her pace along the broad stone walkway atop the battlements, a walkway that was lit only by flickering torches, widely spaced.

She seethed as she walked the parapets, and swore half-remembered oaths taught to her in childhood by a family retainer more years ago than she tried to think about. As she passed the guard station, both of the soldiers leaped to a brace, despite her standing orders that everybody simply stay out of her way but otherwise ignore her during her nightly walk.

She would have stopped to discuss the breach with them, but she was too tired, and felt that if she stopped, she wouldn't be able to start again. Besides, she already had an appointment to put a scare into some soldiers; there was no need for an appetizer before the meal.

On to the next guard station . . .

There were fourteen such stations along the outer wall of the keep; she had now passed a dozen, and had but two more to trudge past if her count was correct, which it was, more often than not.

She had been making an effort to count of late. It felt as though the last few guard stations got further and further apart every day. She was getting too old, that was the problem, and while that problem would cure itself eventually, the rest of it wouldn't. This daily

walk—rain, shine, sleet, or hail—around the top of Castle Biemestren's walls helped to keep her going, but tenday by tenday, it took
more time and more effort, and the climb up the ninety-three steps
to the parapet got harder and harder all the time.

But iron will would succeed where soft flesh alone would have
failed, and before she stepped off into the Great Dark, her son would
be secure on his throne and his new dynasty established. Her nightly
walk didn't just help to keep her thick old blood oozing slowly
through her veins; it was a time to help her focus her thinking. The
Widow of Biemestren Castle, they called her, and the walkway above
the walls that encircled the outer ward was now called the Widow's
Path, the term laden with equal portions of scorn and fear.

Good. Let them all fear her. Scorn was perfectly acceptable, if
the fear came with it. She had lost her husband and one son to the
cursed Cullinanes, and while that maniac Jason Cullinane, the Cullinane heir, had chosen to abdicate the throne in favor of Thomen,
that earned him and them no good will.

Not from her. Thomen ought to have been the heir in the first
place, not given the crown because Jason Cullinane just didn't want
to be emperor.

Besides, the Cullinane heir could probably reclaim the crown if
and when he pleased. Beralyn didn't believe in fooling herself; while
she didn't share the awe of the almost legendary Cullinanes and their
Other Side friends, that put her in a small minority.

Idiots, all of them.

She had known the late, great Karl Cullinane all too well. He
had been deft with a sword, no doubt, had had a certain air of authority and competence about him, but he had been clumsy enough
to let both Rahff and Zherr get killed in his presence. And he had
been reckless enough to get himself killed—and not leading his
troops in battle, for which there would at least have been some sense
and sanity, but while leading some pursuers away from his son, like
a mother deer leading hunters from her hidden fawns.

He had gotten what the mother deer usually got, and Beralyn
Furnael missed him not at all.

It wasn't like he was completely gone, either. Even dead, he lived on in legend: Karl Cullinane, the Old Emperor.

If she had had any spare spit, she would have spat. On all the Cullinanes. Jason Cullinane was off somewhere, haring about, searching for some childhood friend who was in trouble, knowing full well that even though he was avoiding his responsibilities in the empire, others would look after his barony and his family for him, just as others had looked after his father's responsibilities for him. Jason's mother, Andrea, and his sister, Aiea, now slept safely in a guest suite not two floors away from Thomen, their doors guarded by soldiers from Barony Cullinane and Thomen's explicit and very public command that no harm was ever to come to them.

Pfah. Beralyn could have laughed while they were murdered in their beds. If that wouldn't have made Thomen look like an accomplice in murder. If that wouldn't have made the emperor look like he couldn't even protect people under his own roof. If Thomen wouldn't have known that Beralyn was behind that. If, if, if—the bile rose in her throat at the taste of ifs.

Captain Derinald was waiting for her at the last guard station. He was a tall, slim man with a careful way of speaking in counterpoint to the sloppy hand-waving gestures that spoke of his Nerish upbringing.

"Good evening, Your Majesty," he said, his hands spread wide as though in greeting to a long-lost friend. "It's good to see you looking so well."

She grunted. "I understand that it is quite dark, Derinald, but even in the blackness of nights you should be able to see—and smell, if that tiny nose of yours is good for anything except impressing the ladies with how large the mustache underneath it is—that I'm sweating like a pig, just as you should easily be able to hear that I'm wheezing like a horse. I'm a feeble old woman, and easily gulled— as you well know—but I'm not easily moved by hollow pity or empty flattery."

"Your Majesty is, of course, correct that she is not easily moved by such; permit me to tender my apologies." He offered the crook of his elbow, which she accepted with a quick tightening of her lips in gratitude. Walking up the stone steps was painful, but walking down was dangerous.

"Since you've returned, I take it you found them?" she asked.

"Of course, and as Your Majesty instructed," Derinald said, "they await you in the throne room."

"And my son?"

"Abed, presumably asleep."

"Good."

Thomen probably wouldn't approve of her intentions with the Cullinane soldiers, but what he didn't know, he wouldn't protest. What her son hadn't forbidden, Derinald would know better than to report to him. There were legends that the way a wizard created a thrall was to steal its soul and keep it in a bottle. There were simpler ways to do that if you were the dowager empress. It was merely a matter of finding someone who you could persuade you would reward for loyalty and silent obedience, and who you would even more certainly punish for any lack of either.

It was hardly necessary to ride such a thrall with sharp spurs and a heavy bit. The certainty of punishment and an occasional reward were sufficient in and of themselves; taking the thrall into one's confidence sealed him in his obedience and industry.

In this case, it was in essence a very simple plan, and there was no need to keep it from loyal Derinald.

Thomen had wanted that horrible Walter Slovotsky to investigate that problem in Keranahan, thinking it not much of a problem at all—and, besides, it was his sort of thing. A no-doubt-pretty young noble girl, who needed some assistance? The legendary and entirely overrated Walter Slovotsky was perfect for such an assignment. He would likely charm half the women of Keranahan out of their clothing and onto the nearest flat surface, and if in doing that he—whom Beralyn held responsible for Zherr's murder just as surely as if he himself had wielded the knife instead of Pirondael—might leave his own back open for someone else's knife, Beralyn would waste no tears.

Which was why she had been prevailing upon her son to order Walter Slovotsky to Keranahan.

It was just his sort of thing. He could take a carriage and ride out there, planning on retrieving the girl to Biemestren, spending his days pumping her in the carriage while enjoying the scenery.

He certainly would make himself a nuisance there; perhaps he could just get himself killed.

But Walter Slovotsky had dodged: he had left unceremoniously, in the middle of the night, before Thomen had the chance to make his suggestion and order.

Still, with Walter Slovotsky gone, a few Cullinane soldiers would do.

Either they would succeed in Keranahan, and their success would be hers, although it would only be a small one, or they would fail, and their failure would be the Cullinanes', and Beralyn would make that a major embarrassment. It was like that child's game of egg, rock, and water. Egg floats in water, rock smashes egg, water washes rock.

If your opponent picked before you, you could always win. And if you could force him to choose . . .

She touched at her pocket, where the letter rested.

"Take me to my rooms. I'll want to bathe and change before I meet them."

Derinald nodded. "Of course, Your Majesty. It will do them no harm to await your pleasure."

She gave a derisive sniff at the very thought that one could even *think* otherwise.

Pirojil had never liked throne rooms, and this one was worse than most. Too many memories, some of them personal.

Even before the conquest of Holtun had turned the two countries into the empire of Holtun-Bieme, the Old Emperor—then, technically, Prince Karl Cullinane—had had Prince Pirondael's bric-a-brac self-portraiture stripped away from the walls, the carpets rolled up and put away, and the tables and chairs and rows of benches moved over to the Home Guard mess, leaving the large room stark and empty save for the elevated throne at the far end. The throne room hadn't gotten much use for audiences, not during the war years, and not during the following ones—although the Old Emperor had been known to bring in a bunch of randomly chosen Home Guard soldiers for a practice melee with padded sticks every now and then, giving a special bruising to any one of them who he even suspected might be taking it easy on him.

Pirojil rubbed at his shoulder at the memory. The truth was that he had just been suffering from a spot of indigestion that day—but that hadn't saved him from the Old Emperor.

He suppressed a grin at the memory. He had done a lot more for Karl Cullinane than take a few bruises with good enough grace.

There was a time when he and the other two had ridden through hell at the Old Emperor's side, the sole survivors of the whole troop that Karl Cullinane had taken with him on the foolish escapade that had gotten him killed, as Durine had always known that his excesses would. Nobles didn't go out and risk their own tender hides; that's what they had soldiers for.

But even after Karl Cullinane's death, while Jason Cullinane was the heir and Thomen Furnael but the regent, Pirojil, Kethol, and Durine might have been, at least in theory, ordinary soldiers, but they had been his companions in battle, and that had brought a certain status.

But now it was different. Lush Kiaran tapestries in deep, restful shades of rich forest green and midnight blues covered the walls, and ankle-deep carpets, dark crimson like fresh blood, covered the floors.

The oak tables and chairs and benches were back, and they had spawned others—when Parliament met, the barons and major lords were dined here—and another, equally large and majestic chair had been added next to the emperor's throne.

Kethol's head cocked to one side. "I don't know why she added another throne for him," he said.

Durine just grunted; the big man didn't think it was funny, either.

Pirojil's hand dropped to where the hilt of his sword should have been, would have been, in the old days. The Old Emperor used to grin at that habit of Pirojil's, a habit that Pirojil had to consciously control.

But these days there was no Cullinane on the throne, and there was no sword at his hip. These days, the three of them were to come unarmed into the Residence, on the rare occasions when they were summoned to the Residence at all.

Pirojil turned at the sound of footsteps to see the arrival of the dowager empress, accompanied by Captain Derinald and a quartet of soldiers from the House Guard.

Her dumpy bulk was concealed by a long-sleeved black muslin dress that didn't quite cover the blocky shoes, and her dark gray hair was tied back tightly behind her head, as though keeping it tight kept her lined face from falling off.

Derinald and the rest of the soldiers were decked out in the black and white uniform of the House Guard: black leather tunic over a rough-woven cotton shirt and black cotton trousers for the soldiers; blousy white shirt and black leather vest over silver-trimmed trousers for the officer. There were some that said the House Guard were the very elite of the Home Guard, the emperor's personal troops. And there were others, like Pirojil, Kethol, and Durine, who just thought they dressed better—but Pirojil, Kethol, and Durine knew well enough to think that and not say it.

Pirojil and the other two had come to a stiff brace, which the dowager empress dismissed with a flip of her liver-spotted hand.

"Be easy, you three, be easy," she said, her eyes sunken pits in her piggish face. The flickering light of the torches on the walls enhanced the already-deep hollows in her cheeks.

The bright gold clasp at her throat, holding the collar of her dress tightly closed against her livery flesh, provided the only bright note in her dress, or her person. Her withered lips were pursed into a permanent frown, and her jawline was jowly and doughy, but the eyes still held more intelligence than Pirojil was comfortable with.

Intelligence was an important thing, he had long ago learned to his anguish and pain, but intelligence was not always a friendly thing.

"I have a problem, and I require your help in solving it," she said. "It will require some time and effort."

Kethol nodded. "Our pleasure, of course," he said, lying for all three of them.

"But you haven't heard what it is yet," she said with the slightest of sneers, as though she had taken Kethol at face value.

Pirojil smiled in agreement, enjoying the way that forced her to look upon his ugliness. "True enough, Your Majesty, but whatever you might ask us to do would be our pleasure, of course, once we explain the necessity of our absence to the baronial regent."

She sniffed.

That had been a mistake, and he should have known better; Pirojil forced himself not to wince. Doria Perlstein was holding down that job at Castle Cullinane; and Doria Perlstein was one of the Other Siders, all of whom this dowager empress hated. He shouldn't have mentioned her.

"No," the dowager empress said. "that won't be necessary. Any necessary explanations will come from Biemestren and the emperor. You will go by way of Castle Cullinane, but you are to follow orders, and not let your tongues wag excessively. Understood?"

A pointless demand, as she certainly should have known and almost certainly did know. The three of them were fealty-bound, by oaths of the mouth and intents of the heart, to the Cullinanes. The chance that they would not report in full to the Cullinane regent was, at best, infinitesimally small.

But the dowager empress knew that, which meant that either she was just venting her spleen pointlessly or she had some subtler, deeper motives for giving an order she well knew they wouldn't consider obeying.

Pirojil nodded. "As you wish, Your Majesty, of course." Lying came easy to Kethol and Durine, as well:

"As you command," Durine said.

And from Kethol: "We won't discuss it."

She grunted. "Good. And as to where," she said, pulling a letter out of her pocket, "it is Keranahan. As to whom, it is Lady Leria Vor'sen."

Kethol looked over at Pirojil, who kept his face studiously blank.

Pirojil didn't know where Kethol had gotten the idea that Pirojil knew something about noble families, and he didn't much like Kethol hinting to others that he did. Durine, too, had, over the years, hinted that he suspected that Pirojil had been born noble, perhaps, but from the wrong seed perhaps, perhaps planted in the wrong womb. But there was nothing in that that Pirojil cared to display wantonly even to companions, much less to enemies.

Pirojil shook his head and spread his hands. "We're three ordinary soldiers, Your Majesty; we don't know much about such things."

Her laugh was quiet, but harsh, and held not a whiff of amusement. "I'm sure you'll do quite well, if you try hard enough. Now, Lady Leria is from an ancient Holtish lineage. You've never heard of Lord Lerian? As in Lerian's Vengeance?"

Pirojil could tell from the way Kethol didn't move that he knew what the dowager empress was talking about, but Pirojil didn't and it was only a little harder to tell the truth than it would have been for him to lie convincingly: "Apologies, Majesty, but . . ."

The dowager empress dismissed it with a wave. "Never you mind that, then. It doesn't matter. It probably won't matter to you, either, that she probably could make a good argument that she's the Euar'den heir to the Tynearian throne, but Keranahan and Holtun swallowed up Tynear and the Euar'den lineage five generations ago almost as neatly as an owl swallows a mouse—as neatly as I would have wished Bieme to have swallowed up Holtun.

"The problem is that she is a young, marriageable woman of some property and more potential political importance, placed in wardship to the barony, and she's managed to smuggle a letter out to me, asking my help, claiming that Elanee, Baroness Keranahan, is pressuring her to marry the putative baronial heir."

Durine let out another grunt. When you have spent enough years

fighting and sweating and sometimes swiving side by side with someone, you could almost read that someone's thoughts given only the
smallest of cues, and Durine's grunt spoke volumes. Durine thought
it was a trivial matter to involve the dowager empress and themselves.

He was wrong. Pirojil would have shrugged and explained it to
him if it had been politic. Anything involving the movement of money
or power toward the baron's family might not be important, but it
wasn't trivial.

Barony Keranahan was a conquered Holtish barony. The Keranahan family had given their name to the barony over which they
reigned, but they didn't rule, and while imperial policy under the
Cullinanes had been to quickly return loyal Holtish baronies to home
rule, that had slowed during Thomen Furnael's emperorship. Pirojil
thought that wise, but it didn't much matter what a common soldier
thought about it.

"It's just a minor matter, perhaps, of an overly romantic young
girl," the dowager empress went on, "but she has appealed to my
better nature, and I want to be sure that things go well with her."

Well, that was surely a lie: the dowager empress didn't have a
better nature. And Pirojil didn't believe for a moment that the fate
of one girl was something that Beralyn cared about.

But it still would bear looking into. There really shouldn't be a
problem. The baroness of a ruled barony shouldn't have had enough
authority to force any such thing.

Where was the governor, and what was he doing? Sitting on one
thumb, counting his graft with the other?

It wasn't the fact of it. An overbred, spoiled chit had been forced
into a politically convenient marriage before, and surely would be
again. But the implications bothered him.

His thoughts must have been too easy to read on his face, because the dowager empress was looking him in the eye.

"The governor's name is Treseen," she said. "His regular reports
to the emperor suggest no such problems, and while there have been
some occasional interruptions in the telegraph from Neranahan, his
reports do come in regularly, suggesting that there's nothing at all

serious wrong." She sniffed. "Except, perhaps, one hysterical girl who overreacts to an obvious sort of suggestion from the baroness of an alliance that should benefit both families, the barony, Holtun, and the empire. Or perhaps the girl is not hysterical, and is merely reacting to the head of a snake, while the body lies concealed? You will investigate, and report fully, do you hear? *Fully*."

"Of course." Pirojil nodded. "Understood, Your Majesty. But—"

"But nothing." She turned to Captain Derinald, who handed over three scrolls, each wrapped with a ribbon and sealed, although with what seal, Pirojil could not have said.

"This," she said, holding up the first one, wrapped in a beige ribbon, "is your orders, unsigned; the second is the copy for the imperial archives." She paused for a moment, as though she had changed her mind about saying something, and then went on: "You'll need to get it signed by either Baron Cullinane, if he's honoring his home with his presence," she said, her voice dripping sarcasm, "or the Cullinane regent. You'll want to present these orders to Governor Treseen, as I doubt he'll take you seriously otherwise. You leave at first light; Derinald will travel with you to Castle Cullinane, see that the orders are signed, and will return with our copy. Just so there will be no problem later."

The third scroll she held hesitantly. "This is a death warrant, signed by my son. The name is blank, although the . . . object of the warrant is described as 'a noble or subject of Barony Keranahan.' " She smiled briefly. "Yes, I know the story of Pirondael's Warrant, and while I think it's merely a tale, I've learned from it. If you were to use this, I would have to explain why to my son, and although he's a patient listener, I'll not try his patience unnecessarily. You are very simply not to use this unless you're willing to explain the necessity to me, and I am not a patient listener. But if you find it convenient, you may threaten somebody with it." She looked from face to face to face. "Do we have an understanding here?"

Pirojil nodded. "Yes, Your Majesty. But I do see some problems."

Her mouth twisted. "Oh?"

"For one thing, there's the matter of supplies and such. We're just ordinary soldiers, and while I'd be happy to spend the little I have in your service . . ."

"Adequate monies will be provided," she said.

Pirojil ducked his head. "We are grateful for—"

"I said adequate, not generous. And there will be a full accounting, so I'd suggest you practice some economy. If you've need of coin for luxuries, you'd best speak to your patron, and not expect it from the Throne. This is not some furlough to be paid for by my son from the pittance he's able to eke out in taxes, and I'll look very unkindly on anybody who sees it otherwise. Do you all understand me?" She was looking very directly at Kethol for some reason.

Kethol nodded. "Of course."

Durine did, too. "Understood, Your Majesty."

"I understand, Your Majesty," Pirojil lied.

That was the problem. He didn't understand, not really. There was a lot about this that he didn't understand at all. He doubted that the dowager empress was lying to them, not exactly, but there surely was much she was leaving out, and that could easily be much of the same.

"Good." She turned to Derinald, and laid a wrinkled hand on his arm. "You will leave with them, first thing in the morning." She turned back to Pirojil. "Now get out of my sight."

When they stayed in Biemestren, the three rented a pair of rooms at a rooming house near the imperial barracks, just down the hill, at the base of the road that led up to the keep which dominated the city below.

It was far enough away from the Biemestren refuse heap that they didn't have too many rats, and a row of two-story buildings provided enough shade that their rooms didn't heat up too much during the day.

For a small bribe to the cooks, a fresh, covered tray from the soldiers' mess arrived twice a day, which kept them out of the way of the officers. House Guard officers all too often felt that they had to keep billeted baronial troops busy with doing something, and Pirojil had mucked out enough stalls, cleaned and oiled enough pole-arms, and walked enough extra guard patrols in his time.

Besides that, their pair of rooms gave them a private enough place to share an occasional whore brought up from the city. Safer than a dungtown brothel, and cheaper, too, when you split the cost three ways.

Arranging for the rooms had taken a bit of the sort of barracks politics that Kethol always despised aloud, that he said his father, a soldier-turned-huntsman, used to swear was the ruin of good soldiering, but Pirojil didn't much mind when such things brought the sort of privacy that he and the other two liked for their own private reasons.

If Durine was moved by it, or by anything else, he didn't show it. It was the usual pattern: Kethol complained, Pirojil endured, and Durine didn't mind. Or at least he didn't mind aloud, not even to the other two.

It was one thing, of course, to be a private soldier, another to be a valued retainer, and yet another to be an expendable baronial man-at-arms in an age when private loyalties were being dissolved in an imperial soup, like overcooked turnips turning into textureless mush.

Pirojil had been a soldier long enough not to flinch at eating what was set before him, but he had been raised far away, in a house where one ate with one's backside on a well-carved chair and one's boots on a polished wooden floor, not on stools on packed dirt, and he had been used to dishes cooked properly and separately, each having its own character, not thrown in a pot to be turned into indistinguishable, neutral mush.

Pirojil had little use for mush, in any sense. If he had to be somebody's hireling, and he clearly did, he'd rather serve the Cullinanes, each of whose faces he knew, and not some dough-faced dowager empress or, much worse, an empire. You could put yourself in the way of a sword—and he had—thinking that it was your job to protect the sleeping children of the man who made sure you were housed and fed, or you could do it for the food and housing and money . . .

But not for a faceless mush of an empire.

Durine shook his massive head as he sorted through the scattering of gems and coins scattered across the rough-hewn surface of the table. "It looked better on the street," he said. "But it's still an edible piece of meat."

"Well," Pirojil said, "if it fills the belly, it will serve."

"Aye," Kethol said.

They never spoke among themselves about money and valuables, except by indirection. You did the best you could to be sure you weren't overheard, but maybe the best wasn't enough, and it was of a certainty that uncountable throats and bellies had been slit for much less than this.

Pirojil picked up one gem, a fine amber garnet with only a minor flaw, and that just a speck close to the surface. It probably hadn't been visible when mounted.

Fairly cheap gems, certainly—he had hardly expected to find Durine taking a bag of rubies and diamonds off a pair of street thieves—but the garnets were good, and the crimson quartz was superb.

Kethol had been listening at the door long enough. At Durine's and Pirojil's nods of agreement, he joined them over by the small brazier they kept in front of the unlit fireplace. They always kept it lit, carefully stoked with expensive hard coal from Tyrnael, banked to a low heat, a cauldron of vile-smelling water useful for boiling fouled pistols clean always ready.

Durine took a couple of hooks from his rucksack and used them to lift the heavy cauldron. He took one careful step to the side, then set it gently on the dirt floor, while Pirojil and Kethol donned gloves and carefully moved the iron brazier itself.

A flat stone was set underneath, intended to give the brazier a flat surface; Durine took up his hooks again and lifted the stone up, revealing a hole beneath, and a leather bag, which he handed to Pirojil, who opened it.

The bag was opened to reveal a pair of leather strips, carefully intertwined with small, mostly silver but some golden imperial marks, the leather to prevent the money from jingling together.

The gems were unceremoniously dumped into the bottom of the bag—they wouldn't clink; the bottom quarter of the bag was filled with wool yarn, and the coins held jewels against it—and the bag closed.

Pirojil smiled, and while Durine pulled up his tunic and shirt, Pirojil strapped the bag to the big man's broad and hairy back. All three of them carried ordinary pouches containing the few coins that an ordinary soldier might have, but this was their cache. An ordinary soldier couldn't put away a lot of money, not on cot and stew and a handful of coppers at the end of every tenday, but if you kept your eyes and your mind open, and hung around with the right sorts of people, it was entirely possible to quietly put away a little something to see you and a couple of friends through your old age, on the off chance that you should reach an old age.

Particularly when you spent time as bodyguard to nobles who were less concerned about money than a commoner had to be. Money was hard to come by when you couldn't simply tax for it.

They replaced the flagstone lid over the hole in the floor, Kethol carefully setting three telltale pebbles in place before covering it with a light layer of dirt and making some sort of woodsman's mark in the dirt. The brazier was replaced, and the cauldron over that. While they would take their money with them, they would try to rent this same set of rooms the next time they were billeted in Biemestren, and if this hiding place remained undetected, it would be useful then, too.

Pirojil lay down on his straw bed, his sword and pistol beside him, and wrapped his cloak about him.

Durine would have preferred that the cache be kept somewhere in Castle Cullinane—the old castle had secret passages and hiding places galore—but Kethol agreed with Pirojil that they were best off keeping it with them.

Pirojil wouldn't have left it to two-out-of-three, anyway. Not on this. Not when it came to trusting a place. Places could betray you.

Pirojil could recall a time when an ugly young boy had been kicked out of what had been, up until that moment, his home, sent out into a cold and rainy night with nothing more than his cloak, his blade, and a spavined horse, to ride far away. He had sat all night in the rain, on a hilltop overlooking that place, figuring that surely, certainly, it was all a mistake, that it would be corrected, that somebody would come after him, to apologize, to explain, to bring him back into the dryness and the warmth.

In the morning, shivering in the damp cold, his eyes finally dry, he had gotten on the horse and ridden away.

Since then, he had too often let himself get attached to people, but never, ever to places. A place would let you down, a place would betray you, and there was no way to erase the pain of that betrayal. Not when you tried to forget it, because you couldn't. Not when you tried to live with it, because it burned at you.

And not even when you returned in the middle of the night and burned it to the ground, watching from a nearby hilltop while flames and screams turned to ashes, because even after that, and even after you pissed on the ashes, the betrayal still stung.

No. Put not your trust in places. Put your trust in small bags, and watch the small bags. If you kept it with you, it was yours.

As long as you could fight to keep it.

He was quickly asleep.

3

✠ Doria

L ike mice scrabbling in a constantly panicky but utterly futile attempt to escape from a closed cardboard box, spells pushed at the back of Doria Perlstein's mind, as they had for years.

It would have been simplicity itself to let one of the few remaining ones spew out, pleasantly vomiting from her mouth into the warmth of the baronial study, gaining substance and reality, hardening in the air like streams of melted sugar turning into hard candy, a dream given flesh.

One of the spells could have persuaded the annoying, handsome Home Guard captain of anything whatsoever, and the same impish sense of humor that used to get her into trouble as a child was tempted to make him believe he was a duck. It would be more fun than she had had in years to watch him fold his arms back like wings, squat, and quack his way around the study.

But no. The years with the Hand had taught her self-control in ways she was still learning to appreciate, and suppressing that sort of urge had been an early lesson. If you were going to be a Daughter of the Healing Hand, dispensing healing comfort through a gentle touch even more often than through a healing spell, you had to manage yourself before you could begin to manage others' hurts.

Doria had no regrets. She had given up the Hand, and with that the possibility of the Hand restoring a spell, once used. Spending one of her few remaining utterly irreplaceable spells on a moment of amusement for herself and embarrassment for a pretentious, pompous twit wasn't worth considering seriously.

But the thought did relax her.

She sat back in the overstuffed chair next to the man-high fireplace and considered the captain over the rim of her cup of herb tea. She had been thinking over it too long; the tea had gone lukewarm, nowhere near the almost scalding heat she preferred. She grimaced. It was her job to handle things like this—that was what Jason Cullinane had made her regent for, and the emperor had approved it himself—but it would have been nice to have some advice.

But Walter Slovotsky and Bren Adahan and the dragon had hared off after Jason—via the Home colony in what the Therranji elves still stubbornly insisted on referring to as the Valley of Varnath—and Andrea and Aiea were still in Biemestren.

Walter Slovotsky's wife and daughters were still here, of course, but Kirah didn't have a lot of sense, Doranne was a baby, and Janie had her father's impetuousness. Best to keep them out of the way. Handling this was her responsibility, after all, not theirs.

You're the regent, she said to herself, *so rege.*

"So," she said, "Thomen's mother wants to send those three into trouble, and she wants me to order it for her."

"That's not the way I would put it, Regent." Derinald's hands fluttered like an Italian's. "I would not put it that way at all, but I don't object if you do."

She let a smile creep across her face, and recrossed her legs, conscious of the way the slit in her long skirt revealed them to good advantage. "Call me Doria."

He returned her smile, with interest that didn't feel simulated. Hmm . . . that was unusual for Beralyn. She usually chose flunkies who preferred men, as the generally unspoken but very real prejudices against such could bind them more tightly to her. This Side or the Other Side, if you held the key to somebody's closet, you owned what was inside, and if they were inside, that meant you owned them.

On the other hand, even if this one liked women, it would be beyond credibility for Beralyn to send one her way whose loyalty could be turned in bed, even if Doria was willing to.

"Very well, then: Doria. Doria, I hardly see it as much trouble,"

Derinald said. "It makes sense to have the matter looked into, and to do it without creating the sort of disturbance that an official imperial envoy would mean is simple courtesy."

"You mean politics."

"Can it not be both?"

"Well, I'll have to think on it some," she said. It would have been good to have somebody who she could discuss it with, although thank God Jason Cullinane wasn't around. Jason was a good kid, but he had probably made the best political decision of his life when he had abdicated the imperial throne to Thomen. Politics wasn't exactly a Cullinane family specialty, unless the politics involved shooting, slashing, or punching. The Furnaels were much better at real politics, and wasn't that a two-edged sword, eh?

Too bad Jason's mother wasn't here, though.

She could talk things over with Andy, and then do what seemed sensible. But Andrea Cullinane and her daughter Aiea were in residence in Biemestren, albeit temporarily, and while they weren't overtly being used as hostages, there was always that implication. There was a reason why kings and emperors enjoyed having their subordinate nobles and their families pay a call upon them every so often, effectively baring their throats to the ruling swords.

And why did Parliament—well, what they called Parliament; Doria would have called it the House of Lords—meet at Biemestren?

"That's certainly a reasonable request," Derinald said carefully. "I can't see how anyone could give voice to a complaint were you to sleep on it tonight, and then give your answer in the morning. But Her Majesty did emphasize to me that she doesn't think of this whole matter as particularly negotiable."

The veiled threat again. A threat was nonetheless real for being less than explicit.

"I'm shorthanded here, though," Doria said, "what with most of the baronial troops either on occupation duty in Holtun or off in Barony Adahan chasing down those orcs. But some of them are due back any day—I'd rather keep these three around at least until we're back up to some minimal strength."

The best way to deal with it was to delay, at least until she could decide which way to play it. Ellegon was due in a few days, and having a telepathic, fire-breathing dragon sitting out in the courtyard was a definite asset in any set of negotiations.

"I can understand why you would want that," Derinald said, shaking his head, "but I doubt that Her Majesty will brook a delay. She's not the most flexible of women, and perhaps wouldn't see the necessity." He sipped at his wine. "Particularly since I'd have to report that I've counted at least a dozen soldiers' beds in use in your barracks. Not, certainly, anything more than a skeleton crew, but I can't see how she would see that another three would be essential."

"I—"

"Doria, there's a problem," U'len said as she burst in, ahead of schedule, wiping her hands on her ragged apron.

U'len was a massive chunk of middle-aged woman, comfortably homely from the wart on the side of her nose that had three wiry black hairs projecting from it down to the preposterously battered toes that peeked out from under her skirts. Her blouse, a dingy gray to start with, was spattered with grease and bits of food and God-knew-what; she had been in her kitchen since before dawn and would be supervising the two junior cooks until past midnight, supported by an occasional sip from a clay bottle of hideously sweet blackberry wine and two short naps, one after serving breakfast, one after lunch.

Doria rose to her feet slowly, carefully, simulating regret probably not well enough to fool the imperial captain, but he probably wasn't disposed to be fooled. It wasn't as important to fool him as it was to stall him.

Some problems could handle themselves, if you just left them alone, and political machinations in the capital might well turn Beralyn's attention to some other matter, or time alone might give Doria some other opportunity to duck this problem without confronting it directly.

"What appears to be the problem, U'len?" she asked. "Surely there's nothing and nobody about at this hour who needs attention."

"It's Verden. The warden from Lenek village."

Doria was irritated. U'len was supposed to have had Doria called away on a matter out at the Farm, and if Derinald insisted on coming along, a fast rider would have been dispatched to the Farm to be sure there was at least some problem out there that the baron or his regent would have been disturbed for, but U'len was obviously improvising. Lenek was one of the closest villages to the baronial keep, and certainly one could expect loyalty and obedience from the village warden, but it was unlikely that whatever emergency could be improvised there would stand close scrutiny, and the threat of looking closer was another card that Doria didn't want put in Derinald's hand.

And what if Derinald wanted to see Verden? What if he offered to help with whatever the problem was?

He was already on his feet. "Might I be of some assistance?" he asked, with a smile that could have been merely friendly. "I do have a small troop with me, if there's any—"

"No, I don't see any need, after all—" Doria swallowed her improvised excuse when U'len beckoned Verden inside the study.

A village warden wasn't a lofty noble position; it was a commoner's job, and Verden looked like the peasant he was, from the simple sandals strapped to his feet to the rough haircut that could have and probably had been done with a wooden bowl and a pair of farming shears. It paid to look less prosperous than he in fact was. As the tax money passed through his hands toward the baronial keep, it was likely that a copper or two would stick to those hands, but it wouldn't do to either let that show or alienate his neighbors by putting on airs.

His face and arms were covered with dust and sweat, and his breathing was still ragged as U'len led him into the study, although he had the presence of mind to keep his dirty feet on the wicker runner.

"There's trouble at the village, Lady Doria," he said, without preamble. "One of those urks, or orcs, or whatever the foul beasts are called, has broken into the house of Ingrel Leatherworker and made off with his baby boy." He spread his hands helplessly. "The village is up in arms, and torches are lit from one end to the other, but . . ."

"But that won't do any good," Doria said.

Nor, likely, would it do any good for the child, who was probably already dead by now.

Trouble had arrived ahead of schedule. The orcs hadn't been seen this far east, not yet, although the troops in Barony Adahan, across the river in Holtun, had been busy clearing out a hive of them near New Pittsburgh, accompanied by most of the small contingent based at Castle Cullinane.

Trouble always arrived ahead of schedule, though, and the hulking creatures that Walter Slovotsky had named orcs that had flowed out of the breach between Faerie and reality were definitely trouble.

"U'len," she said, "send for my riding gear, if you please. And for Durine, Kethol, and Pirojil. Horses for all four of us."

"They're just outside—the soldiers, I mean—and—"

"Then get them, get them. Find a bed and some food for Verden after you call for the saddle horses."

"Excuse me, if you please." Derinald held up a restraining hand. "But this is foolish. Dashing off into the night to chase down some hulking, claw-handed beast? That's not only unlikely to do you any good, it's unsafe, and I've always hated to see a lovely lady do something dangerous, even when it's not this unwise. Assuming you're so unfortunate as to find the creature—and I think that's not going to happen, not if it doesn't want to be found—do you want to find it jumping out from behind a hedge in the dark? No. This is not a matter for a regent and soldiers at night, it's a matter for huntsmen, in the morning." He patted the air, as though telling her to sit down.

Doria shook her head. "The gamekeeper and his son have been off hunting for several days now; I expect we'll see them in a day or two, with some dressed-out deer and perhaps a boar. This is a small barony, Captain, and we're quite civilized, but I don't have endless gamekeepers sitting on call. Most of our meat comes from the Farm, not the forest. Unless—"

"May I make a small suggestion?" Derinald smiled and bowed.

"Perhaps you could use the assistance of another huntsman's son, one who has spent most of his adult life in service to the Crown, but who still remembers how to follow a trail."

"You?"

"None other." He smiled and bowed again. "In fact, two of my troopers are also experienced in trailing; they were a scout and a ranger during the war. I prefer to keep a balance of talent in my troop. With your permission, we shall leave before first light; I'd ask that you have fresh horses and provisions ready." He turned to Verden. "And I'll have you hold yourself ready as guide to your village, man."

Verden looked to Doria before nodding.

The peasant started as Durine, Kethol, and Pirojil walked into the study.

Kethol, long, lanky, a tangle of red hair and an easy smile that spoke of an easygoing attitude that his clever eyes denied. Durine, the big man, a head taller than Kethol and twice as wide, built like a barrel and covered with black hair from the bushy beard that looked more hacked than trimmed to the backs of his hands, hands with fingers that were too thick to use anything more delicate than an ax handle. Pirojil, the ugly one, his face heavy-jawed, and with an eye ridge that would have made him look like a Neanderthal if the forehead had sloped back. He should have worn a beard. A beard would have covered the double chins and the twisted mouth, but there was nothing much that could have been done about the sunken, piggish eyes.

Without a word or gesture, the three of them spread out, as though dividing the room among themselves. But there were no hands on weapons, or any overt threat, and in fact Kethol leaned back against the doorframe while Durine moved closer to the fireplace as though to warm himself, and Pirojil just watched.

They didn't say anything.

"I'm sure you heard what's happened," Doria said. "We'd all better get some sleep," she went on. "We've got a ride in the morning. Early in the morning. U'len—"

"I'll have Harria have food ready for you," she said firmly. "I'll be sleeping in, in the morning, myself."

Despite the situation, Doria smiled. "Oh? You will, will you?"

U'len nodded grimly. "It'll be a long night, but I won't sleep anyway, not with these orcs or urks or whatever you want to call those horrible monsters lurking about."

Derinald smiled indulgently. "No need for fright, old woman. The keep ought to be more than safe enough—"

"I'm not worried about the little stringy meat clinging to these old bones," she said with a derisive snort. "Besides, any such creature would surely gag and choke to death on my flesh. But my babies sleep upstairs, and I'll be sitting up outside their rooms tonight."

Derinald looked her up and down, no doubt noticing the wrinkles and gray hair that suggested that the time for her to have babies was many years past, but he just smiled and nodded as she turned about and waddled out of the room.

Doria didn't explain that U'len's "babies" were the Slovotsky girls, particularly little Doranne. Ever since Kirah, their mother, had taken up with Bren Adahan, the girls had been getting less attention than they needed, and U'len had always been fond of Doranne and Janie, and had them under her wing.

Hell, most nights Doranne fell asleep on a pile of blankets in a corner of the kitchen, carried up to her room by U'len before U'len turned in for the night. The keep was a lousy hunting ground for any creature, but if U'len had decided to spend the night sitting up outside the girls' rooms, no doubt with a heavy cleaver lying across her lap, Doria knew better than to argue with her.

"And so, Captain," Doria said, "we'd best see about getting you settled in for the night." She turned to Pirojil. "See to his men, if you please, and make sure they have fresh horses in the morning, when we leave."

"We?" Derinald shook his head. "I think it best if you simply leave this to us, to myself and my men."

Durine grunted. Whether that meant he agreed or disagreed was something that Pirojil and Kethol probably could have figured out, but not Doria.

"No," she said. "I'll want to look into it myself. I trust that these three can keep me safe while you hunt down whatever it is."

"Accidents can happen," Pirojil said. He looked her in the eye, then at Derinald, and then back. Yes, accidents could happen, and they could be arranged.

She shook her head once. No. "No, accidents can't happen. It's your task to make sure that they don't. It'd be a bad idea if anybody got hurt."

Sure, if it had been necessary, Derinald and his troopers could be killed, their bodies buried somewhere. But questions would be asked, and the explanations would not satisfy those who wouldn't want to be satisfied. You just didn't go around killing imperial troops, not without a damn good reason, and the irritation with them for conveying the dowager empress's machinations wasn't a good reason.

If Derinald had the sense to feel the menace in the room, he also had the sense not to show it. "As to these three," he said, "I'd feel better about haring off after some rampaging creatures if I could explain to Her Majesty that they had been dispatched, as instructed, to Keranahan."

"We can discuss that in the morning," Doria said. "Perhaps."

Doria had assigned Derinald a room across from her own, just around the corner and down the hall from where U'len sat in an overstuffed chair hauled from the late baron's game room.

"I hope you'll be comfortable here," she said, setting the lantern down on the nightstand.

"I've no doubt I shall. Much nicer accommodations than I'm used to," he said.

It was a nice room, at that. The bed was a large one, and the feather mattress on top of the broad, interlaced leather straps was always freshly aired. The walls had been whitewashed recently, and were decorated with an opposed pair of small tapestries—deer frolicking in a meadow on one side, a familiar-looking fire-breathing dragon coming in for a landing on the other side. The nightstand held a pitcher of water, a corked glass bottle, and a pair of mottled green glasses, while a gleaming porcelain thundermug and basket of corncobs stood in the far corner.

In the morning, the barred window would look out on the apple tree standing at the top of the grassy knoll at the west side of the inner bailey. A pleasant view.

It was a pleasant room, always left prepared for an unexpected guest, and the metal bar hidden behind the heavy oak door could be instantly inserted into a brass socket hidden in the hall floor under the carpet and then jammed into the door, turning it into a comfortable prison, just in case.

It also had the advantage of U'len being down the hall on one side, and the staircase at the end of the hall on the other side leading down past the kitchens, where U'len's assistant cooks and the housemaids were busying themselves with the night's cooking and baking. Feeding a troop of imperials in addition to the household was something that the staff was ready for, but it required pressing some staff into unaccustomed duties.

Keeping a close eye on visitors, on the other hand, wasn't an unaccustomed duty for any of the castle staff.

Derinald hung his sword belt from a bedpost, and then pulled a small bottle out of his leather bag. "I hope you'll join me in a drink."

"I don't think—"

"Please," he said with a smile. "I find it helps me sleep, but I've long had a problem with the bottle, and find that I can best manage it by never drinking alone. And this is a particularly fine Holtish wine, the grapes, so I'm told, grown from vines a thousand years old."

"Well, if you insist," she said.

He poured them each a small glassful. She liked that. An indirect overture, not just a ploy to get her drunk.

"Barony Cullinane," he said, raising his glass.

"The empire," she returned. She sipped at the wine. It was sweeter than she usually liked, but rich and inky, a taste of berries and sunshine that lingered on the tongue.

He smiled at her over the glass, one eyebrow raised in a question that could have been about the wine, but wasn't.

Well, Doria decided as she set the glass down and went to him, there was more than one way to make sure someone didn't prowl around the castle unaccompanied.

Morning broke over the castle threateningly, gray clouds on the western horizon more promising than threatening a storm.

The horses whinnied, and the soldiers holding the reins had to struggle to keep them from bolting. The horses sensed something, although Doria wouldn't have wanted to guess what. It couldn't still be nearby, could it?

The leatherworker's wife stood red-eyed next to her stony husband, occasionally turning to hush at the children hiding inside the low, wattle-and-daub house at the end of a row of such houses. Shutters over a shattered window told where the creature had gotten in, and out.

Doria wanted to go to her, to say something. But what? What could she say? She shook her head. There was nothing to say, and it wasn't her job as baronial regent to comfort; it was her responsibility to see that this thing was chased down and killed.

Durine eyed the path into the woods, and then Doria, and then took another step toward the midpoint position between the two, while Kethol and Pirojil, each with a pistol in hand, kept watch.

Pirojil, in particular, seemed to want to position himself between Doria and Derinald, perhaps as a way of expressing disapproval of last night.

She assumed he knew. Castle life didn't leave one much privacy. Her morning plate of biscuits and pot of almost bubbling-hot cinnomeile tea, along with her riding clothes, had been just outside the door of Derinald's room, and if Pirojil and his companions didn't know how she spent her night, it was because they didn't particularly care to. Maids always gossiped.

Last night had been the first time in longer than she cared to think about, and Doria had apparently been storing up some appetite. She wouldn't have changed a moment of it, but the truth was that she was sore, and while long habits and training had forbidden more than casually considering the idea of using healing draughts to make it less painful to sit a horse, it was still a temptation. Bouncing up and down on a hard saddle was painful enough normally, but the stableboy had picked a robust young mare for her, light-footed and spirited, and the damn horse had felt obligated to keep pace with Derinald's big bay gelding.

But while only remnants of her magical abilities persisted, there had been more to being a daughter of the Hand than simply spurting spells, and she took the few moments of relative quiet to perform an exercise she had both learned and taught.

Pain was important. It was a warning, perhaps of danger, perhaps of an excess of pleasure, but it was a good thing, something to be grateful for, not to fear. It was a matter of recognizing her various aches and pains, accepting them as they were, and then dismissing them, with thanks to her body for reminding her of its limitations.

The pain was still there, and it would still be there, but it was put in context.

That was enough.

Derinald grumbled to himself as he looked at the ground behind the leatherworker's small wattle-and-daub shack. "Too many feet, too many feet shuffling around the ground," he said, motioning with one idle hand for the rest to keep back while he squatted, looking at the ground, squinting as though he was trying to read words in a foreign language.

Finally, he shook his head. "No good at all." He waved a hand toward where a raised path toward the forest separated two cornfields. "Probably went that way; let's see if I can pick up the trail."

One of his men, a crooked little man with a face like a ferret, gestured at a gap in the corn, where perhaps half a dozen stalks had been knocked down. "Perhaps there, perhaps, Captain?"

"I think not, Deven," Derinald said as he shook his head, looking more closely.

"You never can tell, Captain. Even the big animals can fool you. I've seen—"

"Yes, and nobody's hunted anything like these monsters for a dozen generations, but if he was clumsy enough to leave a hole like that, he would have knocked down some stalks going further in." The rows were closely spaced, and there was room enough for somebody to walk between them without knocking against them, but just barely.

Durine grunted. Kethol walked toward one side of the gap while Pirojil eased to another side, all three of them drawing swords and pistols.

The ferret-faced little man grinned, revealing a missing front tooth. "I think the soldier-boys are worried about him hiding there, Captain, I do."

"Well, let's show them better." Derinald picked up a rock and flung it sidearm into the gap. The rock whipped through the leaves, and some yards away, a small bird that had been hiding fluttered into the air and arrowed away, just skimming the tops of the plants . . . but there was no motion. Nothing.

"No, there'd be no reason to hide there," he said. "Not overnight." Motioning at the rest to stay still, he walked down the path and disappeared into the woods.

In a moment, he was back, beckoning at Deven and another, larger man. "It went this way, some hours ago. Probably long gone, but the two of you see if you can pick up the trail."

He had a quick whispered conversation with Deven, who nodded and retrieved a leather bag from his saddlebags before heading into the forest.

Derinald walked over to Doria. His face was grim, and pale.

"You'd think," he said, "that one gets used to such things, but . . . we'll search for the creature, and most likely run it to ground. Clumsy thing; doesn't pay attention to where it's putting its feet. But it ripped the head clear off the child, and left it just a short way in," he said quietly. "The boy probably was screaming too loudly, and frightened the thing. Were it my choice to make, I'd say it would be enough if we tell the parents that we know it to be dead and leave it at that, but it's not my choice, and I'll not intrude."

Deven, walking, while the rest followed along on horseback, led them along the web of an old hunting trail back up toward the hills at a good clip, scouting ahead and picking up traces of the creature's flight that Derinald apparently saw as well, but were utterly invisible to Doria.

As the trail forked and split, Deven was able to find some indication of which way to go, even though in a couple of cases he made them wait at the fork while he jogged down first one path, then returned to find some spoor and lead them up another.

A scraped tree here, some broken brush or disturbed leaves there, an occasional partial print in soft soil was all that the two of them needed. There had been spots where the creature had left the game trails and cut through the woods, but it kept returning to the beaten paths. Understandable, really; the forest was dense, the ground covered with brush in the shade of the leafy giants, their crooked limbs arching above in a green canopy that kept the forest cool and musty.

Around midmorning, they forded a shallow stream to catch up with Deven and his latest find: a small bone by the side of the trail. Deven made as though to throw it into the woods, but stopped at Derinald's gesture, nodded, and handed it over to the captain, who in turn handed it to Doria.

The ants had gotten to it first, although there barely was a gobbet of flesh on it. Part of a femur, maybe six inches long, and it had been thoroughly chewed. She wrapped it in her scarf and tucked it in her saddlebag.

"Ta havath," the captain said. "Easy, now. It could be anywhere, anywhere at all." He frowned at the trees around them.

"No, Captain." Deven shook his head, his voice low, barely carrying the few yards from where he squatted up the trail. "Paw marks up here—but I think we're getting close. They're fresh, and he's not even trying to keep his claws in. I think he's tired—prints are getting less regular, like he's gasping for breath. No piss markings, but you wouldn't expect that, not here, not now."

Derinald glanced at Doria, then back at Deven. He would make his point later, no doubt, about how Doria and her people couldn't have followed it, not that he was right, but—

Her horse's nostrils widened, and it whinnied as a vestige of Doria's old sensitivity flared brightly in the back of her mind, hot and red with hate and fear.

"It's here—" She started to turn, as Kethol sprung from his saddle, Pirojil and Durine a heartbeat behind.

A black, hairy mass leaped from an overhanging branch behind her, pulling one of Derinald's troopers screaming from his saddle and down to the ground. It was a huge beast, half again as tall as a man and covered with short hair or fur, like a bear, and for just a moment Doria thought it was a bear, except that, thick as it was, it was too slim, too humanlike in its shape.

But it wasn't human. Claws slashed at the screaming man's face, and a mouth filled with sharp teeth sank into his neck, turning the scream into a horridly liquid gurgle.

Doria's horse panicked, whinnying in terror, rearing back. She tried to cling to the saddle, but she hadn't been braced for it trying to throw her, and she tumbled off, falling hard on her side on the trail, her right foot caught in the stirrup for a horrible second before it twisted loose, her horse bolting.

She was surrounded by sounds and stomping hooves, and it was all she could to do roll off the path and into the brush, ignoring the way it clawed at her, her hands covering her face to protect her eyes.

Shouts mixed with the loud neighs of the horses, the screams of the injured, and the growls of the beast.

Doria staggered to her feet, the brush grabbing and clawing at her before she could pull free.

The horses had scattered, taking the imperials with them, but

Kethol, Durine, and Pirojil had somehow dismounted before their own mounts had fled, although none of them had managed to remove his flintlock rifle from his saddleboot in so doing.

The orc was still shaking its prey. Kethol took careful aim at the creature's broad back with his flintlock pistol. It fired, with a gout of flame and smoke accompanied by a surprisingly quiet report.

The creature shuddered, dropped the battered, bloody body of the imperial trooper, and spun, not even slowed by the shot as it dropped to a three-point crouch and leaped for Kethol, claw-tipped fingers outstretched. Two other shots rang out, although Doria couldn't see where they came from.

Kethol had managed to get his sword out, and had it extended, but the orc reached out a hand and twisted it away, ignoring the way the sharp blade sliced its thick hairy fingers to the bone.

It claws had barely touched Kethol when Durine hit it in a full-bodied tackle that took both it and the big man to the ground. Pirojil, moving more delicately and precisely than a man that big and ugly should have been able to, danced in among the flailing limbs, his sword tip jabbing and probing. One booted foot stomped down hard, pinning one of the creature's arms to the ground.

A swipe from a hairy hand caught Durine on the side of the head, but Durine just shook his head as though to clear it and fastened both his massive hands on the orc's neck. His growls mingled with the orc's as he squeezed, harder and harder, his own beefy face reddening with the effort, while Pirojil's sword, now bloody halfway to the guard, continued to probe and stab.

And then, with a shudder and a groan and a horrible flatulence, the creature went limp, and dead.

Maybe Durine didn't believe that it was dead, or perhaps he just didn't like to take chances; he didn't stop squeezing until Kethol patted his shoulder and said, "Ta havath, Durine."

Dead and still, the orc somehow looked smaller than it had in life and motion as it lay stretched out on the ground, flies already gathering in the pool of blood and shit.

It reminded Doria of pictures she had seen of Bigfoot, back on the Other Side, although it was perhaps somewhat slimmer, and the dark coarse hair shorter than she remembered, over the years. A ragged muslin breechcloth lay across its loins, tented in the middle in a way that Doria couldn't, despite the situation, help finding vaguely comical.

"Dead, but not forgotten." Pirojil poked at the breechcloth with a stick, pulling it aside to reveal a surprisingly small pink penis peeking out through the fur. The tip of the penis was ringed with a crown of barbs, like a male cat's.

"Well." Kethol chuckled. "No wonder they've got a bad temper. The orc bitches, I mean. Hmmm . . . come to think of it, no wonder they *all* do."

"I don't know," Pirojil said idly, his smile something ugly. "Could be that once you have one with spikes on his prong, you never go back."

Durine grunted, and pulled his belt knife. He looked over at Doria. "Well?"

"Well what?" She was more than vaguely disgusted. "Do you want a trophy?"

She knew she'd said something stupid when all three of their faces went blank and expressionless.

"No, Regent," Pirojil said quietly, calmly. "Do you want me to make sure that this is the one that ate the little boy?" He rested the point of the knife against the protruding abdomen of the orc. "It would be a shame to turn around and go back if we haven't gotten the right one, to leave the one we're hunting still out there."

He was right, of course. It wouldn't really make any difference whether they knew or not. This probably was the one, and the baby was probably in pieces in its stomach, and they could just tell the parents that they were sure.

But no, not knowing didn't make it better. It made it worse.

She worked her mouth, but no words came out. It was all Doria could do to nod.

❖   ❖   ❖

Pirojil was helping Doria down from her horse when U'len stormed out of the kitchen and pushed more through than past the imperials, leaving scowls and rearing horses in her wake.

"What have you done to her?" U'len wailed as she shoved Kethol aside, then snatched at Pirojil's sleeve.

Durine, still looming above on horseback, took in the scene with his usual equanimity as he returned Pirojil's grin. Yes, any of the three of them could have gutted the fat old woman like a trout; no, they'd no more think of raising a hand to U'len in protection of the regent than they would in protection of the Cullinane children: U'len was as loyal as a good dog, and she was a good Cullinane dog. Every bit as expendable in a crisis as, well, Pirojil and Durine and Kethol were, of course.

Doria held up a hand. "Be still. I'm . . . not unwell."

"Oh, you're not unwell, are you? And are you not quite undead, as well? And would you then decline to deny that you do not appear to be other than not unhealthy, too?"

Derinald's too-pretty face was split in a too-easy smile as he stepped forward, his arm extended. "If you'll permit me? Lady Doria and I have matters to discuss."

"They can wait. Now get yourself and your little men out of my way, and—"

"It's nothing, U'len," Doria said. "Just a strenuous day, and I'm not used to so much riding."

U'len's snort threatened to drown out the snort of the horse just behind Pirojil. "Be that as it may, child," she said, "you need a hot cup of tea, and a hot bowl of soup, and a hot bath before you'll be discussing anything with anybody."

She started to lead Doria away, but Derinald interposed himself and laid a gentle hand on her arm. "Please, Lady, permit me," he said, the familiarity of his tone and manner grating in Pirojil's ears.

Durine's mouth twitched, and he cleared his throat loudly enough to get everybody's attention. Pirojil wouldn't have seen

Kethol quietly reclaim his own gear and move away if he hadn't been looking for it.

In fact he didn't see it—he was deliberately focusing his attention on Durine, just as the big man wanted.

"I think, Captain, you'll stop right there," Pirojil said, trying to keep his voice light despite the metallic taste in his mouth. "I think, Captain," he said, deliberately ignoring the way that the dozen or so horsemen were moving into a shallow arc around where he confronted the imperial captain, "that you'll lay not so much as a finger on the hem of her garment without permission. Twice."

His body felt all distant, but precise, as though he was outside it, manipulating it from a distance that lent objectivity to his every word, to his every motion. Or maybe it was that it wasn't just his body, wasn't just his mind, but all three of theirs. Perhaps it was a mind that the three of them shared, that had Durine's horse backing up a few steps and turning away so that the big man's hand was covered as it dropped to where his long saber was lashed to his saddle, that had Kethol, only slightly out of breath from his run up the stairs and to a keep window, his bow strung, an arrow nocked, and a half-dozen others set point-first into the flooring, while Kethol stood back from the window, concealed in shadow from the sight of anyone, but not from Pirojil's knowing what he would do.

"Pirojil." Lady Doria's voice was firm, if quiet. "Stand aside."

"Let it be, Lady," Pirojil said. "Now's as good a time as any, and this is a fine enough place." There were a full dozen of the imperials, and only three of them, but if it were to be necessary, this was the time and place: the old watchman would drop the gate upon command, trapping the imperials in the killing ground. Durine was well placed to cover U'len's and Lady Doria's retreat into the keep, and Kethol was ready and able to send half a dozen shafts whispering through the air before anybody could possibly tell where he was and where they came from.

Pirojil and Durine would be unlikely to survive, of course, but you couldn't have everything. In life you had to keep your priorities straight, and Pirojil's priority was that that smirking pretty boy, Derinald, not touch the Lady under their protection without her permission.

It could be now, or it could be later, or it could be never at all.

Derinald's face paled beneath his even, aristocratic tan. He had seen Pirojil, Durine, and Kethol in action against the orc, and had some sort of idea of what the next few moments held in store for him.

"Let it be, Lady," Pirojil said again as he turned to Derinald's men. "My name is Pirojil," he said loudly, "and I rode with the Old Emperor on his Last Ride, as did my companions, I promised him before he died my loyalty to his family and friends, and I don't think that includes letting some imperial lackey lay his overly familiar hands on the Lady Doria."

It would keep the politics simple, at least as simple as the politics ever got. The three of them would disobey Lady Doria and kill more than their own weight in imperials in the doing. It would help to maintain the principle that it was unsafe to mess with the Cullinanes without putting the barony into open conflict with the dowager empress. Cut through Beralyn's machinations, and if that left blood on the ground and bodies stinking in the sun, well, that was the end result of most political maneuverings anyway.

There was only one problem with it.

"No." Lady Doria stepped in front of him. "That's not a suggestion, Pirojil. Step aside, and let my friend Derinald help me inside. *Now.*"

Pirojil's ears burned red as Derinald escorted her inside the keep, but Durine just shrugged, and high above came a deep laugh from Kethol.

Doria sat in front of the fireplace, a cup of hot tea at her elbow, the orders Beralyn wanted her to sign on the writing desk next to her.

It would be possible to ignore Beralyn perhaps, she decided, particularly now. One orc, even one rogue one, without companions or weapons, probably presaged the appearance of others. And while

Derinald and his men had been able to track it, it had been her three who had brought it down, and there was a good argument for keeping them around. She could explain that to the emperor, if she had to, and she probably would have to.

"May I interrupt?" Derinald stood in the doorway. His hair was wet from the bath, and his clothes were fresh and clean, the crease on his trousers razor-sharp, his loose shirt white as an egg.

She nodded. "Of course." She gestured to a chair on the other side of the fireplace.

"Hederen's resting comfortably," he said, sinking comfortably into the chair. "He'll have a few scars to brag of, but he'll keep the eye, most likely—those Spidersect healing draughts were none too potent in the first place, and they'd probably been sitting in my bag too long."

"There was a time . . ." Doria shook her head. There was a time when she could have put out her hands and let the healing flow into him, a current of power and magic warming her even while it drained her. But that time was gone, and most of her powers along with it. She had defied the Mother, and had been excommunicated from the Hand, and while she had often regretted the fact of it, that was done. "I'm glad he didn't get hurt worse."

Derinald's fingers fluttered. "Yes. It could have been much worse. Those three, they're quite good at what they do, aren't they?" he asked. "Their horses spooked just as badly as the rest of ours did, and every bit as quickly. But the three of them were out of their saddles at the first warning."

"They were, at that." She smiled. "Yes, there's a reason why they've survived when others haven't, and it's not just luck. Nor is it just loyalty."

"Yes. But I'm still surprised that they've survived this one. One would think that they really wanted to spit themselves on my men's spears."

Was he *really* that stupid? No. He couldn't be. Anybody with half a brain could see that Kethol was a heroic suicide, looking for a place to happen, and Durine and Pirojil weren't much better. Dying didn't scare any of the three of them. What was important was that they preserve themselves until they found the right place to die.

She shook her head. "No. It's important to them that they serve the Old Emperor, and his death only made that more complicated for them, and they're three men who do not dote on complexity."

"Which is why you're not going to order them to look into things in Keranahan, correct?" He shook his head. "I think that unwise, but . . ."

"No," she said. "I am."

"Eh?"

"I said I am sending them. I'll sign the orders tonight, and they'll leave in the morning."

"I see." He smiled knowingly, smugly. Stupidly.

She smiled back, not meaning it for a moment.

Men were men, no matter what their profession. A soldier, a sailor, a bookkeeper, a farmer, a mechanic: most—all?—of them thought themselves magicians who could cast a spell over any woman with the magic wand that sprouted from between their legs.

But last night had been pleasure, and today was business.

Chasing the orc had reminded her of something that she would have liked to forget, or at least to ignore: Barony Cullinane was, like all the others, dependent on the empire. During the Holtun-Bieme war that had created the empire, the barony had had no more chance of holding out alone against the Holtish forces than any other, and the Holts had spent much of the war simply slicing off barony-sized chunks of Bieme, selling peasants off to the Slavers Guild to finance their war, and were in the process of cutting up Barony Cullinane— then Barony Furnael—when Karl and his people had taken a hand.

Peace hadn't changed things, not permanently. There were bordering countries to worry about, and with the flush of magical things from Faerie over the past few years, it was entirely possible that the barony would need much help from beyond the borders.

Pirojil had only illustrated the problem with his manufactured confrontation with Derinald. In a conflict between the barony and the empire, the empire's needs had to be considered, even if at the moment the barony could prevail.

Yes, Pirojil and the other two could have killed the small troop of imperials, and perhaps the crime could have been covered up, or more likely swept under the carpet ... but what good would that have done?

It was the classic individualist dilemma, on a baronial scale instead of a personal one.

As long as things went well, as long as the rest of the universe cooperated, it was possible to go it alone and make it work.

But you couldn't go it alone, not always. The world was not a gentle place. A person needed a family, a community, a nation, perhaps. And there had to be a balance between what you gave and what you took.

Yes, Kethol, Pirojil, and Durine had handled that one orc by themselves, and they could have taken on more.

But what if it had been a dozen? Doria might well have had needed Derinald and his scouts to track down the orc before it did a lot more damage, and while Durine and Kethol and Pirojil had been the ones who put it down, it could just as easily have been Derinald's troopers.

And what about next time?

One rogue orc wasn't all that important, not by itself.

Derinald being a trifle overfamiliar was nothing; she could have handled that with a glare or a gesture or a word.

But both the orc and Derinald's overreaching could serve as a reminder that the balance was always there, was always precarious, and that whatever Doria's feelings were about that dried-up bitch Beralyn Furnael, she represented, in a very real if not a formally legal sense, the empire that kept the scales even and unshaking, that would provide help and would demand service, as well.

And if three soldiers would have to be risked to keep that balance, even if the three of them had just saved Doria's life, well, they were expendable. Even if they had just shown themselves willing to die to prevent a slight-that-was-barely-a-slight.

Even though they were more loyal than a good dog, they were

expendable. And it was her job to expend them, if necessary.

She was vaguely disgusted with herself as she reached for her pen.

But she dipped it in the inkwell anyway.

4

✠ A Night in Riverforks

The wizard had been drinking for hours, Pirojil decided. Most of them looked half-drunk most of the time, but this one's eyes were barely able to focus as he raised a finger to signal for more of the sour beer that already had Pirojil's head buzzing.

The Wounded Dog—Pirojil had asked for an explanation of the name of the place, and had promptly forgotten it—wasn't the best of the inns in Riverforks that catered to travelers, and it wasn't the cheapest, but it was the only one that had a private room to let . . . at least for the likes of the three of them.

They could have gotten off cheaper by taking floor space in the common room at the Bearded Thistle and spent the night sleeping in turns to avoid the predations of some light-fingered thief, but they weren't that eager to save the dowager empress a few marks that they would probably try to cheat her out of anyway, and their room down the hall from the bath wasn't excessively expensive.

Kethol had bolted down a bowl of stew before finding a game of bones in the common room with a bunch of teamsters, and Durine had stalked out into the night, probably looking for thieves rather than a whore. Riverforks, having become a trading center of sorts, was more than big enough to have its own criminal class . . . in addition to the nobility, which you had everywhere.

Kethol would probably relieve his newfound friends of their loose coin and head out into the night in search of another game, but Pirojil was content enough to sit over a pitcher of beer while he waited for his turn in the bath. It would be nice to be clean again, at least for a while. After even a few days on the road, it felt like the road had ground its dirt into you beneath the skin, as well as into it.

The innkeeper, rawboned and surprisingly skinny, brought another wooden pitcher of beer over to the table where the wizard sat alone in his stained gray robes, stopping for a moment to chat before he hustled back through the swinging wooden doors to the kitchen.

Over in the corner, a half-dozen or so dwarves bent their heads together over their pitchers—the dwarves shunned simple mugs—in quiet conversation. Pirojil had been raised in a country that had been pretty much free of the Moderate Folk, and they still looked funny to him: as broad as a muscular man, but barely chest-high. The knuckles on the hands that rested on the table looked like walnuts. Broad faces, with heavy jaws covered by thick long beards, and brows even more solid than Pirojil's own. Pirojil could remember slamming in the face of a soldier who had once suggested that Pirojil should go hunt himself up a dwarf sow because she might not find him as ugly as any decent woman would.

Pirojil would have tried to join them in conversation—he spoke a fairly good dwarvish, although his accent was too nasal—but that would have drawn attention of a sort that wouldn't be wise. The idea was to keep a low profile here, to get in, find out what this minor matter in Keranahan was really about, and then get out without a fuss.

It would have been nice to know what the dwarves were doing here, though it could have been any of a hundred things, and not just the mining that they were famous for. The Old Emperor himself had hired a company of Endell dwarves to redo the sewer system in Biemestren, for example; and dwarf warriors were awfully handy to have around in a fight.

Pirojil caught the wizard watching him watching the dwarves, so he raised his own mug in a friendly salute, and then looked away, not particularly wanting to get involved in a conversation or draw attention to himself by trying to avoid one.

But the drunken wizard took his movement as an invitation and staggered over to the table, mug in one hand, pitcher in the other, and seated himself in a chair opposite Pirojil. In the flickering of the overhead lanterns, his face was lined and tired, his gray beard forked into two uneven tufts. "A good evening to you," the wizard said, his voice slurred. "Do you drink?"

"I've been known to," Pirojil said, lifting his own mug and taking a measured sip. "I'm called Pirojil."

"Erenor the Magnificent," the wizard said, refilling Pirojil's mug with a surprisingly steady hand. "Formerly of glorious Pandathaway, and now of this . . . somewhat less glorious place."

Pirojil could have rolled his eyes. Every third drunken hedge-wizard seemed to claim origin in the Pandathaway Wizards Guild, no doubt having studied under Grandmaster Lucius himself. Pitiful. Predictable, but pitiful. Couldn't one of them bill himself as, say, "the Moderately Competent"?

Pirojil's thumb stroked against the hidden gem of his signet ring. Yes, it was pitiful. As pitiful, perhaps, as a simple soldier reminding himself every now and then that he'd been born noble, as though that made a difference in his present estate.

Did it matter if it was true or not? No. Not for him, and not for this wizard.

So he just nodded. "Interesting place, Pandathaway," he said.

"Ah." Erenor raised an eyebrow. "That it is. You know it well?"

"Not well." Pirojil shook his head. "I was there just once, some years ago." He was tempted to mention, say, the fountain at the end of the Street of Two Dogs, just to see the reaction—the street existed; the fountain didn't—but what point would there be in making the drunken old wizard out a liar?

Particularly if he was, as seemed likely. Tell the ugly truth about a man, and he'd never forgive you. Pirojil had looked at his own reflection in too many mirrors, too many pools of water, too many faces, to think that knowing the truth was always a good thing, and had cut too many men for speaking it to think that saying the truth was always safe.

"So. Tell me about Riverforks," Pirojil said. "A good place to live, is it?"

Erenor shrugged. "There's worse, and there's better. I spend most of my time doing farming magic these days—helping to get a barren mare with calf, casting preservative spells on granaries, the like. Death spells, of a certainty—but only on rats." He smiled slyly. "But there's always call for love philters among the nobility, and I've quite a hand with those, as well."

"A lot of those, eh?" Pirojil doubted this disreputable wizard had much connection with the nobility, but he could always be wrong, particularly in Holtun. Pirojil didn't have quite the same feel for Holtun that he did for Bieme. The Holtish nobility had always been more stylish and overly formal than the Biemish, and while the Biemish victory in the war that had created the empire had modified that, it hadn't changed it totally.

"Well, yes," the wizard said, producing a small vial stoppered with wax. "Take this one," he said. "Not just your ordinary love potion, mind, one that will make a resistant woman more willing. But sprinkle this over your food and your lady's, and you'll find her eyes wide and loving as she stares into even yours, I mean even as she stares into your eyes."

Pirojil knew what he meant. Even drunk, the old wizard could see a man too ugly to get a woman other than a rented whore, and would be happy to sell a traveler a potion, and if the potion worked, all the better, eh?

It was one thing for inbred nobility to play at games of love and dominance, a love potion seducing an already half-willing girl for a night. It was another thing for somebody like Pirojil to use one.

The kind of love that even an effective love potion brought was cheap and unsatisfying and would turn to hate and disgust the moment the spell wore off, which it would. Pirojil had tried that, only once. Only once that was long ago, only once that was far too recently. Only once that was far too many times.

"Or, if that didn't suit your fancy, a seeming, perhaps," the wizard went on.

"Of course." Pirojil snorted. "A seeming. Thank you, no. I've no use for seemings."

"Ah? And that would be because . . . ?"

"Because it's just an illusion, a vapor, dispelled by a touch or a breath or the morning sun. There's no truth to it, no substance, that's why." Even a major seeming was easily dispelled, and a minor seeming would flicker when seen out of the corner of the eye. And neither would make Pirojil any less ugly. That was the way it was. Why? Did it matter? He was ugly.

"Ah. You suffer from the common fallacy. Permit me to persuade you otherwise." The wizard muttered harsh syllables under his breath, barely audible.

Pirojil tried to hear them, tried to remember them, but he couldn't: they vanished on his ears like snowflakes on a warm palm.

But the wizard changed. Stains faded and vanished from his robes, and his crooked back straightened; his beard shrank and receded while it darkened. His wrinkled skin grew smooth and young, and while his eyes remained glazed, they grew brighter and sharper.

"As you can see," he said, his voice still low, but now the more powerful voice of a younger man, not the wheeze of an old one, "there can be substance to a seeming."

Pirojil would have liked to slap the grin from the wizard's face, but attacking a wizard would be a stupid way to get killed. And besides . . . "But a seeming is just that," Pirojil said. "It's not real. It's just illusion. One touch, and even if it doesn't all fall apart, it doesn't have any reality to it. It just—"

"Try it," the wizard said, extending a hand. It wasn't the wizened hand that had poured Pirojil's beer moments before; it was a strong, unlined hand, that of a powerful young man.

Pirojil took the hand in his, and the wizard smiled and set his elbow on the table.

"Wrestle arms with me, Pirojil," he said, "and perhaps I can show you that a seeming is, in the proper hands, sometimes more than just a momentary illusion."

Years of working out with polearm and bow and sword had left Pirojil's arms as strong as a farmer's, and while there certainly were stronger men than he, even a young wizard should be no match for him, and this one man . . .

Unless, of course . . .

"So," Pirojil said, placing his own elbow on the table and gripping Erenor's hand in his own. "You're ready to cast a spell of weakness on me, eh? Or perhaps one of strength on yourself?"

"No." Erenor grinned wolfishly. "Of course not; I intend nothing of the sort."

Pirojil grimaced. "Of course not."

"Truly, friend Pirojil. Would you not take a wizard's word on that?"

"Do I look like that kind of fool?"

"Well, perhaps not." The wizard shrugged. "One never knows."

"You place a geas on yourself, bind yourself to use no magic, and perhaps I'll believe it. But I'm willing to let you win a spot of arm wrestling, with magic." There was no shame in losing to magic, after all.

"I've a simpler way." Erenor lifted his beer mug with his free hand. "I'll hold a mouthful of beer while we arm wrestle. If I spit it out before the back of your—before the back of one of our hands rests against the table, I'll admit myself full and fairly defeated. I can hardly murmur instigators or dominatives with a full mouth of beer, and while I could barely move my tongue for hegemonics, that would do me no good without the rest, eh?"

Pirojil was suspicious, but he was more curious. "I assume we're doing this just for our own amusement, eh? There's no local custom that the loser of an arm wrestling match serves the winner as a body servant for years, or buys the winner's wares, is there?"

Erenor's smile was a row of sparkling white teeth. "Buying the winner some beer, perhaps, would be but simple good manners. But I ask nothing more of you, my suspicious friend, than simple good manners. Do you care to try, or do you care to dither and delay and try my patience?"

The tavern was quiet, and if Pirojil hadn't been drinking he would probably have already noticed that most eyes were on him and Erenor. The dwarves over in the corner had risen from their benches and moved in close. Wrestling was considered a high art among the Moderate People, and while Pirojil had never heard of them being involved in this simpler sort of contest, their interest was not surprising.

One beefy man in a cotton tunic split down his hairy chest to his ample belly snickered out loud and whispered behind his hand to one of his fellows, and there was a comment whose origin Pirojil couldn't quite place about how ugly men usually weren't cowards.

It had been many years since he had given up accepting a dare for fear of being called a coward, and as many years since he had given up declining a dare for fear of being thought a coward, because if they knew that you feared something, they owned you.

You could fear anything as long as you didn't let anybody know. And you could even let others know as long as you were willing to do what you had to, no matter what anybody said, what anybody knew, what anybody feared.

"Very well." Pirojil gripped Erenor's hand tighter. "Do let's try."

Erenor took a deep breath, and then a deep swallow of the beer, then slammed the mug down on the table with unexpected vigor, then gripped back at Pirojil's hand. His grasp was stronger than Pirojil had expected, but Pirojil's own hand was strong.

An old stableman who worked for his fath—an old stableman had taught Pirojil how to do this long ago. It was all in the grip. If you could squeeze your opponent's hand hard enough so that he couldn't grip you back, his strength would fade.

So Pirojil squeezed back, hard, and pulled, hard, harder. He was a strong man; there were few stronger. Durine, certainly. Kethol, possibly, if you gave him the right leverage. But few, damn few. Strength wasn't just in the arm, or the back, or the leg—it was in the mind, the spirit, the resolve.

But there *was* strength in the arm and in the hand, and Pirojil used it, too.

He squeezed, and he pulled, and while Erenor's own arm trembled with exertion, it didn't move. The wizard's young face was impassive, and his nostrils flared wide, although his mouth didn't open.

Pirojil pulled harder, his feet flat against the floor, braced for maximum leverage, putting not only his whole arm into the contest, but his body. He concentrated, harder, harder yet, until his whole body shook and quivered.

And still, Erenor's arm didn't move.

Pirojil hated himself for having been duped, although he couldn't figure out how he had been duped. But while it galled him, there wasn't anything he could do about it except pull yet harder, until lights danced in front of his eyes and his breath came in little gasps.

And slowly, bit by bit, Erenor's arm began to push his own down.

Pirojil's left hand rested on his left thigh, and it would have taken but a moment to snatch up his belt knife and plunge it into the wizard, but as angry as he was, he let his hand rest where it lay . . .

. . . until his right hand was pressed back, hard, against the table.

Erenor released his hand and spat his mouthful of beer out onto the floor in a long stream. "And that, friend Pirojil, may suggest that there's some virtue in a well-crafted seeming, now and then, eh?"

Erenor was clearly more of a magician than he had thought, as he had figured out a way to give more body and shape to a seeming than Pirojil had thought possible. What was such a powerful user of magics doing in Riverforks?

"It isn't permanent, of course," the wizard said. "In the morning I'll look as I usually do, and have no more than my usual strength. But the morning is another matter, perhaps, for a man who would wish to, say, bed a beautiful woman and be gone before sunrise?"

Or who would wish to not be fooled by such. "Perhaps there is some business we can do, after all," Pirojil said, rubbing at his arm. "I assume there's an antidote to such a seeming? And that you might, for a price, be willing to part with a sample of such a countermeasure?"

Erenor's youthful smile broadened. "Ah. It would appear that you are a wise man, after all." He patted at Pirojil's aching right arm. "In addition to a remarkably strong one, as well. You did very well."

❋   ❋   ❋

Kethol caught up with Durine outside of a riverfront tavern.

Durine had been leaning against a railing overlooking the embankment, mostly doing nothing: just relaxing, listening to the quiet whisper of the river beneath, watching the water dance in the flickering of the overhead stars, and the slow, green and blue pulse of the Faerie lights above.

The quiet was nice.

The Faerie lights were in a quiet mood tonight, going through a gentle pavane from a deep red and understated orange through a series of quiet blues and finally to a cool green, and then back again.

There were times when one or another of them would pick up the pace, as though trying to whip the others into a faster rhythm, only to finally, regretfully subside into the same slow beat of the other Faerie lights, either dragged down to their gentle somnolence or moderated to a reasonable pace, depending on how you looked at it.

Inside the riverfront tavern, past the mottled glass windows, smiling young men and young women raised their voices in laughter and song, accompanied by the clattering of dishes and the ringing sounds of glasses, their needs served by a bevy of buxom barmaids.

Durine smiled to himself. There was a reason why ripe young women of peasant stock would often seek work in a city tavern, and it wasn't just to make a few extra coppers now and then from a tumble in the hay. It was a gamble that could pay off much better than that: if the bones fell right, a woman might find herself a young tradesman or perhaps even a merchant to marry, and be free of the farm forever. Spending one's life working a plowed field during the day and herself being plowed at night by a farmer who stank of sweat and pig shit was something that a young girl of attractiveness and ambition might well want to avoid these days.

Of course, far too many of them ended up back on the farm, accepting what was available, and a few always found that the occasional tumble turned into years on their backs in a lower-town brothel, but there were risks to everything, and Durine had no more desire than ability to rescue endless hopeful young girls from their destinies.

Hero was, after all, just another word for *fool*.

Durine heard the footsteps behind him, and for a moment grew hopeful at the thought of a footpad, but then he recognized the footsteps.

"A good evening to you, Kethol," he said.

Well, he could hardly be surprised. A man as large as Durine would be an unlikely target to choose when there were so many others, from the nobility crowding this tavern to the drunken sailors from the ore barge making its way downriver toward Barony Adahan and New Pittsburgh.

"Fortune, or intent?" he asked Kethol.

"Eh?"

Durine would have shaken his head if he thought it politic. Kethol was the handsome one of the three of them, good-looking in an earnest and rugged sort of way. And in a fight he was just as rock-steady trustworthy as Pirojil always would be and as Durine prided himself as being, with a keen eye and a wrist like a striking snake. He could find his way down a trail as well as a true woodsman; he had a better eye for horseflesh than most horse traders; and his abilities at a game of bones would have been legendary if Kethol hadn't been too smart to be so indiscreet.

But when it came to following a simple question, sometimes he was dumb as dirt.

"I meant," Durine explained slowly, "have you found me by accident, or are you seeking me out?"

"Some of both."

"Oh?"

"Well . . ."

Kethol would get to the point in his own time. Durine leaned back against the railing. Below, the river rushed and whispered. Maybe someday somebody would tell Durine what it kept whispering about.

"Not a good evening?"

Kethol thought about it for a moment. "Well, truth to tell, I was looking for another game, but I didn't think much of my chances of getting into the Golden Eye here, much less persuading the young nobles of Neranahan to risk their hard-taxed coin on a fall of the bones with the likes of me."

"Well, now." Durine laughed at the mental picture of a bunch of overdressed dandies bent over a gaming table with Kethol. "I think you've found the right of that."

"On the other hand," Kethol said, "I've heard word that some of the sailors off the Metta Dee are squaring off to toss some bones against some overpaid dwarf copper miners just come to town, and it occurred to me that I might be able to finger a stack or two and turn some profit before turning in for the night, and it would be nice to be able to concentrate on the game for once with somebody else to watch my back and help me make my way out if it comes time to do that. When it comes time to do that."

There would be worse ways to pass an idle hour. Not much more boring, but worse. Durine nodded. "It could be worthwhile, at that. As long as it doesn't go too late; I don't watch backs well when I'm yawning and nodding off, and I do it even less well when I've fallen asleep wrapped in my cloak. You know, I would suppose, where this game is happening?"

"A warehouse, down on the Old Docks," Kethol said. "Probably the fastest way to get there would be along the boardwalk next to the piers."

Well, that made sense; nobody ever said that Kethol couldn't think tactically. Much better to scoot along the boardwalk than to plod along muddy streets.

Kethol led the way down a set of steps that led down the embankment, under the stilt-pillars that supported the back ends of the riverfront taverns and other buildings, giving a wide berth to the overflowing dung heap beneath the tavern's garderobe—which was just as well, as a stream of ordure plopped down just as they passed, and would have splattered them. You didn't make it as a soldier by being overly fastidious, not when it mattered, but that still didn't mean you liked being covered with shit.

The street above slanted down as it curved inwards toward the warehouse district, and the cutaway of the riverbank did likewise. They passed few people at this late hour, and those few hurried along.

Durine was used to that, when he wasn't huddled inside his cloak to minimize his size, deliberately weaving to use himself as bait. He was a big man, in a soldier's cloak and sword, and few tradesmen would want to trust that his motives were benign, not late at night when there was nobody to bear witness and deter misbehavior. The military outpost was out of town, and while the town nightwatch patrolled the streets, true, they were mainly there to keep the street lanterns lit and watch and smell for fire more than crime.

They were about to cross the mouth of a road that cut down the now-lower riverbank, leading onto the docks, when Kethol froze in midstep.

"I hear something," he hissed, his voice barely a whisper. "Up ahead."

Their cloaks were a dull brown by design; they wrapped them about themselves as they faded back into the dark shadows under a riverfront building, Durine stepping aside to avoid a piling. The road was now close enough to the riverbank that the bottom of the building was suspended on pilings not quite a manheight tall: Durine had to bend his head as he stepped back and flattened himself against the wall between two large barrels, although Kethol simply squatted down, pulling his cloak around him, turning himself into a shapeless dark mass.

Kethol's hearing was even better than Durine's; it took a another few moments before Durine could make out the muffled sound of somebody trying to shout or scream or at least make some sort of sound over a gag, and it was a few moments later that a trio of young men dragged a struggling woman down the street and onto the docks, moving quickly out of the splash of light from the streetpole lantern and into the dark.

They were nobly dressed, although perhaps not expensively. Shirts that white, even stained by dirt and wine, were not clothes for the common folks, and while nobles were hardly the only ones to

carry swords, such short basket-hilted rapiers were weapons for du-
els, not for war.

They were also drunk—at least the three men were, as they
dragged their captive off the street and onto the boardwalk, unceremoniously shoving her along. She had apparently given them more
resistance than they had cared for: her right eye was already swollen
shut, and she had been gagged with a wadding of cloth tied in place,
her wrists bound behind her with leather straps.

Durinc wouldn't have wanted to bet that she was overly pretty
under the best of circumstances, and this wasn't the best of circumstances. Her hair was long but tied back, and her shift and coarse-
woven skirt militated against any middle-class origin. Large unbound
breasts flopped under her blouse, and her unswollen eye was wild
over the gag.

One of the men unfastened his cloak and spread it on the boards,
while the other two held her. He made a sarcastically extravagant
gesture and bow, as though cordially inviting her to take her place
on it—and then he dumped her to the ground with a quick cuff and
leg sweep when she didn't immediately comply.

Durine frowned. He shouldn't be here. It was no concern of his
if three local bravos wanted to take their turns riding a local girl.
Yes, Durine would have quickly and economically dispatched anybody who tried any such thing on somebody he was bound to protect,
but some random Riverforks tradesman's daughter or barmaid or
whatever she was wasn't under his protection. The girl would be a
little sore in the morning, no doubt, but she'd likely heal, and getting
involved in others' squabbles was a bad habit that Durine had never
had to struggle to give up because he had never considered taking
it up in the first place.

Durine searched about for a convenient exit, and suppressed a
sigh. There was no way out that didn't involve leaving himself and
Kethol open to observation by the three bravos, and that could be
awkward. They were armed, of course, and might take offense at an
interruption in their fun. Durine didn't think much of their fun, but
he didn't believe in looking for a fight when there was no profit in

it. He was big, and he was strong, and he was fast, but a blade in the hands of a better or luckier swordsman could cleave through his flesh just as easily as it could a smaller, weaker, slower man's. That had happened to him before, and while he would surely have to demonstrate that again eventually, he had no desire to do so to no good purpose at the moment.

The girl's hands were retied to a support post, and two of the bravos each grasped an ankle and pulled them apart while the third dropped to his knees between her legs, unbuckling his sword belt and setting it aside before he untied her skirt and pushed up her blouse, then unbuttoned his trousers.

He was already erect; the exercise had apparently stimulated him.

Well, Durine decided, the best thing to do would be to just wait until they finished with her. There was always danger of the night-watch coming by, and while that risk clearly hadn't dissuaded these three—something that also spoke of noble birth and connections—it would encourage them to be quick with her. Durine had spent enough time in line at various cheap brothels or at whores' tents at the outskirts of encampments to know how quickly men could finish with a woman when they were in a hurry, himself included.

With a bit of luck, Kethol would still be able to try his hand at a game of bones with the sailors and dwarves. Durine leaned back against the wall and settled in for the wait.

It was all reasonable, and to do anything else would have been either risky or downright stupid, so it only came as a vague surprise to Durine when Kethol rose up from where he crouched and launched himself toward the three, barely showing the discretion to muffle the shout that came to his lips.

Durine would have sworn at Kethol, and he gladly would have grabbed him by the shoulders and tried to shake some sense into him, but neither would have done any good, so he just straightened and rose from his hiding place, and followed his companion out onto the dock.

Kethol grabbed the leader's hair—at least, Durine assumed it was the leader; surely the leader would have chosen to go first—and yanked him, hard, off the girl, then booted him smartly in the butt.

As the would-be rapist tumbled across the wood, Kethol drew his sword and, with a quick back-and-forth motion, cut the leather straps binding the girl's wrists to the post. Durine had to admire Kethol's technique and control, if not his good sense—slashing at the straps that way with the tip of a sword was the sort of thing that was likely to get fingers severed, but there was not even a muffled groan from the girl, and the straps fell away, while the leader of the group struggled back to his feet, yanking his trousers up as best he could.

The now wild-eyed youngster had unbuckled his sword belt and set it to one side so it would not get in his way.

Durine figured it couldn't do any harm to put his own foot on the scabbard. There was still ample opportunity to turn this into merely an example of Kethol's stupid heroics and not a full-scale fight, and Durine would try to take advantage of that opportunity if he could. If they let him. If they could let him.

The other two had released the girl's ankles and leaped to their feet; they stepped back, hands on the hilts of their swords.

"Ta havath," Durine said, letting his voice rumble. "Stand easy, the lot of you." His own hand was on the hilt of his sword, but he hadn't drawn. It would have been good to have his sword in his hand, but things were balanced on a knifepoint here, and drawing now would surely start a fight that would profit nobody.

The girl didn't wait to see how it would all turn out: she snatched up her skirt as she dashed off in the direction that Durine and Kethol had come from, her free hand working at her gag. She quickly vanished around the bend, naked legs flashing.

The last Durine saw of her was the bouncing of a surprisingly nicely rounded rump. He didn't blame her for not waiting around to see how it would end. For all she knew, Durine and Kethol would have taken up where the noble bravos had left off.

Kethol had taken a step forward, well within range where a quick bounce and lunge could bring his sword tip through either or both of them before they could draw their own swords. Kethol was, no question, acting like a fool, but at least he was acting like a sensible fool, not inviting them to draw their swords. Nobles had more time to spend practicing with the sword, and most of the time they could count on being able to beat lessers, particularly ordinary soldiers who had to spend their training time mastering bows and pikes—and, in the case of imperial troops, guns as well.

"Be easy," Durine said. "Let's let it end here. You can't expect my friend Erven to stand by while you rape his cousin, and I can't see why it has to get any more exciting than this. Erven," he said again, figuring even Kethol would pick up on the necessity of not using their real names, "let it go. We'll just head back the way we came, and you fine young gentlemen can head back the way you came, with none of us the poorer for it than a few bruises on the girl and a few splinters in the buttocks. Let's all be on our way and gone before the girl summons the nightwatch and has us all hauled before the lord warden to be held for the next judge."

"I'm not afraid of a good Holtish judge hearing of us having a bit of innocent fun with a peasant girl," the leader said. "And get your foot off my sword and I'll show you who is much the poorer," he went on.

He buttoned the last button on his fly, showing either an over-developed sense of dress or, more likely, a feeling of less vulnerability with his suddenly flaccid penis tucked away instead of flapping in the chilly breeze.

One of the others started to make a move, and Kethol took a quick step forward, sword tip out, stopping when his opponent thought better of it.

Durine kept his irritation off his face. But, still . . . Kethol hadn't done anything quite this stupidly heroic since the Old Emperor's Last Ride. But back then they were traveling quickly through neutral territory, trying to get out and away before word that the emperor was vulnerable brought the slavers down on them; as long as they could move faster than any news, they were fine. In those days, in the old days, the right thing to do would have been to just kill the three of them, hide the bodies under the docks, perhaps, and get out of town before the smell would lead to their being found.

That might still be the best thing to do here, but the girl was the problem. If she'd been seen with these three, when they turned up dead, the Lord Warden or mayor—Durine didn't know which governed Riverforks—would surely have the town wardens speak with her, and Durine wasn't sanguine about the possibility of her not giving a description of the two of them if asked.

Loyalty was a tree that grew slowly, over years; not something you could instantly stick in a scared girl by sending her running off naked into the night. He and Kethol should have waited while the three took turns sticking something else into her.

But it was too late for that.

Durine swept his foot to one side, flinging the sword belt over the side of the boardwalk, letting it *thwuck* on the muck at the river's edge below.

"Enough," he said. "It's over. Let it be over." He started to move away, kicking the leader's cloak to one side to clear the way for Kethol to back up without tripping. They could fade back into the night and be done with this.

The other two seemed to relax as Kethol's careful retreat brought them out of range of his sword. That was the most tense moment—would they take it as an opportunity to draw their own weapons and charge? There wasn't much reason to worry about flintlocks in Holtun, except among the most elite and trusted occupation troops. And a man moving quickly, dodging from side to side, would be close to safe from a pistol at all but the closest range. Legend aside, the things were deucedly hard to aim.

So it was all perfectly reasonable that they'd disengage with no further damage, which was fine with Durine. You got in enough fights for necessity and money, after all.

But the leader snatched at the hilt of one of his companions' swords, and shoved him aside in order to draw it.

Well, that was the way of fighting, and of war. It could make all the sense in the world to avoid it, but if anybody didn't want to be sensible, nobody could be.

"Mine," Durine said.

Kethol was the better duelist of the two of them, but it was without protest or even a look sideways that he took a delicate, dancing step to one side and backward, his sword tip momentarily wavering as he brought it into line with the attacker for just a moment, then back to hover near the chest of the remaining armed young bravo, who had the sense to keep his hands up, fingers spread as wide as his eyes.

Durine already had his own sword in his hand, although for the life of him, he couldn't remember when he had drawn it. It wasn't a light duelist's rapier but a heavier saber, rigid and inflexible the way Durine liked his swords, sharpened on the top edge a handsbreadth back, to allow for a backhanded slash that a weaker man couldn't have considered.

Yes, the point was deadlier than the edge, but the point and the edge were deadlier than the point alone.

Yes, skill was far more important than strength in swordplay, but skill plus strength was better than skill alone.

Yes, there were swordsmen who could best Durine, but no, not these swordsmen, not today, not here, not now.

Sober, ready, braced, the young swordsman could probably have given a better accounting of himself, but he was drunk and angry, and too eager. Durine engaged and parried easily as they closed, coming almost chest to chest.

This was where the hidden left-handed dagger was supposed to have ended things for Durine, but Durine's own left hand had already seized his opponent's shoulder as they closed, and his bruising grip, combined with the pressure of the forte of his blade, spun the youngster half around, at least momentarily bringing the hidden weapon out of play, and Durine's raised knee that slammed into his opponent's buttocks, lifting him clear into the air, kept him off balance long enough for Durine to slam the brass pommel of his saber into the other's shoulder, causing his borrowed sword to clatter to the boards.

There was still some—too much—energy left him, so Durine

just fastened the fingers of his free hand on the boy's left wrist to keep the knife under control, at least for a moment, and dropped his own saber so that he could fasten his other fingers on the seat of the boy's trousers. He lifted him up, flinging him easily over the boardwalk's rail and into the water below, where he landed with a loud splash and a louder shout of anger and indignation.

"Follow your friend, if you please." Kethol gestured with his sword tip toward the railing. "No, no, not the stairs. Just jump over the railing."

"But . . ."

"Or take up your weapons," Durine said, straightening with both his own sword in his right hand and the newly acquired rapier in his left, "and since your friend didn't just let this be, let's let it end with you splattered either with mud or with blood and shit, and bodies all over the boardwalk." His lips tightened. "I've had about enough of this, and of you, for one evening. Choose."

They looked at each other, and then the one who still had his sword shook his head and the other walked to the railing, clambered over, and dropped down, while the last of them looked them over very carefully before vaulting neatly over the railing.

Durine hefted his newly acquired sword. A good sword was always worth money, but he didn't have the contacts to sell it quickly and discreetly here, and carrying around a clearly identifiable sword like this one wouldn't be a good idea, so he hid it in the corner near where he and Kethol had hidden, and walked on.

There was probably still time to get to the game, let Kethol win some money, fight their way to safety, and make a profit on the evening.

5

⚜ Leaving Riverforks

Pirojil woke to the scritching of rats. And alone. Except for the rat.

The rat was a large, fat animal, bristling whiskers twitching as its long yellowed teeth gnawed at the seam of Kethol's leather saddlebags. Pirojil quickly had a knife in his hand—but the rat caught the movement and skittered off into the shadows of the corner, vanishing into what was no doubt some improbably small hole. Rats were like that. If you wanted to kill one badly enough—and Pirojil had once been hungry enough to eat rats, and eat rats he would again, were he again that hungry—you had to think ahead of them.

He levered himself out of bed and stood unsteadily. His bladder was full to bursting, his head ached, and his gut clenched like a fist at the smell of food coming from somewhere. The reek of cooking sausage made him gag.

Too much beer last night.

The chair was still propped under the door latch, which wasn't surprising. The other two would have woken him when they returned so he could let them in. A chair propped up against the door wasn't a guarantee against a middle-of-the-night invasion, but it was much safer than trusting to keys provided by the owner.

Dawn light more oozed than streamed in through the dirty greased-paper window.

He was vaguely bothered by their absence, but Kethol could have found a game and Durine an all-night whore. Or they both could be dead. Either way, it could wait.

He quickly checked their cache—it was intact—and pulled on his trousers and boots before heading down the hall to the privy at the end of it.

It must have been the hangover; the smell of rotting excrement made him gag badly enough to vomit up what was left of whatever he had eaten last night. He quickly finished relieving himself and headed back to their rooms, then rinsed out his mouth with a deep draught from the water pitcher.

Beer. A quick mug of beer would clear his head and settle his stomach.

The common room was busy in the morning, although not in the noisy way it had been at night. Over in the corner, the six dwarves from last night—at least, Pirojil assumed it was the same six; he had trouble telling dwarves apart—were busy bolting down their breakfast of bread, onion, and that nauseating-smelling sausage, while the teamsters took their time over huge wooden bowls of stew. Erenor the wizard was nowhere to be seen, but you wouldn't expect that an old man would be up that late at night and again up this early in the morning.

The innkeeper wasn't in evidence, either, so Pirojil poured himself a large mug of sour beer from an open firkin and sat down at the same table he'd had last night, the one where he had lost the arm wrestling match to Erenor.

Well, it wasn't the best beer he'd ever had, but it did wash the taste of vomit from his mouth, and that was something, and in a little while, it had cleared the fog from his brain and the fire from his stomach enough that he was starting to think about food.

A ragged boy of about ten, maybe twelve, pushed through the inner set of swinging doors into the common room, his ferretlike face scanning the room before he settled on Pirojil.

"Is your name Pirojil?" the boy asked.

Pirojil didn't see any need to deny it. "Yes."

"Your friend said you'd give me a copper."

Pirojil smiled. "And why would he say such a silly thing as that?"

"He said to tell you that—how did he say it?—once a woman's had an orc, she won't go back, whatever that means, and that when I said that, you'd give me a copper."

It meant that the boy had come from Kethol. Maybe nothing more, but . . . but Kethol wouldn't be sending a boy if there was no problem.

"Fine," Pirojil said, digging into his pouch and coming out with a small copper quartermark that he set on the table.

The boy reached for it. Pirojil slapped his hand down over the coin. "What else did he say?"

The boy hesitated, then shrugged. "He and your big ugly friend are in the jail, and they thought you would pay to know that."

Pirojil stood steadily. Breakfast could wait. He pulled another coin out of his pocket and held it up for the boy. "Where's the jail?"

Getting in to see the Lord Warden was impossible; the Lord Warden was off hunting or tax collecting, or flogging peasants, or sitting under a tree writing poetry, or whatever such a worthy would spend his time doing.

Getting in to see Durine and Kethol was a lot easier. Getting them out would be the problem.

The jail in Riverforks had been carved into the stone of the riverbank itself, the entrance just above the high-water mark. Pirojil walked down the carved steps. There was another way in, of course, but Pirojil had no particular desire to be dropped down through the gratings at the top, or even lowered via a ladder that would be withdrawn before the grating would be sealed.

Some spring, the river would rise enough that a flood would fill the jail and drown its occupants like rats, perhaps—but maybe Pirojil was just being ungenerous. The jail wasn't a dungeon, after all; it was mainly a place to store a troublesome traveler until the arrival of somebody who would pay their way out of trouble—as well as the occasional more serious miscreant, who would have to wait for the high justice of the baron's or emperor's judges, when those worthies got around to Riverforks.

Getting in was no problem. The bored jailer was used to having a barge captain or farmer come to see an abashed sailor or farmworker and hear his protestations and promises before agreeing to pay his fines, and the bribe was smaller than Pirojil had expected.

Pirojil surrendered his sword belt at the entrance and was led down a dark, dank corridor to a barred cell where Kethol paced back and forth while Durine stretched his bulk out on a pile of straw, seemingly asleep.

The bars of the cell were flat pieces of black iron, riveted together at the junction. A good dwarven metal saw could cut through any of the bars, perhaps—say, a night and a day of sawing, if you had to do it quietly—but it would take a good eight, ten, maybe a dozen cuts to create a hole big enough for Kethol, and Durine would require a larger one. There was one gap large enough to pass a slop bucket or food bucket in and out, but that was hardly big enough for a baby.

No door at this level. The only entrance or exit was the barred hatch in the ceiling, more than a manheight above their heads.

Pirojil didn't say anything for a moment. Then: "What happened?"

Kethol shook his head. "We ran into a little trouble last night. I . . . started a fight with a trio of young bravos, and it turns out that one of them is Lordling Mattern, Lord Lerna's son."

"It seems that this Mattern broke his leg in a fall he took, vaulting over a fence and into the river." Durine's eyes didn't open. "With some help from the Spider, he's limping around on it, but he's not happy, and Lerna isn't due back in town for a full tenday. The Lord Warden's not going to want to let us go without his permission."

There were a dozen questions that Pirojil would have liked to ask, for effect if not because he didn't know. Like why, if Kethol had started a fight, Durine had been drawn into it. But he knew the answer.

The question wasn't how to make the two of them feel like the couple of idiots they were—you just didn't get into fights with the nobility—but how to deal with the problem as it was, and preferably without drawing a lot of attention.

"I'll see what I can do," he said.

He would need help, and the only two friends he had in town were in jail, so he couldn't count on them. For a moment he toyed with the idea of the wizard Erenor and a seeming, but he couldn't figure out a way to turn that into an escape.

Hmm . . .

There was another option.

The dowager empress would surely have forbidden it if she had been here, but that was the nice thing about Riverforks:

She wasn't here.

He quickened his pace. A quick jog-trot would clear the beer and sleep and cobwebs from his brain.

The local military garrison was an old castle on a hill a short ride outside of town. The wall was low and narrow, Euar'den style, and the ramparts were crumbling in spots; until it had been taken over by imperial occupation troops, it had probably stood empty for a generation or more. The main gate was closed, and the grass growing in front of it showed that it wasn't in common use, so Pirojil rode around the dirt path circling the hill.

A single sleepy-eyed guard slouched against the postern gate, and made no objection when Pirojil asked to see the captain. With a good chunk of luck—say, the sort that Kethol habitually had over the bones table—the captain would be somebody Pirojil knew from the old days of the Holtun-Bieme wars, or from Biemestren during the Old Emperor's time, but Pirojil's luck wasn't in.

Captain Banderan shook his head. "I don't see a lot that I can do," he said. He probably had cut a fine figure in his uniform and armor in the old days, but he had run to fat, and what had probably been a strong and noble chin was just sagging jowls. "Steady the horse, will you?"

He gave a testing tug to the halter that kept his large black gelding fixed to the hitching post, and moved his three-legged stool back to the rear of the horse. Pirojil took a solid grip on the halter, and gave the horse a reassuring pat on the neck while Banderan sat himself down and bent up the horse's leg, digging clotted dirt and dung out of the bottom of its hoof with a dull knife.

Pirojil wasn't sure whether to think less of an officer who couldn't trust his own stablemen well enough to make sure they gave proper attention to his horse, or to admire him for doing it himself and being sure it was done right, so he settled on both.

Life was like that.

"You said you're from Furnael," Banderan said as he picked up the stool and moved around the back of the horse to the other rear leg.

"That's right." No, it wasn't right, but Pirojil didn't correct him. Legally, the barony was Barony Cullinane, but it had been the barony of the Furnael family until Thomen had become emperor.

"Well," Banderan said thoughtfully, "I might be able to put in a good word with Lord Lerna if I could tell him you were old companions from the war, and I guess that's close enough. I could talk to the Lord Warden, but he's going to want to wait for Lerna. He has to wait for Lerna, really. And he's not going to want to go to the governor over it, and neither am I." He tapped the knife against the heel of his boot to clear it, then spread his hands. "And the jailers are mainly his relatives. Doubt you'd find them wanting to let your friends go for any kind of money you'd be likely to have. Family's important around here."

"It would be best if my friends and I are well out of Riverforks and on our way as soon as possible."

"I don't see how that could be arranged." Banderan shook his head. "Although, for all my opinion's worth, your friends probably should have beaten Mattern worse. He's the second son, and always been a wild one." He frowned derisively. "His brother's off on the borders, leading a company chasing down those orcs, while Mattern rides around the city and the countryside, chasing down peasant girls to stick something entirely different than a sword in them." He raised an eyebrow. "Your friends must be good with their blades, though, if they managed to disarm him without doing more than that. Mattern's back from Biemestren just this year, and in between jumping the local girls he was supposedly studying the sword with some decent swordmaster, some fellow with a good reputation."

"Wartsel?"

Banderan smiled. "Well, that's the name I heard. You know him?"

"I've heard the name, and I think I may have seen him once or twice, but no, I don't know him." Pirojil shook his head. A soldier didn't have a lot of time to take lessons with a swordmaster in the finer points of dueling. What you learned, you learned in the troop, and if you were of a mind, from some extra sparring. And if you had actually picked up more skill than you were supposed to, it was best to minimize it, not brag about it.

"An honest answer, eh? I like that." Banderan pursed his lips. "Tell you what: you tell me what three Cullinane soldiers are doing prowling around Neranahan, and perhaps I'll see what I can do to get your friends out of jail as quickly as I can."

"But I told you we're out of that now. We're off seeing if there's some good work in Holtun, something maybe more profitable than soldiering for the Cullinanes."

Banderan shrugged. "Yes, that's what you told me, and it's not something I particularly believe." He dropped the horse's hoof and straightened, wiping the scraper on the sole of his boot. "Care to swear to that on your sword?" His light smile dropped. "I knew a man who beswore himself on his sword once; it twisted out of his hand the next time he drew it."

Pirojil never much liked swearing on his sword, not even if he was telling the truth. Asking for magical intervention was too much like asking for trouble, and Pirojil had always found trouble easily enough to come by without asking for it.

Still, telling the truth might not be the stupidest idea here. Banderan and his light company might be well settled in, but they were technically still occupation troops—Biemish, not Holts—and would be unlikely to be offended at the idea of somebody investigating some problem in a Holtish barony, as long as it wasn't *his* Holtish barony.

And besides, he didn't have much of a choice, not if he wanted Banderan's help.

Pirojil didn't have much of a lie ready, but he did have the signed orders and the death warrant in his pouch. "Well, perhaps I'd better explain everything to you."

Banderan unwrapped the scroll and read it. And read it again. "Well," he said. "Now that you've brought me into this, it would seem that I'm best off making sure the three of you disappear and are never heard from again if I don't want the dowager empress to take a personal interest in me, which, if this goes wrong, she quite possibly would. Which means that I'd better see that all three of you are quietly buried in unmarked graves, or perhaps I'd best help you."

Pirojil nodded.

Banderan raised an eyebrow. "You don't happen to have a few golden marks on you? I could use a bribe myself, and it always helps to spread some money around."

Pirojil shook his head. He had more than a few golden marks stashed, but admitting that in a keep surrounded by Banderan's men didn't make a lot of sense. Yes, if you could fight to keep it, it was yours, and all that was fine, but looking for opportunities to prove it yours that way wasn't something that appealed to Pirojil.

"Didn't think so. Well, we'll have to see if loyalty can still buy what coin might." He looked Pirojil in the eye. "I've always set a high value on loyalty myself," he said quietly. "I expect that's understood, no matter how the bones finally fall."

Pirojil didn't know quite what the fat man was getting at, but he nodded anyway. "Loyalty and honor are not something I talk about much."

Banderan's mouth twisted into a grin. It didn't look like a comfortable expression on his face. "Just as well. A man who talks too much of loyalty and honor isn't one I'd trust." He sighed. He handed the scrolls back to Pirojil and straightened himself. "Well, let's get a solid meal in our bellies; there's much to do before nightfall." He beckoned toward a soldier. "I'll need some volunteers, Ereden. Let's start with you, Alren, Manrell, and the blacksmith."

A cold wind was blowing in, scattering wispy threads of clouds through the night sky.

Pirojil crept through the night, keeping to the shadows near the buildings. The last thing he wanted to do was to draw attention to himself.

Their horses and gear were hidden down the road, watched over by one of Banderan's men, Pirojil hoped, and three others were now in Riverforks, waiting for the midnight bell, their signal to begin their parts of the plan.

Meanwhile, Pirojil hid himself in the shadow of a warehouse overlooking the jail. The five hatches over the cells were secured by a metal ladder that was used to climb in and out of the cells: the ladder was slid through two huge staples on either end of the row of hatches, then chained and locked in place. Picking the lock would perhaps have been possible for a dedicated thief, but he would then have been faced with the problem of sliding the ladder out and away without drawing the attention of the jailer below, who could quickly ring the alarm bar, waking the whole city within moments, including the nightwatch.

It wasn't an arrangement that would have been useful to keep somebody locked up for years, but that wasn't the purpose of the Riverforks jail, after all. Elves would—had—turned offenders into trees for transgressions that a human might not even be able to understand. Dwarves might lock a miscreant in a tunnel that required expanding or perhaps reshoring and reward him with food only as the work was done, but the Moderate People were different. Justice in the empire was often formal, but punishments were swift, be it a whipping in the public square, a fine, or an execution.

It would have been nice to have a detachment of dwarves right about now, Pirojil decided. They would be able to tunnel into the cells faster than a human who hadn't seen them work with stone could have thought possible.

Or, better yet, Ellegon the dragon. Ellegon could land, tear up the hatches with his immense claws, and be in the air with Pirojil, Durine, and Kethol practically before the jailer would have finished soiling himself.

Of course, these days, that might not be safe. With all the strange things that had flowed out of the breach between reality and Faerie, the cultivation of dragonbane had become more and more common, and many bowmen made it a point to keep their arrows tipped with fresh dragonbane extract.

But it didn't matter much. The dragon might answer to the emperor, and he—it? Pirojil was never sure how to figure out the sex of a dragon—probably would answer to one of the Cullinanes or Walter Slovotsky, but the dragon wasn't about to place himself at the disposal of the likes of Pirojil, and on balance that suited Pirojil just fine.

A fire-breathing dragon that could read your mind wasn't his idea of a pleasant companion.

The night was cool, but not cold, and the guard had chosen to sit outside the jail, his chair propped back against the jailhouse wall. It would have been easy to silence him—permanently—but that assumed not only that he was the only one within earshot, but that Banderan and his people would put up with a deliberate killing in the freeing of the other two.

Well, that simplified things.

Pirojil dropped down lightly behind the jailer, and as the blocky man turned, Pirojil slipped a canvas bag over his head and jerked him out of his chair, kicking him carefully in the pit of the stomach to knock the wind from him.

It was a matter of moments to tie him, hand and foot, and just a few moments more to pull up the bag for a moment and gag him thoroughly. He was disposed to struggle at first, but the prick of a knifepoint against the back of his neck disposed of that inclination.

Silencing the guards was always a lot easier when you didn't mind if they ended up dead, but the idea here was to get Durine and Kethol out with as little fuss and attention as possible. An escape from jail would be forgotten more quickly than a murder.

And besides, this wasn't an ordinary escape from jail.

Pirojil snapped his fingers once, twice, three times. Two men moved out from the shadows, and headed for the ladder that secured the cell's hatches. Everen, the troop's blacksmith, was quick and deft enough with his lockpicks to quickly and quietly open the padlocks, while his partner, whose name Pirojil either never learned or immediately forgot, thoroughly greased the staples holding down the ladder, so the two of them could slide it out quietly.

So far, so good.

Pirojil lifted the hatch on the third cell, and with the aid of both of Banderan's men lowered the ladder.

Kethol swarmed up it, a cloth-wrapped sliver of stone in his hand, relaxing only when he saw Pirojil holding one finger to his lips.

Durine was next, and Pirojil pushed the bound guard to the lip of the hole. "It was magic," he said, his voice low and guttural. "Some sort of magic. You were just keeping watch, and then there was a flash of light and a puff of smoke, and you were inside the jail, unable to speak, while your charges were gone, leaving behind nothing but a foul smell." He forced a chuckle. "The other choice, of course, is that you paid so little attention that not only could you be overpowered, but you helped find the keys and free the prisoners without even being tortured first. So it must have been magic, and what's a poor jailer to do, eh?"

The bound man nodded, and Pirojil guided him toward the ladder, freeing his hands with a quick admonition to leave the bag over his head in place.

The guard slid down the ladder, which was quickly withdrawn. Banderan's soldiers disappeared back into the shadows, and were gone. Pirojil didn't blame them much; there was no point in hanging around.

Pirojil beckoned to Durine and Kethol. Half done; the rest to go. The wizard was a wizard, after all, and his loyalty could be obtained with coin.

In the gray light just before dawn, the sign over the door read ER-ENOR, WIZARD. This was followed by a string of fuzzy symbols that ran down the sign onto the doorframe and onto the door itself.

The sign looked newer than Pirojil would have expected. He had been expecting years of weathering, but the letters and runes were freshly carved, not more than a few tendays old. Strange. Hedge-wizards tended to stay in place pretty much forever; it was a sinecure sort of job.

Low pay, perhaps, as magical occupations went, but without the risks that major magic involved. The worst danger was probably boredom.

The door had no lock, which didn't surprise him at all. Wizards didn't tend to use locks; they had better ways of protecting themselves and their property, and Pirojil had no desire or intention of becoming a demonstration of that.

He knocked hard on the door, and then even harder.

There was no answer.

There was always the window—Erenor had a real glass window—but it would be protected, as well.

So he just knocked again, then drew his knife and pounded the hilt against the wood. There would be no danger to that; a door was supposed to be knocked upon, as long as it was done by somebody not trying to break in.

"I'm coming," a voice grumbled from inside. "Just hold on; I'll be there in a moment."

There was a whisper of hushed voices from inside, and as the door opened Pirojil saw a flash of slim naked legs vanishing through a beaded curtain into a dark room beyond.

It seemed that the wizard had been busy.

"Oh," Erenor said. "It's you."

He was dressed only in a pair of blousy pantaloons. His seeming as a young man was back in place; strong muscles played under sweat-soaked skin. There was, it would appear, more use for a seeming than simply winning a bout of arm wrestling in the bar.

No, that didn't make sense.

Seemings were by definition relatively minor spells—even major seemings were easily broken.

If Erenor had developed a spell of such power as to turn a seeming real and could employ the energies and forces necessary simply to spend a night in bed with a girl, he wouldn't be spending his days as a hedge-magician in Riverforks.

Henrad, the emperor's own wizard, certainly wasn't capable of such a thing, and Henrad was supposedly quite good at what he did.

Pirojil was no expert on magic, but . . .

No. Erenor wasn't that good.

Which meant that Erenor had been using a seeming in the tavern, but not to make himself appear young and strong. It had been used to make him—a young, strong man—appear old and feeble, and all he had done had been to dispel it, and then legitimately beat the surprised Pirojil at arm wrestling and sell him a useless amulet.

"I've come to talk to you about this amulet you sold me," Pirojil said. "The one that dispels these powerful seemings of yours." He reached out and touched it to Erenor's sweaty chest. "How fascinating! It doesn't appear to be working. Imagine that."

"Well," Erenor said, "one wouldn't expect—"

"That a wizard of such power and wisdom would be here in Riverforks. And I should have, not being a local buffoon. And if I'd been sober, I'd not have thought twice about it. But perhaps a minor, young wizard, barely more than an apprentice, a man of more cleverness than learning, would find himself a town to spend at least some time in while selling impotent amulets, before moving on. Magic has value, but belief in magic has more, eh?"

Pirojil pushed Erenor aside and stepped into the wizard's shop, something he wouldn't have considered moments before. Erenor was more of a scoundrel than a wizard, and Pirojil had no particular fear of scoundrels.

Pirojil tossed Erenor the amulet he had bought. "Get rid of the girl," he said. "We have a deal to make."

"But—"

"Just do it."

"So?" Erenor poured himself a drink from a mottled clay bottle, not offering one to Pirojil. "You have some sort of offer to make?"

Pirojil didn't like working with wizards. But there could be some advantages to having one around who had more cleverness than talent, and there was no advantage whatsoever in leaving this one behind to swear that the escape from the jail had involved magic.

"Given your skills," Pirojil said, "I assume you know how to ride a horse very fast."

"Because . . . ?"

"Because you've probably had to ride it very fast out of town on more than one occasion. Here's another one."

"And I should do this because . . . ?" Erenor sipped at his mug.

"Well, because there's been an escape from the jail that may be thought to involve magic just a short while ago, and if you're not around to investigate the magical source of it, you're likely to be suspected of being involved. So you'd best be riding out."

"Which is why I'd want to be sure to stay here, no?"

The point of Pirojil's sword was at Erenor's throat. "No," he said. "Particularly given that my friends are faster than I am, and far more irritable, and they would much rather the local lords be fearfully considering chasing a wizard rather than bravely riding in search of us."

Erenor smiled weakly. "I see their point. And yours, as well."

"Do you need much time in packing? Or would you prefer to decide things here, between the two of us?"

Erenor was a younger man, with a right arm that he no doubt

kept strong and powerful with exercise in order to cozen the credulous, but Pirojil wouldn't have given a copper shard for Erenor's chances against him in a real fight, not even one that didn't start with Pirojil's sword out and ready.

Erenor took barely a moment to come to the same conclusion. His smile was too broad by half, but it was a smile of concession. "I've a bag packed and waiting."

"I'd have thought so."

Kethol and Durine were waiting with fresh horses at the north end of town. Banderan had been generous; there were six horses, and while they were hardly highbred Biemestren warhorses, they looked sound enough. Kethol and Durine had each picked a brown gelding; Pirojil took the remaining saddled horse, a large gray mare, and boosted Erenor up to the bare back of a small bay, adding the wizard's bag to the gear strapped to the coal-black packhorse.

Let the wizard bounce along on bareback.

"It occurs to me," Kethol said, "that after we're clear of town, Erenor here might want to turn around and ride back here, perhaps to clear himself with the locals, perhaps setting them upon our trail in the doing."

"It's occurred to me, too," Pirojil said. "I think we'd better have a new companion, at least for a time."

Erenor spread his hands. "It would be my pleasure, of course. I so much enjoyed being woken this morning to find that I have to flee my all-too-comfortable existence here that I'd not think of departing from your company." His mouth tightened. "But if I did decide to part ways with you, I'm not fool enough to return here. Too much attention would have already been drawn to me, and I'm unfond of that." He patted the neck of his horse. "Now, shall we go?"

"In a moment." It might be handy to have a wizard along, even one who was barely an apprentice. Pirojil opened the wizard's bag and dug through it until he found three leather-bound books.

"Now, friend Pirojil—"

"Be still," Durine said, his face grim.

Pirojil pulled out the smallest one, a slim book bound in brown leather and fastened shut with a buckle and strap. He unbuckled the straps and opened it. It was impossible to focus on the letters on the page; they shifted and swam in front of his eyes. It wasn't just that they were out of focus, either; it was like trying to read something in a dream, where you knew you'd never be able to, but your eyes couldn't help but try.

He closed the book, and wiped at his eyes. He didn't have the gift of magic, and he'd no more be able to read the words than he'd be able to fly. It was painful to try, in a way he couldn't have explained to anybody else.

The two other books were thicker, and bound in finer black leather, but they were the same inside.

Pirojil tossed one book to Durine and another to Kethol. "We'll hold on to these for you, for the time being."

"Well, that does seem reasonable, under the circumstances," Erenor said, sounding pleasant enough about it; he should probably have gone into acting rather than magic. "I see no problem with that. And perhaps we can discuss it further at some later time, eh?"

Kethol opened his mouth to say something, but Durine frowned him to silence. "Discussion later," the big man said. "Let's get out of here before we get into worse trouble."

Erenor actually chuckled. "I would hardly find that likely."

6

A Night on Woodsdun

Night on the flat-topped hill overlooking the village of Woodsdun was crisp and cold, but too dry without beer. Durine missed beer.

At least there was food, even if the food was military field rations. The best part of it was the amazingly fresh-tasting, cedary water from the water bags and the tiny pieces of honey candy wrapped in greased paper. The rest, though, was unchewable hardtack—you had to break off a piece and let it soften to tastelessness in your mouth—accompanied by a handful of tiny, dried smoked sausages that looked like a crooked old man's dismembered fingers and probably tasted about the same.

On the other hand, Durine thought, the meal was also without bars or walls that it would take a dwarf to tunnel through. That was, all things considered, not the worst possible deal.

Take the sort of simple mound that small children make in the dirt, enlarge it to giant size and cover it with grasses and brush, then slice off the top with a giant's sword, and you had the hill that the locals called Woodsdun, same as the village below. Parts of an old road twisted up the side toward the top, but much of it had been overgrown.

Some rocks and rubble remained, ruins of a castle that had overlooked the surroundings long ago, but only the largest and smallest stones; the bones and guts of a dead castle were useful for building more mundane structures, and anything both large enough to be useful and small enough to be easily portable had long since been loaded on sledges and dragged down the hill, or perhaps just rolled downhill to help build, say, a house or a road in the village below.

Woodsdun was a smallish village, a cluster of perhaps thirty or so hovels where the road crossed a creek, but there probably was at least a towner with a room or a barn to let for the night. On the other hand, the top of the hill was a much better place to wait and see if a band of a lordling's men-at-arms was riding in pursuit, and Kethol and Pirojil had pushed all four men and all six horses hard to make it this far by dusk, harder than Durine would have.

Horses were stupid creatures—push one too far, too hard, and it would up and die on you. Better to bet on your fighting arm, and those of your companions, than on a horse's sense of self-preservation.

This time, the gamble had worked. The horses had worked themselves into an unhealthy lather, but they were grazing peacefully downslope, twist-hobbled against wandering far off during the night. By morning they would be ready to travel again.

What really irritated Durine, though, besides the presence of the wizard, was the lack of a fire. It was unlikely but possible, of course, that a villager below would notice the sparks from their fire on the hilltop, so there was to be no fire this night, not while they couldn't be sure there was no pursuit. No fire didn't just mean cold food. Durine had been a soldier far too long to really worry about food, as long as there was enough of it to fill the belly.

But there was more to fire than something to cook with. Durine liked fire; it warmed him in a way that went beyond the physical. Even with his horse blanket beneath him to keep the ground from sucking the heat from his body, even wrapped in his cloak, it would be a cold night, and even if it hadn't, he would have wanted a fire.

Durine knew himself well: tonight he would dream of stones heated in a campfire, then buried under a thin layer of dirt beneath his bed of cold ground. His dreams—as opposed to his nightmares—were always satisfying to him, as they filled in whatever lack he most felt during his waking hours. When he was younger and more hot-blooded, his dreams had been filled with blood and thick yellow worms of intestines writhing on the ground, but he had long had enough of that to satisfy any such lust, and his red dreams had turned all pale and sallow, the color of a dead man's face.

His dreams had been about food from time to time, and even now, every so often it was a woman, although those urges had long started to wither and fade. Even for a long while after he had found himself partnered with Kethol and Pirojil, he had dreamed of being able to leave his back unguarded, but those dreams were gone.

Warmth was the thing that he would miss most tonight, and he would miss it until he fell asleep. And then all would be fine; he would spend his sleeping hours wrapped in the warmth of dreams of warmth, and if he awoke to a cold reality, so be it.

Kethol had already wrapped himself in his own cloak and fallen asleep. Or pretended to, perhaps; if he hadn't grown tired of Pirojil's long discourse on the stupidity of Kethol's heroics in Riverforks, he was the only one of the three listeners who hadn't, including Pirojil— and Pirojil had volunteered for first watch, as usual.

Pirojil would take first watch; Durine, who could easily wake up for his own watch and then fall back asleep when it was finished, would take the second; and Kethol, the third.

Erenor, of course, wanted to stay up and talk, but that was fine with Durine. He would learn quickly enough when traveling with the three of them that you slept and ate when you could when you were on the road, and if that lesson were to cause the wizard a day of misery on the next day's ride, that was more than fine with Durine, as well.

Durine wrapped himself in his cloak and stretched out on his horse blanket, his sword under his right hand, a sack of feed grain as comfortable a pillow as there was. He lay back in the cold, and listened to them talk though the haze of oncoming sleep.

"Well, I had a disagreement with my master, back when I was an apprentice," Erenor said, "and all things considered, it seemed wise to strike out on my own."

"Disagreement?" Durine didn't have to turn his head or open his eyes to see Pirojil's twisted smile in his mind's eye. "What did you try to steal from him?"

"Stealing? No. It wasn't a matter of stealing," Erenor said. "And that's such an ugly word. It was an issue of how . . . advanced an apprentice I was. He felt that his spell books were perhaps too, oh, sophisticated for me, and that my talents should be better focused on sweeping out his quarters, preparing his food, and waiting upon his needs, both professional and personal—with my only reward that honor, plus an occasional bit of training of a minor cantrip or trivial glamour. I felt that my fires were banked too deeply, and might go out without proper feeding.

"So, after some perhaps overly vigorous discussion, we parted ways, and I've made my own way since then. It's not a bad life, and those seeming spells I've managed to master, I'm really quite good at. I doubt there's a man in Riverforks who doesn't think that the wizened wizard is the real me, and the muscular young man an illusion I find convenient to make seem real every now and then."

"You went quickly past that discussion. Did he survive it? This discussion, I mean."

"Possibly."

Pirojil laughed. "So you didn't quite cut his head all the way off and burn it separately from the body, eh?"

"Now, now, now, we're not talking about Arta Myrdhyn or Lucius of Pandathaway, after all, the sort who have prepared spells to regrow a cut tongue and spoken the dominatives and all the rest with a tone of permanence, needing but a tongueless grunt as an instigator. My . . . belated and lamented teacher was a fine wizard, certainly, but not the sort to survive losing so vehement an argument. He made a point or two, certainly, but I felt I got the better of the debate, and well, since I wasn't quite competent to take his place—"

"You weren't good enough. And you'd have had your head hacked off for killing a useful wizard."

"You have a way of putting things so unpleasantly. Could we not say that my abilities are not unlimited, and leave it at that? The good people of my teacher's home abode had come to expect perhaps a higher level of competence than I was immediately ready to demonstrate, and I found it expedient to depart for less demanding fields of endeavor."

Pirojil laughed.

Kethol woke to a rush of wind like that of a violent storm, and the loud flapping of leathery wings beating hard against the crisp, cold night air. He didn't remember throwing off his cloak and blankets, but he was already on his feet, sword in his hand. Durine was already on *his* feet, his cloak wrapped about him and flapping in the wind, his sword sheathed.

Good evening, sounded in Kethol's mind. He had heard that mental voice before, and while he knew people who were comforted by it, he wasn't among them.

The dragon dropped the last manheight to the ground, shaking both Pirojil and the wizard out of their sleep.

Pirojil rose slowly, although the wizard only struggled.

If it hadn't been for the dragon, Kethol would have had to laugh out loud. Durine or Pirojil had clearly tired of watching out for the wizard and taken the appropriate precautions against the three of them being knifed in their sleep: Erenor had been bound, hand and foot, with a rope around his neck tied to a nearby bush. Any excess movement would have rustled the branches, and on the road, not one of the three would sleep through a warning sound like that. They might be able to snore through the tromping of horses or the cries of a drillmaster on the field or the cries of a market outside, perhaps, but not something as threatening as the rustling of branches.

You had to keep your priorities straight, after all.

The dragon craned its huge neck to look down at Kethol with huge unblinking eyes, each larger than the formal dinner plates that the Old Emperor used at table. The dragon's head was vaguely like a forest lizard's, except that it was longer, teeth the size of a man's forearm showing even though its mouth was closed.

It was a huge beast, its body the size of a large house, even excluding the immense leathery wings that it folded down around itself with a few quick final flips that sent sand and dust whipping into the air.

Is there some problem?

Kethol had faced things he feared more, but nothing before that made him fear stuttering.

"Little enough, Ellegon," Pirojil said, saving Kethol the embarrassment. "A cold night—"

And a fire would be unwise. I understand all too well.

Durine grunted. "That I'd doubt."

The dragon snorted. Derisively, Kethol presumed.

Then you're a fool. With all the things that leaked out of Faerie not too long ago still about during the day and particularly the night, the number of arrows and bolts and wall-top spikes coated with dragonbane has gotten to the point where it's enough to make even the most daring dragon nervous, and I've always been the cautious type, myself.

The bush that Erenor was tied to was shaking hard. If Erenor could have escaped by wriggling across the ground like a snake, he would have been gone quickly. His eyes were wide in fear, and he couldn't stop trembling, and from the stink that made its way to Kethol's nostrils, he'd been unable to control himself in other ways as well.

I'd just as soon you not untie your new companion, the dragon said. *Unless you're sure there's no dragonbane within reach.*

The Old Emperor had once said that one thing you should never do was lie to the dragon. Lying to yourself was much safer.

Ellegon didn't often choose to read minds, but . . .

"No, there's definitely some," Kethol said. "The arrows in my quiver are coated."

Kethol gestured toward his gear, but he didn't make a move toward it. Yes, the dragon could certainly read his mind well enough to know that he meant it no harm, but what if it didn't bother to? Kethol had seen a man die, writhing in dragonfire, more than once. It wasn't something you forgot. Particularly the smell. It could be argued that the dragon was the most important weapon that turned

the war Bieme had been losing into the Biemish victory that had
created the empire.

*So, you, too, have dragonbane on you, eh? Should I be con-
cerned? Or vaguely irritated?*

"Nothing to do with you, Ellegon," Pirojil said. "But, as you said,
with things having rushed out of Faerie, it seems reasonable to have
some around, no?"

Umph. Folding its tree-trunk legs beneath its body like a cat,
the dragon settled down to the ground. A netting of ropes tied to its
huge torso held a collection of lashed bags and boxes. In its spare
time—when it wasn't busy doing whatever it was that a dragon did;
the way Ellegon spent his time wasn't something to be shared with
the likes of Kethol and his friends—the dragon had been known to
help out the emperor by carrying the imperial mail faster than the
imperial messengers could, and in far greater bulk and with much
greater secrecy than the telegraph.

Steam whispered out from between its leathery lips. *And it
would be reasonable to have some dried, powdered aconite root in
your spicer kit, just in case you wanted to poison a fancier of
horseradish, eh?*

For some reason, that made Erenor stop struggling for just a
moment.

Kethol realized that he still was standing with his sword in his
hand, and that was a silly thing to be doing under the circumstances.
Ellegon meant no harm, and even if the dragon did, a sword would
be as useful against it as a curse. Less; the dragon might be offended
or insulted by a curse, but an unenchanted sword had no more
chance of cutting through those scales than a leaf did.

So Kethol just stooped and resheathed his blade in his scabbard.

The dragon's massive head turned toward where Erenor lay
bound. *I see you have a new pet.*

Pirojil laughed. "It was convenient to have a wizard along."

*As it might still be. Keep your eyes and ears open in Keranahan.
I'm delivering some dispatches there,* the dragon said.

"I know," Pirojil said. "We've been sent by the—"

By the dowager empress to investigate some arranged marriage. Yes, I know. She tried to get Walter Slovotsky to look into it, but he was smart enough to slip away before he was exactly ordered to do it, and then didn't have to have any discussion with Thomen or Beralyn about what his status was or is.

"I see."

And it seems, the dragon said as it rose to its feet, *that some people aren't as smart.*

There was another explanation, of course: the possibility that it had nothing to do with being smart or not being smart, but that Kethol and the rest were simply obeying orders, that they simply had had no choice . . . That possibility didn't occur to the dragon.

Oh, that occurred to me, Kethol, truly it did, the dragon said. *But it just didn't occur to me that it was an important distinction.*

The dragon craned its neck toward one of the larger rocks. Its massive jaw parted slightly, and a gout of orange fire issued toward the rock, fingers of flame licking and caressing the rough surface for only a few moments.

Heat washed against Kethol's face, even when the dragon closed its mouth and then leaped into the air, massive wings beating hard enough to drive dust and sand painfully into the lids of Kethol's now-tightly-closed eyes.

But, it said, as it rose into the sky and flapped away, *there's no reason that even the stupidly obedient shouldn't be able to sleep with some warmth and comfort.*

7

⚜ Treseen and Elanee

Governor Treseen was just returned from the Residence when the message arrived.

It had been a slow and pleasant ride back from his breakfast with the baroness out at what used to be the baron's country home, and a leisurely ride was a rare treat these days, what with the work of his office.

It wasn't like the old days, but then again, these days he slept in a clean bed, a warm meal resting comfortably in his belly. There was much more to be said for the new days than the old days.

And the future was bright with promise.

He doffed his riding coat and tossed his gloves to the chair in front of his desk and sat down.

Work, work, work.

There were tax reports from the village wardens to go over and scouting reports from the occupation troops on the borderlands that had to be read. A case of fulghum rot had hit outside of some of the northern villages, and it was proving resistant to the Spidersect spells that should have stopped it cold. He'd have to have a word with Trewnel the wizard about that, and while he had little faith in Trewnel's honesty, it was either him or Baroness Elanee, and his plans for intimate talks with the baroness didn't include much discussion of the diseases of plants.

Running a barony was an amazing amount of work, and it was barely possible to get in a couple days' hunting each tenday, not to mention the birds that he had been neglecting. His young sparrow hawk was ripe for training—and a sharp-eyed little killer she was!—and it was all he could do to hand-feed her every now and then. Yes, she would come to the lure, but only if the lure was in the hand of his bird keeper, Henros. He had no intention of spending the mountains of coins it cost to feed and take care of his birds merely for the pleasure of that oily Henros.

He had heard but mostly ignored the clattering of hoofbeats outside his window. There was always somebody coming and going, and usually they were coming and going in a hurry. That was the trouble these days. Too much hurrying. It was one thing to ride quickly into battle, but another entirely less noble, less interesting thing to hurry and scurry forth on matters more mundane.

He turned back to the papers on his desk and got to work.

"Governor?" Ketterling stood in the doorway, an envelope in his hand.

"Yes, yes, what is it?"

"Message, Governor."

Treseen frowned as he took the envelope. The imperial mail rider wasn't due for a couple of days yet, and the telegraph line barely reached into Barony Neranahan; stretching it into the hinterlands of Keranahan was a low priority. There was good and bad in that; Treseen was not eager for more imperial supervision. An occasional troop of the Home Guard coming through was more than enough for him.

"Where?"

"It's from old Banderan, sir."

Treseen smiled. Banderan was a companion from the old days, and while there was little to recommend the old days in comparison with the here and now, loyalty and dedication were tested far better with the clash of steel than with the clink of copper.

"But how did it come in?"

"The dragon Ellegon, of all things."

Treseen swallowed heavily. He felt vaguely nauseous. "Ellegon. Here?"

"He was. Last night. He's long since gone." Ketterling pursed his lips. "I've never much cared for that creature, Governor. He knows too much about too much and tends to find out more about more." Ketterling brightened. "Even when, of course, as I well know, there's nothing to worry about anybody finding out."

Treseen nodded tolerantly. Ketterling was an idiot.

There was always something to worry about. One could have the most innocent intentions in the world, but if those innocent intentions might result in some benefit, there was always somebody else who would want the benefit for himself. One might, for example, wish to marry a baroness—an appropriate reward for long service first to Bieme, and then to the empire, and then to the baroness and the barony itself—and it was entirely possible that that would interfere with the plan or preference or even the whim of somebody in a position to stop it.

One might have urged the emperor to put off the naming of the heir as baron for just that reason, and yes, the baroness finding that out was something to concern oneself with.

The dagger that Treseen had once carried into battle lay on his desk, holding down a stack of papers. It looked different these days than it had at that time. It had been an expensive blade, the manufacture of which had cost Captain Treseen half a year's salary, made from a small ingot of dwarven wootz that Treseen had managed to come by as a battle prize.

But in the old days, the blade was kept merely working-sharp, not honed to a razor's sharpness—too sharp an edge could chip, and Treseen's arm was strong—and it had had a hand guard, to catch and deflect another's blade. It had long since been remounted with a simple bone-inlaid handle, and it lay on his desk merely as a letter opener, and a reminder to Governor Deren Treseen of any number of things.

He used it to slice off the wax thumbprint with which Banderan had sealed the letter, and quickly scanned the contents.

Ah. He should have guessed.

Banderan was merely overreacting, as had always been his wont. Three ordinary soldiers from Barony Furnael—Treseen knew he was now supposed to call it Barony Cullinane, but his thoughts were his own—had been dispatched in response to some note that silly little Leria had managed to smuggle out—Elanee would want to know how that had happened—and which had ended up in the clutching hands of the dowager empress, of all people.

Well, if that was all this was, there was nothing to worry about, and certainly nothing to do. Leria was resisting the idea of marriage to Miron, and while that was a minor complication for the baroness, it was hardly a problem that justified or needed imperial scrutiny.

Which was fine.

Much more important: it was a problem that could easily stand imperial scrutiny.

Some minor reconciliation issues with the taxes collected and those passed on to Biemestren was another matter, but that wasn't the sort of thing that three ordinary soldiers—or a hundred soldiers—would be about to try to sort out, much less be able to sort out.

Besides, if enough coins flowed through one's hands, one or two could only be expected to stick to one's fingers now and then. After all, a man did have to think of his future, and as Treseen's father had always said, it was just simple good sense to put more than one arrow in the air.

And Treseen had more than one arrow in the air.

Until Leria married, her lands were administered by Treseen, and that was perfectly fine with him. Tax money went for roads and mills, and Treseen had used some of that to help sponsor a company of dwarves from Endell who had wanted to take up residence in the Ulter Hills. Wherever dwarves came, money flowed. And the more money that flowed, the more that might be diverted without notice.

Looking at it that way, Elanee's attempts to urge Leria into a marriage with Miron were just a minor problem.

To him, that is, it was a minor problem, but from the point of view of the baroness, it might seem more than minor. It might, in fact, be utterly embarrassing for somebody as adept as Elanee thought herself to find the dowager empress taking a personal interest in her minor machinations.

Which certainly boded well for a man who could handle such a minor/major problem, or at least point the way toward a solution. There was, perhaps, more than gold to be had out of it, and in an empire that had been created by a usurper, what limits could a man with intelligence and ambition have?

"Ketterling," Treseen said, "have a fresh horse saddled, and an escort mounted. I'm afraid I'll have to ride out to the Residence again shortly."

"Yes, Governor."

Treseen sat back in his chair and thought about how he would answer the note. The trick would be to thank Banderan without thanking him too much, but surely Treseen was capable of that much subtlety. Drafting such a message should take but moments.

And if not, well, if Treseen wasn't able to easily manipulate a loyal and straightforward old soldier, who was he to marry a baroness, eh?

Elanee knelt down on a folded blanket and considered the rosebush in front of her.

It was lush and full, dense with thorny branches and dozens of flowers the color of fresh blood, their musky perfume filling the late afternoon air.

Definitely wrong. She suppressed a tsking sound. It never paid to reveal your feelings, even when you were alone. She had neglected this bush too long; it had grown too dense, with far too many flowers, a puffball of a plant. A rosebush was not a wheat field, after all, to be judged by the weight and volume of its yearly crop.

It was a work of art.

This one should, she decided, be cut back to perhaps half a dozen branches, each bearing one or two roses as far from the base of the plant as possible. Let it dominate as much space as it could with its beauty, but let it do so subtly: and let the empty space make the crooked branches stand out more.

She took her favorite tool, a slim serrated knife, and set to work. The trick was to cut enough to bend the bush to her vision without cutting so much that the plant would die.

Nobody—nobody—was allowed in the inner gardens when Elanee was working with her plants. Were an interruption absolutely necessary, there was a bell by the gate that could be rung by anybody willing to quite literally bet his or her life that she would have them killed for relaying whatever the matter was. The bell had never been rung, for that purpose or any other, and Elanee had been mildly amused to discover, some years before, that servants always kept a fresh, dampened rag wrapped about the clapper to prevent it from an accidental ring.

Certain kinds of privacy came easily with her station; others were simply unavailable.

She could easily arrange to be left alone in her bath, or in her room to sleep or read or eat or, more frequently, to think; she could not possibly arrange for a walk about the Residence itself without encountering somebody—it took a large staff to maintain even such a simple country home—and it would not only be beyond stupidity but remarkably noteworthy for her to go for a ride by herself across the countryside or even there without an escort.

The pile of branches on the black soil next to the bush grew slowly, as did the separate pile of roses. There was no need to waste them, after all; a servant would separate the petals and add them to her bath. Tonight.

After, of course, Elanee abandoned her garden for the day.

The privacy of her garden was special. It belonged to her, not to anybody else.

It wasn't just a matter of her privacy, although that would have been sufficient in and of itself. There was also the matter of vanity, and Elanee considered her vanity an asset, not a liability. She was remarkably unbecoming and appeared to be very much a woman of her age with her hair tied back and wrapped in a cloth like a peasant woman's, her face protected from tanning by a floppy straw hat, wearing a loose pair of man's trousers, an oversized shirt, and a pair of pigskin gloves to protect her hands.

She didn't mind getting dirty, be it with dirt or blood, should the situation require it—she was, after all, the Euar'den heir to Tynear, even if the Euar'den Dynasty had long since ended its rule of Tynear, and Tynear itself was swallowed up by Holtun five generations before—but part of what made her what she was was her insistence on appearing above it all. Tanning like a peasant wouldn't fit with that, and neither would it do to be seen wrapping herself up to avoid it.

The hardest thing to do in life was to float through it without effort. Elanee had never managed that, but floating through life without apparent effort was a sufficient substitute.

Elanee tended her roses herself, working slowly and carefully. There was no reason to rush, and one of the reasons she maintained this section of the gardens herself was as a reminder that there was no reason to rush many things.

Patience had been one of the two virtues she had been born with, and while exercising them came naturally, she enjoyed the exercise as much as she presumed a born horseman like her son, Miron, enjoyed the feel of the powerful animal between his legs. She smiled a private smile. That was an enjoyment that, in an entirely different way, she shared with her son. And would share in a third way, someday soon.

The bush was now what she wanted it to be: a scant half-dozen crooked branches, each terminating in a single rose. It reminded her of a crippled old woman extending rich fruit in a supplicatory pose.

Very pretty.

She rose to her feet, ignoring the pain in her lower back from her long crouching, and stretched. The sun lay on the castle walls, and it was time for Elanee to leave her garden for the day.

Life was so unfair, so demanding sometimes.

Elanee, fresh from her ablutions, swept down the staircase and into the great hall, with its table that could have seated a hundred but was set for three. It was a matter of standards, and one of the many battles she had won with her late husband: supper would always be eaten in the great hall.

Miron was waiting for her at table, Leria across the table from him. She could tell from his hand motions and her patient expression that he had, once again, been regaling her with some hunting story.

He rose at her approach. "Good eve to you, Mother," he said.

She regarded him with a sincere affection, although she flattered herself that it was an affection tempered with a sense of reality. He was a remarkably handsome young man, something of her own strength in his face, and his legitimacy as the son of his late father evident only in the squareness of his jawline and the broadness of his hands, with their very un-Euar'den stubby fingers.

The rest of him, though, was classic Euar'den: curiously warm and compelling blue eyes above an aquiline nose and a generous mouth that seemed always ready to part in a smile or a laugh; the body long and lean, shoulders as broad as a peasant's, and a posture that reminded her of her father's father: motionless but never at rest, as though balanced to move from utter stillness into sudden activity at any moment.

She had never seen him with a leg thrown lazily over the arm of a chair, and she never would.

Leria was on her feet, as well, and Elanee forced herself to broaden her smile. "And you look so lovely this evening, my dear."

"Thank you, Baroness," Leria said.

Elanee was pleased to see what appeared to be a flicker of genuineness in the girl's returned smile. Elanee, in her own way, spent as much time and effort courting her as Miron did, and much more than the long-absent-and-unmissed Forinel, who had seduced her apparently without effort and certainly without Elanee's help or blessing.

Leria was a pretty little thing, although her pert little nose and rosy lips were a trifle overdainty to Elanee's way of thinking. But there was determination in her pointed little chin, and she was slim and willowy enough to be clearly of noble and not peasant ancestry.

Perhaps she was too slim—she really should have had a strand of gold chain at the waist of her dress to emphasize its smallness, or had the bodice cut fuller to call attention to the slight swell of her firm young breasts. But the soft black satin had been a good choice in her dress, even if the cut was too ungenerous for such a young girl. It set off her smooth white complexion dramatically, and even somehow enhanced the flow of long golden hair that fell to the girl's shoulders—although the shoulders should have been bared.

Ah, if only the problem were educating the little twit into how to display herself better. Elanee could have handled that in an idle afternoon.

Elanee took her place at the head of the table, allowing Miron to seat her, and waited for the maid to bring in the first course.

Footsteps echoed behind her on the smooth marble, but they were heavier than they ought to have been. She turned to see Thirien stop and draw himself to attention.

The Old Emperor had allowed her late husband to expand his personal guard, and Thirien, who really ought to have commanded nothing larger than a single troop, had found himself in charge of the whole company. His chin was weak and his ears large—he wasn't handsome, he wasn't bright, and he wasn't much of a leader, but he was loyal as a good dog, and that was good enough for Elanee. Intelligence in servants was an often overrated commodity. Elanee had more than enough of that quality, she had long ago decided, and valued other characteristics more in others.

Keeping her guards loyal was important, even though it was so easy.

They were just men, after all.

"Your pardon," he said, his usual parade-ground bark muted, "but Governor Treseen is here."

She raised an eyebrow. She had, in theory, dismissed Treseen after breakfast, and had not expected to see him for several days at least, at least not out here.

"I'll pardon you, of a certainty, but I don't recall having sent for him." Technically, of course, she could no more send for Treseen than she could send for the emperor himself. Barony Keranahan was under imperial governance, and while she was every bit as much baroness in theory now as she had been before Holtun had been conquered, it was the governor who ruled.

That was a technicality only, as long as he ruled as she pleased, just as it had been a technicality when the late baron had ruled as she pleased. Elanee was not concerned with the forms as much as with the substance, and the substance was that he was here uninvited.

So she made a special effort to put a precise measure of coldness in her smile as she rose to greet him.

He was a handsome enough man, his raven-black hair turning quite becomingly silvery at the temples, despite the way that in middle age his chest had started to slide down and become a belly slopping over his sword belt. But there was something wrong, something weak about his eyes, as though he could never quite focus them properly.

Not even when looking at her. Pity.

"I'm sorry to disturb your dinner," he said. "But I foolishly left my seal out here this morning, and there are reports that have to be promptly scaled and sent off to Biemestren. A troop of soldiers slithers along like a snake on its belly, it's said, but an empire sails along on a sea of paper."

A clumsy lie. Either Treseen was more of an idiot than she thought he was—which was always possible; it was a capital error to underestimate an adversary, and everybody was always an adversary— or he couldn't possibly have expected to be believed in that.

"Now, now, Governor Treseen," Miron said, rising politely, "if I didn't know better, I'd think that you're so much taken with my lovely Leria here—" the girl frowned briefly at the possessive, but Miron didn't pause "—that you couldn't bear to wait until you next saw her and left your seal behind as an excuse to return today."

Leria looked Miron square in the eye. "I? I'd think, were I asked—"

"Oh, please, please," Miron said. "Do tell."

"I'd think that perhaps the governor is more likely to be taken with Baroness Elanee than me, were he to be taken with anybody."

Miron laughed. "There certainly would be a point to that, and as a devoted son," he said, with a quick bow toward Elanee, "I'm embarrassed that I wasn't the one to make that observation." He walked around the table and crooked his arm toward her. "Please, Leria, help me hide my shame with a short stroll in the gardens. I couldn't bear to sit at table and blush."

Clearly despite herself, Leria laughed, a sound light and bubbling.

She rose and took Miron's arm.

Elanee waited until they had exited through the doors that opened on the portico overlooking the gardens before she turned back to Treseen.

This had best be important, she thought.

His light expression had grown somber. "I'm sorry I couldn't think of a better reason than that pretext about the seal," he said, patting at his belt pouch to indicate where it, quite properly, still rested. "But I thought you would want to see this without a wait."

He produced a piece of paper. "It seems that the dowager empress herself has taken an interest in your . . . domestic situation. My first thought was that it's an unimportant matter, one worth waiting to inform you of, but my second thought was . . ." He shrugged.

"Now, Governor—"

"But your son is quite right, as I'm sure you know, and I shamelessly employed it as an excuse to see you again." He started to tuck the paper back into his pouch. "I must apologize for disturbing the tranquillity of your meal, and hope you'll both pardon and excuse me." He bowed, and made as though to leave.

"Please, please." She hoped her smile warmed him; she would have preferred that it burned him. "Now," she said, "you know you are always welcome here, Governor Treseen, that I think of you as a dear friend—" The most she had ever allowed him before was "good friend," but this was no time for half measures. "I'm so delighted to see you that I couldn't be so rude as to scold you. Please, please join me for dinner," she said, gesturing him toward Miron's seat. "And if you think that this . . . message is something I should look at, well, I'm only a woman, and know little of politics and such, but I'd be happy to look at it and will listen with great interest to whatever sage advice you'd be generous enough to offer."

She didn't need his intelligence—what there was of it—but she did need his position.

Treseen returned the smile. He figured he'd won something, and perhaps he had.

For the moment.

8

Dereneyl

The road twisted down into the side of the valley, entering and emerging from a small stretch of forest that fringed the farmlands of Keranahan. Out in the fields, peasants in floppy hats and carrying weed bags stooped to pluck out unwanted plants growing among the green leafy plants that they were tending.

Whatever the plants were. They didn't look familiar. Durine didn't know, and he didn't much care.

It had been years since the war had ended, but the baronial capital still showed scars from the war, particularly if you knew where to look, and Durine knew where to look.

Some things never heal.

The castle on the hill overlooking the town was the easiest sign to see. The breach in the wall had not only not been repaired, but it had been expanded into a very broad and permanently open gate. The gatehouses at the other two gates were gone as well, leaving them permanently open. What remained of the wall was useless for defense, and would probably eventually suffer the same fate as the Woodsdun castle, of being disassembled, stone by stone, for construction down in the town. For the time being it was the residence of the governor and his troops, but even if and when control of their baronies was fully returned to the Holtish barons, they wouldn't be returning to their castles.

Holtish nobles were not going to be permitted to hole up in their castles and resist a siege.

A castle wasn't just a place to live. In fact, as a place to live, it was a lot less comfortable than an unfortified house.

It was a weapon.

It was a stronghold, a safe place from which to hold out to fight at the owner's time, on the owner's terms. Certainly, the empire could crush a rebellion in any one barony at a time—as long as the borders were quiet, of course, and you could never count on that, particularly these days, with magic turned loose in the Eren regions, upsetting balances of all sorts, political included—but that just encouraged coalitions and conspiracies among the barons. A wise emperor didn't encourage such things; they grew aplenty without nourishment.

But Durine didn't much care about that, either. Conspiracies could be solved with some complicated political maneuvering—or, better, with the sharp edge of a good sword slipped between the right ribs, or a pair of massive hands fastened around the right throat.

But that was other people's problems. He was just the sword, just the pair of hands.

Not caring was the safe way, the good way.

Everything, everybody he cared enough about died on him. There had been a couple of women—well, four, if you included his mother and his sister—and two horses, and once an officer he had served under, and a stray dog that followed him and these other two around for a while. But they had all died on him. He had had to kill the dog himself.

The last person he had truly loved, truly cared about, was the Old Emperor, and the inconsiderate bastard had blown himself to little bloody chunks protecting his son, Jason.

All the bastards died on him.

Except, he thought, keeping a secret smile, for Kethol and Pirojil, except for these two.

But he had solved that one. Durine had finally figured out a way to cheat fate: he just didn't let himself care about them. They were his companions, certainly, but that was all. He didn't like them as much as everybody thought he did, as though the three shared some deep and intimate bond. Kethol was too brave and reckless, and ugly

Pirojil not nearly as smart as he thought he was, and both of those qualities grated on Durine in a way that he constantly thought about, constantly picking at a scab so it wouldn't ever heal.

Erenor was complaining again.

"So why do I have to be outfitted like a servant?" he asked, his voice whiny.

The pack he had kept ready for a quick exit contained, among other disguises, a soldier's cloak, sword, and belt—the wizard didn't seem to want to have to use a seeming as part of a quick exit. Erenor looked silly with a sword in his hand—typical for wizards—and Pirojil had decided that he would pass as their servant. A silly idea, three ordinary soldiers with a private servant to cook and clean for them, but Pirojil probably had some scheme in mind. He usually did. There was a brain behind that ugly face, even if it didn't work as well as Pirojil thought it did.

Erenor was decked out in a light cotton tunic and leggings that they'd procured in Woodsdun. The tunic, belted with an ordinary rope belt that held only a belt pouch—not even a knife—gave him an entirely inoffensive and decidedly unwizardly air.

"You want reasons?" Kethol asked, letting himself smile. "I'll give you three. One: Pirojil says so. Two: Durine says so. Three: I say so."

"How persuasive," Erenor said.

"I'll give you five." Pirojil counted out the reasons on his fingers. "One: because Erenor the wizard is being looked for for his help at Riverforks, so you don't want to look like a wizard. Two: because there are two soldiers who escaped jail, and we being three soldiers and a servant, we aren't them. Three: because servants sometimes hear things that others don't. Five: because nobody but a wizard is going to be able to pierce that disguise, and maybe not even a wizard."

Erenor sniffed. "I'll thank you not to try to teach me about magic. Any wizard is going to be able to see at a glance what I am. It takes a lot of skill to bank your flame down to the point where another can't see it, and I don't quite have that skill yet."

Pirojil laughed. "Meaning you aren't anywhere near powerful enough."

"That's another way to put it, certainly. And you missed the fourth reason."

"No." Pirojil shook his head and frowned. "No, I didn't. I just used a seeming to make it invisible."

Erenor's laugh sounded genuine. "You're not likely to forgive me for outwitting you, are you?" He tugged vigorously at his forelock in a sarcastically overdone display of a peasant showing respect. "Very well; I'm a servant."

Durine permitted himself to like this Erenor person, just a little. He wasn't much of a wizard, perhaps, but he had been smart enough to swindle Pirojil, and that was unusual in itself.

And he had been useful in getting Durine and Kethol out of jail and as a sinkhole for some of the blame that would go with that. And while he resented his sudden change in station, he at least had a sense of humor about it. With any luck, Durine would learn to like him just enough to get him killed, but not enough to care about it.

Kethol preferred to keep things straightforward when he could, and the other two didn't have a problem with that, not this time.

It took some time to talk their way past the guards at what had been the castle, but Keranahan had been at peace for too long, and eventually they were let in without escort and pointed toward what had been the southeast corner guard tower. The keep at Keranahan was older than the one in Biemestren, and had been built with but a single wall, rather than the double-walled arrangement that had been more common for the past while. Surrounding the keep with two walls added a tremendous amount of protection: if the first wall was breached and enemy forces entered the outer ward, they could be attacked from above from both walls, from both in front and behind. Attackers would have to not only breach the outer wall, but at the very least evict the defenders in order to have a real chance to try their luck with the inner wall and the relatively soft meat of the inner ward beyond.

But this castle had had but a single wall, and a single ward, and with the wall breached and never repaired it was no longer a castle, just a collection of stone buildings surrounding the donjon.

There was something pitiful about that, if you could feel sorry for something made of stone and mortar.

The ward of the castle was now the home of the occupation troops, with ramshackle wattle-and-daub buildings set up against the inside of the walls as barracks and stables, as well as storehouses and such. The grasses and low shrubs of the ward had long been war casualties; it was bare dirt, baked and hardened in the sun, weeds growing at the juncture of what remained of the walls and the ground.

They had been pointed toward where the governor was, and soon found themselves climbing up the absurdly long, winding staircase to the top of what had been a corner guard tower in the old days.

Knock down the walls on either side of a corner guard tower, and it isn't good for much. A lookout tower, perhaps, but if you really need a lookout tower, you really need castle walls. Not much of a place to live, not with hundreds of stairs on the long, winding staircase to climb in the dark every time you dragged your weary body home to sleep. About the only benefit Kethol could think of, offhand, was that with the garderobe that high off the ground, even the lightest breeze would blow the smell from the dung pile away.

Treseen had put his birdery up there.

What had, in the old days, been a useful place was now filled with wooden cages, five of them holding big scowling birds, the rest empty, save for a big one in the corner that held a dozen or so pigeons on various perches, either too stupid or too sullenly pessimistic to figure out what their purpose was. One curved wall held a curved workbench, tools and gear set out on it in careful order. A straw mattress lay against the wall behind the big cage. Kethol figured that it probably wasn't Treseen who slept up here.

Of all the silly ways that the nobility could waste their time while the rest of the world worked to support them, Kethol ranked falconry somewhere between discerden and dueling. There was nothing wrong with hunting rabbits and such. But why not just leave that to a peasant's snares? There was a certain efficiency in turning the pests that fed on a peasant's crop into his dinner, but this was just a matter of sport to the nobility. As a way of procuring food for the pot—not that they needed to—it was just plain silly. Nobles didn't need to hunt their own food.

And Treseen wasn't even nobility. He had been a commander under General Garavar during the war, and the Old Emperor himself had put him in charge of the troops occupying Keranahan, and eventually he had replaced the governor.

And was busy putting on airs, it seemed. He ignored them while he adjusted the hood on the small falcon clinging to his left forearm, which was protected by a thick glove that covered him up to the elbow, and then tickled its beak with the end of a long shred of meat, carefully snatching his bare fingers back when she snapped it up.

His assistant, a wild-haired little man whose face and arms were peasant-brown, scowled. There was something about the way Treseen was doing this that bothered him, or maybe he just didn't like Treseen in the first place.

Treseen fed the bird another few pieces of meat, then sighed and returned the bird to the cage. Stripping off his glove and tossing it to his assistant, he shook his head. "Think she'll be ready for the jesses soon?"

"I think she's ready for the jesses now, and I can prove myself aright in that by telling you that I've had her out on them seven days of the last tenday," the little man said. "She'll be ready to fly free for the lure before you know it," he went on, just the faintest emphasis on the word *you*, "and bringing down game soon after."

Treseen ignored that, or at least affected to. "Good," he said. "The sooner the better."

"That, of a certainty, is true."

He had been ignoring them long enough. Kethol cleared his throat.

Treseen turned to the three of them, and his gaze wavered for a moment before he settled on Kethol. "Yes? Well, what is it?"

Kethol glanced over at Pirojil, who nodded microscopically. Kethol would have preferred that Pirojil handle Treseen, but it didn't look as though he was going to be given much of a choice. "We've come from Biemestren, Governor. We've been sent to look into a problem here," he said.

Treseen arched an eyebrow. "By whom?" He snickered. "The emperor himself, perhaps?"

"Almost." Pirojil dug the papers out of his pouch. "Perhaps you should look at these, sir," he said. "They'll explain it all."

Treseen walked to the window and held the papers out in the light. Kethol would have sworn that the man's hands didn't tremble in the slightest. Which meant that he was brave, although it probably didn't have anything to do with his innocence or guilt.

"I see." Treseen shook his head. "I can't see what the problem is, and why the dowager empress has had to involve herself, but there's nothing to it. Just a matter of a nervous little girl with some overly romantic notions about—well, about life, and such."

"As may be." Durine frowned. "I don't doubt that."

"But . . ." Pirojil seemed to be choosing his words with extra caution. "We haven't been ordered just to come out here and talk to you, Governor. We've been told to talk to the girl herself, and find out what the situation is, and I'd not care to explain to the dowager empress that we came all this way and then didn't do what we've been told to do."

"You have done what's necessary," Treseen said. "You've spoken with me. Do you doubt my word? Is that the courtesy they teach soldiers in Barony Cullinane these days?" His lips tightened. "These are not the days of the Old Emperor, you know, where insolence is rewarded, where—" He stopped himself with visible effort and raised a hand. "But enough of that." He turned his back on them. "You may go."

"Very well," Pirojil said. "As you will, Governor. We certainly can't flout your authority to order us out of Barony Keranahan and go back, empty-handed, frustrated, and ignorant, to Biemestren."

Kethol looked over at Pirojil, whose eye closed in a wink. They'd be looking up the baroness immediately, more likely than not. The dowager empress wouldn't take their word on the governor having ordered them out of the barony, and in fact he hadn't. Not in so many words.

Nor would he. Treseen turned back. "I didn't say that, now, did I?" He frowned. "I'm irritated with you doubting my word, and I can tell you that there will be a note dispatched to Baron Cullinane about your manners, I can promise you that. As to ordering you out of the barony, I didn't say anything of the sort. Do what you will. It seems like a lot of fuss over a little problem that I understand has already been well settled, but . . ." He handed the papers back to Pirojil and turned back to Kethol. "But far be it from me to interfere with the wishes of the dowager empress."

He placed his palm on his chest, over where his heart was supposed to be. "I've been a loyal servant to Bieme and to the empire for my whole life, and I'll not stop now. If you insist on seeing Lady Leria, then go ahead and do so. She's at the Residence."

"Residence?"

"Before the war, it was the old baron's preferred place to spend most of his time. I can understand that: it's out in the country, away from the sights and sounds and smells of the city. He kept the castle as a going concern only in case of need. Ever since the war, of course, the family's been in residence there, and it's been called the Residence, out of deference to them." He smiled slyly. "I understand some of the other Holtish barons suffered rather a lot more, but then most of the others weren't as cooperative as the late baron."

Kethol suppressed a snicker. It was easy for the last of the Holtish barons to be conquered to see the benefit of cooperation.

He shook his head, as though to dismiss the thought. "You can ride two sides of a square of the roads around the forest, but there's a nice path through. It's a pleasant ride, and I'd guide you there myself, but I'm otherwise occupied this morning. Tell the captain of the guard to have Ketterling draw you a quick map; there're only three or four forks on the path." He cocked his head. "And tell him that you've the run of this place, and you can be billeted in the barracks, if you'd like, or you can find lodging in town, if that's more to your taste."

He turned back to his bird assistant, dismissing them. "Now, about the jerfalcon . . ."

As they walked down the long, circular staircase, Kethol could practically hear Pirojil frowning.

"That went awfully easily," Pirojil said. "I've seen token resistance before, but . . ."

"Yes. And you've seen it again." Durine grunted.

It had gone too easily.

But why shouldn't it? Kethol thought.

It was just another one of the spats and arguments that the nobility used to occupy their time instead of honest work, and having somebody see that the problem had been resolved, while it might irritate the governor, shouldn't be a big deal. He could guess what it was: the overbred little bitch had decided to marry the man the baroness had insisted that she should, and it was all over.

All they had to do was ride out to hear that, then ride home and tell the dowager empress that there had been nothing to it, and let the old biddy live her little victory: she would have proved that she could get men from Barony Cullinane to run a minor errand for her, and that would be that.

Durine grunted again.

Kethol nodded. It could be that easy, it could be that simple, but it wouldn't be.

9

✠ Simplicity Itself

The little country home, of course, was nothing of the sort. Pirojil had expected as much. His . . . he had known some nobility in his youth, and the only dwelling he could recall that one of them owned that was little and ordinary was a primitive hunting lodge high in the mountains, little more than a shack.

They paused their horses on the crest of a hill. Below, a stream twisted beneath the Residence, which had been built on the rocky crest of a further hill along Darnegan lines: a central, generally cubical stone building that rose a full three stories, flanked on either side by a long two-story wing, each wing fronted by a full-length portico. The whole structure was overgrown with ivy, and twittering birds fluttered in and out of nests hidden in the green tangle.

There were the outbuildings one would expect: a stable next to the barracks, although Pirojil expected that was a remnant of the old days, and the barracks would be occupied by a skeleton guard. It was one thing to permit the occupied barons to have a small force of guards; it would be another thing to allow them to raise armies.

A quick series of whistles shattered the afternoon quiet, sending a flock of birds fleeing into the air from their nests, a few minutes later followed by a half-dozen mounted soldiers issuing from the barracks, who quickly cantered in their direction.

Well, Pirojil thought, at least somebody was paying attention. That was nice. Maybe.

The men were lancers, their spears pointing innocently toward the sky, for the moment. It was possible for a swordsman on horseback to take on a mounted lancer—if you could get past the steel-clad point, he was yours—but it wasn't easy.

The leader of the squad was a big black-haired man riding a huge black gelding. The horse had overly thick legs that spoke of some plowhorse ancestry. The man had thick legs and arms, as well. Pirojil was tempted to ask if they were related, but he figured that probably wasn't a good way to start off the conversation.

The big black gelding came to a prancing halt. "You are . . . ?"

"Pirojil, Kethol, and Durine," Pirojil said, not introducing Erenor. Erenor was just a servant, after all. "We've been sent from Biemestren. We're here to see the baroness, and the lady Leria." *And why,* he thought, *don't I have any doubt that we're not telling you something you don't already know?*

Well, if so, that boded well. If the baroness had just decided to have them killed, they'd already be dead.

The leader waited a measured two beats before answering. "You've a letter of introduction to show me?" he asked, his hand out.

Pirojil pulled his copy of his orders out of his pouch, and handed it over. The paper was getting a bit ragged around the edges; he'd been pulling it out a lot lately.

"Hmmm . . ." the leader said, "this seems to all be in order."

Then why are you holding the paper upside-down? Pirojil didn't ask. He just accepted the paper back, and stowed it away.

"Follow us."

Their horses unsaddled and let loose in an empty corral to be fed and watered by Erenor—who accepted the reins with a grumble and some quiet muttering—the three were led inside the Residence. Pirojil's eyes took longer to adjust than he would have liked, but that was the way of it on a bright day.

The afternoon was getting hot outside, but the great hall was cool and dark, and there were two women waiting for them, seated at the end of the long oaken table.

The woman at the head of the table was in her forties, an age at which a peasant woman would long ago have gone all dumpy and faded, but she was no peasant woman, and the years had only added a depth of character to her face. Twenty years ago, perhaps, when she was younger and more rounded, her chin would have been weak and her cheeks chubby, but now her face was angular, her cheekbones high and exotic, and the eyes that watched Pirojil seemed to radiate both power and sexuality.

Her hair, black and shiny as a raven, was done up in a complicated braid that left her slender neck bare, and made his hands itch.

She rose at their approach, tall and trim, a smile that was only polite, no more, on her lips. "I am Elanee, Baroness Keranahan," she said. Her voice was lower than Pirojil had expected, and more musical. Her eyes swung past Pirojil and Durine and settled on Kethol.

"I've been told that you wish to see me," she said, addressing him, "and Lady Leria."

The girl was lovely, although Pirojil thought her a little slim and boyish for his tastes. Her long blond hair was faintly curly, as though it had just been released from some sort of braid. Probably something as complicated as the baroness's; a noble girl would hardly have her hair in a simple braid, after all.

"Yes," Kethol said. "We . . . we've been asked to look into a message she sent to the dowager empress." Strange. Kethol didn't stutter, not usually.

The girl didn't quite blush as she lowered her head.

"Oh, that silly thing," The baroness shook her head. "It was just a mistake, and the matter has long since been handled. Isn't that correct, my dear?"

The girl nodded. "Yes, Baroness. I was . . . it was a mistake."

Kethol looked over at Pirojil. He should be handling this, but the baroness assumed that the tall, rangy, good-looking one of them was the leader of the group.

"Mistake?"

"The baroness and I had a misunderstanding," the girl said. "I . . . I thought she was pressing me into a marriage."

"When," the baroness said, "nothing could be further from the truth." She rested a hand on Leria's shoulder. "I would swear on the blood of my son that I'd not want to force this lovely girl into a marriage with anybody at all." Her voice had the ring of truth, but of course that was often the way with liars.

The baroness gestured them to seats, picked up a small bell, and gave it a quick ring. A housemaid, a plain girl in a plainer white shift and gray apron, walked through the door almost instantly, as though she had been waiting just outside, as she probably had been.

"These men," the baroness said, "have had a long ride out here; they'll need cold drinks and some sustenance. A platter from the kitchen, if you please, and hurry about it."

"Yes, Baroness," she said, scurrying away.

"It's common knowledge," the baroness said, turning back to Kethol, "when my husband was still alive, Leria had a . . . a flirtation with Lord Forinel, my stepson." She smiled tolerantly. "Understandable, really: Forinel was a fine figure of a young man, and had quite a way with young girls. And he was the heir apparent to Keranahan, which still does mean something, even these days?"

Was?

"And where would Forinel be?"

"I'm not at all sure." She spread her hands. "He was a romantic young man, very much taken with the idea of making his own way in the world and not simply inheriting the barony." She smiled tolerantly. "I think, perhaps, he heard too many stories about the Old Emperor and his . . . exploits."

Which exploits got the Old Emperor killed.

"Three years ago," she said, "Forinel rode off for the Katharhd, so he said, to—now how did he put this?—to 'prove himself with sword and lance and bow, and to show that the blood of Keranahan does not run thin.' I think he resented the occupation, and perhaps his father's quiet acceptance of it, at the same time that he worshipped the Old Emperor." She shrugged. "I thought it foolish, but—" she spread her hands "—I'm but a woman, and my counsel wasn't heeded." She shook her head sadly. "He's not returned, and we've had no word of him." Her mouth set itself firmly. "And with his father dead, he's the heir to the barony, but . . ."

"But if he's ridden off to the Katharhd and hasn't come back, maybe that's because he's dead," Kethol finished for her. "Which would make your son, Miron, the heir and the baron."

She nodded. "Eventually, the emperor himself will have to decide. I've not pressed the point; it would be unseemly." And it would make her the dowager baroness, as well, although she didn't mention that. For now, with the barony under military government, perhaps the distinction wasn't much, but it was something.

"Perhaps poor Forinel will yet return," she said, "and perhaps not—but for me to push for the accession of my own son would be improper, at best."

And, Pirojil thought, if Forinel was dead, which seemed likely, there was no rush, not with Keranahan still under the authority of the governor. Particularly if the governor could be influenced by those dark eyes as much as Pirojil wanted to let himself be. On the other hand, it didn't take a wizard squatting over the guts of a chicken and muttering unrememberable spells to divine whom the baroness wanted Leria to marry. Tie a young woman with a good heritage and a large inheritance to her son, and she and her son would remain a power in Keranahan even if Forinel returned.

Assuming, of course, that he was alive.

Assuming, of course, that she hadn't dispatched an assassin to kill him and leave his body buried in some unmarked grave. No, she would have been unlikely to do that. The dowager empress was a suspicious type, and what if she insisted on testimony under the influence of a truth spell? Or what if they simply called in Ellegon? The dragon didn't like to read minds, but he could tell a lie from the truth if he had to.

Pirojil would have shaken his head. There was a lot about this that he wasn't required to understand. It was his job to do things. But he did know that the statement of the girl under the baroness's roof, with the baroness herself present, wasn't going to be given much weight. Not by the dowager empress, and not by him and Kethol and Durine.

"Well," he said, "that explains that, but I see a problem. We've ridden a long way, and the dowager empress has gone to some trouble and expense to send us out here. We can't just ride back and tell her that this was a mistake—"

"But it was."

The baroness's lips tightened. "Now, don't interrupt, dear, it's not seemly." She turned back to Kethol. "I've a letter," she said, "apologizing for the misunderstanding." She tapped an envelope that rested on the table. It was wax-sealed at four points. "All you'd need to do is to take this back to Biemestren. It explains everything." She gave a shrug. "I'd have posted it by imperial messenger, but Leria only confessed her . . . indiscretion to me the other day, and we've been discussing how to handle it with the least embarrassment. The letter was written but a few days ago, and we've not had the opportunity to send it into Dereneyl and the . . . the governor's residence, as of yet."

A fascinating coincidence, if true, which it wasn't. Just too much of a coincidence.

Kethol looked to him, while Durine grunted. No, that wasn't going to do. "I think your first thought was right," Pirojil said. "Send the letter by imperial post. I'm sure that will . . . ease Her Majesty's mind, while we ride back to Biemestren—"

She smiled.

"—with Lady Leria."

The smile vanished. The baroness sniffed. "I couldn't possibly agree to such a thing. Subjecting a delicate young girl to such a trip? And with the . . . well, that hardly seems proportionate punishment for such a small flight of fancy on her part."

She had been focusing her attention on Kethol, but now it was Pirojil's turn. Her expression was haughty and distant, but there was something about her eyes.

They locked on his, and he found that his heart was beating hard, so hard he could hear it, could feel it thumping in his chest like a drum. She was a lovely woman, and those were eyes to die for, to kill for. For the life of him, he couldn't tell what color they were, but it didn't matter. He had seen beautiful women before, and he had wanted beautiful women before, but it hadn't ever been like this. That had always been the sort of pressure he could relieve with a quick trip to the nearest brothel.

These eyes not only aroused, but they promised. Pirojil was glad he was sitting down; he found himself suddenly, painfully erect. At her slightest nod, he would have laid his sword at her feet, begging for the touch of her hand on his head. He was hers.

No.

His will was his own, and he was not the vassal of this woman. He would not be.

Pirojil forced his eyes away from hers as he shook his head. "She has nobody to blame but herself, Baroness," he said, hoping nobody else heard how ragged his voice felt. He swallowed once, hard, then turned to Leria. "Lady, your station will, of course, be respected, but if we were to return with nothing more than a piece of paper, I'm confident that Her Majesty would not be satisfied. She thought it important enough to have us sent out here, with letters of authority, and with very specific instructions. I'm sure you'll find it inconvenient and awkward to travel with us, and we'll certainly borrow a coach and team for your comfort, but that's the way it must be. You can explain it yourself, in person, to Her Majesty, that you meant nothing of what you said, and you can let her . . . acceptance of that burn your ears."

He looked over at the baroness. Her expression was hard to read, but he didn't like it. Was there a trace of amusement in her smile? Or was it just contempt and arrogance?

The baroness looked them over for a long time. "Very well. But I'll hold the three of you responsible for her safety. I'm fond of this young girl, and should word come to my ears that any of the three of you has so much as—"

"Please." Kethol held up a hand. "We know our place, Baroness."

"Well, since you seem to have the authority, and since I've been given no choice, I'll surrender with what dignity I can muster." She smiled graciously. "She's in your charge." She turned to the girl and patted her knee. "Don't worry, my dear. We'll have you packed and my coach rigged immediately."

Her eyes fixed on Pirojil's, and again it was all he could do to control himself. "Will you three be able to manage the coach, or must I provide you with a coachman?"

Why the rush? Pirojil wondered. Surely, waiting the rest of the day wouldn't make a difference. And why the sudden switch from resistance to almost eager compliance? Fair questions, certainly, but the baroness's expression made it difficult, perhaps impossible, to ask.

And besides, it was vanishingly unlikely that they'd get an honest answer, and completely impossible that they'd get one they could trust.

"We'll handle it," Durine said. "Unless you've got too many people serving you, and need to cut the number down."

She laughed. "Ah, no, there's barely enough staff to keep this old house running; I've none to spare idly."

A group of three young serving girls arrived, each bearing a tray. All three were slim and lovely, the tan shifts that served as livery cut to emphasize their small waists. The baroness liked to surround herself with pretty girls, something that Pirojil understood. He would have liked that, too.

The prettiest one, a blond girl with a delicate face and full lips that reminded Pirojil of another time and place, was barely able to repress a shudder as she looked him in the face. He would have tried to smile reassuringly, but all he could do was stare at her until she first looked him in the eyes, and then dropped her gaze.

Yes, he wanted to say, I'm ugly. I've been ugly all my life, and lovely young women have been shuddering at me all my life, and I'm used to it, and it doesn't bother me anymore.

Most of that would have been true, more or less.

But not now. If he had been another man, he could have—

But never mind that. He wasn't, and he couldn't, and so be it.

The three girls set the trays down on the table in front of them, and then scurried away.

The bread was a basketful of fist-sized rolls, almost too hot to the touch, as though they had come fresh from the oven. Fresh apples, clearly sliced but moments ago into thin crackers, just barely starting to brown in the fresh air, surrounded tiny, finger-sized sausages that reeked of garlic and perimen. Another tray held wedges of cheese, one a buttery yellow, another just a shade off pure white, delicately veined with a rich blue; yet another, a rich dark brown the color of tanned deerhide. The last held a half-dozen ramckins, each filled to the brim with a different compote.

"Enjoy this small collation," the baroness said as she rose. "Leria and I shall go help the maids pack, while I'll call for the carriage. Please, refresh yourselves, and before you know it, you'll be back on the road." She took the girl by the arm. "And the sooner begun, the sooner ended, yes, my dear? I'm not sure how Her Majesty will deal with these three for having discommoded you so much over so little, but I doubt that will be your problem, and I'm sure it won't be mine."

She smiled genially at the three of them, and then swept away.

Durine checked the rigging again of the four-horse team that was necessary to pull the carriage. Erenor had already checked it—he was taking well to the role of a servant, surprisingly—but Durine had to be sure not only that the horses were properly hitched, but that he himself could not only unhitch them when they stopped for the night but put the whole mess back together in the morning. None of the three of them had had a lot of experience driving teams, and these harnesses were rigged differently enough from the ones they used in Barony Cullinane that he would have been nervous about it, if he got nervous about such things.

He was more irritated than anything else. Durine would have grumbled if grumbling would have done any good. More trouble and expense feeding four dray horses, and more trouble hitching and unhitching the team every night—couldn't the little chit just ride on the back of a horse? She had been born to spread her legs for some nobleman to bear more noble brats—couldn't she just spread them over a saddle?

But no, not nobility. She had to ride like the lady she was. Riding was a sport for a lady, although with all the time some of them spent riding, she was likely better at it than any of the three of them. But it wouldn't do for her to have to ride. For travel, it was a carriage.

Pfah.

With the carriage, they couldn't take the hunting path back to Dereneyl; the carriage needed a wider road. And that would mean a longer trip back than out, as they would have to stick to the main roads. You could ford a stream on the back of a horse, but a carriage would break a wheel or an axle, or just get stuck and not be able to move.

Enh.

Well, there was a good side to it. At least the carriage was of the old Euar'den style, with a flat roof where the baggage could be tied down. With a little effort in rearranging it, once they were out of sight, it would be possible to leave a space between the bags where you might lay down a blanket and stretch out. Kethol prided himself that he could sleep anywhere, and if it was possible to sleep while traveling, that would be nice for Kethol.

Pirojil tied his horse's reins to the hitching rings at the rear of the carriage; he'd take the first turn driving the team from the driver's bench. It was a plain wooden bench, of course, not the leather-upholstered couch for the passenger inside. If the jouncing of the coach bruised a pair of buttocks, it wasn't going to be the occupant's.

He beckoned to Kethol, and Durine walked over, as well.

"Eager to get back to Dereneyl?" he asked, his voice low but casual.

Kethol shrugged. "Not particularly."

Pirojil nodded. "There's more than a little strange going on here." He patted his saddlebags. "We've got enough water and field rations to keep you a couple of days, if we pool all of ours. Once we're out of sight of the Residence, are you willing to sneak back and take a look around? I'll have Durine ride out with your horse and meet you on the trail, say, sundown, day after tomorrow."

Kethol? The hero? Durine grunted. No. Not a smart way to do it.

Pirojil raised an eyebrow. "You've got a better idea?"

"Yes." Durine nodded. "Me."

Kethol was more of a woodsman, and was better at keeping out of sight, but he wasn't better at keeping out of trouble. He had demonstrated that in Riverforks, and as a result they'd been saddled with Erenor, and had had too much attention drawn to the three of them. Durine didn't like that. Attention was something that you got enough of when you were big and strong, but being big and strong didn't make you invulnerable. You were the first target for an archer, or a lancer, or even a swordsman, because they always saw you as the dangerous one.

There were times when you could use that to advantage, but those times were rare . . .

Kethol frowned. "Sounds more like my kind of thing, I'd say."

"Well . . ." Pirojil rubbed the back of his hand against his misshapen, bulbous nose. "Durine's got the right of it. Kethol, you can probably do better at charming Lady Leria than he can. You just ride beside her and chatter brightly with her when I give the signal. Durine will drop off."

Erenor had joined them. "And my part in it?"

"Two things," Pirojil said. "You take the reins of Durine's horse, and then you just ride behind the carriage, so that she can't see you."

"I can do that. Or I can do better than that," Erenor said brightly.

"Eh?"

"If friend Durine will be kind enough to cut off, say, a lock of hair, and wrap it tightly in a rag, then bind it to his saddle, I can put a seeming on it." He looked Durine up and down, his head cocked to one side. "It won't be able to talk, or anything of the sort, but for a few hours, it'll look like him enough to fool a casual observer, certainly." He pursed his lips thoughtfully. "I will need one of my spell books back, though. The smallest one."

Durine thought about it. Erenor was probably good enough with illusionary magic to make himself disappear, but in the long run, trying to hang on to him against his will would probably be impossible, and besides, even if Erenor had one of the books, the two others were still safely stored, and that probably anchored Erenor to them.

And if he wasn't going to let the wizard do magic, then what was the point of keeping him around? They didn't need a servant, particularly one they couldn't trust.

So he nodded. "As soon as we're on our way."

"And why wait until then?" Erenor shook his head. "You are blind, aren't you?" He jerked his chin toward the house. "The baroness has the Talent. I can see her flame from here."

"Which means that she can see that you're—"

"Please." Erenor rolled his eyes, as though imploring some magical help that would make it possible for him to deal with the stupidity of such as the three of them. "Would I be standing here casually talking to you if I thought for a moment that she could see that I was, well, what I am, rather than just a servant? I've taken to my heels before, and I can't imagine a better time." His lips made a thin line. "It's a raw flame, as we call it." His mouth worked as he groped for the words. "She's got the Talent, but she's no more trained at the use of it than you are." He looked again toward the Residence. "I'd swear she's getting some use out of it, but . . ." He shook his head. "It's not focused the way it would be if she had even the rudiments of training, and I'd just be guessing as to what."

"Guess," Durine said.

Erenor shrugged. "It could be something sexual, perhaps. Women can do that to men ordinarily, without magic. If she found, when she was a young girl, that she could twist men to her will with a smile and a flash of leg, it could be—and I'm just guessing—that her Talent might have started to express itself that way. It would be like exercising a muscle she didn't know she had, but that wouldn't mean she couldn't make it strong with enough practice."

"Yes." Pirojil nodded. "That's entirely possible," he said, trying to keep his voice level.

Durine would have chuckled. Pirojil had practically drooled over the baroness, as though he was sure he had found some sort of bliss in her face or could find some between her thighs. Well, maybe he could, for a few moments. It never lasted longer than that.

Durine smiled. It was clearly time for Pirojil to find himself a whore when he got back to Dereneyl. Pirojil would bristle at the suggestion—Pirojil broke out in fastidiousness at the strangest times—but Durine could have a quiet word with Kethol, and the two of them could brace him together. Shit, if it would make it easier for Pirojil to concentrate on the job ahead, Durine would be glad to pay for it himself, and Kethol would probably go halves on it.

Pirojil frowned at him. You wouldn't think that face could get any uglier, but somehow Pirojil managed it. "What are you grinning about?"

"Nothing," Durine said. "Just eager to be going."

"Then let's get going."

Durine's departure went smoothly and easily. At the first bend in the road, the moment that their procession was out of sight of the Residence, the big man slung his bags over his shoulder, dropped to the ground quietly enough that he probably couldn't have been overheard even without the clopping of the horses to cover it, dashed quickly and quietly through a gap in the trees, and was gone.

Erenor, riding beside Durine's big bay, had already opened his spell book, his reins clamped between his teeth while his fingers danced through the pages until he found what he was looking for. It took him just a few moments to impress the words in his mind, apparently, for he quickly stowed the book and turned to the small bundle bound to the rings at the front of Durine's otherwise empty saddle.

Pirojil didn't make any effort to overhear the words. The wizard's voice was too low, and he'd been through this too many times. Without the spark of Talent, the words could no more remain in his mind than a wisp of paper could survive in a raging fire.

The air over the saddle wavered for a moment, like the air in the distance on a road on a hot day, and then Durine was there.

Well, almost.

It looked like Durine, and it was dressed as Durine had been, and the figure even swayed appropriately with the movement of the horse, but while the left hand was clenched as though it held the reins, it didn't. And then there was the head and the eyes. Durine wasn't the fidgety type, but he was always looking around, always aware of his surroundings. That was one of the reasons that Pirojil trusted him. It might not be impossible to take Durine by surprise, but it wouldn't be easy.

And there was something else, something that Pirojil wished he could have put his finger on. He would have known at first glance that that was just an illusion, and not Durine.

Kethol caught his eye, and smiled. He'd been riding on the other side of the carriage, chattering with the girl while Durine made his exit, but he'd first let himself lag behind, then kicked his horse into a short canter to bring himself with where Pirojil sat on the driver's bench.

The illusion wasn't great, but it was good enough, good enough to fool anybody who was watching them ride away.

Good enough would do.

10

A Night in Town

In the ruins of what had been the castle of the Keranahan barons, there remained at least one well-appointed suite for visiting notables, and it was a matter of but a few words with Treseen's lackey, Ketterling, to see Lady Leria safely settled into it.

Despite Kethol's attempts to engage her in conversation, she had been quiet during the ride out, which didn't particularly surprise Pirojil. Making idle conversation with ordinary folks, he said, was not something that nobility had a lot of use for.

Giving commands was more their style.

She was settled in for the night, two of the governor's guards at her door with instructions from Ketterling that the governor himself would be personally offended if any harm came to her—unlikely, in Kethol's opinion—or she wasn't there in the morning, which was much more likely. She had been quiet to the point of being almost monosyllabic, and it didn't take great insight into the noble mind to figure out that this whole trip wasn't something she was looking forward to.

Kethol didn't blame her, but it wasn't about blame. It was about putting this little blond thing in front of the dowager empress and then getting back to the barony, where not every face was a stranger's. Home was where if, say, you found yourself protecting some innocent girl from being raped by a bunch of drunken dastards, it would be the would-be rapists who would find themselves in fear for their lives, not the rescuer who would find himself in a jail.

That was the trouble with the here and now. Back in the old

days, on the Last Ride, the rule was cut—as in slice—and then run, leaving bleeding enemies, bruised feelings, and indignant nobles behind.

Here, now, in these supposedly more peaceful days, you were supposed to get proper permission before slicing into some deserving piece of crud.

Pfah. It made him wish he'd never gone a-soldiering. There was much to be said for the life of a huntsman.

Pirojil wanted to go settle in at the barracks, and wasn't only resistant to Kethol's idea of heading down into the town and finding a game, some beer, and a whore—in just that order—but just this side of forbade Kethol from doing the same thing. That irritated Kethol. It wasn't what Pirojil said—the three of them were companions, not officer and followers—it was mainly the knowing look on his ugly face, as though it had been Kethol's fault for the trouble in Riverforks.

But, shit, it wasn't his fault.

Things had just turned out badly, but the idea was right.

So they headed across the dirt ground for the barracks. In the old days, it had clearly been a stable—the loft spoke of that—but the occupation forces needed more stable room than the small contingent of baronial soldiers stationed at the castle had, and the stable was now one of the long wattle-and-daub buildings built up against what remained of the keep's outer wall, while the former stable had been converted into barracks.

Pirojil sniffed, as though he could still smell the reek of horse dung—which he couldn't; it had long since been cleaned out.

It smelled like a barracks, with the peculiar reek of old sweat that made some people gag. Kethol didn't mind.

It had been a good move to turn the stable into a barracks: you could fit a lot more soldiers into a given space than you could horses. Quadruple-rack bunks, their mattresses intertwined leather strips, stood in rows, while above, the loft had been divided into small rooms, presumably for the decurions. The officers would be billeted in the former castle, which was better for everybody. You couldn't get a good game of bones going with some captain or his subaltern looking over your shoulder all the time.

But the bunks were almost empty, except for perhaps a dozen men, one all alone in a corner bed, interrupting himself every few moments with a loud and heroic snore that caused him to shift and then settle back down. Not a pleasant way to sleep.

A short soldier limped over. Not a big man, not a small man, but there was something about the way his eyes searched theirs before his hand moved away from the hilt of the knife it had seemed to drift near that impressed Kethol.

"You the ones from Barony Furnael?" he asked. His voice was cracked around the edges, as if he'd strained it by shouting at one too many troopers.

"Barony Cullinane," Kethol corrected, more feeling than seeing Pirojil's glare out of the corner of his eye.

"Sure." The other man shrugged. "Barony Cullinane, fine. My name's Tarnell. I've been left in charge of the barracks, not that there's a lot to do." His forehead wrinkled. "They said there was four of you."

"The other's down in town right now. He'll join us," Pirojil said. "When he's finished . . . running an errand or two."

"Errand, eh?" Tarnell chuckled. "Ah. The girl got to him, eh? Or was it the baroness?" He licked his lips and made a sucking sound between his teeth. He shook his head, as though dismissing the thought, then looked Erenor up and down with an expression of distaste. "You have your own little servant, eh?" he said, although the top of his head was barely level with Erenor's chin. "I guess I should have gone soldiering in a different barony."

Kethol started to bristle, but Tarnell held up a palm. "No, take no offense at an old soldier's griping," he said. "Things are too quiet around here right now, and complaining is about the only sport around that doesn't cost anything." He jerked his thumb at a quadruple bunk. "You can take one of those racks over there," he said, "and you'll find blankets in the big chest over at the far end, if you don't have enough of your own. If you're the sensitive sort, there's mattress bags in the chest, too, and you can fill them with straw over at the stables. Me, I'm not the sensitive sort, and don't mind the feel of leather under my aging back."

Pirojil's mouth twisted. "Where is everybody? Seems kind of late for an all-hands patrol to still be out."

Tarnell shrugged. "Yeah, it does, at that." He started to turn away.

"Is there some secret?" Kethol asked, letting his irritation show in his voice.

Tarnell turned back, and stared him flat in the eye for a moment, for long enough for his silence and flat expression to say that he wasn't going to be pushed around by anybody, and that if it was going to be his single knife against two swords, that was the way it was going to be. Amazing that he'd lived so long with that kind of attitude, but stranger things had been known to happen.

Pirojil cleared his throat. "Kethol's manner sometimes leaves something to be desired. He spent the afternoon riding back from the baroness's residence, trying to get a conversation going with Lady Leria, and she . . ."

Tarnell grinned, and the tension in the air dropped away. "And she didn't have any more use for an ordinary soldier than you'd expect, eh?" He laughed, and shook his head. "I've seen that before. Not met her, although I've heard she's supposed to think kindly toward us lesser types." He laughed again. "Some things never change, eh? Let's get you settled in." He picked up one of Pirojil's bags and guided them over to the bunk he'd indicated before, setting it down on the flat leather straps that served as the mattress. "And there's no secret, not particularly. Somehow or other, the governor got word of some orc trouble on the border, and he sent most of the detachment off to run them down." He shrugged. "There's maybe a dozen of us left here, but this hasn't exactly been overflowing with real soldiering to do for the past few years. We spend more time accompanying the tax collectors to Neranahan than anything else except for this orc-chasing."

"Easy duty, eh?"

"Enh. Boring, most of the time, unless you like haring after orcs. Or bandits." Tarnell grimaced. "We had to chase down a nest of bandits a few tendays ago, but the hard part of that was tracking them down. After that, it was just a matter of getting a couple of archers in close enough to do their sentries, and then an ordinary slaughter—a dozen lancers could have done it, but the governor's never believed in sending in one man when a hundred will do."

Kethol smiled. "Neither did the Old Emperor."

"Naturally." Tarnell snickered. "Of course. Knew him real well, did you?"

A sharp response was on Kethol's lips when Pirojil cleared his throat.

"We're going down into the town," Pirojil said, "and see if we can find a game or a drink, or maybe some other entertainment. Feel like coming along?"

Tarnell raised an eyebrow. "You take your servant drinking and whoring with you?"

"We—"

"I'll stay here, if you don't mind, good sirs," Erenor said, tugging at his forelock. "I know you'd like me pouring your beer for you, but I've got your clothes to wash, and your beds to make, and suchlike. I'll be happy to watch over the barracks for you, if you'd like to go along with them, Tarnell."

"You never did any soldiering, did you?" Tarnell shook his head. "I like swapping lies over beer and bones as much as anybody else does, and more than some, but I'm on duty. Just because there's only a few of us here doesn't mean that the captain doesn't expect us to do our jobs, eh?"

There was a game of bones going on in the corner of the Tavern of the Three Horses, and Pirojil wasn't surprised to find Kethol quickly working his way into the small group of men watching the play, some making side bets, others, perhaps, waiting for their chance to get in the game.

Not much of a crowd, but the place mainly catered to the occupation troops, and most of them were off after the orcs.

Pirojil wished them the best of luck. The beasts were tough and mean, and he would just as soon they die on somebody else's sword rather than his.

The night was getting cold; Pirojil picked a spot near the large fireplace, and sipped at his beer. It was sweeter than he really liked, but it did wash the grit and the taste of road dust from his mouth and throat, and that was all he really expected beer to do.

Three burly men walked into the tavern in company. All wore swords, but they were plainly dressed in coarse-woven loose tunics over blousy, equally coarse-woven trousers and boots. Not nobility. If these three tried to rape a local girl, Kethol could carve them into bloody little chunks, for all Pirojil cared.

They had already been drinking, they were visibly weaving as they made their way to a table over in the corner, and one held up three fingers when he caught the taverner's eye. The fat, bald, sweaty man reached a mug deep into the open hogshead, coming out with it full of beer. He set it on the counter, and then bent over the hogshead with another mug. Why he had the top off the hogshead instead of putting it up on a table and tapping it at the bottom was something Pirojil wondered about idly. Easier to turn a tap than to constantly be reaching over, after all.

And why, come to think of it, were most taverners fat, bald, sweaty men, anyway? He'd known quite a few—in most villages and towns, there was little to do at night except sit around and drink—and more than half of them were fat, bald, and sweaty. Fat made sense, maybe. They were around food all the time, and it would be easy to make the day a nonstop eating binge. And sweaty? Well, working around cooking fires and all, rarely getting outside except to step out the back door for a breath of fresh air every now and then, that probably explained it. But bald? If you ate too much, did sweating make your hair fall out?

Or was it that if you sweated a lot, eating too much made your hair fall out?

Cold wetness splashed down the back of his neck, wetting him across the shoulder. He turned in his chair quickly as the remaining two mugs dropped from the swordsman's hand, drenching his leg as they splashed on the floor.

"You mangy son of a half-breed Katharhd," the swordsman said, his voice slurred with drink. "You bumped my arm, and look what you've done." He reached out a hand to grab at Pirojil's tunic, but Pirojil blocked it easily as he rose. "And look at you," he went on. His eyes seemed to have trouble focusing. "That face of yours is the ugliest thing I've seen since the hind end of a pig, and there's some pig's asses I'd rather look at. Makes me want to puke, it does."

Getting into a fight with a drunk wasn't what Pirojil had come down into town for, and while under other circumstances he would gladly have given the dolt a lesson in manners—preferably with his bare hands; there was something satisfying about doing it that way—this wasn't the time or place.

"Ta havath," he said. "It's just spilled beer."

"But it's my beer." The other took a wild swing at Pirojil, which Pirojil again blocked, grabbing the wrist and twisting it up and around behind the fellow's back easily.

"Now just go back to your table and I'll have the taverner bring you over your mugs, eh?" He pushed the wrist up until the other grunted. "Eh?"

His friends were on their feet, but the taverner was suddenly in between them and where Pirojil stood, a short staff, ferruled in brass at both ends, in his hand. His face was creased in an irritated frown, but he looked comfortable holding the staff in his massive hands, the knuckles the size of walnuts. Big walnuts.

"I don't mind fights in my tavern," he said. "Can't sell beer to men who want to drink themselves drunk without having a fight every now and then, and a fight means some smashed furniture and broken barrels. But I'll want to see the silver you're going to use to pay for the damage before you go after each other." One of the two seated drunks set his hands on the table and started to rise, but the taverner slammed one end of the staff down barely short of the ends of his fingers, scoring the wood but stopping the movement cold. "Sit, I said, and sit I meant."

He waved the end of the staff toward where Pirojil stood, still holding the drunk with his arm twisted up behind his back. The fellow lifted his right boot—probably to stomp down on Pirojil's foot—but Pirojil just twisted the arm up higher, forcing something halfway between a scream and a groan from the other's lips.

"Now, as to you, you with the ugly face," the taverner said, "you just let him go, and let's be done with this, since I don't see anybody eager enough to fight showing some coin to pay for the privilege."

Kethol had been trying to get into the game, but now he was working his way through the suddenly quiet, suddenly attentive crowd. He'd made no move toward his weapon, or any sound at all, but it wasn't a coincidence that he was positioned to move against either of the seated men if they tried to get up, or that one of his hands gripped the back of a chair, ready to use it as an improvised weapon.

Pirojil didn't look directly at him. Kethol had his flaws, but you could count on him in a fight, even if the fight hadn't started.

The taverner took a half-step toward Pirojil. "I won't tell you three times to let him go," he said, his voice more threatening for its quietness.

Pirojil shoved the drunk away, and took a careful step back to get himself clear from any sudden back kick.

Kethol caught his eye, made a slight jerking movement of his chin toward the exit, and then quietly started to edge his way around the crowd, toward the door. Pirojil didn't need the advice: he was covered in beer, his head still flushed from the sudden rush of anger, and he wasn't thirsty anymore.

He tossed a copper coin on the table. "I'll be leaving now. I'd appreciate it," he said to the taverner, "if you'd buy them a round of beer on me, and see they stay to drink it."

The taverner shrugged. "Just get going. They're too drunk to catch up with you, if you make yourself gone quickly enough."

"Coward," one of the three said.

"An ugly coward, at that," another snickered.

"Run, run, run," the third muttered, his voice, if anything, thicker and more slurred than those of the other two. "Men fight; cowards run."

Pirojil, Kethol at his side, bowed graciously toward the taverner, spun around, and walked swiftly out and into the night.

The way back through town toward the main road that twisted up the hill toward the keep was a long one, but Pirojil didn't mind the walk. It gave him a chance to calm down, or at least fool himself that he could.

He had more than once drawn on somebody who had made fun of his ugliness, and he had both given and received the scars to show for it, and not just blade scars. There had been this fellow back in Biemestren—a baron's man, not an imperial—whose ear Pirojil had bitten half off, and he still remembered the feel of the flesh rending between his teeth, the warm taste of the salty blood in his mouth, and the way the snickers had turned to squeals of pain.

Silently he cursed the dowager empress for putting him in a position where he had to take the abuse a drunk wanted to dish out. He cursed the taverner for stopping the fight, because even though it was stupid, he wanted to carve the drunk's face until it was uglier than his own.

Pirojil could have justified fighting back. He probably should have. Kethol certainly would have, and so would Durine. The drunk had not only splashed beer on him, but he had thrown the first blow. If his steel had started to clear its scabbard first—and a quick move toward the hilt of his own sword could have persuaded the drunk to draw—Pirojil could have drawn and killed him without a qualm. Nobody who had ever held a sword in his hand expected you to take it easy on somebody who had started a swordfight just because he was drunk. It wasn't like hand-to-hand, where anybody with any backbone would look down on you for beating up an obviously in-capable opponent. Swords were sharp and steel moved quickly, and the blade of even an incompetent, blind-drunk opponent could find its way to your heart or through your neck if you let up on him for even an instant.

Kethol kept quiet as they walked. Say what you would about Kethol's judgment, but, just like Durine, he was a good and loyal companion.

They had turned down a side street toward the main road that led up to the keep when Kethol nudged him. "Footsteps behind," he whispered, then stopped in his tracks, bending over in a fit of coughing that covered his moving his hand toward his sword, while it let Pirojil move a few steps away, close enough to aid him, not so close as to get in his way.

Pirojil stopped, and looked back at where Kethol was half bent over. There was nobody on the dirt street behind him, and the shops that lined the street were shuttered and locked up for the night. Kethol hadn't just been hearing things—whoever it was must have ducked into the alley.

Kethol must have thought the same thing, because he continued his coughing fit, staggering toward the darkness of the alley.

Very well. If Kethol was handling the alley, that left it to Pirojil to deal with another threat, if there was another threat.

"What is it now?" Pirojil asked, not letting his voice get too loud.

It was then that the two men came from around the corner, swords glistening in the starlight.

They were, of course, two of the three from the tavern.

"We have some unfinished business, ugly one," the heavyset man who had slopped the beer on Pirojil said. He didn't sound quite so drunk now, if indeed he ever had been drunk at all. "Coward."

Pirojil set his hand on the hilt of his own sword. "You use words like 'coward' quite a lot," he said. "Are you brave enough to come at me one at a time, or do I have to skewer both of you at once?"

Kethol's coughing fit seemed to worsen; he leaned up against the wall next to the alley.

The heavyset man smiled thickly. "Oh, I think I'll be able to handle you myself," he said, stepping forward, while the other stood waiting.

Pirojil drew his own sword. It was hard to see it by the dim light of the overhead stars; its coating of lampblack made it difficult— well, impossible—to handle without getting dirty, but it also put an opponent at a disadvantage in a fight in the dark, and made no difference in its ability to cut or stab.

He closed, and engaged blades, tentatively testing the other's defenses. A quick feint that could have preceded a lunge drew an instant parry—not the delayed movement of a drunk. No, this man wasn't drunk, and he hadn't been drunk in the tavern, not with reflexes like these. There were those who could hold their beer well, but it did not sharpen the eye or steady the wrist.

Another series of equally tentative moves drew only defensive responses. This fellow was at least an adequate swordsman, and a cautious one. The time you were most exposed was when you were on the attack, and it was a matter of simple strategy to try to draw a predictable attack, allowing your opponent to bring his arm, particularly his wrist, into your range.

Great swordsmen and greater idiots could show off by trying for the heart or the belly, but anybody with anything less than a master's touch and anything more than a cow's brain went for the extremities, for the sword arm or the legs. An amazingly small cut to the wrist would make it impossible for your opponent to fight, even if he could still, just barely, clutch his sword. A jab to the knee, or the thigh, or as little as a thrust to the toe could slow your enemy down enough to let you control the space, the timing, and if you could control the fight, you would win it.

Pirojil was still feeling around the other's defenses when he heard the sounds of fighting behind him, followed by a bubbling groan and Kethol's laugh.

Pirojil's opponent's eyes widened, and he retreated several paces while Kethol rejoined Pirojil, his sword extended, the blade darkly wet.

Even out of the corner of Pirojil's eye, Kethol's grin was warming. "Seems there was a bowman waiting in the alley for you," he said, walking crabwise away from Pirojil's opponent to engage the remaining man. "The idea, I suppose, was for you to be busy watching the one in front while an arrow pierced you from behind."

The three of them carried healing draughts in their pouches—that was one of the benefits that came with working for the Cullinanes, who insisted on it, despite the expense. But even the best healing draughts would do no good whatsoever to a man who had been injured by an arrow—not if the swordsman in front of him had used the injury as an opportunity to run him through.

Remove the arrow and thrust a sword through the wound, and what you had lying on the ground was the loser of a duel, somebody who had been run through. Maybe slash his wrist and sword arm a few times, too, to make the killing wound look like the last of several blows.

Steel clashed on steel as Kethol engaged with his man—Kethol was always eager, perhaps always too eager—but Pirojil didn't let himself get too anxious. A sword fight wasn't won as much as it was lost.

"Put up your sword, and tell us who sent you and why," he said, "and you'll go free." He raised his voice. "Kethol, that goes for the other, too. The first to surrender lives."

Pirojil's opponent started to speak, but all he made was choking sounds. "I'd like to," he said, with a friendly smile. "But I'm afraid that just won't be possible. Not this—" He interrupted himself with a quick feint toward Pirojil, probably hoping to draw a response.

"Not this time?" Pirojil said.

His opponent shook his head. "I'm afraid not," he said, suddenly lunging toward Pirojil. "My regrets." Perhaps next time his assassin wouldn't agree to having a geas put on him, one that would make the back of his throat close up tight if he tried to tell who his employer was.

Then again, if there was a next time, Pirojil wouldn't be around to care about it.

Their blades clashed again as they thrust and parried, counter-thrust and riposted. Pirojil's opponent left his wrist high and exposed momentarily. Pirojil feinted toward it, then thrust low and in, under the other's blade, in full extension, the tip of his sword slicing high into the other's thigh, near the groin, while his opponent was busy sticking the point of his sword high into the air where Pirojil's arm was supposed to be.

Pirojil recovered instantly, beating his man's sword aside as he did, and he took a few cautious retreating steps while blood fountained from the other's thigh like a stream of dark wine pouring from a keg with its bung pulled.

Despite the deadly wound, the heavyset man was game enough: he took a half-step forward, but he grunted as a bloody sword point thrust out of the front of his chest. He barely had time to look down and see a hands breadth of steel thrusting through his ribs before he was flung forward as Kethol kicked him off his sword, twisting it as he did so.

He was dead before he hit the ground, although the body did twitch for just a moment before fouling itself with an almost funny flatulence, followed by a horrible stench.

Kethol's man was down and dead—Pirojil had been too busy with his own fight to take in the details—his throat cut open, most likely to finish him off. Kethol was aggressive, but not likely to go for the throat until his opponent was down.

Kethol cleaned his sword on the cloak of Pirojil's dead opponent. "I think we'd best wake up the governor and report."

"Before somebody else does." Pirojil nodded.

"Who do the three—two of you think you are?" Treseen fumed. "You had me taken from a soft, warm bed in the middle of the night to tell me that instead of simply retiring for the evening, you found yourself a drunken duel, and that three men lie dead on the street?" His hair was disarrayed, no longer covering the bald spot that it had so assiduously been combed over, and he had not bothered to put on shoes when he had pulled on a fresh tunic and trousers to come downstairs.

It wouldn't do to get into a fight with the governor, of course—the guards weren't close enough to hear a low conversation, but a shout was another matter—but if it were to happen, Pirojil would start off by stomping, hard, on the governor's toes. It was a trick he had learned from Durine so long ago that he had almost come to think of it as his own, so long ago that he almost didn't wince at the memory.

Pirojil let Kethol do the talking. Treseen had decided that Kethol was the leader of the three, and that was fine with Pirojil.

Kethol shook his head. "No, Governor, that's not what we're saying. We're saying that those three were looking for us. First they tried to pick a fight with Pirojil, and then when that didn't work out, they waylaid us. Two of them were supposed to draw our attention while the third filled us full of arrows from behind."

"Pfah." Treseen's mouth twisted into a sneer. "That's hard to believe. Abrasive and offensive the three of you are, surely, but I can't see how you could have irritated anybody here so much as to dispatch three armed men after your blood." He cocked his head to one side. "On the other hand, perhaps you have the right of it. So, those nobles you went out of your way to offend in Riverforks decided not to let things rest so easily. Eh?"

What he was suggesting just wasn't possible. In order for these to be from Riverforks, whoever had sent them would have had to locate three assassins, hire them, get a wizard to put a geas on them to prevent them from speaking his name, and put the assassins on their trail—and do it all quickly enough that these men had arrived in town less than a day after Pirojil, Kethol, and Durine had. With the local wizard in tow.

No. It hadn't happened that way, and it hadn't happened by accident.

There was only one question in Pirojil's mind about the assassins: was it the dowager empress or Elanee who had targeted them?

Either made sense. If they had been killed in what would be

portrayed as a drunken brawl, as Treseen had put it, that would have reflected badly on Barony Cullinane, and perhaps that was what the dowager empress had intended all the time. It would have been nice to know if these three had been on their trail since they had left Biemestren, perhaps waiting to make their play until Kethol, Pirojil, and Durine had managed to get Leria out of Elanee's hands.

That way, if they failed, Beralyn's agents wouldn't have had to do anything at all. And if that was the case, then was Treseen working for the dowager empress, too?

Or was it Elanee? She had given in perhaps too easily at the Residence, and let them take Leria without protest or obstruction.

But that would have meant that she would have had to have had the assassins standing by, already her retainers. There just hadn't been enough time for her to go about recruiting such, even if she knew just whom to see and where.

Either way, it wasn't just a bar fight gone serious, and it wasn't a retribution for Riverforks.

Pirojil couldn't quite figure out whether Treseen was willfully avoiding the obvious explanation or was just stupid. The Old Emperor used to say something about not ascribing to malice what stupidity could explain, but the Old Emperor had always had a better feel for the amount of stupidity in the world than he'd had for the malice.

"No," Pirojil said quietly. "No. It wasn't because of Riverforks. And I think you know that very well, Governor."

Treseen raised a finger. "I would be very careful, were I you, of making wild accusations, soldier. I'm not disposed to listen to such, and I would suggest that you not dispose yourself to making such." He sighed. "But enough of that, and enough of all this. You've a long trip to start in the morning, and the Lady Leria to guard. Perhaps it would be just as well if you did so well rested, eh?"

11

Uneasy Lies the Head, Part I

The emperor's dreams were soft and gentle this night, for a change.

He was out riding a large ruddy horse through fields of clover, under a sky of pure blue decorated with huge, fluffy clouds.

Not hunting, not trying to escape the endless infighting among the barons and the staff, not getting exercise—just riding. He pricked at the horse's side with his heels, and the huge animal broke first into a canter, then a full gallop, Thomen's legs straight as he stood tall in the saddle.

Usually, when he dreamed of riding, it was all smooth and effortless, but this time, it felt real—it took all his skill and most of his strength to go with the motion, to prevent the saddle from smashing his tailbone into splinters.

It was wonderful.

The horse didn't think so. It raised its head and snorted at him, its neck craning around at an angle that would have broken its spine in real life.

"Wonderful for you," it said, in his mother's voice, "but what of the realm?"

That took all the fun out of it in an instant. He was suddenly in his office in the west wing of Biemestren Castle, his desk rammed against the corner of a box canyon whose walls were gigantic piles of paper that threatened to tumble at any moment, smothering him in their dull grayishness.

And the horse was still there, and still sounding like his mother.

"It's about time you got married," it said, its face changing into hers, then back. He tried to tell himself that he had never noticed the similarity before, but Thomen Furnael didn't like lying to himself. Or to anybody else, for that matter.

Yet another reason that he shouldn't be emperor. Deception was an important tool of statecraft. Not as useful as fear, perhaps, but at least as important as loyalty.

"Mother," he said, "we've had this discussion before, and we'll no doubt have it again." He climbed up on his desk and then made his way up the sheer wall of paper, clinging by suddenly bare toes and fingers to the canyon walls. Another tax request from Parliament was coming undone, and if he didn't push it back into place in time, it all would fall in.

Not that it mattered what he did, mind. But he had to look at it, pretend to consider it, and, while hanging by toes and fingers from the walls perhaps ten, fifteen stories above his desk, sign it.

It should have been somebody else. Thomen was a second son, and while myth and legend had second sons as being poor relations of their elder brothers, Thomen had always thought it the best of things to have the privileges and wealth that came with nobility without the responsibility. Second sons were wastrels, yes, by popular consensus—but it would have been nice to have been a wastrel.

But Rahff was long dead, and Father was long dead, and the Old Emperor was long dead, and Jason Cullinane had abdicated the throne and the Silver Crown in Thomen's favor, and if there was a path out of this dead-end paper canyon, he couldn't find it, not in his waking hours, and not in his sleep.

And, truth to tell, in a sense he didn't want out. There were days—few of them, but some—when he thought that he was doing a decent job of all this. Knitting together two formerly hostile principalities into one empire and eventually one country took a certain touch, and maybe a certain sense of history as well as proportion. The Old Emperor might have had some of the latter, but not a trace of the former.

"Well, then," his mother/the horse said, "if you have any sense of history, young man, you'll understand that the first duty of the ruler has always been to survive, and the second duty has always been to perpetuate his line." She/it punctuated the sentence with a sniff that was both pure Mother and pure horse at the same time. "You've not so much as a bastard child, much less a proper heir."

Yes, that was the plan, be it sleeping or awake. Bind him tightly with a wife and children, and he would be trapped in this canyon forever, without any possible means of escape.

"Escape?" A new voice chimed in. Walter Slovotsky stood in front of him, one hip thrown over the edge of Thomen's desk. He was taller than Thomen, both in dream and in reality, but not much, and while age had begun to let his chest fall and become belly, that war was by no means over. His beard was well-trimmed, and his eyes seemed to smile genially, but the grin that seemed a fixture on his lips was neither friendly nor hostile, but entirely one of self-appreciation. Any realm wise or lucky enough to host Walter Slovotsky deserved to be graced by that smile.

Thomen didn't know whether he loved or hated Walter Slovotsky, but he had always liked and resented him.

"I know," Walter Slovotsky said. "Now tell me about this escape, if I heard you aright."

"Yes, escape," he said, gesturing at the paper walls. "From this."

Slovotsky chuckled. "Now, let me understand this. You work in a nice, clean room, with food, drink, and companionship on call and available at any time; you get to make decisions that count—in fact, that's your fucking job—and you don't have to deal with hairy, smelly strangers who want to slit you from guzzle to zorch and back again; and you complain that all this is a trap from which you need escape."

Put that way—and if Thomen could be sure of nothing else, he could be sure that Walter Slovotsky would put it just that way—it didn't sound bad at all.

"Well, of course it doesn't," Slovotsky said. "And that's because it isn't that bad. In fact, it's as soft a touch as you're likely to find outside of a dream."

His mother was suddenly behind Slovotsky, her arm raised, an improbably long, improbably needle-pointed dagger clenched in a white-knuckled fist. Slovotsky made a face and, and without looking around, reached up and grabbed her descending hand and twisted the knife out of it, looked at it for a moment, then tossed it aside, into nothingness.

"Now, now," he said, chiding her in a gentle voice that in real life would have enraged her, but in the dream actually served to calm her down. "That's not nice. I'm just telling him the truth. You wouldn't slay the bearer of bad news—" He stopped himself and raised a palm. "Never mind. Of course you would."

He chucked Thomen under the chin with the hilt of the knife that he had just tossed away. "Always a bad idea, kiddo. If you punish people for bringing you bad news, then the only people who will bring you bad news are those whom you can't punish. And you want to get your bad news hot off the presses, while there may still be something you can do about it. By the time you reach the point of your pyramid-shaped society, the point is sharp enough to cut you, and will be most unpleasant if the universe decides to shove it up your backside."

Well, Walter Slovotsky in a dream still had much in common with the real-life Walter Slovotsky: Thomen could only understand about half of what he was saying.

At best.

"So," the Emperor asked, "what is this bad news that you're bringing me?"

"It's pretty horrible." Uncharacteristically, Slovotsky looked shy. "I hesitate to even mention it in front of your Imperial Majesty, for fear."

"For fear of what? That I'd have you killed?"

"Well, no. Not in a dream I'm not. I mean, you could have me killed, but, this being a dream and all, it wouldn't quite take."

"Then what are you afraid of?"

Slovotsky sobered. "I'm afraid I'll hurt your feelings. Wouldn't want that." His smile was back in place, and Thomen's mother was gone, vanished as he wished—as people only do in a dream.

Thomen's mouth was dry. "I'll live," he said. "Tell me."

"Okay: the truth is that you like being Emperor. The truth is that it tickles you to hold the closest thing to absolute power that you're ever likely to see. The truth is that you think you do a fairly good job at it. And the truth is that you wouldn't give it up. Your mommy wouldn't let you, and if she was dead, you'd find another reason. You like having the Ladies accompanying the barons to Parliament trying to sneak up to your room to have you father an heir on them, and you like—"

"Do you really think I'm that shallow, that venal?"

Slovotsky's face went blank. "Doesn't matter what I think. This is only a dream, after all. The problem is that *you* think you're that shallow, that venal—or at least you're afraid that you are."

Mother was back again. "This is the man," she said, her jaw tense, her lips and knuckles white, "who got your father killed. How dare you, his son, just lie there and let him speak to you that way?"

Thomen's jaw was tight. "Because," he said, "I think he's right. Anybody can say anything to me, as long as they're right. I need to hear truth, Mother."

"Hey, take it easy." Slovotsky laughed, and took a step forward. "It's a fucking dream, kid. You don't have to be rigidly fair. You don't even have to be honest with yourself. If you're mad at me for living a life, wild and free, doing what I want when I want, well, then, go ahead and hurt me for it—in a dream. I won't mind. Really. I won't even know." He slapped Thomen once, lightly, across the face. "But, shit, if this'll make it easier for you . . ."

Thomen Furnael, former heir to what was now Barony Cullinane, former judge of the realm, former child, former younger brother to Rahff Furnael, now prince of Bieme and emperor of Holtun-Bieme, awoke from his sleep to find himself on his knees in his nightshirt, trying to choke the life out of his blanket.

12

✠ Durine

Deer were amazing creatures, Durine had long ago learned. He had seen them run silently out of brush you'd swear a mouse couldn't make his way through, and bound across a trail into even denser brush without so much as a hoofbeat. It wasn't as though they were quiet; it was as if your ears couldn't work to hear them.

Durine wished he was a deer just about now.

As he worked his way through the woods toward where forested land broke on plowed ground on the far side of the baroness's residence, he sounded to himself a lot more like a cow trampling through the humus and detritus littering the forest floor.

Well, be that as it may, he had volunteered for the job, and it made a lot more sense for him to be doing this than Kethol. A better woodsman, certainly, but too much the hero.

Branches and twigs clawed at his clothes and body, but the few scratches were nothing to worry about, even though every insect in the forest seemed to be using his cuts and scratches as dining troughs. As long as his eyes were left alone, the cuts could be healed.

It took him longer than even the generous amount of time he had allowed himself to work his way through to the far side, and the sun had set by the time he peered out onto the fields. He was bone-tired, hungry, and thirsty enough to consider another draught from his half-empty water bag, but that was to be expected.

What wasn't expected was the party at the stables saddling up for a ride, a half-dozen soldiers led by a woman in riding breeches and cloak, her hair tied back, who looked for all the world, even from this distance, to be the baroness herself. It was, of course, possible that she was fond of a nighttime ride every now and then, and it would certainly be prudent to take along a bodyguard or seven, but Durine didn't believe that for a moment.

Where was she going? And why?

Saddled, the party clopped away at a slow walk on a dirt road that led away from the Residence, the baroness in the lead. An extra horse trailed along behind, pulled along on the end of a rope by the last of the horsemen, barely able to keep up, even though it was unencumbered by a saddle or a rider. Why they wanted a spavined old horse as a spare was something Durine couldn't quite figure out; the others all had decent mounts.

They quickly disappeared over the hill, and in a moment, even the sound of the hooves had faded in the distance.

Well, this wasn't the first mistake Durine had ever made, and he hoped it wouldn't be the last. Kethol, long-legged and lanky, could probably have followed them for quite some distance at a fast soldier's pace, a dogtrot. Kethol could keep that up as long as he had to.

Durine, well, Durine was large, and he was strong, but he wasn't Kethol.

Cursing himself silently for a moment as he stripped off his cloak and wrapped it around the rest of his gear before hiding the package under a pile of brush—it wasn't that he was really angry at himself, but it gave him something to do—he shook his head.

Well, if Kethol wasn't available, then Durine would have to do the best he could. He worked his way through to a path that exited the woods, and plodded his way along the edge of a wheat field toward the road that the baroness and her party had taken. He was exposed for at least a short while to anybody looking out the back of the Residence, but it was a risk Durine would have to take; it would have been impossible to make his way through the woods around to the road that the party had taken before dark, and he wasn't a dwarf, able to see in the darkness.

As it was, the sky had gone slate-gray and the stars and the distant pulsing Faerie lights had begun to show by the time he reached the spot where the riders had vanished over the hill.

So far, so good.

He started off at a slow walk, getting into the rhythm of walking before gradually picking up the pace. The road was as good as a dirt road ever got: baked in the heat of the sun since the last rain, it was relatively free of holes and divots, although it was by no means the sort of solid road that the imperials built and maintained. His slow walk became a faster one and he forced that up into a jog, with each step landing on the heel of his boot and pushing off from the balls of his feet. Running wasn't something Durine was built for, but this whole mission was something that none of them were really built for, anyway. You just had to do the best you could, and hope that was enough, and hope that was enough not to get you killed.

His scabbard kept slapping against his leg, so, without slowing or stopping—he had the sense that if he had the sense to slow or stop, he'd turn right around and go back, instead of chasing horsemen on foot—he unbuckled his sword belt, then rebuckled it and slung it over his shoulder. His pouch still bounced against his right buttock, but that didn't bother him. It was kind of reassuring, really, and helped him keep the rhythm.

It was said that a man could run down any other animal, if given enough time, and surely that had to include a horse carrying somebody.

Of course, it wasn't said that *any* man could pull that trick. A one-legged cripple certainly couldn't. A young child unsteady on his first legs couldn't.

And maybe Durine couldn't. His heart thumped madly in his chest, and his lungs burned with a horrid fire. His feet hurt from blisters broken open and bleeding, and his shirt hung damp with sweat. It should have been Kethol. It should have been Kethol.

He began running to the rhythm of that thought.

It should have been Kethol.

It shouldn't be me.

It should have been Kethol.

It shouldn't be me.

It should . . .

He never could remember how long he held that thought as he held that pace, but the thought and the pace carried him down the road as it twisted across the landscape, up and down hills.

The hardest moment came as he approached a wide wooden bridge that arched above a stream. Running across that expanse would sound like somebody beating a drum, and would carry probably into the next barony. So he let himself ease down into a slow walk, wondering if he would be able to force himself to run again.

Durine had been wounded more times than he cared to count, and there had been a time, somewhere high in the mountains, when he had come down with an awful fever that had left him not only in agony but hallucinating, wanting to run away, even though that would have meant falling down the mountain in the dark. It had been all the other two could do to hold him down and keep forcing water down his throat.

But he had never tried to run down a horse before, and while Durine was used to doing what he set out to, there was no sense in trying to fool himself. It would have been useful to know where the baroness and her party were going, but . . .

He walked slowly, quietly, across the bridge. Maybe just a little further, and then he could, in good conscience, give up.

Just a little further, he thought, his feet breaking into a brisk walk.

Just a little.

Just a little.

Then he would rest.

The brisk walk became a trot, the broken bloody blister on his right heel stabbing up into his leg every time he landed on it. He had developed a stitch in the side that felt like the blade of a thin, sharp knife. His breath was ragged and his heart felt as if it would burst out of his chest and splatter all over the road.

A dark storm was rolling in from over the horizon, blotting out distant stars and Faerie lights. Wind whipped dust into the air, and into his eyes.

Just a little farther, he thought.

The road climbed up a steep hill, and Durine accelerated, just out of pigheaded stubbornness, even though the effort caused him to hurt even more.

He stopped dead in his tracks at the top of the hill, then took a few shaky steps back. He dropped to the ground, gasping for air like a fish on the bank of a stream. Near the bottom of the hill, where a dark hole—a cave? a tunnel? Durine couldn't be sure—opened on the side of a rocky hill, a half-dozen or so horses waited in a small corral.

It was awfully large for a dwarven tunnel—dwarves tended to dig to their own scale, whether for habitation or mining—but it was regular and even enough to be. Most of the original dwarven inhabitants had long been driven out of the Middle Lands and most of the Eren regions, but some of their burrows persisted, those that they hadn't sealed up behind them or been sealed up in. The Old Emperor had invited some to move back in, but that was mainly out in Adahan, not here.

Had Elanee persuaded some to take up residence here? Was this some sort of mine?

If so, no wonder she didn't want any attention. Gold could do magical things, in more ways than one, and the imperial tax on mined gold was intended to concentrate the wealth into imperial hands. The last thing the emperor needed was some Holtish baron with a secret cache.

Whatever the origin of the tunnel, a lantern had been placed in a niche carved neatly into the rocks just outside the cave, and in its flickering light four soldiers crouched over a small fire, although the night wasn't particularly cold.

Durine could understand that, though. There was something about a fire that made you feel safer from whatever lurked out in the darkness.

Even if it was only a big, sweaty, tired man, whose every bone and muscle ached. It would have been awfully nice to be the one sitting around the campfire instead of out here in the dark and the cold.

The soldiers were keeping a lousy watch; they seemed to spend most of their time watching the entrance, rather than the horses, as they talked quietly among themselves.

The night was bright, and Durine had good night vision—for a human, at least—but he couldn't make out anything inside the entrance to the tunnel or cave. If the baroness and the other two had gone in, what had they gone in for?

A familiar kind of whinnying scream filled the night air, giving the four men in front of the cavern entrance a start. A horse's scream of terror and pain is a distinctive sound, different from anything else. Durine had heard it before, more than once.

And here it was again.

The baroness certainly had impressed Durine as capable of cruelty, but that wasn't what this smelled like. If she had simply wanted to torture an animal, she could have done it out at the Residence, if she didn't mind others knowing. She couldn't expect her guard not to talk at all, so even if they were closemouthed, whatever she was doing she didn't mind them knowing about.

Unless—

There was the slightest of sounds behind him, barely audible over the whispering of the wind through the trees.

Durine rolled to one side as the bearded soldier behind him charged, sword thrust out in front of him. He scrabbled back, crab-like, the heels of his boots kicking against the dirt of the road, ignoring the damage that stones were doing to the palms of his hands.

But not quickly enough. The sword point took him high in the right thigh, only stopping when it grated against bone.

The man took a step back, and lunged again, but Durine was able to kick the point of the sword aside with a sweep of his good leg while warm blood poured from the wound in his thigh. It hurt surprisingly little—more of a shock than pain, although as he tried to stand, he found that his leg would barely support him.

Somehow or other, he had managed to get the hilt of his sword in his hand, and whipped his arm to clear the scabbard and belt away.

By the pulsing crimson and purple of the overhead Faerie lights, the enemy's face shone with sweat as he smiled. "Oh, so you're faster than you look, are you," he said, beckoning toward Durine with his free hand. "Come on, let's see how your steel moves, eh?"

The fool. With his lifeblood pouring out of his wound, all the other had to do was keep Durine occupied, retreating if need be, until the loss of blood led to loss of consciousness and Durine fell. But the idiot wasn't having any of that—

No. He was smarter than he wanted to appear. As he closed, his lunges and parries were only tentative. He didn't approach closely enough to be within a short lunge of Durine, and Durine was in no condition to lunge at him.

He was just toying with him, and there wasn't much time. With every thump of his heart, Durine's blood was dripping away, his life was dripping away.

Durine had a flask of healing draughts in his pouch, but his pouch hung from the belt that held up his trousers, and on the right side. He was right-handed, after all, and—

That was it. He switched his sword to his left hand, and dropped back into a ready stance, holding his opponent's gaze with his eyes as his clumsy fingers tweaked at the mouth of his pouch.

"Ah," Durine said as the man's eyes widened. His words were ragged and harsh in his throat. "You don't like fighting a left-handed swordsman, eh?" That was true enough—and common enough—but Durine wasn't a left-handed swordsman, and in a moment the other would realize it, and at that moment it would be all over but the dying.

His fingers seized the brass capsule and he spun the cap off and away with a quick, hard motion of his thumb.

Smooth as smooth could be, a glass vial, sealed with wood and wax, slipped into his hand. If he'd had the time, Durine could have scraped away the wax to pull out the wooden plug, and poured perhaps a quarter of the contents into his wound. That would surely be enough to seal it up, to heal it up.

If he had had the use of both hands, he could have simply snapped the vial open over his wound and let the healing draughts pour in. He really only should have needed part of what was inside.

But he needed one of his hands for his sword, and there was no time at all.

So he brought the vial up and into his mouth, and bit down, hard, glass shattering and grinding between his teeth.

His gums stung in a dozen places, for just a moment, and then the pain was replaced by a sense of warmth that flowed into his jaw, then across his face, down his neck and through his body, wiping away not only pain but even the memory of it.

He felt his muscles seize together and knit, while the aches in his body were washed away as though they had never been. He stood firmly on what had been blistered feet, and he spat out the fragments of glass, then spat again.

The bearded man closed, but this time Durine didn't retreat.

Instead, he pushed both of their swords to the side, then dropped his blade to wrap his arms around his opponent, his blunt fingers locking tightly behind the smaller man's back, lifting him up and off the ground.

Durine squeezed, as hard as he could.

The other's sword fell from nerveless fingers, and his hot breath, reeking of garlic and onion, came out in a whoosh across Durine's face. He writhed, trying to escape, trying to bring an arm or a knee up, but Durine held him too tightly, and squeezed harder.

Durine squeezed and squeezed, until bones cracked and the air was foul with the stink of shit.

And then he dropped the corpse to the ground.

It would have been worth a few moments to try to hide the body, but there was no real point. The dirt road was splattered with Durine's blood, and while nobody would be able to make it out by starlight and Faerie light, in the morning the evidence of a fight would be written on the dirt for anybody to see.

Whatever was going on down in the cave was a matter for another time, and Durine would make sure that there would be another time. With the right weapons and the right companions, he wouldn't hesitate to try to sneak up and take on a half-dozen men in the dark. But not now.

He must have been more shaken than he realized. He almost forgot to retrieve and empty the dead man's pouch before he turned and limped down the road in the dark.

But only almost.

13

✠ The Road

Day broke all dark and wet and mean, with streams of water running down the single set of stairs down from the top of what remained of the curtain wall. One end had been blocked with rubble, it seemed, and a gutter from the flat roof of the keep had been extended not quite far enough to dump the water beyond the wall.

Pirojil stood at the window, thinking about how nice and dry it was here, and how wet and miserable Durine must be out in the woods. There was only so much you could do to stay dry under the best of circumstances, which this wasn't.

Kethol probably should have been the one to go spying on the baroness; let the would-be hero once again suffer the irritations of his heroism. That seemed only fair, and while life wasn't fair—Pirojil had heard that more than once—Pirojil tried to be. It was something he had gotten from the Old Emperor.

Damn little else.

Erenor was at his elbow. "Nasty day out. I take it we stay here until things dry out?"

Pirojil shook his head. "No. Kethol's seeing to the team. It won't take us more than a few moments to pack up. We're leaving this morning, as planned." The sooner they were out of here and back in Biemestren, the better. And more: the sooner they were out of here, the better. Dereneyl in particular and Barony Neranahan in general weren't good places to be spending a lot of time. "Go help Lady Leria pack."

"Of course. I live but to serve." Erenor smiled. "It will be my—"

"No."

The wizard raised an eyebrow. "No, what?"

"No, don't," Pirojil said. "Whatever you're thinking, don't. The lady's above our station, and even though I've little doubt your oily charm and perhaps a small cantrip or two could get past that, don't do it. You're a servant for now, until we drop her off in Biemestren." And then the wizard could go his way and the three of them could go theirs. Setting himself up in a new town would be no new thing for Erenor, and it would do Pirojil good to see the back of him.

But for now, having him along had already proved handy, and it might be invaluable.

Wizards were not common coin.

Erenor frowned broadly. Had he been on stage, even the patrons in the back row would have thought it overdramatic. "Very well," he said, with a tug on the forelock. "I shall go be a lady's maid, and help her to pack."

By the time Pirojil got back down to the stables, the rain had eased to a sodden drizzle, and Kethol had the team hitched and his own horse saddled, with Durine's large bay, its back bare, hitched to the back of the carriage. He took a look out through the open doors toward the rain.

"I figured that Durine wouldn't mind if we didn't leave his saddle and blanket out on his horse's back to get all wet," he said in a low voice. He pointed his chin toward the carriage boot. "Plenty of room in there; our Lady Leria packed lightly, all things considered."

The stable storeroom produced some extra oiled slickers, which would at least keep them less wet for a while, and a selection of wide-brimmed hats. With march provisions provided by Tarnell stowed away, it was just a matter of waiting for Leria and Erenor.

That was the point at which Treseen showed up, half a dozen of his guardsman trailing along.

"I really think you should reconsider leaving today," he said.

"The weather is horrid, in case you have not bothered to notice."

And you brought along enough swordsmen to kill us easily if we don't reconsider? Pirojil kept his face studiously blank. "I have, Governor. But my orders are clear, and they don't say anything about staying out of the rain."

"Be sensible, man," Treseen said. "It would be a nice change." He gestured out at the downpour. "Yes, the paved roads will be passable for the carriage—except where they're in need of repair, perhaps—but anything unpaved has already turned to mud, and you're likely to get the lady's carriage stuck, and then where are you?"

Kethol grunted. "So we'll stay to the paved roads, at least until the weather clears."

"This isn't an inner Biemish barony, completely rebuilt since the war. All the roads, even the old prince's road, are gapped in spots."

Pirojil nodded. "Yes, we've seen that. But if peasants have been known to remove paving stones from roads for their own use, perhaps that's something the governor should take up with them, and not with us. We have our orders, and one of our number has already been dispatched as pathfinder."

Kethol nodded. "Amazing fellow, Durine. You'd think with his bulk he'd not be good at that, but not only can he slip through the woods like a spirit, he can scout out a path better than any man I've ridden with."

Pirojil's mouth twisted into a grin, but he made it a confident one. "The man is something to behold. When you can behold him."

He saw that Treseen took their meaning: So if there's going to be a bloodletting here, Governor, word will get out, unless you manage to bring Durine down, too, and you won't be able to do that.

Even if he didn't believe them about Durine, the implicit threat might keep the governor cautious. Pirojil wasn't sure how far Treseen would go, or why he was so nervous about them. But there were few witnesses, and if a fight broke out that left Pirojil and Kethol dead on the ground, perhaps that would solve several people's problems—

—unless one of them were free to tell another side of the story.

Were they being overly cautious? It was hard to say at all, and impossible to say for sure. Treseen was fealty-bound to the empire, after all, but . . .

"Really," Treseen said, bristling.

Pirojil felt Kethol shifting slightly to one side. It was going to happen now. His mouth tasted of steel and blood, as though he had, as he once had before in the service of the Old Emperor, stopped a blade with a chomp of his teeth. He forced himself not to swallow, not to drop his hand to the hilt of his sword, not to take a step back into a fighting stance.

No need for Pirojil to begin it. He would let the governor start it all.

And then Pirojil would kill him, while Kethol took out Tarnell, and the two of them would see how many could be brought down before they, inevitably, fell beneath the swords of the local soldiers.

The governor went blithely on. "I wasn't aware he had returned at all. I hadn't heard—"

"No, Cap'n," Tarnell put in. "He was here, all right. Came in last night, dropped off for a quick sleep, and then was out into the rain while it was still more black than gray out." His mouth twitched. "Not that he came in all that quiet; I could hear the clomping of that little chestnut mare he was riding long before I saw his ugly face."

Treseen clearly wanted to question them all further, but he was interrupted by the sight and sounds of Erenor splashing his way through the mud, his hair already plastered down tightly against his head by the rain.

"The lady is ready, Governor," Erenor called, peering out from under the hand shielding his eyes from the worst of the rain. "May I tell her that her carriage is ready for her?"

Treseen's mouth twitched. "Of course."

Tarnell eyed him levelly, as though to say, *I didn't do it for you. I'm not afraid of you.* He looked over at Treseen, and barely moved his chin to indicate the governor.

Pirojil nodded. He hadn't needed to be told. The old soldier was still protecting his captain, and never mind that Treseen was not the man he had been twenty years ago. That wasn't something that Tarnell was to judge, any more than Pirojil would have thought it his place to judge the Old Emperor.

"I see no reason to delay the lady's journey," Pirojil said, returning Tarnell's smile.

Treseen misunderstood whom the nod and smile were for, what the nod and smile were for.

He thought it was relief that Erenor had intervened in their argument—the effete, sag-jowled idiot actually thought that Pirojil was smiling in relief.

He probably never would understand that it was a salute from one warrior to another, and Treseen wasn't the other warrior—Tarnell was.

Tarnell would have leaped at Pirojil's throat if his legs still had the spring of youth in them, and he would have whipped out his sword if that could have protected Treseen.

But, instead, he'd just said a few words, disarming the situation as neatly as a master swordsman, with a flick of a muscular wrist, could send a novice's blade tumbling end-over-end through the air.

Of course, that maneuver had saved Tarnell's life along with Treseen's, and Pirojil's, and Kethol's—but Pirojil didn't for a moment think that was the reason.

Tarnell's lips tightened into a thin smile that didn't quite hide the old lion's teeth.

No, that wasn't Tarnell's reason. That wasn't his reason at all. He might not even see it as a benefit.

Pirojil nodded, and raised his hand—slowly, carefully—in salute.

They caught up with Durine exactly where Pirojil had expected they would: at the opening in the forest, where the path through the woods to the baroness's residence split off from the main road out of town.

At first, there was no sign of him out in the dreariness and the rain, and for a moment, Pirojil thought that something had gone dreadfully wrong, and that Durine wasn't where he was supposed to be. What would they do? They couldn't go after him, and not just because that would bring Leria into danger, but because searching for him in the rain would be—

But then a large and soggy mass detached itself from the underbrush and straightened into Durine's familiar bulk. The big man shook himself off like a dog, and, shivering, plodded his way through the mud toward the carriage, while Kethol carefully stopped his horse next to the carriage so as to block any possible view from inside.

"What is happening?" came from the carriage in Lady Leria's voice, higher and sharper than it had been before. "Is there some problem?"

Kethol leaned his face in through the window. "Not at all, Lady," he said. "Durine has just returned from scouting for us, and Pirojil is taking his report. Nothing of consequence, nothing to concern yourself with."

Durine's grip was every bit as firm as usual, but his hand was icy cold as he accepted Pirojil's help up to the driver's bench. It had been a long, cold, and wet night. Which was to be expected: the only way to stay dry if you were outdoors in a storm was to get indoors. Silently but with obvious gratitude written on his gray face, he accepted a heavy woolen blanket from Erenor and a corked bottle from Pirojil. He drank heavily, thirstily, until his huge hands stopped trembling.

"Long, wet night, eh?" Pirojil asked.

"Yes." Durine grunted. "I've had shorter and drier, and that's a fact." He eyed the bottle with naked longing for a moment, and then recorked it with a steady hand. "And the sooner we get back home, the sooner they can send out somebody to find out what is really going on out here." He bit his lip for a moment, just barely drawing blood. "If they were to ask me, I'd say they start with a dozen troops of the Home Guard, or better yet, Ellegon. There's something wrong here, and it's more than the three of us can handle."

Kethol had joined them while Durine quenched his thirst. "Three?" he asked with a smile. "You're not counting Erenor?"

That drew a smile from the big man. "No," he said.

Durine had finally dried off by the time the clouds finally began to clear in late afternoon, just as the sun had finished clumsily trying to hide itself behind the wooded hills.

The hard rain had given way to gray drizzle, which had slowly wheezed to a stop. Pirojil had taken a turn riding point, and then another turn driving the carriage, leaving the soft, clean seats inside the carriage to Kethol, Durine, and Erenor. Lady Leria didn't enjoy looking at his face. Not that she said so, but she didn't have to.

Who would?

"Right about now," Durine said, as he rode up alongside Pirojil, his eyes not leaving the road ahead, "I'm thinking that we have an obvious plan for the night, and I don't much care for that."

"Well, I didn't like the baroness at first sight, but that didn't matter much, either."

"It would be nice if, for a change, what you and Kethol and I liked and didn't like made much of a difference." The life of a soldier wasn't largely about doing what you wanted. Life wasn't largely about doing what you wanted.

"Well, it would be a change."

"True enough."

Ahead, the road twisted along the curving ridgeline, ducking in and out of the fringes of the forest as though it were a rocky thread, left behind when some ancient giant had hemmed the world. It also provided more places than Durine cared to think about for an ambush, although there was nothing that he could do about that. Kethol had the sharpest eyes and perhaps nose, as well, and he was riding point.

Down the slope, a village spraddled across the silvery cord of stream that marked the valley floor. It was a short ride off the road, and the web of dirt roads around it proclaimed it used to visitors.

There would be an inn suitable for travelers, and that was the obvious place for them for the night.

"Yes," Pirojil said with a nod. "You think we should do something different?"

Well, there were advantages to trying the village—innkeepers were professional gossips, and it would be nice to see if anybody had an idea as to what Baroness Elanee was up to. And if there had been anybody looking for the three—no, four of them and their charge— they could pick up word of that down there. Definitely better than spending the night out in the open.

Probably the best thing to do was to keep riding until they were clear of the barony, but they had to sleep sometime, and the border was easily two days' ride away.

Durine said as much.

Pirojil's face twisted into a frown. "I don't like it, either way. If we keep riding until we're so tired that we have to stop, none of us will be in any condition to stand watch. And that would be the worst case."

Durine nodded. "So, the village, you think?"

"I don't like that either."

Durine was tempted to say they had to make some sort of choice sometime, but Pirojil already knew that. Ah. Of course. "The local lord, eh?"

Pirojil smiled. He was particularly ugly when he smiled, what with the way that it revealed his gap-laden, yellowy teeth. He pointed the topmost of his chins at a wisp of smoke rising from behind a hillock ahead. "It took me some time to figure that out, too—I'm out of the habit of traveling with nobility."

That made sense. While three traveling soldiers would not be expected or welcomed at the local lord's keep, the presence of Lady Leria changed the whole recipe—she, of course, would be welcome, and given how inbred the Holtish ruling class tended to be, she was probably a medium-close relative. And while Durine and the others normally would not be welcome even to sleep in the stables there, their commission would give them the right to sleep across the door-

step of her room. It was a lot warmer and more comfortable on soft
blankets over a stone floor than it was in damp hay in a stable.

Fewer rats, too.

"I'll tell the lady," Durine said, dropping back. He quickly dismounted from the broad back of his gray gelding, hitched its reins
to a bracket at the back of the carriage, then ran alongside until he
could get the door open and his foot on the brass mounting peg. He
pulled himself up and into the carriage, ducking his head to avoid
smashing it on the doorjamb. "Lady, may I?"

She nodded. "Please," she said, and reached out a hand to help
him in. Durine tried to keep his surprise from his face. He had
expected perhaps to be permitted in, but he certainly hadn't expected
her to reach out her hand to him. It was all Durine could to do keep
his balance as he drew himself into the carriage, no more pulling on
her hand than he would have pulled himself in by grabbing onto her
breast.

It was a small hand, smoother than his callused one, and warm,
like a blanket on a cold night. He released it quickly, and then let
the jerking of the coach drop him into the bench opposite her, next
to Erenor.

"You're looking better," Erenor said. His smile was a figure's-
width too broad to possibly be sincere. Durine had to remember
that. If he didn't watch himself, he could end up liking the wizard,
and that wouldn't do at all. Be a shame when he got killed.

Durine shrugged. Yes, it had been a cold and uncomfortable
night, but admitting that didn't, wouldn't, couldn't make it feel any
better. "Nothing of any importance," he said. "Nothing that a servant
need concern himself with," he went on, giving Erenor a pointed
look that he hoped went over Lady Leria's head.

She pursed her lips together, as though she was going to say
something, but subsided instead. An awfully pretty little thing she
was, but then again, with her inheritance, she could have a face like
Pirojil's and still have the suitors breaking down her door. A face like
Pirojil's? She could have a face like Pirojil's backside and still be
more than very marriageable.

Erenor gave him a knowing smile. Durine would have liked little more than to slap that smile halfway down the road, as impractical as that was at the moment. Still, thinking about it warmed his insides almost as much as the brandy had before, even more than Leria's surprising act of kindness.

"Lady," Durine said, "we think it best to arrange for you to stay the night with the local lord. That would be—"

"No," she said, "no." Her cheekbones flared crimson. "Lord Moarin and . . . and I, we . . ." She shook her head. "No."

Erenor leaned forward. "I have been talking with the lady, Master Durine; it would appear that Lord Moarin is—well, has been—one of the lady's suitors. An old and wrinkled man, so I'm told, with a most unbecoming potbelly, and, no doubt, breath that reeks of garlic and wine."

It would be awkward, certainly, but not as awkward as she was making it seem. They were both of the nobility, after all. "I understand," Durine said, "but there are no other—"

"No," she said. "I simply can't stay under his roof. He . . ." She shook her head. "I can't." Her blush deepened.

Ah. So that was it. Moarin was a lecher and Leria was nervous about sleeping where he could get at her. Durine spread his hands. "Lady, you are in no danger while you're with us."

He tried to grin reassuringly, but it had no apparent effect. "I'll sleep across your doorstep myself, a knife in hand."

Her eyes widened at that, and a faint gasp escaped her lips as she shook her head. Durine kept his own irritation from his face. He had not so much as smiled at the girl; she had nothing to fear from him, and she should have been smart enough to work out that the dowager empress would not have sent somebody so ill-trained as to not know his place around noblewomen.

But there was, of course, no way that he could simply say that. He looked over again at Erenor, wondering what it was that the wizard had been doing that had Lady Leria's nerves so on edge. Not that he spent a long time wondering.

"Erenor," he said, "I think it would be best if you rode with

Master Pirojil for the rest of the day." *And,* he thought, *it would be even better if you were dragged along behind the carriage for the rest of the day.* But to do that would require taking notice of his having made advances toward the lady, and that could only embarrass what clearly was an easily embarrassed young woman further. Durine didn't want to do that. He and the others were committed to protecting Leria, and that protection wasn't limited to physical harm.

Erenor opened his mouth to protest. Durine had had enough from him, but that wasn't why he opened the carriage door with his left hand while he reached out with his free hand, grabbed the smaller man by the front of his tunic, and unceremoniously pitched him out the open door. It wasn't for the cry of surprise and the very pleasant splashing sound Erenor made as he tumbled to the muck. It was to reassure the lady, in a way that words simply couldn't, that he and the other two took their responsibilities seriously, and would brook interference from no one.

He didn't expect gratitude—that would have been far too much like the Cullinanes—but neither did he expect the expression of anger and even disgust on Leria's face. He would have expected the back of her hand across his face, but she simply sat, glaring, her eyes burning into his.

"I'm sorry, Lady, for any . . . inconvenience my servant has given you. I—"

"He did nothing." Her lips tightened. "And I still don't want to stay at Lord Moarin's. I won't. I won't."

Well, that was as direct as direct could be. If it was a matter of life and death, Durine would have overruled her—much easier to explain an angry lady to the dowager empress, if need be, than a dead one—but this wasn't that, and it was definitely better to do as she wanted, if possible.

Durine bowed his head momentarily. "As you wish it, of course."

Tennetty's Village had had another name before the war, the innkeeper explained, when it had housed a Holtish regiment, but it had been spared being put to the torch during the conquest of Holtun at, so it was said, the request of the Old Emperor's personal body-guard herself, and had been renamed in her honor.

"Truly?" It was all Pirojil could do not to snicker. He had known Tennetty all too well, for all too long, and the odds of that skinny, crazy, one-eyed attack bitch requesting anybody, anything, anywhere to be spared anything were somewhere between tiny, slim, and none.

But let the villagers live with their myth; it wouldn't hurt any-thing.

Kethol, on the other hand, snickered. "Tennetty's Village, eh?" He may not have noticed the way his right hand dropped to the hilt of his sword, but Durine did: the big man took Kethol's wrist be-tween his thumb and forefinger and placed it on the table. He pursed his thick lips and shook his head. Kethol shrugged. "I knew her. Once had to pull her off the—my master's son."

"You knew her?" The innkeeper nodded too quickly. "Of course, of course."

Kethol grinned. "I get the feeling you don't believe me." It wasn't a friendly grin.

"Ta havath," Pirojil said.

Shut your mouth, he meant. Showing off for the girl wasn't just stupid, it was very stupid. It was also pointless, in fact, what with Lady Leria outside in the carriage and the three of them in here.

The trouble was that Kethol probably didn't even know he was trying to impress her. Which didn't make it any better; he probably thought that he was just handling the situation well, impressing the innkeeper that he wasn't to be trifled with. Which only made it worse. If Kethol was going to be stupid, as he had been in Riverforks, at least he should know he was being stupid. Deliberate stupidity was always better than the accidental, unconscious type.

Either could, of course, get you killed.

Durine looked at Pirojil, and Pirojil looked at Durine. Well, Riv-erforks had been Durine's turn, at that. "Kethol," Pirojil said, "I need to see you for a moment. Outside."

"But—"

"Now, please." He turned to go, Kethol reluctantly at his side. "Durine," he went on, "can negotiate our lodgings just as well without us as with. And Durine, please don't lose your temper this time. It cost the lady most of her purse last time to pay for the damages, and that innkeeper will never quite be able to sit down comfortably again."

One of Durine's eyes closed in a broad wink. "If you insist, Pirojil."

There was a reception committee, of sorts, at the carriage: Lord Miron and three other men, in varicolored filigreed tunics and leggings that looked entirely normal on Miron, and ill-fitting and awkward on the other three. One of them held the carriage in place, while another stayed on horseback, holding the rein extensions of the three dismounted men's horses, and the third stood on the ground between Erenor and the carriage.

They might as well have been wearing large signs, with a drawing showing soldiers taking off their livery and uncomfortably donning civilian garb suitable for minor nobility.

Erenor was, as Pirojil could have easily predicted, standing around uselessly, his face studiously blank, his eyes shouting for help. Miron had evicted him from the carriage and taken his place next to the lady.

"Lady Leria informs me," he said, his hand resting insolently on her smaller one in a way that made Pirojil want to break his fingers one by one, "that you lot have for some reason decided to spurn Lord Moarin's hospitality before it is even offered."

Pirojil grunted. "I've always thought that the best time," he said. "Safer, too."

Miron let that go past without comment. "I—we, that is—we are concerned about her well-being. I thought it wise to join you, and ride with you, at least to the border. Bandits, you know."

Four of them? Pirojil thought about it for a moment. He didn't like it, but there didn't seem to be any way around it, at least not at the moment.

"We'd be honored, of course," he said. "Durine is making arrangements for our own housing for tonight; I'm sure there will be ample room at the inn for you and your noble company, as well."

Miron's face was impassive. Which probably meant he was surprised.

Pirojil stepped up on the mounting peg and offered his hand to Lady Leria. "If you please, Lady," he said, resenting but ignoring the way Miron openly eyed the swell of her bosom as she rose to a crouch to make her way out of the couch.

"Very well." Miron's lips pursed. "Yes, we shall take rooms here. And you shall join me for dinner in my rooms, Lady, if it pleases you."

"She'll have the three of us at her side," Kethol said, too quickly.

"I think it would be crowded in your rooms," Pirojil said. "Perhaps the main room of the tavern would be better."

"Much better." Kethol nodded.

Miron opened his mouth. "Are you suggesting that she wouldn't be safe in my company, my man?" His voice oozed an oily threat.

"I'm—"

"No," Pirojil said, "he isn't suggesting that." *And he isn't your man, either.* "He is, though, suggesting that whether the lady dines in your rooms or in public, she'll have us at her side. And he is suggesting that the lady has been put in our safekeeping at the orders of the dowager empress, and that in our safekeeping she will remain until she reaches the dowager empress." He offered her the crook of his arm. "Lady? If I may see you to your rooms?"

Miron was an expansive host, once he got a skinful of wine into him. "Well, now, and what did the Old Emperor do then?"

The sitting room was heated by a huge fireplace, easily as wide as Pirojil was tall.

Pirojil sat back in the too-comfortable chair. Miron wasn't the only one who had been drinking too much. Leria's face was flushed, and Durine was holding himself with an unusual stiffness. The wine was deceptively strong—there was a taste of some piney resin that masked the spirits' strength.

Only Kethol had settled for a single glass of wine, diluted that with half again as much water, and sweetened it with honey, Salket style. Not that Kethol was a Salke, of course, but . . .

"He drew himself up straight," Kethol went on, pausing to take another minuscule sip from his glass, "and announced himself in a voice so loud that it shook walls. 'I am Karl Cullinane, prince of Bieme and emperor of Holtun-Bieme,' he said, 'and if I do not see that miserable excuse of a baron of yours standing before me in ten heartbeats, I'll see him dancing on the end of a spear before the dawn finishes breaking.' "

"And Baron Arondael tolerated that?"

Durine gave out a rumbling chuckle, and Kethol laughed. "Yes, he did more than tolerate it. He came ascurrying and bowing and scraping, and begged the emperor to accept the hospitality of his castle."

"All because of one swordsman and a handful of soldiers? Amazing."

Pirojil kept quiet. Could it be that Miron was as stupid as he was pretending to be? Or was he just trying to draw them out?

Kethol, of course, took the bait. "No, it wasn't just any handful of soldiers, and the emperor wasn't just a swordsman. He was . . . well, he was something. I swear he could have torn down that castle by himself, stone by stone."

Durine grunted. "He wasn't by himself, either. I think Tennetty—the woman they named this village after—had already silenced a half-dozen guards." He drew a blunt thumb across his throat and made a wet sucking sound with his lips. "Tennetty always did like silencing guards."

Kethol nodded. "She did, at that," he said, warming to the subject. "She had this way with a knife, where she'd snake an arm around from behind and do this stab-and-twist thing, and all you'd hear was a low gurgle and—"

"And then," Durine put in, "there was an army marching on Arondael—under Neranahan and Garavar, by the way—and the dragon Ellegon flew overhead."

"Yes," Kethol said, "his leathery wings a-flapping, fire issuing from his roar, the sulfuric stench of all filling the air until all you could do was choke. The baron was more than happy to see things our way, under the circumstances. He was something, the Old Emperor."

Durine smiled thinly. "I can still hear him shouting. 'Baron!' he shouted, his voice loud enough to shatter walls, 'when the emperor comes a-calling, it had best not be because you have refused his hospitality.' "

Miron spread his hands. "But, still . . . one man? Or even a dozen?"

Durine nodded wisely. "You have a point, and it is well taken. One moment." With a loud scraping, he pushed himself back from his chair and rose, then half-staggered toward the arched doorway that led to the hall, returning in a few moments with two items, one in each hand: a large onion, still with top and trailing roots, dripping water as though it had just been rinsed moments before, and a small bright knife, wooden-handled.

He set both down on the table in front of Kethol. "The stew is a bit bland for my tastes," he said, his voice only slightly slurred. "Could you help?"

"Of course." Kethol had already produced his own knife, as Pirojil had known he would, and quickly trimmed off the roots and the nubbin left behind, then decapitated the onion with one quick motion. Two quick longitudinal slices, and the brown outer skin was gone, leaving behind only the pale green flesh of the onion.

Kethol set it down on the rough-hewn surface of the table and quickly sliced it in half, then took one half, set it flat on the table, and made six quick parallel cuts, then another six perpendicular to the first. A half-dozen quick chops, and the onion half had been cut into tiny diced pieces, which Kethol quickly scooped up in one hand and sprinkled over the top of Durine's stew.

The big man's breath would smell painfully bad in the morning, but Miron was nodding.

"One cut at a time, eh?" His fingers toyed with the remaining half of the onion. "I see your point," he said, taking at first a delicate nibble, and then a full bite, smiling through the entirely emotion-free tears that ran freely down his cheeks and into his beard.

He took big bites, and enjoyed raw flavors. Pirojil couldn't help but like that in him.

Of course, should the situation arise where killing Miron seemed to be the right thing to do, that wouldn't stay his hand for a heartbeat.

He smiled back.

14

✠ Biemestren

Clouds concealed the night stars, but not the Faeric lights. The east wind blew cold and damp, the sort of wind her husband used to call the Wind of Foreboding. It chilled her to the very bone, but Beralyn Furnael, dowager empress of Holtun-Bieme, persisted in her walk, neither quickening nor slowing her pace.

It would take more than an icy wind to divert her from her routine, and more than a diversion from her routine to divert her from her resolution.

So let the wind blow, cold and hard, chilly and inflexible as a man's heart. She would still enjoy her stroll about the parapet.

The Faerie lights were all in blues and purples tonight, and half-hidden in the clouds. They pulsed through their narrow spectrum quickly, like a heartbeat, then vanished, like sheets of silent blued lightning.

It was only iron will that prevented her from shivering as she rounded the last of the guard stations and started down the steps, slowly, carefully. The climb up to the parapet was difficult, and painful to the knees and that cursed right hip that not even the Hand woman could do much with. But the climb down was dangerous. One crumbling step beneath her feet, one failure of knee or hip or muscle, and she would pitch forward, with nothing to break her fall but the steps beneath her and the too-solid cobblestones of the yard below.

It occurred to her that a lesser woman would have clung to the stone railing that ran down the side of the steps, but Beralyn was

not a lesser woman. Her womb had long since dried up, and no man
had warmed her bed since her husband had been murdered by Pirondael through either the connivance or the incompetence of the
cursed Cullinanes, but she was no lesser woman.

She was the dowager empress, and mother of the emperor himself, and until she held her grandson and future emperor in her
hands, she would maintain.

But she had had enough of today.

Let tomorrow's troubles be what they may; they could wait until
tomorrow. It was all she could do not to glare at Derinald as he
waited, his hands behind his back, just inside the archway. She had
not summoned him, and that did not bode well. But her long-dead
husband had once chastised her for her tendency to blame the augur
for the augury, and it was all she could do not to duck her head and
whisper, Yes, Zherr, I shall never do that again.

The years had, despite her wish to the contrary, dulled her pain,
if not her resolution. But it was at moments like this that her voice
and hands quavered at the horrid realization that never again would
she be held in those strong, warm arms.

"I had best change my route," she said, using all her resolve to
keep her voice from trembling, her look daring him to recognize her
failure. "I am becoming too predictable in my old age."

"Not at all, my empress. Rather, I think of it as a duty and a
pleasure to know where to find you."

He had a pretty way with a compliment, but she was having none
of it. "You'd rather lay me out on a slab for burial, and don't deny
it," she said. "What need does a young man like yourself have of a
withered old woman?" she asked, as she walked toward the doorway
into the keep, ignoring the way the guard leaped to get the door for
her. She had her control back; as long as she could keep her anger
and hate warm and sharp, the pain would recede to the background.

Derinald grinned. The buffoon. "I'd rather think of you as reliable, ever steady, my empress," he said, his smile too broad, too
apparently sincere to possibly be real. "Which does make you a stanchion of security in an always-insecure world, an utterly steadfast

anchor for my restless and ever uncertain mind to cling to."

"And what news do you bring that will bind this stanchion ever more securely to you?" she asked. This was ridiculous. She was an old woman, living on tasteless food and salty anger, more set in her ways than any stanchion, but once again this charming captain had her taking on his style of speech, as though she was still a young chit whose head could be turned with flattery and flowers.

Beralyn had been young once, long ago, but she had never been *that* young.

He pursed his lips. "News? I wouldn't say it is precisely news, but a fast runner was dispatched by Governor Treseen to the telography station, and his reports have reached here tonight." He tapped at his chest. "I was just on my way to deliver this to the emperor, although as I understand it he will be retiring—"

A distant gong rang, then again, and again, and a final time.

"—just about now," Derinald went on, his smile returning, "although it is nothing that needs his attention before morning."

She held out her hand, palm up.

"I'm very sorry, Your Majesty," Derinald said as he removed a small leather pouch from inside his tunic. He held it up to the flickering light. There were two seals; one was Derinald's familiar curlicues that always reminded Beralyn of a handful of snakes trying to escape from a wicker basket, and the other was one of those engineer glyphs. "The emperor himself ordered all messages to him sealed, for reasons I can't explain."

"Can't, or won't?"

He shrugged away the difference. "I'm hardly one to read the emperor's thoughts at all, and I'm not one to repeat the emperor's words unbidden."

Nor was he one to keep a secret from her, even though ordered to by Thomen. That was good. It showed that he understood his situation.

"And why is it sealed by your ring, as well?"

Derinald's lips pursed. "Well, it's been my custom to bring a tray of tea and trifles to the poor fellow on evening duty at the telegraphy station, just about the time that the new telegrapher at Neranahan comes on."

She snickered. "And he doesn't wonder why a captain in the guard would be acting as his servant?"

"Engineers," he said, his tone making the word a pejorative. It occurred to Beralyn that if he used that tone in public frequently, his oh-too-pretty face would not have remained so pretty, unless he was very good with the suspiciously decorative sword that stuck out impudently from the right side of his waist, at the angle of a young man's erection.

"It is a lonely job," he said, spreading his hands, "and surely no simple soldier could possibly read the tickety-tickety-tackity of the telegraph."

"Oh, really?" She raised an eyebrow. "And you can, you say?"

"I hope I said nothing of the sort, my Empress." He raised his palms. "I would not lie to you, and I am loath to confess my inadequacy so very bluntly, but since you insist, so be it: I cannot. It's just a clickety-clickety-click to me, and nothing more."

It wasn't like Derinald to present himself a failure. She waited, letting just a trace of impatience show. Yes, the guard captain was a useful retainer, but there were times when his predilections for drama and self-aggrandizement made her wonder if he was more trouble than he was worth.

So: he couldn't make out the code of the telegraph. But he was not announcing failure.

"Very well," she said. "Go on."

"I can, however," he said, "read upside-down." He stuck his hand into his pouch. "And my memory is quite good." He extracted a folded sheet of paper from his pouch, and held it out to her. "It would seem that the three Cullinane men have successfully extracted the girl from the baroness's possession, and are on their way back to Biemestren, having left something of a mess behind them."

"So even if they are successful . . ." she said, and let her voice peter out. She was too old, and there was not enough time left. A younger Beralyn would not have revealed her thoughts to one such as Derinald, even though he likely could have guessed them anyway.

He took her silence as an invitation. "Yes, even if they are successful, they'll have engendered sufficient ill-will in Keranahan to reflect badly on their master."

And, of course, there was little reason to assume, and less to hope, that they would be successful, in the final essence.

"Well?" she asked. "Isn't there something you ought to be doing?"

His eyebrow lifted, but his composure didn't waver for a heartbeat. "Your Majesty?"

She kept a gnarled forefinger against his chest. "I think the emperor is awaiting the message you carry. I don't imagine he'd want you standing about and jabbering with a useless old woman."

"I am sure that is so, but I cannot possible imagine how that would have anything whatsoever to do with Your Majesty," he said, bowing as he took a step back. "But, nevertheless, I'm sure the emperor would not thank me for dawdling even in such pleasant and noble company, and if I may be excused, I shall be on my way."

She smiled at his back. Well, at least the boy had enough spine for sarcasm.

Meanwhile, it was time to heat things up for the cursed Cullinanes.

A quick telegram to Governor Treseen, explaining her wish that the baroness be apprised of Beralyn's unhappiness with the way that Leria had been treated, and her intention to listen to the girl's full report before deciding what punishment to recommend to the emperor . . .

That ought to stir up some action, and if that action caused anybody to overplay his—or her!—hand, then so be it.

She picked up her pace, and if she hadn't long since been incapable of smiling, she probably would have smiled. For some reason, Beralyn's joints weren't hurting as much as usual.

15

The Road, Again

awn was threatening to break; through the windows, the outside had gone from black to an incredibly dull taupe, and was now settling on a nice dark gray.

Kethol rose silently from his bed and crept across the floor to the door. He listened for a moment, and then another, and stayed motionless, listening, until Pirojil wanted to shout at him to get on with it until he nodded.

Pirojil threw back his blankets and rose quickly. He had slept fully dressed—save for his boots, of course, and it was just a matter of moments to lace them up and tie the laces tightly, and then belt his sword about his waist.

He took a small tub of grease from his kit, opened it, wincing at the smell—that goose had died far too long ago, and the expense of having a wizard put a preservative spell on the grease seemed trivial, in malodorous retrospect—and dipped his index finger in it, then carefully lubricated the hinges on the heavy door that led to Lady Leria's room. It was the only door in or out of that room; their suite was the usual one for a noble with bodyguards.

She lay sleeping peacefully, her chest barely moving with gentle breaths, her golden hair spread out across her pillow as if it were floating there. Had she been some common wench, she would have woken with his left hand across her mouth, if not with his right holding a knife to her neck, but he could hardly lay familiar hands on a noblewoman with no more reason than a strong desire for silence.

So he stood well away from her bed. "Lady," Pirojil whispered. "Lady."

She came awake suddenly and sat up, her breath coming in a loud gasp, quickly focusing on Pirojil standing near the door, his finger flying to his lips.

That was a mistake; he could barely stop himself from gagging at the smell of the long-rancid goose grease. There had been time to clean his hands, he supposed, and it would have been well to use it.

"Lady," he whispered again. "It's time we be going."

"But . . . the—I mean, Lord Miron—"

"Should still be asleep, given the amount he drank and the time he retired, and we'll be well on our way before he wakes, with any luck."

You made your own luck, and if it took a drinking contest that still had Pirojil's temples feeling as if somebody was pounding on them with a hammer and his stomach ready for heaving with a moment's notice, well, so be it. He and Durine could function with hangovers, and Kethol's head had been kept clear for a purpose.

"Quickly, quickly," he said, then closed the door behind him. If he'd had his way he would have yanked her out of her nightclothes, stuffed them in a bag and her in another, and thrown her over his shoulder, but she was a lady, and he would have to wait

He was surprised—pleasantly so, for once—that she emerged from her room only a short while later, hair pulled back and tied with a ribbon, and a dark green cloak covering her brown traveling dress. She actually was carrying one of her bags herself, with her own hands.

Not your typical noble lady, Pirojil decided. Not typical at all.

"You said we had to hurry, Pirojil," she said, her voice a low murmur, her head tilted to one side in a way that made her even smile seem crooked. "Shall we be off ?"

✿　　✿　　✿

Durine leaned hard against the traces, ignoring how much his fingers ached, the way that his thighs, powerful though they were, complained with every step.

From a leafy branch overhanging the road ahead of him, the bright eyes of a jackhen peeked through the dimly lit leaves in the gray light, and cawed a noisy laugh. Durine didn't reach out and crush its head and body with his hands not just because the bird's perch on the branch was at least two manheights out of his reach, not just because even if the branch had been within reach the bird would have flown away at his first motion, not just because even if the bird had been nailed to its perch—a pleasant idea, that—and the perch had been within Durine's reach, his hands were occupied with the traces.

Durine didn't blame the bird. If he had been the one sitting comfortably on a branch, he would have laughed at the idiot below, pulling the carriage up what had looked, at first, to be only a shallow rise.

It had seemed like a simple idea yesterday, and in fact it still made sense.

Sort of.

The harness straps didn't cut into his shoulders—any more than they would have cut into the dray horses' thick hides—but the trouble was keeping his hands tight on the harness. The next time they did this—hah!—he would have some saddlemaker make him a harness. If Durine was going to pull a carriage, he could bloody well at least be hitched properly to it. Horses didn't have to blister and bloody their hands.

He wouldn't mind skipping the iron bit between his teeth, though.

The way Pirojil had explained it, it had all made sense: it wouldn't be possible to hitch all the dray horses to the carriage and then clop off down the road without making enough noise to draw the attention of Miron and his companions, but it was possible for Erenor to quietly lead the horses out of the stable one by one and hitch them all, one at a time, to a stump a far ways down the road, and then the only problem was bringing along the carriage without the clop-clop-clop of hoofbeats.

That was the trouble with Pirojil: he thought too much. Spent too much time worrying over every little problem, like a dog worrying a bone. Made life too complicated.

Life should be simple.

Of course, he thought, when you let life be simple, you found yourself the one stuck pulling the carriage while Pirojil and Kethol got to walk, so maybe there was something to this complication stuff after all.

He recognized Erenor's footsteps—far too noisy, far too self-assured, far too Erenor—before he saw him crest the hill.

What was it with this wizard? He was all fresh and clean and well combed in the morning light, even though he had gotten less sleep than Durine had, and had been spending his time making trips to and from the stable for the horses. There was something suspicious about a man who looked too good this early.

"That was the last one, Master Durine," he said as he approached, his voice too loud. Without so much as a by-your-leave, without even a raised eyebrow in inquiry, Erenor reached up to the seat of the carriage and pulled down a set of traces, quickly slinging them across his own shoulders and leaning into them, just as Durine had.

Hmm . . . he really was as strong as he looked; the weight against Durine's hands lightened, and his pace quickened.

They crested the hill easily, and before the carriage could pick up speed, Durine slipped out of his traces and quickly boosted Erenor to the driver's bench.

Durine let the carriage roll past, and got a grip on the straps he'd tied to the tailpiece. He was about to caution Erenor to use the brake, carefully but firmly, to avoid letting the carriage break into an unguided roll, but even before he could open his mouth, he felt the carriage slow—but just a trifle, just enough to keep the pace at a fast walk, but not so fast that Durine couldn't swing the rear wheels to the right, and then correct to the left, keeping the carriage in the middle of the road.

It wasn't the easiest thing Durine had ever done, but it did beat hauling this hunk of wood and iron uphill, at that.

There was the temptation to let the carriage build up speed so as to roll-at least partway up the next hill, but, surprisingly, Erenor was smart enough to resist it even without specifically being told to, although, unsurprisingly, his resolve weakened and the carriage sped up as it approached the bottom of the hill, so much so that Durine had to break into a dogtrot to keep up with it until, too soon, it slowed and, iron-rimmed wheels grinding against the dirt of the road, stopped.

Back into the traces Durine went, Erenor again at his side.

Years ago, with the emperor, he had flown over this barony, and from high above, on the dragon's back, the land had seemed gently rippled, like a lakeside beach after the water receded. They might have been gentle ripples from cloud level; here on the ground they were bloody big hills, and Durine hoped that this was the last one.

At the top of the hill, the road curved away, twisting down the slope toward where a glistening stream divided woods from plowed land. A path had been worn along the streambed, and it was on the path that their horses stood, each carefully hitched to an overhead branch and then twist-hobbled. Pirojil's big bay was the first to notice; the amber-eyed gelding lifted its muzzle from the water and snorted, sending the other horses shifting nervously.

Off in the distance, each burdened only by a bag on his shoulder, Pirojil led Lady Leria down the streamside path, while Kethol, ever watchful, brought up the rear.

Where was the rest of the gear?

He turned to Erenor, favoring him with a glance that would have shriveled a less self-confident man. "You didn't leave the rest of our gear at the inn, did you?" The idea was to be gone, long gone, before Miron and his companions were awake, and they were getting a late enough start as it was.

Erenor ducked his head in simulated humility and then gestured a thumb toward the carriage's boot. "No, Master Durine, I wouldn't think of it."

The arrogant brummagem wizard had had Durine haul the bags up hill after hill, like a plowhorse, when he could have simply loaded the gear on the horses? The nerve of him! Durine would have liked to strangle him one-handed, right here on the road.

"The bags, eh, Master Durine?" Erenor might as well have been reading his thoughts. "That is what angers you now? And if I had left them here unguarded, when I could have kept them safely with you and me, Master Durine, would you not choose to be angry at me for that?" He gestured toward where the hobbled horses stood. "And were I to have left them somewhere else, would you not be angry at me for that, no matter where they were and how safe they might have been?"

Durine's fingers twitched.

"Ah," Erenor said, "very good, Master Durine: strangle me here on the road, and surely that will solve all of your problems, for I am unquestionably the cause of all of them." He turned his back on Durine, and—after pausing for a moment as though challenging Durine to strike him from behind—set the carriage's brake before dogtrotting down the hill toward the others.

Durine nodded to himself. The wizard might lack a lot of things, but he had style.

Of course, style was an often overvalued quality.

It was all Pirojil could do to avoid whistling as he wheeled his horse around and kicked his heels against her slab sides, sending her into an easy canter, the cloppity-clop of her hooves a pleasant rhythm that kept time with the bouncing of the saddle.

Life was good.

High in the crook of an old oak, a trio of jackjays sang in a harmony that was nonetheless pleasing for its raggedness. At a walk or canter, the air was crisp and cooling without being cold, and in the bright spattered light that filtered through the canopy of leaves overhead, there would have been no problem even at the fastest gallop to anticipate the necessity of ducking under or guiding the horse to the side of the odd branch that stuck out over the road.

That was annoying, and a sign of the decline of the times. Back when the Old Emperor ruled Holtun, patrol captains would tally any failings in the roads and fine the barons accordingly until woodsmen were dispatched to cut down overhanging branches, or dig out fallen boulders, or repair bridges, or whatever. Roads were an imperial resource and a baronial responsibility.

But attention to detail—or, rather, the requirement that others attend to detail—was not one of the virtues of the emperor Thomen, and Pirojil decided that he might as well resign himself to that.

At least it was better than it had been under Prince Pirondael. If Pirondael had wanted somebody's opinion, so the wags said, he would have tortured it out of him.

It was too nice a day for such black thoughts.

Things were going their way for once. His belly was full and warm with a nice horseback lunch of sausage, onions, and bread, and the still-wet waterskin lashed to the saddle was filled with fresh stream water.

The fork in the road lay ahead, this one less acute than some others. Pirojil decided that it was perfectly logical that someone would have ridden in a generally northern way and then turned east, so he didn't hide what tracks his horse made on the dirt road. Carriage tracks led back the way Pirojil had just come, and that would—or should, anyway—be enough for their erstwhile escorts.

Closing in on a capital—be it simply a baronial seat or Biemestren itself—was like following a river toward its mouth: smaller roads tended to join into larger ones, and as you rode on, your path became more and more predictable, carrying you toward the capital like a river sweeping you to the Cirric. The good side of that was that it was easy to avoid getting lost—as long as you kept heading in the direction of the capital, the odds were that any road would do—but the bad side of it was that it made tracking you easy.

For now, at least, they were riding more away than toward, and every fork in the road represented yet another opportunity to lose any pursuers.

By the time the sun had reached its zenith, they had passed through three forks, and now Pirojil had covered their tracks and was on the way to rejoin the carriage, not caring if he tired his horse in the process.

Kethol was the old woodsman among them, and each time he had thrown a bale of branches down to drag behind the carriage, while either Pirojil or Durine had ridden at least a short way down the path they'd not taken, then turned about, each masking his own path with another bale dragged behind the horse.

Yes, if young Lord Miron was following them, he and his party would likely be able to double back as well, perhaps even before reaching the turnaround. But there was a trick to this: when Pirojil rejoined his companions, he would swap the sweaty ruddy mare for a fresh mount, one that hadn't been carrying the weight of a man on her back, and let this horse rest at a carriage-paced walk. It wouldn't take much backing-and-filling for the pursuers, if any, to tire their mounts, even if they spun about at each place the decoy rider did.

More likely, they would give up and go home.

And if not, that would be suggestive.

Of what, though?

Pirojil didn't know. There was a lot here that didn't make sense, from the baroness who was feeding something out in the back country, to the young lord who was far too friendly to be sincere, to the imperial governor who was more interested in not seeing anything than in whatever it was that was going on.

But it wasn't Pirojil's job to make sense of things; it was his job to get the girl to the dowager empress, and then get out from under her eye at Biemestren and back to the life of a private soldier, soldiering as little as possible while raising and storing away as much money as possible. Gold was always a more reliable friend than any nobility, particularly those that—

Pirojil cut that thought off, and stopped fiddling with the ring that he wore, signet side in, on his hand. It was a country far away, and if the fire he had set hadn't burned away those wounds—and it hadn't—and if the years hadn't healed them—and they hadn't—there was no point in dwelling on it.

Besides, even the Old Emperor had betrayed him by dying. Pirojil hadn't quite forgiven him for that, even now, but there was, as usual, nothing that could be done about it.

Pirojil took a deep draught of cold water from his waterskin, then splashed his face with some more to rid himself of some of the road dust.

There was nothing to be done about it; it would just have to be lived with. On a nice day, that was easier than otherwise.

Pirojil had been paying attention to the distant rattling of the carriage and the clopping of hooves; when Kethol spurred his horse out of the trees he started. But he kept his right hand on the reins, away from the hilt of his sword, although his left hand did rest on the butt of the pistol stuck in his belt, concealed under his tunic. If it hadn't been Kethol or Durine or Erenor, it would have been just a matter of rip, grab, and then cock-and-blam. With Pirojil's limited marksmanship, it was silver marks to slimy meatrolls that he would miss even at close range, but so be it. The noise easily could distract an enemy long enough for Pirojil's sword tip to find his wrist.

"You can do better than that, Piro," Kethol said, tsking. "You can't fool me so easily into thinking you actually didn't spot me, rather than waiting to see what my move was to be."

Pirojil smiled. "We all have our days."

Kethol was, at times, an empty-headed hero, but you could always trust him to give a friend so much the benefit of the doubt that doubt itself was banished.

"I think it's about time we figure we've lost them, eh?"

"That suits me." Kethol nodded. "No more of this back-and-fill? Yes, that suits me, I'll tell you." He cocked his head to one side. "Still, all in all, it pays to be careful. Let's keep it up for the rest of the day, and leave one behind on watch."

If we were so careful, we'd be in a different line of work, Pirojil thought.

But he said, "You or me?"

Kethol snorted, as though the idea of Pirojil being up to his own standard of watchmanship was a silly idea. Well, maybe it was, under the circumstances. Kethol's woodcraft was better than Pirojil's, and so was his horsemanship. Which was surprising. Kethol had been a foot soldier almost since childhood, and had only taken to riding when tapped by the Old Emperor, while Pirojil had spent many a happy hour in the saddle.

He cut off that thought, wishing he could cut off memories with a knife. His thumb felt at the signet in his backwards-turned ring. "You," Pirojil said.

"I'll watch the trail, and catch up to you before nightfall. Mark any fork." Kethol brought his horse from its normal to-and-froing to a statuelike stand with one quick tug on the reins and a squeeze of the knees, then rose to a precarious balance, standing on his saddle. He produced the knife from his sleeve and made three small, parallel slashes on an overhead branch. They were easy to see if you were looking for them, but trails were blazed, be it intentionally or unintentionally, at eye height, not above the eyes of a mounted man.

Pirojil would have stood high in his stirrups and used his sword to make such a mark, but you could trust Kethol to do it another way.

"Very well," Pirojil said. "But just to make things difficult for anybody after you, we'll mark the ways not taken."

Kethol smiled, wheeled his horse about, and cantered off. "See you by tonight, or perhaps tomorrow."

16

Bats and Owls

They stopped for the night at a burned-out old farmhouse that Durine had scouted for them. The sunken fields around it had been planted with bitter oats, now almost waist-high, and the road across the top of the berm that led to the island of blackened timbers and tumbledown stones was overgrown and narrowed by weather and time. They unhitched the horses, and pulled the carriage off the road into the woods, hiding it from casual view with branches and brush.

It once had been a prosperous farm; Pirojil could tell by the number of outbuildings. There had been a barn or stable, and a knee-high circle of stones was probably the corpse of a granary. Presumably the hulk of the building that had straddled the stream that twisted its way across the property and into the woods had been a water mill. The water barely fell over what had been a dam. Another few years, and all evidence of that would be washed away, unless of course some beavers got to it first and made it their own dam for their own damn purposes.

But the land hadn't been abandoned. Just the farmstead, which was probably why it had been planted with a crop that took little weeding and less attention, like bitter oats. Not the best use of farmland, perhaps, but one that only needed attention at planting and harvest—if, of course, you didn't mind the deer going at the young stalks, which they obviously were: the edges of the fields looked as if they'd been nibbled on by a giant.

The horses were unhitched and unsaddled, and secured in what was left of the barn—the waist-high wall of stone was broken in few enough places that they could be sealed off with rope and brambles, horses hitched into stalls. It would have been nice to put some hay down to soak up their piss and shit, but one night of standing in it wouldn't do them any harm.

But the timbers that had once held the walls had been standing out in the sun and the rain for long enough that they didn't even smell of smoke anymore, and it was easy enough to rig a pair of tarpaulins to give Lady Leria some privacy for sleeping, and a simple lean-to, past the remnants of the silo, to shade the hastily dug privy from which Leria returned, her face clean-scrubbed, her traveling dress exchanged for a heavy cotton shift belted loosely at the hips.

Pirojil offered her a mug. "The stream water is quite good, Lady," he said.

She smiled her thanks. "I know, Pirojil. I've just washed in it. Cold and refreshing, better than a fresh dipperful from a well bucket."

Erenor frowned at that last, but returned to preparing their cold supper. He had gone to work with a knife and a wooden cutting board, and had turned an ordinary cold road meal of bread, sausage, cheese, and onion into an attractive arrangement of slices and wedges. The sausage had been fanned out like a fallen stack of coins, and the onions had been cut thin enough to read through. The whole arrangement was bordered with some leafy green thing that looked like lettuce that Pirojil was sure hadn't been among their travel rations.

He wielded a pair of silver tongs—Pirojil didn't have the slightest idea where they had come from, either—with dexterity and flair, piling layers of meat and cheese atop a slice of bread which he presented on a plate to Lady Leria, and then repeated the performance for Durine and finally for Pirojil.

It was the same bread, sausage, and onion he had had for lunch, but somehow the whole presentation of it made it taste better, or maybe it was just that Pirojil was so hungry that the sole of his boot would have tasted good.

Still, Erenor might not be much of a wizard, but he did make an excellent servant, from time to time.

Leria smiled around a bite of her food. Her mouth was quite properly closed, but there was something strange about her smile.

She swallowed heavily. "Very tasty, Erenor; you have my thanks," she said.

The way she put that bothered Pirojil, although he couldn't quite figure out why.

"I'm grateful," he said, "that you aren't unhappy that we couldn't start a cookfire."

She raised her eyebrows. "Really. It had not occurred to me that such a thing would be possible." She pursed her lips together. "Or desirable."

"It's possible. Not desirable," Durine said, his voice a bass rumble, like distant thunder.

"Oh?"

"Draws attention," he said.

When you were fleeing, the last thing you needed to do was start a fire. During the day, even a wisp of smoke would point like a finger toward your location; at night, even a carefully banked fire might send up a few stray sparks, and would of a certainty send the fragrance of woodsmoke downwind.

If it hadn't been the local sausage, Pirojil wouldn't have even considered letting them eat such spicy stuff, for fear that their trail would be marked by the smell of their shit, or worse—Kethol claimed, perhaps with only a little braggadocio, that he could smell a sailor's salt-pork-and-cheap-wine sweat half a barony away, and a dwarf's mushroomy fart even further.

"Yes, Lady," Pirojil said. "We've spent the day trying to hide our trail from Lord Miron and his friends. It would be . . . unwise to cry out 'Here we are!' for the sake of a cookfire."

She nodded. "But how will Kethol find us, then?"

"It would depend," Pirojil said. "If he comes along within the next hour, there's a good chance he'll see us before we see him."

"And if not?"

Why the interest? Was she just making conversation, or was there something going on there?

Durine caught his eye, and shrugged. Well, if there was, she'd hardly be the first noblewoman to want to sport with a handsome soldier, and she wouldn't be the last.

"No problem," Pirojil said. "He'll catch up with us tonight, or tomorrow sometime." Kethol had spent a night alone in the woods before, and would again.

Kethol tsked quietly to himself as the wind brought him the distant sounds of conversation and the sour smell of moist air across humus and bitter oats, with just a hint of horseshit and a distant musky touch of skunk, both smells that Kethol liked in small doses. At dusk, he had dismounted and walked his horse—overhanging branches had a tendency to grow twigs and barbs that could slash at a face and eyes in the dark—and what with his leisurely pace, he hadn't caught up to them until well after sundown.

Well, he hadn't actually caught up with them, not yet. But even if Pirojil hadn't marked the turnoff, Kethol would have known that they would use the ruins of the farmhouse as a campsite for the night. You don't spend too many of your waking hours with two other people without developing a feel for how their minds work, even if their minds usually work better than yours.

There was the temptation to rejoin the party, but . . . But there was an advantage to having a night to himself, to not sharing the watch, to not having to watch the way his tongue tended to tie itself in knots around Lady Leria. Kethol liked a good night's sleep and for once he would have one. For once, let the two—well, three, if you included Erenor, although Kethol would have bet marks to chits that Pirojil and Durine wouldn't—split the watch. His horse was hobbled in a nearby clearing to graze for the night, and it was more than slightly unlikely that some night traveler would stumble across her. Yes, she would whinny and whicker at an approach, if she noticed it, but Kethol couldn't fall asleep with only the horse to watch over him, not out in the open.

There was a better way.

A light string tied to his belt, Kethol climbed high into the old gnarled oak, then seated himself carefully before pulling up his gear bag. He pulled out a roll of leather hide, unrolled it, and threaded two strong ropes through its reinforced hems.

It was part of his share of their communal gear by his choice. Stick two fresh-cut poles down its hemmed sides, and it was a stretcher. Dig two shallow parallel trenches spaced for hips and shoulders, cover same with corn husks or straw or nothing, cover that with a blanket and cover the blanket with the leather, and it was a comfortable bed.

Or thread two ropes with it, tie them appropriately tightly to two branches high in a tree, and you had a comfortable hammock, high above the ground, safe from prowling animals—particularly the two-legged kind. Of course, if you were the sort to roll over in your sleep, it was also a fine way to drop to your death, but Kethol had learned to sleep in a tree when he was a boy, and he'd yet to fall out.

There was, of course, always a first time for everything, so he tied another rope under his arms, then hitched the free end to an overhanging limb. If he fell out of bed, it would be a painful fall, but it wouldn't kill him.

He used the rope to lower himself carefully to the hammock, then stretched out with just a quick pat at his pistol and sword to be sure they were in place, as of course they were.

The night was alive with sounds and smells. Kethol liked that. He never understood city folk, who found the distant clickety-click of tappetbugs irritating and the calls of birds an annoyance. They were the music of the forest, and every forest played a different tune for your pleasure, if you only were a quiet audience. His long-dead father had taught him that, along with how to sleep in a tree.

A tightness in his bladder reminded him of something else his father had taught him, about relieving yourself before you climbed a tree to sleep.

Well, at least he wouldn't have to repeat the whole process, he thought as he carefully lifted himself out of the hammock, untied the chest strap, then climbed down the tree. The hammock would still be there.

He could have just unbuttoned his trousers and relieved himself right there, but the whole idea of sleeping in a tree was to avoid announcing your presence. Besides, on the way in, he had smelled fresh wolf sign on a tree, and that would make good enough cover for his own spoor.

He found the spot easily in the dark. Memorizing his way in was second nature to him, and while he moved as quietly as he could, nothing human could move silently through the forest, so he didn't let it bother him. He was good at this, and anybody else would announce their presence to him long before he announced his presence to them.

He unbuttoned his trousers and relieved himself. There was something absurdly pleasurable about a good piss in the woods at night, although Kethol wouldn't have admitted that to anybody else; it seemed funny and embarrassing to him.

He made his way back to his tree and up to his hammock, and stretched out.

The music of the forest would have lulled him to sleep quickly if he'd have stayed awake to let it.

Leathery wings beat against the night sky above the field of bitter oats. The night was filled with gnats, and bats by the dozen had come out of somewhere to feed. They were only shadows flittering against the star-spattered sky, but still Pirojil shivered.

Bats. Pirojil hated bats. It was something about their featherless wings, and the evil faces. He wasn't sure why—much worse had come flapping out of Faerie during the Breach, after all; and he had worn an uglier face than any bat all his adult life—but ordinary bats bothered him.

The Old Emperor used to say that bats were beneficial, that they daily ate their weight in noxious insects, and, he'd add with a secret smile, there was another virtue or two they had, as the Engineer would swear—but he would never explain what that was all about, or why caves where bats lived were Engineer property by imperial fiat.

The Old Emperor had hinted once or twice that it might have something to do with the secret of gunpowder. Pirojil didn't know much about magic—if you couldn't see the glyphs, what was the point?—but maybe bat wings were an ingredient that made gunpowder make bullets fly.

No, that seemed unlikely. After all, bullets flew straight, and bats didn't. They twisted and turned and capered in the night sky in their search for some preposterous number of bugs. Somehow—perhaps they had night vision like dwarves?—the bats never seemed to bump into each other as they fluttered and fed, as though they had their own system of precedence, with presumably commoner bats staying out of the way of noble bats.

Back when he was—

Pirojil cut off the thought with a savage shake of his head. He had tried to burn those memories away, and even the screams in the dark were long forgotten.

They had to be.

—back a long time ago, somebody Pirojil had known had taught him a trick to do with bats.

His blunt fingers felt on the ground for a round pebble, and flicked it underhand, high, high into the air over the bitter oats field.

A small shadow dove on it, then fell almost to the ground before it righted itself, and chittered its discomfort as it climbed into the dark.

Instead of a nice juicy gnat, the bat had found itself trying to swallow a pebble that probably weighed as much as it did, and it didn't like that much. Pebbles weren't supposed to be flying through the night sky; just bugs and other bats—must have been frustrating for the little creature.

Off in the distance, an owl hooted three times, then three times again.

Pirojil's mouth twitched. Trouble.

❄   ❄   ❄

Kethol had come awake with a start. Not enough to move, but his whole body twitched.

There was something wrong, and it took him too long to place what it was:

The night was quiet. No chirping of insects, no *taroo* of a distant gray owl chortling over a fresh field mouse, not even a distant wolf's cry.

Nothing.

Anybody who had spent as much as a night in the woods knew what that meant: something was moving out there, and that something was either human or worse. Orcs hunted at night, by preference, and their bitter smell of sour sweat would be enough to frighten anybody off.

It probably meant humans, and humans moving at night ought to be making a lot of noise clomping down the road. Animals had learned to avoid that noise.

But it was silent. No sound save for the rustling of the leaves and the almost deafening *lump-lump-lump* of his own heart.

He willed it to be silent, and was unsurprised when the noise in his ears dimmed.

The night was awash in shades of grays and blacks as Kethol climbed down out of the tree, moving slowly, scanning all around with his eyes. That was the trick of the night: you saw better out of the corner of your eye than with the middle, and that was the mistake too many city people made out in the dark. The dark had its own ways, and you could either live with them or die with them.

Miron had had four men with him, and five against three would have been bad enough odds even if Lord Miron hadn't been a noble with so much time on his hands that he could practice the sword for pleasure. Kethol begged to doubt that they could get within sword or even pistol range of Durine without his sounding the alarm, but that would still leave five against two.

There was, of course, another alternative.

His bow was stashed near his horse, with his tack and the rest of his gear. Hauling everything his horse carried around the woods as night was falling had had no appeal for Kethol, and if they had been after deer, while he would have considered having been at a stand at sunrise—there were spots along the edges of the bitter oats fields that just shouted they were deer feeding grounds—but they were traveling fast and light and couldn't afford the time for a leisurely hunt.

For game.

The only problem was that the deer trail that led to the meadow where he had left his horse was a good hundred leagues back, and the meadow was even further down the trail. Getting to his horse and gear meant getting to the road, which was fine, and it meant walking down the road, which wasn't.

Still, there was no choice about doing it. But regardless of what Pirojil said about him, he wasn't so foolish as to rush in without thinking, without listening.

Kethol leaned back against the bole of an ancient elm and listened again. Nothing. No sound except for the breeze in the leaves.

Very well. They were out there somewhere, but he couldn't count on Pirojil or Durine having spotted them, not yet. They had made a good choice in campsites; the farmhouse and outbuildings had been built on a mound overlooking the fields. But it was possible that somebody really good could sneak up through the bitter oats, leaving behind a trail of crushed plants that you would have to be looking for to see in the dark. Walter Slovotsky certainly could have done it easily, and Kethol himself could have.

The wind had changed while he slept, blowing toward the fields, toward the ruins. A shout would have carried, but it would also have announced to all and sundry that they'd been spotted. Better than letting his companions be surprised, but . . .

Better.

He pursed his lips and gave the hoot of a forest owl, as loud as he could, three times. With any luck, Miron and his companions wouldn't know that a forest owl always hooted twice only, or wouldn't notice.

He waited for a moment for the sound of boots crashing through the woods in search of whoever had so badly impersonated an owl, but none came.

Good. Maybe it wasn't such a bad impersonation, after all.

He crept quietly back to the deer trail he had taken most of the way into his hiding place for the night—you didn't want to sleep right next to a trail; that permitted anybody or anything to walk right up to your tree without making a sound.

The night felt as if it had a thousand eyes, and each one of them was fixed on his back.

But the silence still rang in his ears. Which was good. It meant that whatever was going to happen hadn't started yet. Miron and his companions were probably taking their time setting up. By now, Pirojil and Durine would both be awake and looking out over the fields, watching and waiting, their pistols out and ready, their crossbows loaded.

Crossbows. Kethol snickered silently. There was nothing wrong with a crossbow, except that the rate of fire was pitiful, and the accuracy wasn't much better.

But it had its advantages.

You could take a peasant conscript right out of the pig shit, hand him a crossbow, and with even a tenday or so of practice—aided, if necessary, by a clout or two alongside the head to assist in the instruction—he could be a competent shot with a crossbow. Now, that wouldn't make him stand and fight, and it surely wouldn't make him hold his position among a line of archers, but that could be done, too, with only a little more work, another few dozen more clouts, and perhaps a blooding here and there.

But training a real archer took almost as long as training a swordsman.

Reclaiming his bow took too long, and he silently congratulated himself for having stashed his hidden gear on the other side of the meadow from where his horse stood grazing. Not the most observant of animals, she didn't stop in her munching in the dark. Amazing how much clover she could put away.

He strung his bow, and slung his quiver over his shoulders. It would have been nice to use his shooting glove, but while the wooden sear laced into the surface of its fingers made his every loose clean and pure—Kethol had always had to fight a certain amount of pluck in his loose; there were times it got so bad that he thought he should have been a lutist—it also made it impossible to grip his sword with his right hand, and he could easily find himself needing his sword without sufficient warning.

He settled on his left-arm sheath and stalked back down the trail, bow in his left hand, his right hand reaching up to untie the mouth of his quiver, his fingers counting the arrows by touch.

Good.

There was only one more bit of preparation. Kethol carefully set his bow on the ground, then sat down on the hard-packed dirt and removed his boots. He tied them together, slung them across his shoulder, and replaced them with the woodsman's deerskin buskins he kept rolled up in his pack. It had been a long time since he'd worn them, and there was something comforting about their softness, about the gentle way they held his feet.

It felt too good to be wearing buskins again; he had been a soldier too long, and this short respite was like a cool stream flowing through the middle of his soul. A painful stream—his feet weren't as toughened as they'd been when he was a boy, and the sharp rocks on the rough path hurt, but the whole idea was to be able to feel the ground underneath him. Tales told around campfires about heroic deeds almost always had somebody stepping on and breaking a twig at just the right—or wrong—moment, and while Kethol had no objection to heroic deeds, he did have a strong objection to making noise. The idea here was to heroically shoot their attackers in the back with longbow and barbed arrow, not to draw their attention and sacrifice himself.

He stopped just short of the road, and looked and listened. It would have been nice if the wind had been blowing in his face instead of against his back, but it wasn't, and circling around to down-wind from them would have required both a lot of time and knowing where they were.

He moved slowly to the road, and looked across the fields at the ruins.

Nothing.

There was no sign of life or activity, which was either very good or very bad. Kethol would have preferred something somewhere in the middle, something safer—some hulking motion in the darkness that spoke of Durine moving about impatiently, waiting for the attack.

He set his boots and his rucksack down on the ground and stood, still as the boy Kethol had on stand, waiting for the deer to come within range of his bow, and waited. And waited.

And waited.

The night was still quiet. He was beginning to think that maybe he'd been wrong, maybe it had been that clumsy Erenor who had alarmed the creatures of darkness into a warning silence, maybe—

No. It took the wind to show him, but there were dim trails in the bitter oats. Kethol could count ten.

Ten? Where had Miron gotten so many men? He had been riding with—

Never mind that. Three against ten was horrible odds, and Kethol wasn't willing to bet a life he cared about on there being only ten of them.

But one of them was less dexterous than the rest. A dark shadow rose up momentarily in the sea of bitter oats, then ducked down.

Kethol nocked an arrow, and drew it back. Nine against one was almost as bad as ten against one, but . . . You kill a band of enemies the way you slice an onion: one slice, one shot at a time. Nine could be cut down to eight, could be cut down to seven . . .

He drew a deep breath, let half of it out, and held the rest. It would have been nice to have warmed up with some practice shots, but that was hardly practicable.

The string pressed hard against the tips of his fingers, tempting him to a plucking loose. It was all the same whether the target was straw-filled ticking, a deer, or a man. It was a matter of years of learning that burned deep into muscle and mind and bone and soul, so he waited until he was ready, until every instinct and every bit of training told him that the arrow would arc to the spot where the enemy had ducked down, and let fly with a pure loose that sent the shaft on a flat arc that ended in a groan.

A dark shape lunged up and out of the darkness, screaming some painful obscenity.

Everything broke loose at once. A dozen or more other men rose instantly out of the field, some with swords in their hands, at least two with long hunting spears, and rushed the encampment. Kethol already had another arrow nocked, and let fly, but his target was bobbing and weaving as he charged up the slope, and the arrow disappeared somewhere in the dark.

A dozen? The other two didn't stand a chance. Kethol would do his best to avenge them, but even Pirojil and Durine had their limits, and—

The darkness was shattered by a flash of light as white as a cloud, as bright as the sun.

17

Seemings

The three hoots had brought Pirojil fully alert.

For a moment, he allowed himself to smile—three to split the night watch was a lot better than two—until the triple hoot was followed by another, instead of the expected call.

And then by silence.

Durine was already on his feet by the time Pirojil made it back into the ruins of the stable, belting his sword and pistols about his massive waist by the light of a ragged silver of Faerie silver that he had picked up somewhere, sometime. His face was sallow and lined in the pale light, and he looked half again his age.

"Trouble," the big man whispered. A statement, not a question. He slipped the shining metal back into its leather sheath. "What is it?"

"I just heard a forest owl hoot three times."

Durine grunted, and if Pirojil hadn't known better, he would have thought that the big man was smiling in the darkness. "I think, perhaps, he has too much faith in you and me, Piro."

That was certainly true enough. Well, everybody has to believe in something.

Pirojil jerked his chin toward the field. Durine nodded; he cocked his crossbow and nocked a bolt before he moved, much more quietly than one would think such a big man could, toward the skeletal timbers at what had been the front of the stable.

Lady Leria was sleeping in what had been a stall; Durine had made his bed at the entrance to it, as though trouble couldn't simply step over the raggedly waist-high foundation that was all that remained of the walls. Pirojil walked past her stall to the one where Erenor slept, snoring quietly, peacefully.

He clapped his hand over Erenor's mouth. That was the only safe way to wake a wizard—a real one could easily come awake spewing out some defensive spell—although in this case, it was more of a way to prevent Erenor from crying out than spells from issuing from his mouth.

The wizard's eyes snapped open, wide and white above Pirojil's hand. "Quiet, now," Pirojil said, removing his hand only when Erenor raised his palms in a gesture of surrender.

"We have trouble," Pirojil said. "How many times does a forest owl hoot?"

"I wouldn't know," Erenor said quite quietly, his tone saying, *And I wouldn't care* quite loudly.

Pirojil didn't know much about owls, and was about as interested in them as he was in rocks, but Kethol had always had a tendency to go on about woodcraft, and he had mentioned over more campfires than Pirojil cared to count that the forest owl always hooted twice.

"It's one of Kethol's . . . preoccupations." He had stopped himself from saying "obsession." Not in front of Erenor. Pirojil didn't think friendship required one to turn a blind eye to faults, but neither did it permit revealing them to outsiders.

"Forest owls—the big ones, the ones with the deep voice like a silverhorn—always hoot twice over their kills." Why hoot at all? Was it a signal to other owls that there was good hunting, or was it to warn them away from their prey? Or was it simply the owl announcing, with pride, that he had caught yet another field mouse or vole?

"So there's a deranged owl out there who hoots three times," Erenor said. "Thank you very kindly for the lesson, Master Pirojil," he said, "and now may I get back to sleep?"

There was the temptation to slap Erenor until his face sloughed off, but Pirojil manfully resisted it.

"No. What it means is that it's Kethol out there, and that there's trouble." If Kethol was simply announcing his own presence, warning them that he was coming in so that they wouldn't accidentally send a crossbow bolt through him in the dark, he would have quickly followed up with a shout, or a repetition, or something.

It also meant that there was more trouble than Kethol himself could have handled. One scout—Kethol's only problem would have been what to do with the body. Two might be a little trickier, but Kethol would have trusted in his own abilities to take on two, and with the element of surprise on his side, it was a good bet.

Three, maybe. Four, no, But it could be far more than that.

Erenor had worked out at least some of it as he threw his blankets to the side and rolled quickly to his feet. He shot a quick glance toward his own bag. It was packed, ready for a quick grab-and-run; the only thing left behind would be his blankets, and blankets could be gotten elsewhere. Erenor might not have been much more than an apprentice wizard, but he was a master of the quick getaway.

"When it starts, I want you to take Lady Leria and sneak her out of here, into the woods. If we win, if we survive, you rejoin us. If we don't seem to, you can either safely convey her to Biemestren or you can bet your life that none of us live to hunt you down." His lips tightened. "The lady is under our protection, understood?"

Erenor nodded. "Yes, Lord Pirojil," he said.

Lord? Without thinking, he backhanded Erenor across the face, and stopped himself with his sword half out of its sheath.

No. This wasn't the time for that. If he lived through this night, then he would settle up with Erenor for his impudence. Nobody had ever called him Lord, ever, and nobody had called him Lordling for more years than Pirojil liked to think about. And then, his name had not been Pirojil. Pirojil had been the name of his dog. A loyal animal.

Erenor wiped at his mouth with the back of his hand. "No offense was intended," he said. "But you have to understand that those of us who learn much about seemings learn to see past the surface, past the way things seem." Erenor held himself with more dignity than Pirojil could have managed under the circumstances. "You perhaps should look beyond the surface more often, Pirojil," he said, his voice quiet but unwavering.

Pirojil tried to just let it go, tried to ignore it, strained to ignore the blood rushing in his ears.

He didn't hear Durine come up until the big man cleared his throat.

"I count twelve," Durine said, "and they're moving slowly toward us through the fields." He shook his head. "Perhaps this is the time we saddle up and ride out of here fast as we can."

If they could saddle the horses quickly, if Lady Leria was as good a horsewoman as noblewomen usually were, they would still have to ride down the road across the top of the berm, because horses would surely stumble and fall if they tried to gallop through the soft dirt of the fields. And that would make them adequate targets, at least.

But one or two would probably get through. Kethol was out there, and he would have his longbow ready.

"Wake the lady," Pirojil said. "You first, then Erenor, then her, with me to bring up the rear. I'll take your crossbow and your pistols."

Durine eyed him levelly. He knew as well as Pirojil did that the last man out wasn't going to make it out.

"You should," Erenor said quietly, "learn to look beneath the surface, to accept what is." His voice took on a note of command. "If they attack us all at once, they'll overwhelm us, but if they run away in fear, in terror, can you cut them down?"

"With pleasure," Durine said. "How do you propose to frighten them so?"

Erenor's answer was a quiet stream of words, first so low-voiced as to be unintelligible, then rising in volume and timbre. There was a logic and a grammar in the words he spoke, but as each syllable fell on Pirojil's ears, it vanished from his mind, gone where a popped soap bubble goes.

Wrapped in light so bright it should have blinded Pirojil but somehow didn't even hurt his eyes, the wizard grew larger, his form changing as he did so.

✿   ✿   ✿

It should have burned Kethol's eyes into his head, or at the very least left him dazzled, unable to see, but it vanished immediately, replaced by a huge glowing beast, easily three manheights tall.

It looked more like a large, misshapen bear than anything else, although it was easily twice the height of any bear Kethol had ever heard of, and no bear could be that white, so white that it glowed in the dark. And its face was long, like a wolf's, with teeth the size of hunting knives protruding over its lower lip

It opened its mouth with a roar that was loud enough to be deafening, and took two staggering steps toward where the dozen attackers stood, frozen in terror.

Kethol was frightened enough to piss down his leg—that wasn't the first time that had happened to him, and if he survived the night, odds were it wouldn't be the last—but his fingers had nocked another arrow, and without even thinking about it, he had taken aim, and let fly again, his blood and bones knowing that it would fly flat and straight to its target. He didn't even wait for it to hit before he had another arrow in hand, ready to be nocked.

Kethol looked for Miron among the attackers for a scant heartbeat, then cursed himself for that stupidity.

Any target would do. He was leading a stocky man who was scurrying back toward the road when his target shouted and pitched forward, screaming in pain. An arrow or bolt could kill as well as a sword could, but it was the rare shot that knocked a target down immediately.

Kethol picked another target, and let fly again. The monster, whatever it was, wherever it had come from, could wait. It wasn't doing anything but standing there and roaring at the retreating figures. None of it made sense, but it wasn't Kethol's job to make sense. It was his job to nock arrows and send them singing off into the night, seeking flesh.

He bent his arm and his mind to his job.

18

✠ Brutal Necessity

Dawn threatened to break all golden and peach over a sea of bitter oats dotted by islands of corpses.

Pirojil considered the stocky man in a peasant's rough tunic who lay on the ground in front of him, the fletching of a crossbow bolt barely protruding through the back of his jacket.

Well, he was probably as dead as he looked, and Durine was back at the farmhouse with the two survivors they'd taken captive, but it didn't hurt to make sure: Pirojil lifted the hunting spear he had taken off another of the dead men and thrust it carefully into the peasant's back.

It was like stabbing a side of beef. No reaction. No life.

He moved on to the next one.

In the gray light before dawn, dead men lay scattered about the field, their blood and their stink already drawing flies. Pirojil would have to decide what they were going to do with them. There was a strong temptation on his part to leave them to rot where they lay. That's what they had done in the old days, when they'd ridden with the Old Emperor on his Last Ride, cutting through any opposition, leaving clotting blood and shattered bone in their wake.

Those were good days, in their way. Blood didn't bother Pirojil. Neither did the shit-stink of dead men.

But it could be argued that leaving a trail of bodies behind them, here and now, was liable to cause more trouble than it stopped.

He heard Erenor's footsteps on the ground behind him. More tentative than Pirojil's; noisier than Pirojil's and much noisier than

Kethol's, as though the wizard took special care to step on the plants only in the noisiest possible way.

"Do you have another one of those spears available, Master Pirojil?" Erenor asked.

He didn't look like some huge shaggy monster in the gray light before dawn. He just looked like a tired man who had had too little sleep and too much exertion of late.

Pirojil's eyeballs ached. He had some sympathy for that, although he didn't think of himself as the sympathetic type.

He grunted and gestured toward where another spear lay on the soft ground a handsbreadth away from the outflung arm of another dead man. "You can have that one. There's another over that way," he said.

He had expected Erenor to take the spear and himself back up the slope to the ruins, but instead the wizard took it up and thrust it clumsily into the dead man he'd taken it from, and then walked toward where another body lay.

That was the last one. The dead were all dead, and Pirojil could turn his attention to the living without having to worry about an injured enemy at his back.

Erenor cleared his throat. "All in all, it seems to have gone better than it could have," he said.

Pirojil nodded. "By rather a lot."

"Where I come from," Erenor went on, his lips perhaps tightening a trifle, "it's considered good manners for all, from the rudest serf to the most effete noble, to offer thanks to one who has been of some . . . serious assistance."

Pirojil found himself smiling at the wizard's impertinence. But, still, he had a point. "Thank you for helping to save all of our lives, yours included and in particular."

Erenor cocked his head to one side. "Hmm . . . Master Pirojil, it occurs to me that a warrior such as yourself would be more grateful for my having helped save the life of Lady Leria—as her welfare is your responsibility, is it not?"

His contribution to their survival had clearly gone to Erenor's head. But Pirojil had overreacted to Erenor's slip of the tongue last night, and even though he was sure Erenor was taking advantage of that, seeing how far he could press the advantage, Pirojil didn't have the stomach to slap that smile from his face.

Or maybe it had had something to do with the violence of the early dawn. You couldn't be a soldier and not be able to handle death close-up. It wasn't possible to be a warrior if you let yourself be obsessed with the memories of the cries of the dying, of the smells of the dead, of the expressions on the faces of the legions of men you had cut down with sword and knife, with bolt and bullet.

People reacted in different ways. Durine made a fetish of not caring, while Kethol thought of dead enemies as he did of dead game. Tennetty had actually enjoyed the bloodletting, and Pirojil had always found it vaguely disgusting the way she would smile and shake almost in orgasm at each kill.

But you couldn't be a human being if it didn't get to you at all. There was something more perverse in those who felt nothing than there was even in those who liked it.

"Is it not?" Erenor repeated.

Pirojil shook himself out of his reverie. "Yes, it is. It very much is my responsibility, and I'm grateful that you made it possible. Of course, your own life was on the table as well, wasn't it?"

The wizard nodded emphatically. "That it was."

"And if the peasants had simply ignored your seeming, if they had charged upslope and stuck their spears into the hide of the monster—"

"I would have been very, very uncomfortable," Erenor said. "For but a few moments, until I died." He brightened. "So may I thank you and your companions, Master Pirojil, for saving my life? It's not an important life, to be sure, and it's obviously none too precious to any of you, but it is, after all, the only one I have, and I'm rather fond of it, and would like to continue to cling to it for as many years as possible."

Pirojil knew Erenor was trying to get a laugh out of him, but he let himself chuckle nonetheless. "Your thanks are accepted, Erenor," he said.

He wasn't sure why, and he wasn't sure what the terms were, but it felt as if he'd just struck a bargain.

He used the butt of the spear as a staff to help him up the slope.

There were two survivors among their attackers. Both stocky peasant men, both wounded—one with Kethol's arrow still stuck through his thigh—both securely bound. Durine's blunt fingers were surprisingly good with knots, and it was easy to lash a couple of thumbs together if you didn't much care about the health of the thumb.

Lady Leria watched, her eyes wide in horror. That was understandable; nobility—well, female nobility, at least—didn't have to get used to blood and pain, except maybe during childbirth.

And it was going to get worse.

Pirojil heard Kethol making his way up the path from the stream before he saw him. Dressed in a fresh tunic and trousers, he carried his wet clothes in one hand, while his free hand stayed close to the hilt of his knife, not his sword. He was still wearing his woodsman's leather buskins, not his boots. Pirojil smiled to himself. Under pressure, Kethol had reverted to type.

He was still a warrior, and there was still nobody Pirojil would have preferred at his back in a fight, but Kethol had been raised a woodsman, and in some ways that was what he would always be.

Well, it wouldn't take long with his feet in the stirrups for Kethol to remember the virtues of hard-soled boots over the buskins, and maybe by then he'd be thinking like a warrior again.

"Kethol," he said, "why don't you and Erenor take the lady and the horses up the road to where we hid the carriage? We'll want to get moving before it gets much lighter." And, unspoken: *none of us want to see what we're going to have to do with the two captives.*

He and Durine waited, chatting idly, until Kethol and Erenor had led the horses and the lady well down the road before they turned to the captives.

That was a trick he had learned from Tennetty, back during the conquest of Holtun. Always get two captives, if you can, and then let them sit and think for a while before you start in on them.

In a real battle, it didn't much matter most of the time. Foot soldiers—peasant conscripts, particularly—wouldn't know anything of any importance about the enemy's plans, and Ellegon was far, far better at scouting out an army's disposition and strength than even the cleverest spy.

But, every so often, there were some things you needed to know, and there were ways to make people tell you those things.

Durine would do it without hesitation, but . . .

Pirojil knelt down before the closer of the two—there really wasn't much to choose between the two of them—and drew his belt knife. It was shorter than most such knives—when Pirojil needed a blade with a reach, he used his sword—and it was single-edged rather than double, but it was shiny and sharp, and came to a threateningly narrow point.

The peasant was a blunt-faced man, his beard ragged and untrimmed, although his hair had been bowl-cut not long ago. His nostrils flared as he drew in what air he could, probably more from fright than from pain.

His wound—or, at least, the only wound Pirojil could see—had been the arrow to the back of the leg that had hamstrung him as neatly as a sharp knife blade could have. Hamstringing was one of the classic ways to prevent the pursuit of somebody you didn't want to kill, and it was an old slaver's trick for preventing slaves from running off. Until he could find a Spider—Spidersect seemed to have a put a charmed circle around most of Holtun; even the sisters of the Hand were conspicuous by their absence—he would be hopping on one foot or crawling.

Pirojil moved the knifepoint closer to the widening eyes, and slipped it carefully down the cheek, under the thong that bound the gag in place. A quick twist and the thong parted easily. Pirojil waited for the peasant to spit out the gag, then beckoned Durine for the water bag.

"Here," he said. "Your mouth is dry, and you've lost blood." He lifted the horn spout to the bloodied lips. "Drink all you want, and we can get more if you like."

Yellowed teeth clamped down on the spout, and the peasant sucked eagerly, like a child at its mother's breast.

Pirojil took the bottle away. "We need to know who you are, and who sent you."

Durine loomed above, growling. "I hurt him first," he said, his voice a gravelly rumble. "I hurt him lots. Then he talk."

"No, no, we don't want to hurt anybody. We just need to know some things." He turned back to the peasant. "You have a name?"

"Horolf. Horolf Two Fields they call me."

"So, Horolf Two Fields, why were you and your friends sneaking up to kill us last night?"

"No, no, it was nothing like that." He shook his head half hard enough to shake his ears off. "We heard—Wilsh heard about raiders, bandits, encamped on the ruins of old Marsel's farm, and we figured to capture them for the reward. Really, Lord, we had no idea it was you."

Pirojil shook his head. There were about a dozen things wrong with that story, beginning with how easily it came to the peasant's lips.

But mainly it was preposterous. A bunch of peasants trying to attack sleeping bandits? That was like a bunch of rabbits gathering to ambush a wayward hunter. Certainly, peasants would be afraid of bandits—but that was what the local lord was for, and the reward for leading local armsmen to the capture of a gang would be significant, and could be gotten without risk.

Durine slapped Horolf across the face, once, hard.

"No, please," Horolf whined. "I've told you what you wanted to know."

Pirojil shrugged as theatrically as he could. "Well, we only need one. I'll deal with this one; you take the other."

Durine fastened one huge hand on the front of the other peasant's tunic and lifted him easily to his shoulder, then walked out of sight, around the bend down the hill toward the stream.

Pirojil shook his head. He really disliked this, but he had done things he disliked more before, and he probably would again.

There was nothing fun about torture, but he wasn't going to go back on the road without knowing what this was all about. "It's a pity," he said. "Not that we have anything against bandits like your-self, mind, but if you're going to lie to me, we'll just see if you and your friend have any coin on you, and then go about our business."

"Please, Lord. You can look in my pouch. I don't have so much as a copper half-mark on me. None of us have much of any hard money. We mostly trade—"

Pirojil sighed. "That's just what a bandit would say, after he'd swallowed his gold." He shook his head. "I've dealt with your type before, but I've never fallen for it. You dress up as peasants and waylay travelers. Well," he said, drawing his knife, "we'll soon see what you've got in your stomachs, won't we?"

A scream came from over the hill. "I think my partner picked the wrong one," Pirojil said. "You look to be the leader; you've prob-ably got a full ten gold marks in your gullet."

Durine walked back down the path, cleaning his knife and hands of blood with what had been the other peasant's tunic. "Nothing there," he said. "Nothing except the stink of bread and onions in his gut."

"No," Horolf said. "Please. I beg of you, please."

Pirojil ignored him. "Help me stretch this one out. He looks like a kicker to me."

"No, Lord, no. I'll tell the truth. It is gold, but we are not bandits. We didn't want to kill you. We just came for your gold."

Pirojil looked up at Durine. Nobody else would have seen the way Durine held himself still, to prevent himself from reaching for the money vest that held all their savings.

"The gold?" Pirojil asked.

"Yes, the gold. The dowry. For the girl."

✿   ✿   ✿

Horolf had given up any reluctance to tell what he knew, but he was a peasant, not a storyteller, and not only wounded, but half frightened to death. Pirojil was willing to settle for that, but it did make getting the story out of him a longer task than he would have liked.

Somebody had been spreading rumors. It seemed that the word had gone out that three men—a tall, rangy, redheaded fellow; a huge, hulking swordsman; and the ugliest man that anybody had ever seen—together with a handsome, somewhat uppity body servant, were escorting a minor lady of Neranahan to Biemestren so that she could attempt to buy herself a Biemish husband.

Her prey must have been somebody of very high rank indeed, as the three escorts had been personal bodyguards to the Old Emperor himself, and now were fealty-bound to Barony Cullinane and the former heir.

Perhaps her future husband was even the former heir himself? If so, her dowry must have been immense, as Jason Cullinane was probably the wealthiest of all the imperial barons, and it would have taken a great deal of gold to interest him, indeed, particularly since the lady was known to be of violent temper and ugly of face.

(Pirojil grinned at that. Horolf misunderstood the meaning of the smile and voided his bowels. Again. This interrogation was smelly work.)

The size of the dowry had grown as the tale had spread, and when Wilah had spotted them from his croft, it hadn't taken long for a dozen or more veterans of the Biemish war to decide that this was their opportunity, their chance to leave their miserable crofts and this two-nation empire.

Pirojil shook his head. People who hadn't been around wealth both overestimated and underestimated what gold could do. Gold certainly could buy them land and cattle and horses in Kiar or Nyphien or—better—in the lands around and protected by Pandathaway. But it couldn't make them run faster than their pursuers would, and it wouldn't stop men who were better with sword and spear and crossbow from taking their possessions and their lives away from them.

The life of an outlaw was cheap tender, and the life of an outlaw who somehow managed to have a stack of gold on him was absolutely worthless.

But that didn't stop fools from trying for their one chance, and Pirojil was familiar enough with a crofter's life to have more than vague sympathy for somebody who wanted to escape the endless days of drudgery that began before dawn and ended with exhaustion after sundown. There was a lot lacking in a soldier's life, but at least you didn't have to grub your living out of the very dirt you shit in.

Pirojil rose. "Shit," he said.

Durine grunted. "Dowry, indeed." He used the toe of his boot to flip Horolf over, then drew his sword. Best to end this now, and be on their way.

At the sound of steel sliding on leather, Horolf cried out something loud and incoherent, and his body spasmed. He probably would have voided himself again if he hadn't run out by now.

"Oh, be still," Durine said as he sliced through first the leather thongs that bound Horolf's thumbs together, then the ones that bound his wrists. Even if Horolf hadn't been thoroughly frightened—and you could never quite count on fright to stop somebody from doing what he had to; it had never stopped Durine—he was still hamstrung in one leg, and the nearest crossbow was lying in a field a fair walk away.

Durine flipped him back over, then tossed him a piece of broken blade. Cheap local steel wasn't worth keeping, anyway; if it was worth a gold mark a tonne, he would be surprised. "If you don't crawl down to the stream and cut your friend loose, I'll be back for you," he said, letting his voice rasp.

He was lying, but he didn't think Horolf would test him on it.

It took the peasant a long moment to realize what Durine was saying. "But—"

The point of Durine's sword whipped through the air and hovered near Horolf's right eye. "Don't even think me a gentle man," he said. "I've hamstrung him, same as the arrow did for you. You can cut yourselves a pair of crutches and hobble on back to your miserable village and your miserable lives." He touched the point of his sword to Horolf's nose, just barely hard enough to draw blood, although he doubted that Horolf noticed. "I may see you again, once; I will not see you again twice," Durine said.

Pirojil was already walking away; Durine turned and followed him.

Yes, if it had been necessary, or even desirable, Durine could have cut little screaming pieces out of the other peasant all day long.

You did what you had to, after all, and let the rest of it sort itself out. But one quick stab to get one long scream had been enough to prepare the way for Pirojil's talk with Horolf, and while it had been years since Durine had lost count of the number of men he had killed, he had long since come up with an answer for the lot of them when their pale, bloodless faces crowded his dreams, trying to deny him his rest.

Yes, he would say, I've killed all of you, and more, and yes, I probably could have handled many of you more gently, and yes, you can haunt my nights for that. But while I've killed many a man I had to, and probably nearly as many more as I didn't have to, I've never killed one I knew I didn't have to, he would tell them.

And while that didn't dispel the ghosts that haunted his dreams, that was enough for Durine.

Pirojil clapped a hand to his shoulder. "We'd best be moving fast."

"Yes, but where?"

19
Division

It took less time than Pirojil had thought it would to reduce the carriage into sufficiently small pieces. Getting the doors off had been easy, and cutting through the axles only took Durine a few moments with a saw. The hard part had been breaking the walls apart—whoever had built it had built it to last—but after the first corner finally yielded to Durine's ax, it was just a matter of hitching up one of the dray horses to each wall and sending them in opposite directions.

By noon, the carriage was no more, just pieces of wood scattered in the woods. There was something satisfying in the destruction. The carriage didn't bleed and moan and shit itself; maybe that was it.

The five of them gathered in the clearing, packing up the horses. The dray horses made fine pack animals, and anybody who had served with the Old Emperor was long since a past master of lashing odd-shaped gear.

Pirojil ticked off the possibilities as they loaded, while Lady Leria watched quietly. She hadn't said much since last night. Not that Pirojil blamed her.

"One," he said, raising his voice as he ducked under the belly of the gray gelding to give its harness strap a tightening tug, "we can stick together, try to somehow disguise ourselves, and hope that a party of five heading toward Biemestren won't draw every dissatisfied peasant, out-of-work mercenary, or just plain bored soldier between here and there. We can travel at night—"

"Which anybody would expect us to do," Erenor said, interrupting. He didn't stop working, though. "It's only sensible."

Pirojil went on, ignoring the wizard: "—or, two, we can change our destination."

Kethol nodded. "Barony Adahan, and New Pittsburgh. I like that idea."

Durine shook his head, but Kethol didn't catch it.

It was all Pirojil could do not to do the same. It wasn't his fault—Kethol wasn't stupid, not really, but he had blind spots—and Kethol would see that as a good idea. Kethol would count on the peasants and soldiers of Barony Adahan being loyal to their baron, and their knowledge of Bren Adahan's personal friendship with the Cullinanes protecting the lot of them.

Pirojil shook his head. "Even if we make it there—and I doubt we could do it in less than five days, moving at night—you assume too much."

Wizards and women all had their own magical ways of warping a man's mind, but gold, or even the idea of gold, had a magic all its own.

Yes, Pirojil would trust Bren, Baron Adahan, at least in this. But some peasant or soldier or armsman fealty-bound to him?

Fealty did not move as quickly as a fast horse, and it was not as sharp as the edge of a knife or the point of an arrow.

Durine shook his head. "Bad idea."

"There is another possibility," Erenor said, slapping his hands together to clear the dust from them. He rose to his full height. He had dropped his role as a body servant, and while Pirojil thought he could detect a trace of uncertainty in Erenor's manner, there had been a definite change.

Pirojil wasn't sure how he felt about that. Ever since Erenor had provided his seeming-monster distraction, he had been behaving as though he was, well, an equal, not just a lackey pressed into service by blackmail and force.

Well, maybe he wasn't just a lackey, not anymore.

Erenor smiled. "While there are those who would say I'm not much of a wizard, when it comes to seemings, I am—" he paused, presumably for dramatic effect, as his hand fluttered "—demonstrably quite good."

Kethol grinned. "Good? You're magnificent," he said, his smile picked up and echoed by Lady Leria. The two of them seemed to be doing a lot of smiling lately. Pirojil tried not to wonder why that bothered him so much.

Durine shook his massive head. "But can you keep up five seemings at the same time?"

"Hardly. But hardly necessary." Erenor snorted. "Mundanes," he said, the word overlaid with condescension. "You see so much, and observe so little of it—there is always more to magic than magic. Lady, if you would?" He gestured her to sit on the trunk that lay on the ground next to the carriage. "Pirojil, I'll need a spare tunic of yours, and Kethol, your sword belt, if you please."

She wasn't used to being dressed by men, and Erenor was clearly more used to getting women out of their clothes than to helping one into a man's tunic, but it wasn't long before she was wearing Pirojil's tunic over her blouse.

It hung loosely on her, but with the belt tight around her hips rather than waist, it covered her curves quite handily.

Still, she looked like a pretty young woman dressed up as a man, and that—

"Oh, be still, Pirojil," Erenor said. Swift, clever fingers twisted her hair into a sailor's queue, and a quick rubbing of something from Erenor's wizard's bag robbed it of its bright sheen. Some swipes with a damp cloth, then a rubbing of something else from the bag, and she looked like a man who needed a shave, if you didn't look too closely, much as Kethol did.

"Now, I'd despair of teaching our lady to walk like a man, but put her in a saddle, astride a horse, her feet in boots instead of slippers, and—nobody would give her a second glance." Erenor put a finger to his lips and considered Kethol. "Now, Mast—Kethol will be easy enough. I can darken his hair quickly, and while he's tall, he's not tall enough to be unusual."

"And you?"

"Quite easy," he said, pulling clothes from his bag. "I'm a merchant—a buyer of horses, perhaps?—and the four of you are my drovers and bodyguard." He considered Durine and Pirojil. "It's the two of you that are the problem." He shook his head. "Durine is a big man, granted, but he's a big hairy man, and with a razor and some dye for his head, he can become a big bald man. Yes, yes, I know his scalp won't be tanned and weathered," he said, raising a palm to forestall a protest that Pirojil hadn't thought of, "but some stain and a few days of sunburn, and it'll look just fine. A tad uncomfortable, perhaps, but what of that?" He turned to Pirojil. "It's you that I'll need the seeming for, Pirojil. Your looks are—" he hesitated, perhaps trying to see how far he should push his newfound equality " distinctive, that's what they are, and that creates a problem that is best addressed by the Arts."

"No." Pirojil shook his head. "It won't happen."

Erenor made a sound that Pirojil hadn't heard before; it had something of a tsk to it, combined with a fricative of the lips. "Ah. So now you not only know more about when magic is to be used than I do, but *how* to use it? I would think I've more than a little more experience than you have with seemings, Pirojil."

"No," Pirojil said. His stomach felt as if he had swallowed something cold and metallic; he resisted the urge to purge himself.

"But— "

"Leave it be. We have to figure out another way."

"We should listen to him," Kethol said, each word a cut to Pirojil's heart.

After all this time, Kethol, you clumsy, heroic idiot, can't you keep your knifepoint out of my wounds?

Durine looked over at Kethol and shook his head. "There are some things we don't speak of," he said.

Kethol's head was tilted to one side. "Yes, of course, but—but this is important. No, that's not what I meant." He must have realized how that sounded. "It's more important this time."

Lady Leria stood too close to Pirojil. "I don't understand," she said. "We can't travel together, not if you don't let him disguise you."

She laid a slim hand on his arm, and left it there for a long, warm moment, and he made the mistake of inhaling. The scent of her was overpowering. Yes, she stank of Kethol's leather, and there were more than hints of her own unwashed sweat, but mainly she smelled of sunshine and warmth and comfort, and it was all Pirojil could do not to kick her away from him and run screaming away from her smooth youth and beauty.

"No, Lady, I . . ." He stopped himself. Pirojil opened his mouth, closed it. He could argue the point until night fell, but the only way to shut Erenor up would be to beat him, and there was no way he could argue with Leria.

He took a step away from Leria and stood with his arms folded across his chest. "Very well," he said to Erenor, each word tasting of salt and steel, "do your best."

The wizard shrugged. "I don't see what the—well, let's just do it, and be done with it." He licked his lips once, and for a moment his eyes went all vague and distant, as though he was reading something that was simultaneously both in front of him and far away.

And then the words issued from his mouth. Pirojil tried to distract himself with the thought that he had, perhaps, just a touch of wizard in his ancestry, because he could make them out enough to know they sounded familiar, but only for a moment. Then they were gone, burned from his ears and mind like a drop of fresh blood on a hot skillet, leaving behind nothing more than a sound and a scent.

Unfamiliar forces pulled at his face, like fingers tugging at his muscles from the inside of his face, like the time that his—like the time that somebody had used two blunt fingers to push the mouth of the boy whose name wasn't then Pirojil from a frown into a smile.

That smile had lasted, and he could still feel those gentle fingers hours later.

But these just faded away.

The Words left no trace of effect on him. It was as though they had never been spoken. Pirojil had expected that. No—it was more than expected, he had *known* that was how it would be.

You have to live with your own curses, and when one of those curses is your own ugliness, you have to live with that being exposed to the world every day.

"There are some men who can be made to seem something that they are not," he said, rubbing thick fingers against his bearded cheeks. "I'm not one of them." He smiled the lie that it didn't bother him, a lie he had smiled many times before. "No magic, no artifice, can help that."

Leria laid her hand on his arm once more. "I'm sorry," she said. "I didn't mean to—I didn't want to . . ."

He reached up to—gently, gently—remove her hand. "It's of no consequence, Lady. But you do see that this face of mine makes it impossible for me to travel with you now."

Durine nodded. "And I, as well. You'll have sufficient trouble keeping the three of you from looking like, well, the three of you—and Pirojil is going to need somebody to accompany him back to deal with the baroness."

Leria lifted a brow, and Kethol just looked blank, but Pirojil wasn't surprised that Durine had worked that out. There were two noblewomen who had cause—or at least reason—to be sowing caltrops in their path. This smelled more of Baroness Elanee than it did of the dowager empress, although he didn't doubt for a moment that Beralyn was perfectly capable of setting the wolves on them. The life of a minor Holtish noblewoman wasn't of any great importance to a former Biemish baroness, and if the lives of Pirojil, Kethol, and Durine were of any value whatsoever to the dowager empress, the three of them wouldn't be here now, smashing the remnants of a carriage into unidentifiable flinders.

He hoped it was Elanee who had put the price on their heads. They just might be able to survive that, unlikely though it seemed at the moment. Beralyn was not only beyond their reach, but beyond any reach they could ever develop. Yes, that was unfair and horrible, but the world was unfair and horrible, and eventually you got used to it. Or, at least, you learned to pretend to yourself that you did.

But Baroness Elanee, perhaps, was not beyond their reach. And it might prove sufficiently politic for the blame for this to be laid upon her grave, even if the dowager empress was the one who had, in effect, put a phantom price on their heads. Life was unfair and horrible and often shorter than it ought to be, and perhaps now was the time to explain that, quite quickly, to the baroness.

"In any case," Durine said, his voice the rumble of an approaching thunderstorm, "it sounds better than running around like a pair of rabbits waiting to find their wolves around the next corner."

Pirojil smiled, and tried to ignore the way it made Leria shudder. "Somehow, I thought you'd see it that way."

Kethol tried not to think as he checked the bellyband on Leria's brown mare for probably the twentieth time. Thinking, it had been brought home to him, was not one of his strengths. "Reminds me of the Old Emperor's Last Ride," he said, levering himself up and into his saddle. "So be careful, the two of you."

Durine chuckled, a low bass rumble that sounded, for once, more of amusement than irony. "We," he said, "we survived that just fine, if you'll recall. It was you that needed enough healing draughts to float an ox." His massive hand clasped Kethol's just for a moment. "So watch your own back, hero."

Pirojil lifted a finger to his massive sunken brow. "Be well," he said. "You watch out for him, Erenor, or you'll answer to me, and I can promise you that you won't like the way I put the questions."

Kethol beckoned to Leria, then kicked his horse into a canter, letting Erenor drive the unsaddled ones ahead of him. It took her a few minutes to catch up with him, at which point he let his horse drop back into a walk. This was a race, yes, but it wasn't a sprint.

She rode beside him, almost knee to knee. "Erenor has this puzzled look on his face."

"Oh?"

She shook her head. "I think he sometimes prefers not to look beneath the surface of things, don't you?"

Kethol shrugged. He didn't know what she meant, but he didn't want to admit that out loud.

"I mean," she went on, "here Durine and Pirojil are heading off to take on a barony by themselves, and both of them warn him about not letting you get hurt."

Kethol nodded. "Yes," he said, taking her meaning. "I get the feeling he has never heard a man say good-bye before."

Her lips pursed tightly. "I have," she said, "and I've never much cared for it."

20

✠ Uneasy Lies the Head, Part II

The emperor of Holtun-Bieme dreamed of rivers of blood coursing down his body, leaving his soil dark and fouled.

Or was it his body? When had his body merged with the rocks and trees and dirt of Bieme or Holtun?

Armies, huge and tiny at the same time as they could only be in a dream, fought up and down across his chest. A troop of cavalry hid in the greenery of the Prince's Woods, while a battalion of riflemen crouched in the badlands near his left armpit.

Some waited in hiding, and some moved into position, ready to attack or defend, but mostly they cut and hacked at each other one-to-one. Their battles raged up and down his land, doing only minor damage to his body—a nick in the skin here, a burned field there, an ache between his toes or some mild injury to his streams—but mostly they bled, and their blood soaked him to the bone, chilling him thoroughly.

He had to remain still. He was the land, and if he moved, if he turned over to brush aside the tiny battling ones, he wouldn't crush just them, but the others, hiding in their thatched huts or crouching under siege in their tiny, delicate castles.

Perhaps if he moved slowly enough?

No.

To do anything, or to do nothing, it was all the same. Blood coursed down him, and the cries of the innocent fought with the clang of steel against steel, with him knowing, every moment, that whatever he did would make it worse, and if he did nothing that would make it worse, too.

And, eventually, he would move. Some village set afire on his kneecap would cause him to move suddenly, shaking all loose, killing everyone.

Wait. There was a way.

It all stopped and went quiet. The battling armies paused in their carnage, while the people crouching behind castle walls or in their ragged huts stopped shaking for just a moment and listened, waiting for him to speak.

He knew how to stop it, suddenly, easily, with the clarity that could only come in a dream. All he would have to do was—

Thomen sat up in bed with a jerk. It was always the same. That was the way dreams were for him. Just when he had the solution to a problem, be it big or small, it would snap him out of his sleep.

He threw off the light blankets that he'd chosen against the chill night air, and got out of bed, bending to turn up the small oil lantern he'd left burning on the nightstand. He didn't like waking in a totally dark room.

His nightshirt was cold and clammy against his body. Well, sweat was better than blood, and even real sweat was better than dreamed blood. He was sweat-soaked all across his chest and back, where the warring armies of his dreams had fought, and when he felt the soft mattress, it was soaked through in spots, too. No wonder his throat was painfully dry.

His hand shook as he poured himself a mug of water from the silver pitcher on his nightstand, and only steadied after he drank it quickly, greedily, then poured himself another and drank it more slowly. His bladder was tight as a drum now, and while there was a garderobe not twenty steps down the hall, Thomen didn't like leaving his rooms at night. His guards were always sleepy-eyed, and embarrassed about that, as though Thomen was going to report them to General Garavar for being tired in the middle of the night.

But there was a thundermug on a stand behind a screen at the far corner of the room, and he moved through the darkness, the carpet soft beneath his feet, found it, and relieved himself, carefully directing the stream of urine against the inner side of the mug to keep the sound down, just as he would have if he hadn't been alone.

It would have been nice not to sleep alone so often, but that was something he had to be careful about. His mother had the bad habit of reshuffling the upstairs maids if she suspected—accurately, more often than not—that one or another warmed his bed every now and then, and any show of favoritism was guaranteed to cause some sort of trouble.

And not just among the house staff, either.

Who would have ever thought that being the emperor would be so awfully lonely? he asked himself once again.

Deven Tyrnael was probably his best friend among the barons, but as Baron Tyrnael, his claim to the throne and crown of Bieme was technically better than Thomen's—and having Deven spend too much time in Biemestren would be a signal to the other barons that Thomen didn't trust him. Jason Cullinane had abdicated the throne in Thomen's favor, and had the sense to stay away from the capital except when called. And Thomen liked Jason. There was some of his father in him.

He sighed. He was actually looking forward to Parliament meeting, even though that was a dozen tendays off. It wasn't just the barons; there would be minor and major lords and ladies accompanying them, and that would, at least, give him somebody to talk to. And, no doubt, with the aid of General Garavar's guards, some lovely young lady would be allowed to sneak into the imperial bedrooms late one night, in hopes of getting herself with the emperor's child.

That, he had to admit, was fun. There were benefits to being emperor, after all. Thomen chuckled. It wasn't only a woman who could visit the Spider, after all. Thomen didn't like to threaten—just about the worst thing a ruler could be known for was making any threat he didn't mean—but if Keverel, the local Spider, ever let it out that the emperor was seeing him to keep himself temporarily infertile instead of treating a chronic shoulder ache, he would live to regret it.

There would be an heir—his mother was right; he ought to marry—but that would happen when he decided on it, and not before. He had lost his father and his older brother; he wanted the empire to be more stable before he left any son of his open to being orphaned so easily.

He stripped off his nightshirt, toweled off his chest and underarms, tossed it toward a far corner of the room, then shrugged into the soft robe he had left draped across the foot of his bed.

Well, he could go alert the guard to get a maid to change his blankets and sheets, but the new night maid, while not particularly attractive, was particularly good at seeing to his needs without fawning over him all the time, and it took less time for him to strip the bed and flip over the down mattress, carefully checking the flintlock pistol that he kept within reach.

It was unlikely, of course, if some assassin or invader reached the donjon at all, much less got up to the third floor and Thomen's rooms, that he would still be asleep, or that one shot from a pistol would make much of a difference, but Pirondael, the former occupant of these rooms, had, after all, used a hidden weapon to kill Thomen's father in just such a circumstance.

The ancient chest at the foot of the bed provided a change of pillows, sheet, and a fresh nightshirt, and after another drink from the water pitcher and another quick use of the thundermug, he slipped back into bed.

Maybe he would have quiet dreams, for once. That would be nice.

He pillowed his head on his hands, and closed his eyes. The flickering of the lantern bothered him now, so he blew it out, turned over, and fell asleep.

This time, thankfully, he didn't dream. Not exactly. But his sleep was a cold, icy thing that seemed to go on forever . . .

. . . ended by the touch of a sword tip to his chest.

His eyes snapped open to see two dark shapes looming over him.

He started to reach for his hidden pistol, but stopped himself: it was now sticking out of Walter Slovotsky's belt, and it was Bren, Baron Adahan, who was putting his sword away.

"Good evening, Your Majesty," Bren said, striking a match and lighting the bedside lantern. The light hurt Thomen's eyes, but it didn't seem that complaining about that was the thing to do.

The thing to do was probably to shout for the guards, but that would only turn an awkward and annoying situation into a dangerous one. You could always start a battle or a fight, but turning it off so that it stayed off was another matter entirely. Walter Slovotsky was an annoyance at times, a help at others, but he and Bren Adahan were hardly here in the middle of the night to assassinate Thomen, and if Walter Slovotsky insisted on some grand gesture rather than simply waiting for an audience in the morning, well, Thomen would oblige him, and only wish that he had arrived earlier, when his dreams had been all red and sharp-edged.

"We've come about a couple of jobs," Walter Slovotsky said. "I think you need a pair of special representatives for difficult political problems. Care to review my qualifications?"

It was all Thomen could do not to laugh. Moving slowly—there was no need to get anybody excited—he poured himself another mug of water. Maybe it was just as well they hadn't woken him early; this time his hand didn't shake. "I had thought I'd offered you such a position not too long ago." That matter over in Keranahan did need investigating, after all, even though it sounded minor—but you could never tell when some minor problem could flare up into something worse, and Thomen had wanted Walter Slovotsky to look into it. Well, no: *Mother* had wanted Walter Slovotsky to look into it, and Thomen hadn't seen any reason to overrule her.

Instead, as he could have, should have, predicted, Slovotsky had ducked out in the middle of the night, stealing Thomen's candelabra either just for practice or to show that he could get past the guards.

Slovotsky shook his head. "No. I'm not talking about running around playing catch every time your mother finds something who likes to throw spears. We may have other projects in the fire every now and then."

"Seems likely. When things quiet down in Pandathaway, I intend to kill whoever it is that sent assassins after Kirah and her daughters," Bren said, without heat, in the quiet way that a death sentence is passed.

Thomen would have asked about that, but it could wait: if any of Walter Slovotsky's family had been harmed, he and Bren Adahan would not be standing here casually chatting in the middle of the night, and it wouldn't do for the emperor to advertise his ignorance.

Bren Adahan raised a palm and nodded, confirming Thomen's thoughts.

"Make that 'we intend'—but save the details for later," Walter Slovotsky said. "We'll work for you, not your mother; and that means we report to you, and not to your mother."

"Whenever we want to," Bren put in. "Even in the middle of the night."

Thomen tried not to laugh. "You seem to have arranged that part of it already."

Theatrically—Slovotsky did everything theatrically—he rubbed at the small of his back, as though it was hurting him. Thomen was skeptical. Not that he would have minded if Slovotsky was hurting. There was something about the arrogance of Walter Slovotsky's smile that made Thomen—even though he really liked Slovotsky—often want to hit him with a stick until he stopped smiling.

"I'm starting to get too old to be jumping in and out of windows," Slovotsky said. "Next time I get to walk in, through the door. Anytime, night or day. That's for a starter."

"And?"

"And him." Slovotsky indicated the baron. "He sits in for you when you're taking some time off."

"The Biemish barons will love that," Thomen said sarcastically. Bieme had been on its way to not only defeat but destruction during the war, and feelings still ran hot and deep. Thomen shared some of those feelings, but an emperor's feelings weren't allowed to matter.

Walter Slovotsky shrugged. "I've been thinking about that, and I've got a few ideas about how to make them like it better."

"You do?" Slovotsky was always full of ideas. But some of them might even work. Still, Thomen would love to hear how a Holtish baron as his deputy would work.

Oh, I think the idea can be sold to them, sounded in his head. Ellegon!

I'd say 'At your service, Emperor,' but the fact is that I spend more time than I'd like at your service as it is. There was a serious, almost accusing undertone to the dragon's mental voice, but Thomen didn't let it bother him. Thomen didn't really understand why most people were so frightened of the dragon.

Well, there is the fact that I can bite people in half or flame them to a crisp. Some folks are just nervous about such things.

"I do," Slovotsky went on, as though he hadn't heard the dragon.

Which he hadn't. He asked me to find a perch nearby in case you decided not to take having your sleep interrupted well. Finish with him, and we'll talk.

"In any case," Slovotsky went on, "you do take some time off— all work and no play makes Thomen a dull emperor. You need to spend more time with your butt in a saddle and less with it in a throne. Bren will keep the throne warm for you."

"And you?"

"I'll run important errands for you, with Bren when he's available, but with whatever support I think necessary: a few bodyguards, a troop from the House Guard, or a baronial army. And a nice title— imperial proctor, maybe. Something that suggests it'd be real unhandy if anything were to happen to me."

"I take it there's more."

"Sure. Our families live in the castle here, under your protection, when we aren't based out of Little Pittsburgh and Castle Adahan. They come and they go as they please, with imperial troops for their security, too." He turned to Bren. "What next?"

"Next, we need to arrange a divorce," Bren said. "And a marriage, as well. Or is it two marriages?" He looked over at Slovotsky.

"I haven't exactly asked her yet," Slovotsky said. "I sort of figured I'd have to dispose of one wife before I take on another one, eh?"

Bren laughed.

And, after a moment, so did Thomen. "Imperial proctor, eh? Well, true enough, I could find some work for you."

"Some work of noble note, eh?"

That was a strange way to put it. "Rather." *What am I going to say, I'll give you pointless jobs with useless risks?*

He's going to be insufferable if he gets away with this, you know. Sneaking into your rooms in the middle of the night and then walking out the front door like nothing's wrong?

It was worse than that. Thomen would have to get the door for the two of them and calm the guard, or the alarm would be raised.

Which probably wouldn't have bothered Walter Slovotsky a whole lot, but Walter Slovotsky probably didn't care if anybody got a good night's sleep. He probably slept easily, softly, happily every night, and most times with some new female companion.

And would you trade places with him?

It was all Thomen could do not to snort. *No,* he thought. *Being emperor is my responsibility. You can't just give away a responsibility.*

I know.

Thomen smiled. "One thing, though?"

"Yes?"

"I don't care where it is," he said firmly, as though the whole deal depended on Slovotsky's agreement, "or what happened to it, but I want my candelabra back. Soon."

Slovotsky pursed his lips. "Done."

Thomen walked to the door, and opened it slowly, carefully.

Outside, the guard across the hall leaped to attention. He had been leaning against the wall, which was the sort of thing that General Garavar objected to but never bothered Thomen.

"Your—"

"Shh." Thomen held up a hand, then beckoned to Walter Slovotsky and Bren Adahan. "Would you call for your replacement, and make sure these two don't get themselves killed by some overeager guard?"

"But—"

"Please." It took him a moment to realize that he wasn't going to remember the guard's name, and that was embarrassing. "I'm not sure you've been introduced," Thomen said, gesturing at Bren Adahan and ignoring Walter Slovotsky's knowing smile.

He only is good at women's names, so he's got no reason to smirk.

The baron drew himself up straight. "Bren, Baron Adahan," he said, "greets you."

The burly soldier was fighting to keep his composure. Even a trooper assigned to the house didn't expect to be treated as a human being by nobility, and what was supposed to have been a quiet shift in the middle of the night outside the emperor's quarters had just turned strange. Soldiers didn't like strange. "Palton, son of Palton," the guard said. "I am at your service, Lord Baron."

Walter Slovotsky stuck out a hand, as though offering to seal a bargain. Palton took it. "Walter Slovotsky, son of Stash and Emma. I'm the new imperial proctor," he said. "And it's my job and privilege to get in to see his imperial muchness whenever I want to, so you don't need to concern yourself with how the baron and I slipped by you."

Home soldiers weren't necessarily the brightest of men; loyalty and skill were a higher priority. It clearly hadn't occurred to Palton that he had failed, somehow.

Thomen nodded, and reached for the thin bell rope, the one that rang down in the servants' quarters. If he was going to summon some guards, it was best to have one of the servitors do it, because ringing the guard bell would get a troop of heavily armed soldiers up here spoiling for a fight that nobody wanted.

There would be time enough in the morning to issue the proper orders. And deal with Mother. That would be the difficult part, but— enough for one night.

The emperor returned to his rooms.

Outside, Ellegon perched on the far wall of the inner keep. In the flickering light of the blazing torches that lined the walls, a few of the younger soldiers stood and stared, although the senior ones had seen a dragon before, and knew the value of a good night's sleep.

"Enjoying scaring the young ones?" Thomen asked. His voice was quiet, barely above a whisper, but the dragon wasn't listening to his voice.

They wouldn't be the only ones scared. The dragon's broad wings curled and uncurled. *Things got a little . . . scary at Castle Cullinane while I was gone. A team of assassins made a try for the family.*

Thomen nodded. That explained a lot about tonight, and about his visitors. Trust Walter Slovotsky to do himself a favor while explaining to Thomen that he was doing the emperor and the empire one.

They all handled it well enough, but . . .

"But it made you nervous." The dragon had a strong affection for the Cullinane family.

Next time you're chained in a sewer for a few centuries, you let me know how you feel about the family of the man that freed you.

Point taken.

The dragon stretched his long neck, and sent a gout of flame skyward. *I have some business in Home to deal with, but after that, I think I'll want to spend some time around here for a while. If that's okay.*

Thomen grinned. "You should probably take that up with Baron Adahan. As I understand it, he's going to be holding my throne down for me while I go hunting." Thomen couldn't remember the last time he'd taken a bow and a quiver and gone in search of rabbit, much less of deer. When he had been an imperial judge, he had made time for hunting and riding, and even when he had been regent he still had managed to get away occasionally.

The dragon snorted flame. *You'll be a good long while setting that up, Emperor. By Parliament, maybe. If you're lucky.*

That was true enough. But it would be nice to get away every now and then. Kiar and Nyphien were making threatening noises, and the preference of many of the barons to simply blame them for some of the border incidents and launch at least a punitive attack if not simply to try to conquer the rest of the Middle Lands—

You could count on my lack of support for that, Ellegon said.

Thomen pounded a fist on the stone wall. "I don't want any wars. I've seen enough of them for one lifetime, and I thought after the Holtun-Bieme war, things would stay quiet."

Yes, you did. Because you were a child. There are always fires to be pissed on, and some of them have to be pissed on from the very top. The dragon lifted its rear leg as though to demonstrate, but desisted at Thomen's grimace. The emperor had been downwind from that once, and it had been just about the worst smell he'd ever had.

Ingratitude, thy name is human. After all I've done for you.

And the dragon had indeed done a lot, particularly in keeping the Biemish barons in line.

Well, the threat that anybody who acted up would have a few tons of fire-breathing dragon landing on top of them tends to make folks think twice.

Well, yes, there was that, and it was no accident that the imperial seal was that of a dragon rampant, breathing fire—

I blush.

—but it would be easy to overestimate that. Ellegon had been of inestimable help back during the war, but the war had gone on nonetheless.

Yes, it had. And it could happen again, the dragon said, stretching out its wings as it leaped skyward with a flurry of wings that sent dust flying from the parade ground even up to the emperor's window. *But do your best, O Emperor, and let's hope that best is good enough.*

Thomen Furnael, emperor of Holtun-Bieme, wiped the dust from his eyes, drank a last mug of water, and returned to his bed.

This time, his sleep was all warm and dreamless.

21

⯎ Miron

This newfound equality was one thing, but the thin, mocking smile that never quite left Erenor's lips made Kethol want to grab the front of the wizard's tunic and slap his face into the next barony.

"Kethol?" Leria caught up with him once more, easily matching her horse's speed to his. Truth to tell, she was a better rider than he was—which was understandable: years of recreational riding probably gave you better control over not only the horse but of your own muscles than the kind of riding you got while soldiering, which consisted more often than not of just sitting on the back of a slowly plodding horse.

The notion that soldiers were somehow great horsemen was something peasants were more easily persuaded of than anybody else was.

"Yes, Lady—I mean yes, Lerian." He couldn't quite meet her eyes. He wasn't sure why. Or maybe it was that he *was* sure why, and didn't dare even explain to himself why an ordinary pair of strangely warm blue eyes could make it difficult for him to think clearly.

"When we reach Horsten?"

"Yes?"

"Do you think we can look for one of the baron's men? I mean, Horsten is, I mean it now is, part of Barony Adahan, and we should—"

"Should." That was a word that always decided it for Kethol.

Since when did *should* have anything to do with anything? No, he would go with what Pirojil and Durine had said, and if that was overly cautious, perhaps Kethol could be overly cautious for once.

Erenor dropped back to join them. "I hope you'll notice," he said, punctuating a sniff with a wave of his hand, "the tendency of horses to wander off on their own when not properly attended."

Actually, Kethol had noticed no such thing. The horses—the dray horses in particular—tended to follow each other, particularly when the big brown gelding that Leria was riding was in the lead. He'd known a drover, years ago, who always believed in riding a stallion, knowing that the mares and geldings would follow. Of course, the drover had died one day when he wasn't paying quite enough attention and his stallion had gotten a sniff of something and suddenly lunged into full gallop. If he had been alert enough to spring out of the saddle, he would have come away with no worse than a few scrapes and maybe a broken bone or two, but he hadn't. And he hadn't been alert enough to cling for dear life, which might have worked. Instead, he had half fallen, dragged along rocky ground by one imprisoned ankle long after he was dead.

Pirojil had a point about how sometimes it was better to not do something at all than only half do it.

But that probably wasn't what this was all about anyway, so he didn't say that.

"Then gather them together," Kethol said, "and bring up the rear."

When they rounded the bend of the road ahead, Leria was the first to notice the flag fluttering from the pole on the far hilltop. "Look," she said, one slim finger pointing in an elegant way that Kethol wanted to correct but didn't quite know how, "somebody is trying to get our attention."

Kethol would have noticed the flag in just another moment or two. Off in the distance he could barely see a blocky figure—a man, although he could only tell that by the way sunlight gleamed on his bald head. The flag was not the red of distress or the white of surrender, but blue, and while Kethol couldn't make out the symbol on it, he was sure that when they got closer it would be the imperial dragon, which, technically, made this a call to parley, but which in practice made it a call to trade.

What else would a farmer want to parley about?

Erenor rode back up, his horse not quite at the canter, but verging on it. He raised a palm to forestall—what?

"Ta havath," he said. "Ta havath, Kethol. There's no problem here."

Well, yes, there was a problem here, and Kethol was talking to it. "What are you talking about?"

"The flag. Technically, I know, it's a call to parley. But if you were a landowner, and you saw three . . . men riding down the road driving what would appear to be trade horses, you'd probably want to make a call to parley, too. If only—"

"If only to see if there was some advantage to be taken," Kethol said. "After all, somebody who has horses, and is looking to sell them, probably wants money. And if he wants money very badly, it may be that there is to be some horseflesh bought for too little coin."

Kethol kept the words level and even, or at least tried to. Regardless of how Pirojil and Durine sometimes treated him, he was not a gibbering, capering, drooling idiot, not always looking to find a problem that could only be solved with a blade or a bullet. He had even been known to, from time to time, solve a problem with an insight or two, hard though that was to believe.

"Too little? Well, we couldn't have that," Erenor said. "Too little, and he'd wonder why we sold so cheaply, and perhaps if there was a reward on our heads for stolen horses."

Leria's grin would have irritated him if her eyes weren't smiling, too. "Perhaps, Erenor, wisest of employers," she said, "hostler among hostlers, it would be sensible of you to simply go and parley with him?"

Erenor's mouth twisted into a thoughtful frown. "No," he said after a moment. "That makes us seem too eager—that makes *me* seem too eager." He dismissed Kethol with a flip of his hand. "Go and see what he wants, if you please."

It made sense. And it made sense not to stand here, wasting daylight, leaving the people up the hill wondering why it was taking so long for these horse traders to begin horse trading, and it made sense not to stand here arguing with his putative employer, but it still felt as if Erenor had, once again, managed to put something over on somebody, and Kethol didn't much like that feeling.

He tugged on the reins and gave a firm twitch of his heels.

Master Sanders—he insisted that he had earned the title during his years as a blacksmith, before he had sold his smithy in a Tyrnaelian village to buy farmland in Neranahan and hire some displaced peasants to work it for him—ran knowing hands up and down the dray horse's withers, then fastened blunt fingers tightly around its lead rope before giving it a solid thwack on the side that would have stunned a strong man but barely caused the horse to twitch.

He was a big man, built like a brick, his skin permanently burned and reddened from the sun to such an extent that his bald head looked as if it had been scorched clean.

He had dismissed his eldest son—a younger, not quite as bald version of himself—and two of the farmworkers, sending them off to do some job on the other side of the long wattle-and-daub house. Two men, sweating in the sun, were busying themselves rethatching the roof, but they were well out of earshot; it seemed that Master Sanders liked to do his trading without an audience. Kethol tried to decide whether that was because he was afraid that others would think he'd been taken advantage of or because he was afraid that another's expression would give some advantage away, and decided that it could easily be both, or neither.

"Not a bad animal, Trader, not a bad animal at all," Master Sanders said, giving the lead rope a quick twist around the hitching pole. He stepped back into the shade of the stable, beckoning Erenor and Kethol to follow. "Seven, eight years old, eh?"

The stable had originally been a well house, which Sanders had expanded into a smithy and a stable, although Kethol couldn't tell in which order. Not a bad idea—it kept a source of water close to both animals and forge.

"Five," Erenor said. "Five years old. No more."

"Naturally," Sanders said. "Five very long years, eh?" His fingers traced their way through the wear marks on its hide. "Spent more time pulling a carriage or a wagon than a plow, but I've never found a horse I couldn't teach to walk a straight line, though a time or two there's been some question as to whether its stubbornness or my hand would break first." He rubbed the back of his hand against his sweaty brow. "If that gray mare and the big brown gelding are the same sort of five-year-olds, I think we can do some business, if you don't want to hold out for the three silver marks you'd get in New Pittsburgh."

"It would be at least five in New Pittsburgh," Erenor said. "But I'd thought we'd try Adahan itself first, and see if there's any interest there—I've been told the Baron Adahan himself has a fine eye for horses, and I'd thought we'd be able to get a good price from his factor."

Sanders chuckled. "I heard that the baron has a fine eye for many things, horses and friends' wives among them, but I've never heard that he has a great interest in dray stock or hard-worked gelding plow horses. Of course, if he's found a way to breed geldings, then we'll all be in his debt."

Master Sanders laughed too loudly at his own joke. He was the sort who would.

Erenor laughed along, although Kethol didn't.

Sanders and Erenor got down to some serious haggling, while Kethol looked out over the fields. Leria—no, Lerian, he reminded himself—had dismounted, and had the horses grazing on a grassy plot down near the fence, gently switching at the little roan, her alternate mount, who tended to stray if not watched carefully. There was just a touch of sway in her hips as she moved, but Kethol was looking for that.

Off in the distance, a quartet of shirtless, sun-browned men worked their way down the green rows, stooping with every step to pick weeds. Sanders had the right idea—if you were going to be a farmer, best to own the land and have others work it for you. Smithing, carpentry, butchering, and all the other work involved in running a farm were bad enough, but could there be anything worse than spending your days stooped over in the hot sun, far from the coolness of the green woods?

Well, yes, there could be many worse things. But not many of them were part of the day-to-day life of a farmer.

"The day gets no shorter," Sanders said, "and there's no better place to make camp between here and Horsten. I'll put the three of you and your animals up for the night—my guesting room for you; a warm stable to sleep in for your men; hay, oats, and fresh water for the animals; beer and stew for the humans—for the sake of the deal, if you'll not hold out for such a ridiculous price."

That would have been a good deal for three road-weary drovers, but it was a danger for the three of them. Leria's disguise would hold up from a distance, but close-up would be another matter.

Erenor apparently agreed; he shook his head. "Well, a ridiculous price it may be; I've been thought ridiculous before," he said. "I think we can get better than five for the mottled mare and the brown, although I'll settle for five for this gelding. We'd best be moving on, then."

"Is there some reason to hurry?" Sanders asked. "Young Baron Adahan is on his deathbed, is he? And he wishes to buy some non-breeding stock before he closes his eyes for the last time?"

Erenor smiled. "Of course not."

"Then why such unseemly haste, when there's food, rest, and a fair price here?"

"Food and rest, perhaps, but as to the price . . . We'd be happy to accept your generosity, provided you'll come to a full four marks for the gelding. Five for each of the others. Shall I have Lerian bring them up for your inspection?"

Sanders rubbed a thick hand against his chin. "No, no, I'll go the four marks, but I'll not buy these sort of five-year-olds for five. Four for this big one; a bargain it is, then." Sanders held out his hand, and after a moment, Erenor slapped his palm in agreement.

Kethol could easily have been wrong, but he figured that Sanders felt he was short only one horse, and wouldn't have bought the others unless the price was low, but not suspiciously low. Probably some overaged, swaybacked plow horse had finally keeled over and died, and Sanders was eager to replace it, preferably by dealing with somebody who wouldn't know his situation and might set a low price on one horse for the sake of trying to get several sold.

Erenor and Sanders sealed the bargain with a quick drink from a brown clay bottle that Sanders took down from a shelf over near the forge. Sanders took a second sip, then passed the bottle to Kethol. It was a soured wine, but fruity for all that, and it washed the taste of road dust from Kethol's mouth.

"Now, bring up this Lerian of yours—a fine name for a simple drover, eh?—and let us drink with him," Sanders said to Kethol. "I've never had a man sleeping under my roof I haven't drunk with, and I'm too old to change and too stubborn to try."

Kethol opened his mouth to say something—he wasn't sure quite what—when Erenor spoke up.

"I'll go and get him," he said, handing his reins over to Sanders. "Kethol, unsaddle and water our saddle horses—they've had a long enough day as it is."

Sanders accepted the reins with a nod, and led the horse into the dark of the stable. Kethol followed. There didn't seem to be anything better to do. Maybe Leria's disguise would hold up, or maybe . . .

No, maybe it wouldn't need to.

Erenor returned in a few moments with a big, brawny man astride a little roan, leading the rest of the horses.

"Good day to you, Master Sanders," the brawny man said in a deep basso rumble that had the pitch of Durine's voice but the rhythm of Leria's speech. "My name is Lerian. I'm told you have a bottle of wine waiting for me."

Erenor smiled genially at Kethol, no trace of a boast on his face.

"I should have warned Master Sanders about Lerian's capacity, but, after all, he insisted."

Kethol grinned back. This just might work.

The night spread out all inky in front of him, lit only by black gashes in the not-quite-black clouds that let some stars sparkle through, and by the distant pulse of a trio of Faerie lights that, for whatever reason, had taken up a position at the turnoff down the road, as though they had been assigned to light the way of somebody, something.

There was something about the night that appealed to Kethol. It was like a dark blanket that could cover and warm you, and once you learned its ways, it was a friend.

Not a particularly good friend, mind, but life was like that. You didn't get many good friends.

He leaned against the doorframe, easily two manheights above the packed dirt below. There were lots of things he liked about sleeping in a stable's hayloft, and this wasn't the first time in his life he had found this sort of shelter. The wind was refreshing, and the animals below stood guard for you, as long as you had enough presence of mind to tell a warning whicker from an ordinary snort in your sleep, and Kethol figured he could probably do that dead.

Yes, there was the occasional rat scurrying about—but if you hung your bags from a rafter, a spare blanket folded properly about them, they would usually leave your food alone, and if one or two happened to be careless enough to get near you, a sudden swipe of your sword would leave a body rotting as a warning to the others.

Not necessarily a warning they would heed, but you couldn't have everything. If your friends didn't listen to your warnings, then how could you expect rats to?

Erenor had been put up in the house—which was nice; the wizard's arrogance was getting on Kethol's nerves, and his having been right and useful of late somehow made that worse, not better.

The trouble was that that left Kethol alone with Leria, who had taken his advice and wrapped herself in a thick blanket, then burrowed her way into a pile of hay.

It was hard to sleep. It had been too long since he'd had a whore, and that only went so far. Not that he had any right to complain about his present conditions. Kethol wondered what Durine and Pirojil were doing now, and decided that they were unlikely to be sleeping in a nice warm stable, their bellies warmed with fresh stew and their heads slightly abuzz with sour beer.

They were also unlikely to be headed anywhere warm and safe, like Biemestren.

It was clear what he would have to do, although how to do it was the problem. Kethol had never been much for talking people into doing things. Not even his brothers in arms. He did what he had to, when he had to, and hoped that they would back him up.

But how he could persuade the dowager empress of anything? The only reason he could even get that close to the imperial family was because he was ordered to report to her—and would she possibly agree to set up an audience with the emperor? He might as well ask to see the matriarch of the Healing Hand.

But Lady Doria would listen to him, and she had some influence.

There was something going on in Neranahan, something that needed investigating, and she would see that. If she could persuade, say, Walter Slovotsky, he could persuade Ellegon, and they could take a squad into the hills north of the baronial estate and find out just what it was that the baroness was hiding there.

A light touch was called for; that much was clear. Kethol didn't know much about politics, but he knew that you couldn't just ride an army of horsemen onto a baron's estate without some good reason, not without making all the other barons—Holtish and Biemish alike—nervous.

A light touch wasn't Kethol's specialty, and even asking for one was not. It should have been Piro who would bring Leria to court. Pirojil was probably the ugliest man Kethol had ever known, but his mind was clear and sharp, and he didn't let his tongue or his reflexes overrule his good sense.

As Kethol had in Riverforks.

But what should he have done? Let those three toughs rape that girl, and just stand there and listen?

The Old Emperor wouldn't have. The Old Emperor would have killed the lot of them for daring to lay their hands on an unwilling woman.

Shit. He could almost hear Pirojil say it: You aren't the Old Emperor.

Truth to tell, the Old Emperor wasn't the invulnerable, all-powerful Old Emperor of legend—his last heroics got him killed, after all.

But everybody dies sometime, Pirojil, he thought. It's a question of what you're doing when it happens, more than anything else.

He heard her move behind him.

"You should be sleeping," she said, her voice low.

"I probably should." He didn't turn. She was wearing a loose cotton tunic as a sleeping dress, and he knew he would gawk and stare if he let his eyes fall on her.

"If you think we need to set a watch," she said, "it's probably my turn."

He shook his head. "No." He gave a practice thump of his heel on the floor, rewarded by a shuffling of hooves and quiet neighing below. "We've good enough watchers on duty."

It was hard enough talking to her without looking at her. There was something in her eyes, something in her smile, something in the way she held herself that made it hard to breathe. It wasn't that the only women Kethol was ever around were smelly whores, because they weren't; he had spent much time guarding Andrea Cullinane and her daughter, as well as Kirah, wife of Walter Slovotsky, and their daughter, Jane.

The Cullinane and Slovotsky women were attractive—very attractive—but, well, he was their man. That made them, if not any more untouchable in law—it would already be worth his life to so much as lay an unwanted finger on any noblewoman—more akin to family, maybe.

Or maybe it made him a trusted pet and them his owner.

If so, he was comfortable with that.

Leria made him uncomfortable. Even after days on the road, under the dirt and sweat she somehow felt and smelled—even though he wasn't close enough to touch or smell her—of soap and flowers, of cleanliness and warmth on a cold night, of the friendly green coolness of the woods on a hot day.

And he could no more reach out and touch that than he could reach out and touch the Faerie lights. She wasn't a girl; she was a lady, and whether he was a woodsman or a soldier, she was far above him, out of reach. If he touched her, would it all burst like a soap bubble? Or, more likely, would she scream and claw at his face?

The pain wouldn't be important—pain? what was pain?—but the betrayal would be.

And which betrayal would that be?

And of whom?

He more felt than saw her move next to him. "It's a pretty night," she said.

He swallowed heavily, nodded. "Yes, Lady, that it is."

Steely fingers gripped his shoulder, and pulled. She didn't have the strength to move him, but it was all he could do to simply let himself turn, to not break her grip with a sweep of one arm while the other sought the hilt of his dagger. "What is it with you?" she asked. "Is it that I'm Euar'den? I'm used to that."

"Eh?" He turned to face her. If he hadn't known that her eyes were blue, the warm blue of the morning sky, he wouldn't have been able to tell. But even in the dim light of the stars and the Faerie lights, her eyes seemed to burn into his.

"Is that why you treat me like I'm some . . . some thing?" she asked. "Or is it that you so resent being sent out to rescue me, the way the others do?"

Kethol didn't have the slightest idea what she was getting at, but he sensed that admitting that would only infuriate her more, although why she was angry in the first place he just didn't know. "I . . . we don't resent you at all. It's not a soldier's job to resent, anyway. We just go where we're told and do what we're told."

"So it's just another job to you," she said. If her voice had been any more flat and level, it would have sounded inhuman. "And such an unimportant one, at that, rescuing a spoiled noble girl from an unwanted marriage. How very trivial a task for somebody who accompanied the Old Emperor on his Last Ride."

"Lady," he said, "I—we—don't mind trivial, easy little tasks. Of course, when half the barony is out looking for us, wanting a carriageful of gold that we don't even have, it's not easy."

For a moment, he didn't know how it would go. But then her hand dropped from his shoulder, and she laughed, quietly, a distant sound of silver bells. "I guess it isn't all that easy, at that," she said. "Is that why the three of you resent me so?"

Kethol wished Pirojil was here. Piro was good at explaining things. "No," he finally said. "Oh, I think Durine probably gets angry every time you shudder when you look at Piro; you'd think we'd be used to that by now as we are to his face. And Durine has always wanted something big and dramatic to die for, maybe. Me, I'm a simple sort. I go where I'm told, and I do what I'm told to do, and I worry a lot more about how than why." Not that he was all that good at figuring out how. But maybe he was good enough.

"And that's all you want," she more said than asked. "Just to go where you're told and do what you're told to do? That's all?"

Now it was his turn to chuckle. But the sound rattled in his throat like dry bones. "I guess it all depends on who's doing the telling. The Old Emperor once told us to ride along with him, and even though the ride was likely to be in only one direction, a lot of us went smiling. The dowager empress told us to go straighten out just a small problem in a small barony, and I don't think any of us is going to be smiling about it."

"But it's not me," she said. "You don't blame me for all this."

It hadn't occurred to him to blame her, or that she could possibly care whether or not any of the three of them blamed her. They were just soldiers, after all, and she was a lady. And a lady no more cared for the opinions of soldiers than soldiers cared for the opinions of their horses. Of course, it mattered a great deal whether or not the horse, or the soldier, responded to orders, kept a steady pace, or was liable to lie down and die instead of slogging on, but the feelings, the opinions?

"Of course not." For that matter—and despite the fact that he would have loved to get her wrinkled neck between his hands—he really didn't blame the dowager empress. She owed no loyalty to three Cullinane family retainers, three men who would happily slit open an imperial belly to warm the chilled feet of the least of the Cullinanes.

Maybe he should have said this all to Leria. But it would be impertinent to explain to her something she knew very well: that he was a different sort of person than she was, and that he didn't really expect her to even acknowledge him as a person, even though her smile warmed him deeper and better than a mug of hot, mulled wine.

He was just a soldier, after all.

She took a tentative step closer to him, and he could feel her warm breath against his neck. "And my being Euar'den doesn't mean anything to you?"

His hands started to reach for her, and then they dropped. "Lady Leria, the wars among the old clans and septs just don't mean much of a muchness to a simple soldier from another country."

"I'm not some untouchable prize, then?"

"No. Or yes." But not because of her ancestry. He was just a soldier, and she was a lady, but he was made of flesh and bone, not of steel and stone, and he reached out and took her in his arms.

Her mouth was warm and soft on his for a long moment, until she pushed back from him, her hands clenched into fists, a quiet "no," issuing from between her lips.

He raised his palms in a gesture of surrender. "My apologies, Lady," he said. "I . . ."

She looked at him, wide-eyed, and fled back into the darkness.

Kethol didn't know what it was that he was supposed to do. Was he supposed to go after her? Didn't she understand that his kind just didn't do that? He could still feel the warmth of her lips on his, the taste of her tongue in his mouth, the nearness of her body pressed up against his—but she had said no, and she was a lady, and he had no right to so much as lay a finger on the hem of her garment.

When there was nothing to say, Kethol thought, perhaps it was best to say nothing.

He lay down, his back to her, and pretended to fall asleep.

The golden light of predawn beat down on Kethol's eyelids; he stretched and yawned silently. He had slept, finally; the pretense had turned real.

It was an old woodsman's trick, to position yourself with a clear horizon to the east. You could sleep better that way, knowing that the morning sun was your ally, that even before sunrise, anybody or anything moving to the east of you might cast a shadow across your face.

It wasn't perfect, of course. Somebody could still sneak up silently behind you and slit your throat before you ever woke up. But even a woodsman or a soldier had to sleep sometime, and if the night was your friend, the sun could be one, too, if not as loyal and valuable.

Or maybe it wasn't the sun. A distant clopping of horses' hooves came to his ears on the morning breeze. At least three; maybe as many as five. Given enough time, he could sort it out by hearing; but he crept slowly, carefully, toward the opening, keeping himself in shadow.

It was Miron and his four men. Somehow they had tracked them down here.

Running would be hopeless. Even if they could saddle their horses and make their way out the other side of the stable, there was no way the two of them could evade pursuit for long. It was possible, perhaps, that Kethol could draw them away and let Leria and Erenor escape while Miron hunted him down. And he might be able to make that last a good long while, if he could get past them to the woods.

But, no, that was hopeless. Erenor wasn't here; he was in the main house, guest of Sanders, and the sort of quick coordination that was needed just wasn't possible, not here and now.

There was another possibility.

Kethol's hands were already reaching for his bow; he strung it quickly, automatically, then took a handful of arrows and stuck them, point first, into the wood beside the door. Putting an arrow through each of the riders before any of them noticed was beyond any one archer's abilities, but perhaps if he nailed Miron and one or two others, the remaining men would flee and find themselves more afraid of what Baroness Elanee would do to them for having failed than they would be eager to hunt down Leria. After all, if anybody knew better than to believe the story about the large gold dowry being guarded by just three men, it would be Miron, who was probably the source of it.

He would have to take them all down now, get Leria and Erenor, and make their escape into Barony Adahan before anybody could raise a cry. And a cry would be raised. Rumors about a carriage overladen with a dowry in gold had already drawn some attention, but that attention, while widespread, was private, not official.

A hostler and a couple of drovers could hardly murder a lord, a baron-to-be, and expect that the local folks would simply bury them in an unmarked grave. Imperial law was firm on matters such as the murder of nobility, and it was enforced by imperial troops when village wardens and armsmen and baronial soldiers weren't up to the task. Pirojil and Durine had the imperial warrant, and its only purpose was to threaten a Keranahan subject; it didn't give Kethol license to go about killing a baron-to-be and his soldiers right and left.

But he was best off forgetting about all that.

Concentrate on the here and now, because the here and now was bad enough.

His fingers trembled ever so slightly as he nocked his first arrow. It wasn't going to work. The Old Emperor might have been able to take on five at once and drop them all, but Kethol doubted that.

Kethol certainly couldn't. But that wouldn't excuse him from trying.

Miron gestured to the stocky man who rode beside him, who

immediately dismounted and headed up the path toward the house.

If it was going to be done at all, now was the time, before they were any further spread out.

Kethol took a half-step back as he nocked the first arrow and drew the string back to his cheek. Miron first, then—

"A good morning to you," a deep voice boomed out, "Lord and minion alike."

Kethol let his point drop, and relaxed his arm. Six, now, with Sanders joining them? And what about the others? That ruined even the slim possibility of fighting his way out.

Too many witnesses . . .

Well, he had known this day would come, sooner or later. It was time to do his best to take them off Leria's trail while they ran him to ground.

He walked back into the hayloft, toward where Leria lay, wrapped in light white blankets like a shroud on a corpse. One hand fastened over her mouth, while the other clutched her shoulder to shake her awake.

Her eyes snapped open, but surprisingly she didn't try to scream around his hand. He let it drop.

"Miron and his companions are here," he said, his voice a hoarse whisper. "They're talking to Sanders right now. They're going to be asking about travelers, and Sanders isn't going to want to make any trouble for them. The question is what you want to do."

Her hair was all mussed and laden with straw, and there was an entirely unladylike trickle of drool at the side of her full mouth. "What do you mean?"

It was ridiculous that a soldier should be lecturing a lady about politics. "If Miron rescues you from me and brings you home safely, he's a hero, and I'm a dead man. And he's a clever one; he might go for it. Erenor and I have been holding you captive, planning to ransom you, perhaps, which is where all this story about gold came from. He kills the two of us, and returns home triumphantly, to your gratitude." She would have to marry Miron, probably; but he was a handsome enough, clever enough man, and hopefully he would treat her gently.

And with worms eating his flesh, Kethol wouldn't miss her warm mouth on his, wouldn't find the nearness of her body both—

No.

Hopefully Durine and Pirojil would hear about it in time to abandon their plans, whatever they were—Kethol hadn't wanted to know any more than he had to know.

"No," she said. "I'll turn myself over to him. And tell him that you're gone, the lot of you."

Miron would never believe that. Kethol didn't have to say that; his expression said it for him.

"No, but he'll *pretend* to," she said urgently. "Miron's clever. He'll understand what the . . . arrangement is," she said. She stood and turned away from him, and as she reached up to the rafters where she had hung her mannish tunic and leggings, she dropped the shift she'd slept in to her ankles.

Kethol had never seen a woman naked in the daylight, not ever. It wasn't the same as with a whore in a dimly lit room, urging him to finish so that she could get on to the next one. It wasn't even the same as a peasant's daughter or two that he had managed to have over the years.

It was all he could do to turn away, blushing, as he heard her dress quickly, knowing that she had distracted him from what was his duty, his responsibility, and that she'd done it neatly, in a way he couldn't defend himself from.

There wasn't time for arguing or discussion. And perhaps that was the best chance she had. Miron and his men could do a better job of protecting her than Kethol could, and if the price of that was Leria herself, well, it was up to her, not him.

There was another possibility. He could let them take her, and then follow them. One against five was horrible odds, yes, but perhaps he could take them by surprise.

And perhaps he could piss on a forest fire and put it out.

No. When they came up the ladder to the hayloft, he would kill as many as he could before they killed him. He had been told by the Cullinane regent to bring her to Biemestren safely, and since he could not do that, he would die trying.

With, at least, the remembrance of the warmth of her mouth . . .

A long iron pole ran through loose brackets on the overhead beams. It was a common enough arrangement for a hayloft—a rope would be threaded through the loop at the end of the pole, tied to bales of hay below, and used to pull the bales up to the loft. It didn't protect it from the rats. Rats could find their way through anything. They could tunnel up through walls, climb columns, and probably walk upside-down on the ceilings, or even climb up spiderwebs, for all Kethol knew.

But it did keep the hay off the ground and out of the damp, and made delivering it to the various stalls below just a matter of dropping it down through any of the several openings in the ceiling.

It was a common enough arrangement, and Kethol remembered seeing children playing on something like it once, one rainy afternoon: they had extended the pole out as far as it would go, then they would swing out on the rope, trying to make their way to the crooked limb of an old oak that was barely within reach, with a running start.

Then and there, there had been an unoccupied pigsty in between, and the boys who missed could count on falling into the soft, wet, smelly ground, and Kethol wasn't sure whether the risk or the actuality of it was the fun.

Here, there was no old oak, and no sty—but there was a rope, and it would be possible to wrap a piece of leather around the rope to protect his hands for the moment, then slide down it and come up behind them.

It wasn't as good a plan as the three of them could have come up with, but it was the best Kethol could do on such short notice, and it should get him at least two of them, maybe three: skewer the first one up the ladder, then kick him away, letting him fall and distract the others. Then slide down the rope, and come up behind them.

His brace of pistols were wrapped in oiled skins in his saddlebags. If there had been more time he would have reprimed the pans and made sure the touchhole was clear, but there wasn't, so all he could do was uncover the frizzens and bring them safely to the half-cock. Kethol was a lousy pistol shot—a pistol had no life to it, not a like a bow—but at the range where you could smell the onions on your enemy's breath, you didn't have to be a good shot, and the noise just might buy him some time to . . . to give a good accounting of himself before they brought him down. He probably wouldn't kill more than two, perhaps as many as three, but it was possible that none of them would walk away uninjured.

How many had the Old Emperor taken with him? A dozen, perhaps? More. Well, Kethol was not the Old Emperor, but he would do the best he could.

Durine, though, Durine had done something clever—yes, that was it. Kethol took his sealed flask of healing draughts from its steel container, and tucked it in the corner of his mouth. It would be important to hold off using it as long as possible, but if he clenched it between his teeth as he fought, a blow to the head hard enough to knock him down should shatter it and give him a few more moments of fighting.

That was worth doing.

Leria was standing silent, dressed now, her eyes wide, her hands open, fingers spread, shaking her head. *No,* she mouthed silently. Please.

It was, Kethol decided, every bit as easy to go out to die with a smile on your lips as not. Durine's and Pirojil's sarcastic comments about heroism aside, it just didn't make any difference, and if you didn't mind trembling a bit at the edges—and Kethol always trembled when he was waiting for it to all hit; that was why he liked to launch himself into the thick of things first, without warning—

For me, she mouthed.

She didn't understand. Shit, maybe *he* didn't understand, but

while he couldn't stop them from taking her away, he simply couldn't
let them do it while he lived.

Some things in life were complicated, but Kethol had been a
simple woodsman and a simple soldier all his life—he liked things
that way.

He was waiting for sounds of footsteps on the floor below when
he heard the scream.

It had been a pleasant evening of talk and drink with Eregen the
supposed hostler, followed by a quick pronging of Horvel's woman—
Sanders took advantage of his privileges with as much gusto as he
took up his responsibilities—and a good night's sleep.

And, as he sat on his front porch and ate his morning bread and
stew—it was better for having simmered all night—and drank another mugful of fresh well water while he watched the sunrise, he
was a happy man. From off behind the house came the sounds of
the field-workers starting their day—they always made a point to
rattle their tools loudly enough that he could hear them—and that
meant that his sons were up and supervising, which meant that Sanders could spend the day in the smithy, catching up on some nail
making and rewelding that scythe that had somehow or other gotten
snapped in two, and perhaps getting a good start on the hardware
for the harness that the new gelding would need. He would probably
have to do more work than he cared to in return for Beneder's making the harness, but by doing the ironwork himself he would avoid
having to deal with that idiot dwarf blacksmith who thought that
humans didn't know iron and steel.

And besides, that would give him a chance to go into town.

Travelers were frequent, but nonetheless welcome for that. Conversation was a pleasure, and when the only people you could talk
to were people who were beholden to you, that robbed it of some
of the pleasure. Maybe it was time he thought about a new wife, a
young one, perhaps with a sharp tongue in her mouth. Some of the
neighbors had daughters who were ready for husbands, and Sanders

just might have himself a decent bride-price handy, shortly.

And, in a few days, there would be a good reward, he was sure. Eregen—or whatever his name was; Sanders didn't know, and didn't much care—was clearly on the run from something, and while Sanders didn't care to try to see if his people could take on Eregen's impressive-looking swordsmen—he had been around steel long enough to know what somebody who could handle a sword looked like, and this Kethol person looked like somebody who could handle a sword—first thing after waking this morning, he had dispatched Kendrel's son to the village with a message that Sanders would like to see the warden as soon as convenient.

There was no rush. Of course, these three and their horses would be on their way by then, but surely whatever they were fleeing would involve some sort of reward. If they had been on the right side of the empire, they could have, would have, asked for the local warden themselves.

He was enjoying his own cleverness as much as the red and orange streaks of the sunrise when he heard the clopping of the horses, and five riders came into view.

His brow furrowed as he got to his feet. It was too soon for the warden to show up—Kendrel's son couldn't have even reached the village by now, much less woken that sluggish warden—and these didn't have the look of armsmen anyway. Four of them were clearly soldiers, although the lack of colors in their livery surprised him. Just whom were they soldiering for?

Presumably it was for the fifth, a youngish man in his twenties, his neatly trimmed beard and brightly filigreed and remarkably clean tunic proclaiming him to be some sort of nobility, although Sanders didn't recognize him. Not local; Lord Florent's folk ran to heavy brows and a permanent scowl—even the women—and this one had a strong but somewhat delicate face, and a smile rather than a scowl. They had clearly camped somewhere nearby last night, as the lordling's clothes were barely touched with road dust, and his hair was still damp, presumably from a morning washing.

Sanders ducked his head politely as they brought their horses to

a prancing stop. "A good morning to you, Lord and minion alike,"
he said. "I am Sanders, a common farmer. Can I offer your horses
water and yourselves refreshment?" There was no harm in courtesy.
Nobles would take what they wanted, and pay if they wanted, and
what was a poor farmer to do? Petition the emperor?

The lordling smiled. "That would certainly do quite well," he
said. "Although I'd be more interested in some information. We're . . .
seeking some friends. Have any strangers passed by recently?"

Well, there was such a thing as coincidence, but Sanders didn't
believe in it. "Not only passed by, Lord, Lord—"

"Miron," the lordling said, as though he expected the name to
mean something to Sanders. Well, it probably would, if Sanders was
native to Neranahan and had much contact with nobility, but he
wasn't, and he had as little as he could. He preferred people defer-
ring to him, rather than the other way around. "Not only passed by,
if these are the men you're looking for, one of them snores in my
house right now, while the other two are sleeping in the stable."

"Men?" one of the soldiers asked. "Just three men?"

Oh. That was it. These three were chasing after that silly rumor
of a dowager with a dowry heading for Biemestren. Sanders tried to
keep the disappointment off his face. His guests would still have
some sort of price on their heads, somewhere, but he wasn't going
to hear the clink of the gold from Lord Miron's purse.

"And they're right here, you say?"

"Yes, yes, yes, Lord." Sanders spread his hands. "Just a dealer
in horses, with a fairly odd collection of mares and geldings to sell."

"Big geldings? Dray horses?"

Sanders brightened. "Then these are the people you're looking
for, perhaps?" He turned toward the stable. "They are in—"

At first, he didn't recognize the sound of steel on leather. Strange
that a blacksmith, of all people, didn't immediately recognize the
sound of a sword being drawn quickly by somebody who knew how
to quickly bring it into play.

"There's no need, Lord Miron," Sanders said, turning toward the
lordling. "They—"

The slashing tip of the sword caught him on the throat, and then Miron drew the dark tip back for a final stroke.

Sanders barely had time to get out a single scream before the final darkness claimed him.

Kethol felt strangely limp as he watched from the darkness of the stable while Miron finished killing Sanders, then quickly remounted and spun his horse about.

In moments, the five of them were off down the road at a fast canter. It was all Kethol could do not to shake, and then he did find himself trembling, his teeth clattering together as though from a chill, his knees first shaking, then buckling as his stomach rebelled, and he fell to all fours, retching.

Leria was at his side, shaming him with her concern. "Kethol? What can I do?"

He shook his head, in part to clear it, in part to motion her away. He couldn't explain it himself. It had been years since seeing a death had affected him like this. You got used to it after a while; that was the sad truth.

But this was different. It wasn't just soldiering. He had keyed himself up to take on five men to protect Leria, knowing that he couldn't, leaving behind nothing to do with all that pent-up fury and violence, and his body was taking it out on him with this shameful weakness.

He spat sour vomit into the hay, and his trembling fingers accepted the water bag from her. He rinsed his mouth with the warm, tannic water. It usually tasted bad, but it was better than his own vomit.

It was a few moments before he could sit, and more before he could talk.

The riding off made sense—this was Neranahan, not Keranahan, and even Holtish nobility from another barony were not welcome to slaughter peasants as they pleased.

But why had Miron killed Sanders? Could it be that Sanders had refused to tell Miron whether or not he'd seen them? Kethol had hardly gotten to know Sanders well—Erenor might have a better understanding of the man—but he hardly seemed to be the sort suicidal enough to dismiss a noble's question with the wave of a hand or a coarse remark.

Leria ducked back into the shadows, and pulled on her man's tunic, quickly tying her own rucksack shut while she gestured at Kethol to do the same.

The scream had drawn people from the house and fields, and Erenor from the house. His hair was mussed, and his tunic unlaced, but he walked up to where the body lay and quickly took charge, sending one man running off down the path behind the house, a stocky woman scurrying back into the house.

He glanced up at where Kethol stood in the open doorway of the hayloft. "Kelleren," he said, "quickly saddle the horses. Master Sanders has been murdered by bandits, and we've got to go tell the village warden or the local lord. Quickly, now, before the murderers escape!"

By the time Kethol gathered his gear together, the peasant woman that Erenor had sent to the house returned with a soiled sheet; she and he managed to cover the body just as Sanders's oldest son, Vecten, rounded the side of the house, panting from the long run.

Erenor seized him by the shoulders before he could speak. "Your father was a brave and good man," he said. "I don't know why the bandits killed him, or what they're after, but quickly, quickly, you must gather all your people together here, at the house, where you can protect them. They rode off quickly, but they took no gold, no horses, nothing with them. They could be back at any moment for whatever it is that they came for."

The questionable logic of that might not have worked under normal circumstances, but Leria and Kethol forced the issue as they brought their mounts from the stable.

"Quickly, Kelleren," Erenor said, "gather our horses together, and we'll make for the safety of the village. We can report this mur-

der to the town warden, and the lord—the local lord—can have a
troop of good men on the murderers' tracks before nightfall."

As they cantered down the path toward the main road, Erenor muttered, "What just happened here?"

"It was Miron," Kethol said. "Miron killed Sanders, and then ran
off."

Erenor looked as puzzled as Kethol felt. "Why?"

"I don't know." Kethol shook his head. "I don't even have an
idea."

Erenor nodded knowingly. "Well, I should have figured that
out."

Under normal circumstances, that would have gotten Kethol angry enough to say or do something, but he still was trembling around
the edges.

Leria got the horses moving down the road, and then dropped
back to let Kethol and Erenor catch up with her. "So what do we
tell the village warden?" she asked.

Kethol didn't understand why Erenor laughed. It was a reasonable question.

"Nothing," Erenor said. "Because we don't stop in the village.
What we do is we get to Adahan as quickly as we can, and let them
run after or before us all the way to Biemestren, if that's their pleasure."

Kethol frowned. Erenor had changed, from an unwilling prisoner
compelled to come along, to an inadequate but convincing servant,
to an equal. And now, somehow, in some way that Kethol couldn't
quite put a finger on, Erenor had taken over. No, he couldn't get
Kethol to abandon Leria or anything of the sort, but it had become
natural for Kethol to follow his lead even when Erenor took charge
only implicitly.

He wondered why that didn't bother him.

"What is in Barony Adahan, then?" Leria asked. "You were so

set against it before—aren't you worried about treasure hunters after my supposed dowry?"

Erenor shook his head. For once, his easy smile was absent. "No. Or maybe yes, I am, but I'm more worried about what went on back there. I don't believe that Sanders was disrespectful to a noble, and I don't believe that Miron would have ridden off to escape pursuit from the local warden, or from a local lord that he could, at the very least, pay some sort of blood-price to." He looked over at Kethol. "You were a woodsman once. Did you ever try to herd your prey into a trap?"

Well, yes, he had beaten through the brush on more than one occasion, trying to spook a deer for a waiting hunter's shot.

But that didn't make any sense. If Miron had known they were there, he and his men could have taken the three of them right then and there. Why let them go?

Erenor shook his head in response to the unasked question. "I don't know. You play at bones, don't you?"

"Yes." And he played it well, at that.

"If your opponent left you an easy pinbone, just waiting to be pulled, and kept urging you toward it, would you take it?"

Kethol shrugged. "I'd at least look at the stack carefully."

Erenor nodded. "Well, the easy pinbone they're leaving us—the direction they're driving us—is Biemestren, by way of Barony Cullinane. What happens when we get there? Is there some charge laid against you to embarrass your baron? Are there bandits waiting in Barony Cullinane to, say, leave our lady raped and dead on Cullinane territory? Or perhaps a detachment of Keranahan soldiers who couldn't quite save her from you?" He threw up his hands. "No, none of that sounds likely, but we're being driven one way, and I don't for a moment think that's being done for our own benefit. I think we go another way. I think we head for Adahan itself, and trust the baron's men, as the best choice we have."

Two days. It would take two days, moving quickly, to make it to Adahan. "But it's only one more day to New Pittsburgh," Kethol said.

"You think that a steel plant is going to solve all of our problems?" Erenor shook his head.

Kethol let his smile show. "No. Not the steel plant. The telegraph."

Erenor touched his finger to his brow. "My apologies, Master Kethol," he said. "I thought you were just another idiot swordsman. You do have two thoughts to rub together, after all."

"I thank you, Master Erenor," Kethol said.

And if you're so clever, how come you didn't think of it first?

But he didn't say that. From the curious expression on Leria's face, and the way her smile met his gaze, he knew she'd asked herself exactly the same question.

22

Pirojil and Durine

Durine stopped suddenly. Pirojil froze. You wouldn't think a big man like that could move so quietly.

Of course, it was entirely possible that whatever noise Durine was really making was drowned out by the thumping of Pirojil's own heart. You'd think that after all these years Pirojil would be used to this, that creeping up on a house would be something he could take in stride, something that wouldn't put a steely, salty taste in his mouth, something that wouldn't make him long for a garderobe or even an outhouse where he could void his bowels.

Durine cocked his head to one side, then moved it fractionally, mechanically, like some bowman sweeping across a field of fire.

"Three," he said, his voice a low whisper that Pirojil more felt than heard. "At least. One's a baby."

Of course it was "at least." Even Durine couldn't hear the heartbeat of a silently sleeping man.

"Understood," Pirojil said. Their line of retreat had already been planned. There was a small thicket just down the road, with a time- and weather-hardened dirt path running alongside it. The brambles would cut and bite, but if you took a running start and launched yourself into the air, you could miss most of them, and the thorns themselves would discourage investigation, although probably not pursuit. There were two alternatives, in case that way was blocked.

The important point was to get in and get them down quickly, before they could raise an alarm. The nearest house was down past the road, at the other end of the communal plot, but it wasn't completely out of earshot, and a scream could carry on the cold night air.

They were almost there, almost in place to deal with the baroness.

The baronial residence was just over the hill and through the woods. All the peasants here were directly fealty-bound, working and living on baronial farmland in return for a portion of the crop.

It should be possible to work their way into the baronial Residence and get to the baroness without being spotted. But just after sundown wasn't the right time for that, and they needed some real rest.

After too many days in the woods, making their way back, they were hardly ready to take on a stealthy entry into the Residence. They were hardly ready to take on half their weight in local soldiers. It wasn't just that Pirojil and Durine both reeked like a pair of boars—but too many days of hiding out and trying to sleep during the day, only moving at night, had taken their toll. Every movement hurt, and while hunger had long since faded into a weak, desperate remnant of what it had been, just the idea of a warm bowl of stew was half worth killing for.

So Pirojil quietly drew his sword with one hand, snatched up his dagger with the other, and walked down the path to the single door of the thatched hut gently opening—smoothly, but not too fast—the door and stepping inside.

In the light of the open hearth, a young woman with an old face was reaching into a cradle to replace a sleeping child. Four other shapes lay huddled, sleeping, in a preposterously small bed, raised off the dirt floor by four stubby legs.

Pirojil was on her in two quick strides, his hand across her mouth.

"Quiet," he said, his voice a harsh whisper, "and nobody has to be killed."

The others were stirring, but Durine's harsh voice and looming form quieted them down. Peasants knew what they were to do if bandits invaded their home: cooperate, put up with the rapine, the robbery, and the beating, give over all you had, and you'd probably be allowed to live.

The logical thing to do was to act like bandits, to give these peasants no reason to think them anything else . . .

Pirojil had done some things in his life that he regretted, some of them bloody, but he had never raped a woman—and he was not about to start by doing it in front of her children, or molest a young girl in front of her parents and brothers.

"We need food, and we need rest," he said quietly. "We need to stay here for a couple of days, eating and sleeping." They would sleep in shifts, of course, with the family well secured. "Then we'll be on our way, and leave behind this."

He held up a single gold coin.

The baby started crying.

Moving slowly, nodding, the young woman with the old face lifted it up out of the cradle, and, at Pirojil's nod of permission, brought it to her breast. "We'll be no trouble to you," she said. "We'll be no trouble at all."

23

✠ The Baroness and the Proctor

Governor Treseen is here, Baroness," the servant girl said quietly, her head lowered.

Elanee, fresh and naked from her bath, looked up in irritation, then put a neutral expression on her face. "I'm delighted, of course," she lied. "Please see to his refreshment, and make him comfortable. I'll be down shortly."

What was it with this man and her bath? She could hardly dip her little foot into some heated water when Treseen, unsummoned, would be at her doorstep with some new problem or complaint. Did he have a spy waiting outside the residence, galloping for town the moment the large copper kettle that heated her bathwater was fired up?

Outside her window, the sky was dark and cloudy; a storm was coming. Despite that, her riding clothes had been set out, it had been too many days since she had made the trip out to the cave, and letting that go too long was a bad idea. It might find itself more attached to its guards than to her, and that wouldn't be good at all.

Well, she would have to go riding this afternoon, come what may, but first she would have to dispose of Treseen. She smiled to herself. No, not that way. But it was tempting at times.

She shook her head as she padded across the floor to her closet.

Treseen was pacing back and forth in the great hall when Elanee joined him.

Details were important. She had dressed casually, in a long skirt and blouse, but not too informally. Details were, as she had tried to teach Miron, everything.

"Good day to you, Governor," she said. "And what horrific event brings you out here, all perturbed?"

"There've been a whole series of messages from Biemestren," he said, pulling a handful of papers from his pouch. "And there's something very wrong going on there."

She waved him to a seat as she accepted the papers and sat herself down to read, ignoring him for the moment.

Treseen, thorough to a fault, had apparently brought every scrap of message that had come over the telegraph and by messenger over the past few tendays. Most of it was trivial—notes of taxes received and due; news of some banditry here and some orc attack there; some reports of rumblings along the borders of Nyphien and Kiar that were probably just cross-border banditry but could be a subtle test; a quick listing of promotions in the Home Guard, as though that was of interest to the entire empire—but she finally got to the message from the chamberlain that the emperor had appointed Walter Slovotsky as something to be called an imperial proctor.

Now, that was interesting. And quite promising, actually, given the situation.

"He's a proctor, you say," she said, relishing the word. "There were prince's proctors in the old Euar'den days, you know, Governor."

Originally they had been merely high-ranking messengers of the Euar'den princes, but when the blood of the Euar'dens thinned, all too many of them became the real rulers behind the throne.

Had the blood of the Furnaels thinned so within a generation that the emperor needed another hand at his plow? Unlikely.

"I'm afraid I don't see what you are so"—she didn't want to say "worried," even though he clearly was—"concerned about, Governor?"

"Walter Slovotsky was the one whom the dowager empress wanted to send to look into the . . . matter of Lady Leria. Now, suddenly, he's an imperial proctor, and you don't see the problem?"

Her lips tightened. She didn't care for his tone. "No, Governor, I do not see the problem. We handed over the lady to those three smelly soldiers, as the Cullinane regent and the dowager empress herself requested, and they're off to the capital."

It wasn't like Leria knew anything important; Elanee had kept *it* completely isolated.

It was just a matter of timing, and Elanee's timing was exquisite.

Treseen leafed through the sheets. "It's not in here," he said. "But it's all over the barony—there's talk of some lady being conducted to Biemestren with a huge dowry."

She spread her hands. "The land that the lady will inherit is rather large, isn't it? And if I recall correctly," which of course she did, "a company of dwarves has taken up residence in the Ulter Hills—with your permission, Governor?"

"Yes, yes, yes," he said. "But—"

"And where dwarves dig, wealth often follows, doesn't it? So she may well come to the marriage bed with a fine dowry, indeed."

Right now, of course, the governor was collecting the taxes on Leria's inheritance. Elanee was quite sure that a piece of gold, here and there, had managed to stick to Treseen's nail-bitten fingers.

But what of that? The emperor wasn't going to name an imperial proctor to go punish some slightly greedy governor for a light bit of graft.

She could hardly say that to him, though.

And, besides, this all boded very well.

Imperial proctor, eh? Either those three awful soldiers would not have arrived back at the capital, or they would have arrived with too many questions unanswered. The only thing that had to be avoided was Miron interfering with their getting there, and her son was smart enough to be able to chase them without quite catching them, contrary though that went to his instincts in other areas.

So three soldiers and an empty-headed girl would arrive in Biemestren, telling tales of strange goings-on, of being chased by rumors, of attempts to prevent them from reaching the capital that they had, heroically no doubt, just managed to thwart.

Perhaps the emperor would be sending his newly made imperial proctor to investigate the strange things happening in Keranahan.

He would have to send somebody.

Would the emperor send a detachment of the House Guard thundering down the road across the baronies, accompanying his newly named imperial proctor, just to investigate something a bit amiss?

Perhaps.

And what would a bunch of soldiers find? Nothing overt. No sign of a barony about to rise in revolt. Yes, Elanee's own House Guard was larger than common, but not large enough to endanger anybody or anything—just large enough to help protect her people from bandits.

But no, the emperor would not send a troop of soldiers tromping down roads and spreading worry and panic.

He would send the dragon, Ellegon. Which was just what Elanee wanted. With or without this imperial proctor, she wanted the dragon here.

She had always had this ability to charm, and it had not only made her a good horsewoman, able to ride the most recalcitrant steed, but it had brought her a baron as a husband, a governor as a devoted retainer, and the loyalty of *it*. No, she was sure that she couldn't control the mind of the dragon Ellegon for long. But she didn't need to control it for long. She really didn't need to control it at all. She just needed to charm it for a few moments. Just as a distraction, while her men put dragonbaned bolts into its scaly hide and left it dead on the ground.

It was like gardening, really. You nurtured your plants—whether they were bushes of roses or clumps of leafy dragonbane—by giving them just enough light, just enough water, just enough manure to encourage them to grow. And then you trimmed here and cut there.

Until you were ready to harvest.

She spent a few more minutes charming, then dismissing the governor. It wouldn't do at all to seem to be in too much of a rush.

Her riding clothes were still laid out.

Normally, she would have chided the maid for that, but this time it was just as well. Elanee didn't see the need to strain her wrist in beating the girl, or her tongue in lashing her, either.

The storm had been threatening to break all afternoon; it finally carried out its threat when Elanee and her guards were within sight of the cave and the corral in front of it.

Above, lightning flashed and thunder roared, sending one of the guards' horses into such a panic that it threw its rider and galloped off.

Elanee's own mount, of course, remained steady between her thighs, and she guided it down the twisting road toward where the cave opened on the hillside, her guards trailing after her.

She left her horse outside—her men would unsaddle it and bring her leather inside—and shook her head briskly to clear the water from her eyes. Her teeth chattered with cold, but—

I can warm you, sounded in her mind.

She smiled. Yes, it could warm her, in more ways than one.

But I'm hungry.

Be still, she thought, firmly but lovingly. *I've come to feed you, of course.* Yes, there were still several decrepit old animals out in the paddock, waiting their turn to become food, but perhaps it would appreciate a fresher animal. Like the one that had bolted underneath one of her guards.

I'll always take care of you, she thought, every fiber of her being radiating sincerity. It made it no easier that she *was* sincere this time, but it made it no more difficult, either. *I won't let those mean creatures hurt you.*

Light flared down the tunnel, and a wave of pleasant heat washed over her.

❖   ❖   ❖

The telegraph stopped its chattering as Walter Slovotsky reached the top of the stone steps.

Which was just as well, as far as Slovotsky was concerned. He knew Morse, he could follow Morse, but it was a distracting sound. He couldn't keep up a conversation and follow it, but he couldn't totally ignore it, either.

Moderation sometimes sucked.

The engineer on duty was a woman Slovotsky didn't recognize. Dumpy-looking, but he gave her the benefit of his smile anyway. There was, after all, no need to deprive her of that.

She returned it with interest. "Greetings, Imperial Proctor," she said, sliding a folded piece of paper to him. "And a good morning to you."

"For me?" He had a name, after all, and the mark on the paper was some symbol he didn't recognize.

"Well, no," she said. "It's for Captain Derinald, but the general said that anything coming in for him should go to you first."

Which was fair enough, given that Walter had sent Derinald and a troop of cavalry to convey his family to Biemestren. He would have preferred to go himself, but there was a confrontation in the offing with Beralyn, and he figured that he really ought to be around for it rather than let Thomen take the heat.

Besides, maybe he could make peace with the old biddy.

Right.

Fat fucking chance.

"Well." He smiled. "That sounds fine. Besides, it's not up to the general. I'm the imperial proctor. Anything the emperor doesn't say doesn't go to me, I can have."

She took a moment to parse that, then shrugged. "Your choice, sir." She leaned against the counter. "If you want copies of everything that comes through here, I've no objection. But you're going to have to get me a team of scribes to copy it all, as I can barely keep up with the traffic as it is." She jerked a thumb at her desk. "I don't mind that the empire flows on a river of paper, but it feels like the whole river dumps out right here."

As if on cue, the telegraph sitting on her desk started up chattering again, and she turned to answer it. "But you'd probably better look at this one soon. It's from one of the Cullinane men. Kethol."

Cullinane? There was no telegraph station at Castle Cullinane. Eventually, of course, all the baronial capitals would be wired, and the larger towns and villages, as well. But miles and miles and miles of telegraph wire took maintenance, and right now most of the lines ran along the major roads into occupied Holtun, where the occupation troops could at least note where the lines went down.

He opened the paper and read quickly. New Pittsburgh, eh? How had Kethol and the others gotten themselves over there? And why?

Oh, really.

Very strange, indeed.

Hmmm . . . maybe there was a way to use this to advantage, and even win a few points with that soured old Beralyn.

She received him in the throne room, alone. He wasn't sure if that was a good sign or not. Well, it was a better sign than her meeting him with a bunch of soldiers pointing swords, bows, flintlock rifles, and pistols at him would have been, but he wasn't sure how much.

The years had taken an unattractive old woman and made her downright ugly. She reminded him vaguely of a cross between Elsa Lanchester and Winston Churchill. There was something about the droop of her frown that accentuated the bagginess under her eyes and chin. Her hands, knobby-knuckled with age, lay folded in her lap.

"Good afternoon, my Lord Imperial Proctor," she said, the sarcasm only in a vague undertone. "You have asked to see me."

"Yes, I did," he said.

"You're seeing me."

"I'd like to make a peace between us."

"Of course," she said, her voice caustic in its casualness. "Nothing could be easier, Proctor."

"You'll need to see this." He took a step toward her, Kethol's message held out in his hand.

She waved it away. "I've never learned this Englits of yours," she said. "To read or to understand. Why don't you read it for me, if you think it's important."

She hadn't taken much of a look at it if she hadn't noticed that it was written in Erendra, and not in English, but maybe that was her strange way of offering an olive branch?

Probably not.

"Well," he said, "it seems that there is, or was, something strange going on in Keranahan. Somebody expended a lot of effort either to make it impossible for Kethol, Pirojil, and Durine to bring this Lady Leria here, or to make it seem like it was supposed to be impossible."

Wheels within wheels, and it was only because Kethol and the others were as good as they were that they had survived. It was fairly crafty of her to make this a Cullinane problem. He had no doubt that Beralyn was responsible for putting the hounds on their tail, and it was entirely possible that an imperial proctor, with a bit of digging, could find out how she had done that.

So he wouldn't. But there was no need to tell her that.

Thomen was her son, but sending men out to get killed merely to embarrass somebody, well, that was a bit much. She was already jealous of the way Walter and the Cullinanes had the emperor's ear— with some work, this could relegate her to the status of a crazy old woman whose son would tolerate her, but that was all.

Maybe. Did she want him to find out? Or did she just want to close the books on this?

"So you admit I was right?" She nodded. "It sounds to me like there's something, something seriously wrong, going on in Keranahan, and the girl was just part of it." She dismissed her original claim, that this was all about Leria, with a convenient wave of her hand.

What it sounded like to Walter was that Beralyn had reasons to make herself look good at Cullinane expense, while Baroness Elanee had every reason to want to force a young noblewoman into a marriage that would enrich her own family.

But he shrugged. *I'll let you be right, old lady, if you'll let me just be wrong.*

He'd want to get over there, anyway. Durine and Pirojil were liable to make a whole lot of trouble, and when this just turned out to be some political maneuvering by two noblewomen with more ambition than sense, that could make things sticky. As in the stickiness of newly shed blood.

How best to find them? They would be making every effort to avoid leaving tracks.

I think that can be managed. Flame roared outside. *Castle Keranahan, here we come, eh?*

Walter Slovotsky smiled. The last time he had ridden on the dragon's back was to sneak into Castle Biemestren, with Ellegon standing by to haul them out if things got sticky; the time before that, it was in fear that he would arrive at Castle Cullinane to find his family dead.

This time, they'd drop in unannounced at Keranahan.

Probably best to pick up Kethol in New Pittsburgh. And, besides, maybe this Lady Leria was easy on the eyes.

But in a day or two, they could drop out of the bright blue Keranahan sky unannounced and unexpected, which should shock the locals, and it sounded like a little shock would be good for this Baroness Elanee. He could make a few vaguely threatening comments, suitable for an imperial proctor to get a Holtish baroness to remember her position—and with Ellegon flying overhead, the point would be made quite easily—then they could drop in and suggest to the governor that even simple soldiers on imperial duty were to receive help, not hindrance, and let Ellegon give a light show at night that would draw the attention of Pirojil and Durine.

And then home.

Neat, sweet, and complete.

After what I've been through lately, this kind of sounds like fun.

"You admit that I was right? That this was something you should have gone to look at in the first place?"

No. Not at all, he thought. "Absolutely, Beralyn," he said.

"Very well, then." She seemed satisfied, and the temperature in the room didn't seem quite so cold. "And you intend to have words with her?"

"Better than words," he said. "I think you need a noble attendant for your own companionship, Beralyn." A year or so visiting in the capital ought to give Beralyn somebody to watch, and with Beralyn watching Elanee, and Elanee looking for some advantage, both of them would be too busy to make trouble for anybody else.

This is going to be easy, he thought. *For a change. So what am I missing?*

Oh, you humans. You have to make everything difficult for your-selves.

Not me.

Walter Slovotsky smiled.

I like it when it's easy.

24

✠ New Pittsburgh

ait, the message had said.

So Kethol waited where he had been told to. That was the way it was when you were a soldier. Durine and Pirojil were out there, in danger, ready to take on a barony all by themselves and get killed in the process, but . . .

Wait, the message had said. He had been told to wait, so he waited.

Despite her appearance, Leria's arrival had been greeted by the majordomo of Bren Adahan's New Pittsburgh home with ill-concealed, almost indecent glee. By local standards, it was a smallish house—there were many minor lords and even more high-ranking engineers with much larger homes—but it was nicely situated near the top of a hill to the west of the steel plants, and it was only rarely that the smoke blew up the hill.

"The truth is, Lady," old Narta said as she guided them up the narrow staircase to the second floor, "that the baron spends little enough time here, and it's hard to keep a house as a going concern when there's nobody to take care of, *even* with such a small staff."

Erenor gave Kethol a knowing glance, and Kethol just shook his head. He'd never get used to nobility. The house had a staff of at least twelve, and not one of them without gray hair. Adahan apparently used this as a place to pension off some of his old retainers, at least until they became too old and feeble to work, and who spent most of their time taking care of themselves.

But they never knew when the baron or one of his guesting

nobles would be in residence, so the larder was presumably well stocked, and of a certainty the tantalizing smell of fresh-baked bread filled the air. The room Leria was shown to was bright and clean, the stone walls freshly whitewashed, with a maid's room off it. A maid who must have been even older than Narta was emerging from that maid's room, bearing pillows and sheets and blankets for the large bed near the far wall.

"A bath's being heated for the lady right now," Narta said, "and we've a dress or two in storage that I can fit to you, so you'll be presentable."

"Presentable?" Leria raised an eyebrow.

"Lord Davin and Lady Deneria have invited you to join them for dinner this evening." Narta's grin revealed several missing teeth, although the remaining teeth were less yellowed than Kethol expected. "It's not often there's nobility from Keranahan guesting here. I'm sure some of the young lordlings and ladies will be gathered to meet you and hear all about your . . . adventures. Things have been quiet here of late, since those awful things stopping streaming out of Faerie."

Kethol opened the shutters of the nearest window and ran a quick eye and hand over the bars, which seemed secure enough.

Narta gave a derisive sniff. "Yes, there's crime enough in the city, but I think you'll find that even thieves know to give the baron's home a wide berth."

Kethol didn't say anything as he closed the shutters, although it wasn't thieves he was worried about. Erenor was sure that Miron was off somewhere, trying to herd them in another direction, but Erenor was always sure about everything. It was one of the wizard's annoying habits. Even though he was right, most often.

In any case, the room should be safe enough.

But this dinner . . .

Narta raised a hand to forestall his objection. "We've already had our orders. She'll be escorted to and from dinner by a company of the baron's troops, and they'll be taking up station outside the house." She sniffed again. Kethol was beginning to dislike that sniff.

"Not that there'll be any trouble here."

Narta ushered Erenor and Kethol outside, and closed the door. "Now, if you'll leave the lady to her bath, I'll show you to your quarters." She grinned. "You'll find your beds comfortable, your food warm, and your beer cold. And," she added with a sniff, "you can use the bath in our quarters to wash yourselves, and I'll find something more . . . something for you to wear, as well."

Kethol didn't argue. It would be good to be clean. And there was no reason to deny Leria the company of her kind this evening. If she wouldn't be safe while guarded by baronial troops, Kethol could hardly make a difference.

It was well after midnight when Kethol met the officer of the guard at the door. In the lantern light he looked too young to be a captain, but he not only wore officer's livery embroidered with the Adahan pattern, he also wore a sword rather than the pikes his men carried.

Pikes would become a thing of the past eventually. Right now, only some troops of the Home Guard carried rifles, but eventually that would change. A change for the better? Probably. You could teach a recruit how to use a crossbow faster than a longbow, and you could train him in the use of a rifle faster than a crossbow.

But Kethol could still put a score of arrows into a man while he was trying to reload a rifle. He would be a useless relic someday, if he survived, but he still had some value now. Yes, there was something to be said for pistols, but for close-up work, Kethol would have bet the young officer would still reach for the sword at his waist even if he'd had a brace of pistols there, as well.

"You're Captain Kethol?" the too-young officer said, coming to attention.

Kethol looked down at himself. Captain? Well, freshly washed, beard trimmed, wearing a fresh pair of black linen trousers and a blousy white shirt fastened at the neck with a silver clasp, he might have looked more like an officer than an ordinary soldier, at that.

He didn't correct the Holt. As far as Kethol was concerned, a regular soldier in the service of Barony Cullinane outranked any officer in Barony Adahan, despite what protocol said. "I'm Kethol."

"We'll be on station, sir," the officer said. "I don't think you'll have any trouble tonight."

"I wouldn't think so," Kethol said, nodding sagely, the way an officer was supposed to. "A fine-looking troop of men you have there," he added. That was an officer sort of thing to say.

It apparently was also the right thing to say; the officer snapped to, then turned about and gestured, and Leria was helped down out of the coach by a waiting soldier, and quickly ran up the path.

Her hair had been done up in some sort of complicated knot that left her neck bare, and the creamy linen dress Narta had found for her clung tightly, emphasizing the swell at hip and breast, as though it had been made for her.

Very different from the dirty-faced woman in Kethol's spare tunic who had ridden into New Pittsburgh this morning.

She waited for him at the top of the stairs. "Well, Kethol, don't you want to hear about it?"

He couldn't say no, although there was nothing he wanted to hear about. That was her world, not his, and she was going back to it.

Well, that was probably all for the best.

"Of course," he said.

Erenor had smiled knowingly and had taken a clay bottle of wine to bed with him earlier, but Kethol slept across her doorway, his head pillowed on a folded blanket. She was probably safe here now, and anybody stealthy enough to get past the guards outside would surely be able to murder him in his sleep.

But he slept across her doorway anyway.

It felt right.

✧   ✧   ✧

She came to him in his dreams. The door opened inward slowly, silently, and she stood there, all naked and lovely under a filmy nightdress. He rose without a word, and she took his hand and led him inside, her nightdress falling away in the red light of the overhead lamp. He started to speak, but she put a finger to his lips and shook her head.

He woke in the early morning light, the door to her room still closed. For a moment, he wondered if it had all been a dream, and it probably was, but —

And then Walter Slovotsky was knocking and bellowing at the door downstairs, and all dreams were driven away.

25

✠ Geraden

The dragon banked sharply, high above Dereneyl, flame gushing forth from its wide jaws like blood from an artery. It stank of sulfur, and it was all Kethol could do not to vomit.

Again.

Below, Kethol was sure, people were staring up at the skies, reminded once again of Ellegon's power.

Hey, if you can scare them, you usually don't have to kill them.

Erenor, on the other hand, was strapped in next to Walter Slovotsky at the foremost position, just behind where the dragon's long neck joined to its huge body. And he was having the time of his life, enjoying every minute of soaring above the common ruck, craning his neck to spot this village and that settlement, probably reflecting over having swindled a peasant *here* and defrauded a merchant *there*, or deceived a noble *here* and *there* and *there*.

Kethol didn't like it, but the altitude did have its advantages. Up here, the air was cleaner, and it didn't stink up here so badly. Normally. He wiped his mouth on the back of his sleeve. The wind rushing past his face drew tears from his eyes, pulled them into his ears.

It was almost over. The imperial proctor had ordered out a troop of Home Guards to escort Leria from New Pittsburgh to Biemestren; she would be safe in Baron Adahan's house until they arrived, and safe on the road to the capital.

And then? That was up to the dowager empress, most likely. Parliament was meeting soon, and there would be plenty of young lords and lordlings eager to make her acquaintance. If the dowager empress didn't marry her off to a scion of a neighboring noble family to consolidate her lands, perhaps she would find Leria a second son to marry, one to give her children and manage her lands.

Without any further problems from Elanee.

They would settle that here.

The dowager empress wanted her as an attendant and companion in Biemestren, and attend her she would. Let the two of them scheme against each other in the capital, under the imperial proctor's watchful eye. It was one thing to wish to increase the baronial lands by encouraging a marriage between Leria and Miron; it was another thing to try to force the girl into it, and yet another to interfere with soldiers on imperial business.

And all the trouble she had put Kethol and Durine and Pirojil and Erenor to? She had tried to get them killed, that was all.

Well, that didn't matter. Just some imperial politics that Walter Slovotsky could dismiss with a wave of his hand.

°And what would you have him do? Put the baroness to death for something he couldn't prove? You don't hold an empire together by wantonly slaughtering off nobility. Makes the other nobles nervous, in the wrong way.°

That was probably so, but the politics of it didn't matter to Kethol.

It was wrong for Elanee to have tried to force Leria into a marriage to Miron, and it was worse that she'd tried to have them all killed—while keeping her own hands clean—when they tried to take her to Biemestren.

°Yes, that's all true. She's a horrible person, not suitable to govern a barony, and she's raised her son the same way. Why do you think Keranahan is still under imperial control?°

So what would be her punishment? A year in Biemestren, waiting on Beralyn. Was that just?

°Well, now, that might turn out to be punishment enough. But if not, well, so be it. You don't think politically, that's the problem.°

It wasn't Kethol's job to think politically. It was Kethol's job to go where he was told and do what he was told, and that usually meant to fight somebody. He understood how to do that . . .

And how to stash away every piece of gold you can for your old age. Which is fair enough. The dragon's wings slowed, and it leaned forward into a long glide. What had taken days and days on foot and horseback was just a matter of moments of flight.

Ellegon came in fast into the clearing, braking to a bumpy landing with a frantic pinioning of huge, leathery wings.

Kethol clawed at the straps that held him in place on the dragon's back, but was the third down: Walter Slovotsky, through greater familiarity, and Erenor, through greater dexterity, had managed to get out of their harnesses, retrieve their gear, and slide down the dragon's side to the waist-high grass before Kethol was fully unhooked.

A little faster, if you please.

Kethol didn't blame the dragon for being nervous. Ever since strange things had started to flow out of Faerie, the cultivation of dragonbane had become more common in the Eren regions, and three pale spots on the dragon's scaly hide spoke of the damage that the extract of that leafy plant could do to magical creatures.

But in a matter of moments, Kethol was beside the other two, and the dragon leaped into the air, wings beating hard as it climbed in a tight circle into the blue sky.

Walter Slovotsky grinned as a long trail of flame flared, high above the trees. "Always good to remind people who's who and what's what, eh?" He shouldered his rucksack and led the way.

The guards were apparently keeping more of a watchful eye this time than the last time Kethol had been here; before they were more than a dozen steps over the crest of the hill, a mounted detachment of six spearmen were cantering their way from the barracks.

"Saddled and ready to ride at a moment's notice, eh?" Walter Slovotsky said. "Thoroughly endeavoring not to be surprised."

Erenor's brow furrowed. "Eh?"

Slovotsky waved it away. "Never mind." He glanced up pointedly. High above, Ellegon was circling.

Ellegon? Kethol thought. But there was no answer in his mind. He had never tried to mindspeak with the dragon from this far away, although he knew that some could. On the other hand, the dragon was there, and the lancers knew it was there, and what wasn't going to happen was that the three of them would be quietly murdered and buried in unmarked graves.

"You worry too much," Walter Slovotsky said as the leader of the lancers signaled for a halt a short bowshot away. "Greetings," he said, raising a palm. "My name is Walter Slovotsky; you may have heard it. I'm here as the imperial proctor, to see the Baroness Elanee."

The leader of the detachment was the same one who had greeted Kethol before; he was an ugly man with a weak chin and large ears. "My name is Thirien. I suppose you have a warrant from the emperor."

Kethol stifled a chuckle. This one couldn't read; what good would a warrant do him?

Slovotsky jerked a thumb skyward. "Yes, and I have a dragon flying overhead. Figure it out, clever one. I'm from Biemestren, with a soldier you've seen before, and I rode over on Ellegon. Do I get to see the baroness now?"

Thirien shook his head. "You can wait for her. She's out for her afternoon ride."

"You saw her leave?"

"Yes, sir, I did," he said, as though daring to be called a liar.

"All by herself, eh?"

"No." The soldier shrugged. "She has a detachment of guards with her. As is appropriate, sir."

"Then they shouldn't be terribly hard to follow. We'll take all of your horses, except yours. You can guide us. Dismount. Now, please."

❀   ❀   ❀

Elanee had saddled and left for her ride quickly, but unhurriedly, when Ellegon's flame flashed over Dereneyl, hoping that she would be followed but not relying on it. There were easier ways this could be done, but it was best to do it quickly, and have it over with. There would be time to sit down and write the emperor a long letter about the new arrangements there would have to be, and much better to gloat after it was all done.

It was just a matter of time, really. She would wait for them at the cave, and they would come after her. If Thirien had persuaded them to wait for her—not that she had much faith in Thirien's powers of persuasion—they would eventually tire of that and come looking.

And, if not, it would be over all the sooner.

She led the goat into the cave.

Just a goat?

Now, now, she thought, *I know you're hungry. You're always hungry. But you don't want a full stomach now. The bad people are coming to hurt us. And you have to be ready.*

I'm ready, Elanee. The mental voice was sure, the way a child's always was.

Well, Elanee wasn't a child, and she was ready.

At the last bend in the tunnel, the goat sniffed the air, and pulled back, hard, on the rope, but Elanee patted it on the head and smiled down at it, beaming a wave of love and reassurance, and it looked up at her with warm brown eyes and stopped pulling, trotting obediently around the bend, its hooves clickety-clickety-clicking on stone.

The chamber was as large as her own great hall, and that's probably what the dwarves had used it for, although it was hard to say; the Euar'den had driven them out ages ago, and even dwarven warrens required some maintenance. Over the centuries, the outer wall had cracked, and a narrow, ragged band of light leaked in from the outside.

And lying in the middle of the chamber was *it*.

The dragon sniffed. °I have a name, you know.°

Of course you do, my darling Geraden.

It was a huge beast, easily five times the size of a dray horse, its scales dark brown, edged in green. Wings curled and uncurled in impatience as it eyed the goat.

But it didn't make a move to rise from where it lay, its legs tucked underneath its body, as though it was trying to conceal the way the left foreleg ended in a stump.

Elanee had let her attention lag, and the goat panicked, its hooves skittering comically on the smooth stone as it tried to gain purchase for a quick break to daylight, freedom, and survival.

But Geraden was too quick for it. Its saurian head snaked out and caught the goat around the shoulders, bones crunching between strong jaws as it lifted the twitching animal high in the air, then swallowed it quickly, in two bites. A yellow snake of entrails hung from the side of Geraden's jaw; the dragon tried to chew at it, but couldn't quite get it.

Elanee walked up and pulled the bloody scrap of intestine from its teeth, ignoring the stench of its breath. She didn't mind getting her hands dirty—cleaning off dirt was, after all, a secondary function of the bath—but she hated bad smells.

°Like the smell of that bad man who shot me with that burning arrow?°

Yes, she thought. *Like the smell of that one.* She patted at its stump. *Yes, he was a very bad man. They all were. Men, that is. Look into their souls and you'll see that, Geraden.*

The dragon looked at her with wet, loving eyes the size of dinner plates. °But you won't let them hurt me again.°

Of course not. That's why I've hidden you here so long, letting you rest and gain your strength.

Verinel had been a terrific archer, and his dragonbaned arrow had brought Geraden tumbling out of the sky. No matter that Geraden, blown out from Faerie like a soap bubble taking form and substance, had been in full stoop, ready to snatch a rider and horse, even if one of the riders was a baroness on her afternoon ride—

I'm sorry. I didn't know you then.

I know, my darling.

She stroked at the stump. On the ground, Geraden would limp, but the few times she had dared let him fly—only at night, and only on stormy nights at that, where a burst of flame might be mistaken for lightning—he had been fine in the air, swift and sure, not lumbering through the sky like that horrible Ellegon, that beast that kept the Cullinanes and Furnaels and their stinking minions in power.

I won't let him hurt you, Elanee. I promise.

He's coming for me, you know, she thought, letting some of the real fear she felt show through. *He hates me because of you. He wants to be the only dragon in the Eren regions, and let the bad men ride high above the clouds, swooping down when they want to hurt me.*

Geraden's mental voice was sure. *I can stop him,* the dragon said. *And then I'll be the only one.*

Perhaps or perhaps not. Many strange things had leaked out before the breach between Faerie and reality had been sealed. The orcs, for one. And there were tales of serpents in the Cirric, and of creatures living high on mountain peaks, away from man. Men and magical creatures didn't get along. Men didn't get along with anybody, be it other men or women.

But for now, he would be the only one.

And the emperor would have to meet her terms, unless he wanted his empire to fall apart in bloody chunks. Maybe the irreplaceable loss of Ellegon alone wouldn't start the avalanche that would tear the empire apart—but would Thomen want to risk it?

He would meet her terms. They all would. The Cullinanes and Furnaels had seized power with bloody hands, and they could hardly protest sharing it with Elanee's cleaner ones, now, could they?

She was not a young woman anymore, but she could still bear children, even if she might need a little help from the Spider or an

Eareven witch to conceive and bring to term. It would be a bit . . . much to ask Thomen Furnael to adopt Miron as his heir, but she could bear him another son.

And Miron could still marry Leria, and consolidate their lands.

It would be nice to give him something to play with.

I can hear horses, Geraden said.

Shh. Hide your thoughts, she thought sternly. *Be still as a rock. No, better, be the rock. Don't let any of them hear you until it's too late.*

An old oaken chest lay under the crack in the outer wall, and next to it an even stack of long wooden poles. She opened the chest, and removed the stone crock that lay within it, setting it down very carefully on the floor before she pried open the waxed lid with her fingernails, too eager to reach for the knife that lay on the floor next to the spears.

Eagerly, hungrily, she took up a spear and coated the head of it with the tarry sludge. Boiling down the dragonbane had been easy, although Geraden had had a moment of panic when the wind outside the cave had changed, bringing the scent to his nostrils, poor dear. But she had reassured him.

The dragonbane wasn't for him, after all.

The trick had been to get the extract thick and gooey enough, and she had finally resorted to pouring most of a jugful of honey into the vat, cooking it down until what was left was a thick, sweet, deadly tar.

It wouldn't do to have the wind whip droplets of it back into Geraden's face. She coated the spear thickly, a full arm length back from the point, and then wrapped the head of the spear in a sheet of leather, binding it tightly with three thongs, like a cook preparing a roast. The force of the point being driven into Ellegon's hide would tear the wrapping loose and smear the poison along a channel as deep as Geraden could gouge.

And Geraden would gouge deeply indeed.

It's time, she thought.

Obediently, Geraden rose, limping over on his three good legs to gingerly take the spear in his mouth.

Don't worry, Elanee. I won't let them hurt you, the dragon said as it limped its way down the passage toward daylight.

Of course you won't. I am relying on you, my dearest darling.

26

Death of a Dragon

He should have made it one of Slovotsky's Laws years before. "It always takes a lot of time to make things go right, but they can go all to hell in a heartbeat."

Walter Slovotsky kicked his heels against the beefy side of his borrowed horse, following Thirien up the steep trail to where the forest broke on daylight.

Below, a dark-mouthed tunnel opened at the base of the far hill, near where a half-dozen men sat around a rough corral filled with horses. Either it had been too long since Walter had spent time around dwarves—he liked the Moderate People, as long as they didn't insist that he share their moderation—or that was awfully large for a dwarven tunnel.

Still, it was possible. And if not an entry to dwarven warrens, then what was it? Kethol had relayed Durine's description, and Walter's first guess was a mine, although not a modern one. One just didn't make mine shafts larger than necessary. A larger tunnel called for more bracing, and was more likely to collapse than a smaller one. You did want to make it large enough so that you could pull a large cart out through it—no matter what you were mining, you'd find it necessary to haul away a large quantity of rocks—but enlarging it beyond necessity quickly ran into the law of diminishing returns, and—

A dragon limped its way out into the sunlight, a spear clenched in its mouth.

Holy mother of shit.

Thirien grabbed his dagger from his belt and lunged for Kethol, while Erenor just sat openmouthed at the sight of the dragon.

Slovotsky already had a throwing knife in his hand, and while his throw went wide and caught Thirien's horse in the withers instead of Thirien himself, that sent the horse bucking, tossing Thirien into Kethol, knocking both of them to the ground.

Ellegon?

The dragon didn't answer; he was either too high or distracted. As who wouldn't be?

There was still talk of the occasional dragon still surviving in elven lands and the Waste, and there was, of course, The Dragon, once again sleeping at the Gate Between Worlds, but dragons were mostly gone from the Eren regions, the Middle Lands in particular. That was one of the reasons that Ellegon was so valuable an ally: it wasn't just that he was powerful, but that he was unique.

But another dragon, here, its dinner-plate-sized eyes blinking in the sunlight?

Things seemed to move slowly, the way they often did when it all hit the fan.

You could spend as much time as you wanted figuring things out, the whole fucking universe could be laid out in front of you, clear as a bell, ripe for the plucking, but you were just as trapped in the slow time as everybody else was, and you could no more escape from it than they could.

They had been had.

The whole thing wasn't some minor play for additional lands for the baroness's son to inherit, and it wasn't some typical backstreet noble politics, even though that could end up with a knife through somebody's throat as easily as not. Walter was barely egotistical enough to think that he was part of the prey that the baroness wanted, but no, he wasn't the target of all this.

It was Ellegon.

Ellegon would land to greet the other dragon—no, he wouldn't. Ellegon had been caught once, and he wouldn't simply fly into a trap. He would wait for the other dragon to rise in flight—

—which meant that that spear in its mouth was coated with dragonbane, and for whatever reason, it was going to kill Ellegon.

It was clear, it was obvious, and if he could have moved quickly enough, he could have done—what?

Ellegon, get out of here, he thought, as hard as he could, trying to shout with his mind. That, at least, made sense—no matter what the game was, it had to be right to get the most valuable piece off the board.

Now.

But there was no answer from the dragon, wheeling itself high across the sky.

His mind was racing, fast, out of control, but he was stuck in this slow time like everybody else was, where Erenor sat stupid on his horse and Kethol and Thirien rolled around the ground, each with his hand on the other's knife arm, as though they were trying to mirror each other.

That was when the rockslide started.

It had taken Pirojil and Durine most of the afternoon to work their way around to the crest of the hill over the cave mouth. It would have been nice to have Kethol around—he had a way of finding a path through woods where there really wasn't one.

But they didn't have Kethol, and they didn't have any paths to follow, and by noon they were well scratched up, as well as tired and sore.

It could have been worse. A couple of days of rest and food had made the two of them half-human again. Not well, not rested, not comfortable nor relaxed, but functional, and that would have to do.

They wouldn't have to watch their back trail closely, although they would; Vester and his family would hardly be carrying tales, not after having put them up for all that time.

Not that it would make a difference soon. The baroness had tried to have not just them killed—that was bad enough—but Leria, as well.

And that was simply not acceptable.

Pirojil shook his head. This had started out as just an annoyance, just an uncomplicated conveying of a silly little chit from one city to another, just another job. When had it become personal? And why? He knew what Durine would have said: It became personal when she tried to have us killed, the big man would say.

But maybe not. People had tried to have them killed before. That was the way it worked for soldiers.

You tried to do it to them first, to do it better, to do it right, but . . .

But there was no need to get angry about it.

Pirojil shrugged. It didn't matter why he was angry, or even that he was angry. What mattered was that the place to take on the baroness was out here, at her mine or whatever it was. The deadfall would take out her guards, or at least some of them, leaving Pirojil and Durine to then slide down the side of the hill to go after the baroness herself, to settle with her.

This was the place; this was the time. Not that it would take much time. Pirojil didn't need much time. He wouldn't explain to her that you didn't send people chasing after somebody that he and Kethol and Durine and Erenor were guarding. He wouldn't explain to her that when you played a game of bones with humans as the pinbones, you had to worry about one of your pieces resenting it. He wouldn't tell her that his life wasn't worth much, but it wasn't hers to take, not while he was serving the Old Emperor's memory, or the Old Emperor's legacy.

No.

If the stones didn't get her, and Pirojil did get to her, it would be just a quick slash to slow her down, and then one thrust to finish her off.

If he lived through that, he could give speeches over the dead body later. The Old Emperor had been fond of that, although Pirojil had never quite found it to his taste. Usually, by the time Pirojil was done killing, he was more in need of a hot bath than a few hot words.

Maybe he would make an exception this time.

Her guard was outside, sitting around the inevitable cookfire, and there was one extra saddled horse in addition to the knacker-ready old beasts in the corral, and the saddle on that horse was all pretty and filigreed.

She was there.

Their flintlock pistols had long since been removed from their oiled skins, and Pirojil was busy repriming the last of them.

No, a pistol wasn't as good as a sword, not for killing, but just the sound of the gunshots would likely panic the horses and send them running. And if you could even disable an enemy with a pistol shot to the sword arm or either leg, that would make him easy meat for the sword, when you got around to him.

Durine carefully fitted another stone into place behind the rotting log they were using as a deadfall. Kick out the stones they'd jammed in front of the log, and it would all happen quicker than a man could die.

There was an argument to not waiting for the baroness to come out, to drop the deadfall now and then go in after her. But Pirojil wanted at least the chance of doing it quickly and neatly, and Durine seemed to read his mind and nodded, his fingers spread in a "let's wait" motion.

And then things all started to happen quickly.

Too quickly.

A quartet of horsemen emerged from the forest over the far hill just as Ellegon's dark shape appeared over the horizon above them, flame issuing from the dragon's mouth to mark the spot in case Pirojil missed it.

Which he didn't.

And if he wasn't—no, he was right. He could recognize Kethol's red hair and his overly stiff way of riding a horse from here, and with Ellegon overhead, that probably meant that he had Walter Slovotsky—yes, it was him.

Durine grinned.

They weren't going to have to deal with the baroness themselves, and while six on five wasn't the best odds he'd ever heard of, they had Ellegon overhead, and while the dragon would be careful to stay out of range of any dragonbaned arrows, he was still—

A smaller, browner dragon limped out of the cave, a spear in its mouth.

Work with somebody long enough, and you end up sharing a mind. Pirojil didn't have to see Durine moving out of the corner of his eye to know that the big man would be going for the left side of the deadfall, trusting that Pirojil would go for the right. He scrabbled across the ground, ignoring the way that rocks chewed at his hands, until his boots reached the rock.

He kicked hard at it with his heel, once, twice, three times, but it didn't move. They had piled too many rocks behind the rotting log, perhaps, or maybe he was more tired than he thought, but the important thing was that the cursed rock wasn't going to move, and that dragon down there *was* going to move.

Could it be harmless, or friendly? He didn't waste a heartbeat on that notion. Ellegon hadn't been lured here to meet a new friend, and the baroness was not only more dangerous than Pirojil had imagined, she was more dangerous than anyone could have imagined.

He kicked hard, harder, then braced himself, back flat on the rocky slope, fingers grabbing for purchase, and pushed.

And failed.

But Durine had more luck, or more strength, and his side of the log began to move, at first barely, but then more and more quickly, until the whole rotting mass of wood slipped away downslope, rocks and rubble tumbling after it.

Chunks of wood fell away as the log rolled and bounced down the slope, but the mass was almost intact as it struck the dragon a glancing blow on the shoulder, and a good third of the rocks hit it in a steady rain that knocked it to the ground.

But the dragon rose and shook itself all over, like a dog drying itself, and craned its neck up toward where Pirojil stood, his hands bloody and empty.

That's right, he thought. *Come to me.* Durine was fumbling with the straps of their rucksack. If he could get to the vial of dragonbane and get it on a knife edge, maybe, maybe, maybe . . .

Maybe they could die, roasted in dragonfire, before the dragon went on to kill Ellegon and their friends.

But wait. That spear in its mouth—the only thing that made sense was that that was coated with dragonbane, too, and if it used its flame it would burn the weapon it intended to use on Ellegon.

I won't let you hurt her. Or me.

Another man perhaps could have reassured it with his mind, or perhaps would at least have tried. But Pirojil wasn't another man, and Durine had coated his sword with the dark oily fluid from the flask and tossed the flask toward Pirojil before he ran, half-stumbling, down the slope toward where the dragon waited below.

Pirojil, trying to do everything at once, stumbled and fell as he went down the slope after Durine, the flask of dragonbane extract bouncing out of his bloody hands. It came to rest on a clump of grass, and he had just retrieved it and started to coat his own blade when Durine reached the bottom and charged the dragon.

He moved quickly for such a big man; if he could only get his sword—

The dragon moved even faster, snakelike, its wings pinioning the air as it backed away, ready to launch itself into the air after Ellegon.

"Fly away," Durine bellowed, daring the dragon with his words as he threatened it with his sword. "Do it: fly away and I'll be rolling her head around the ground like a child's ball when you return. Fly away, and I'll have her guts for garters when you come back. Fly away, and I'll be toasting her heart over a fire and slicing off tasty tidbits."

No. I won't let you hurt her. I won't.* The wind from its wings whipped dust into the air, and sent Durine tumbling back on the hard, rocky ground, his sword flying from his hand.

Pirojil had never seen Durine drop his sword before, ever.

He was never sure whether Durine was already dead when the

dragon lunged forward and its good forepaw crushed the big man to a bloody pulp, as easily as Pirojil could have crushed a raw egg.

It was all clear to Walter, but clarity wasn't the prize here. Survival was the only reward, life was the only medallion, and as the dragon shrugged off the rockslide and then mashed Durine against the hard stone, Durine had lost the prize just as surely as the two of the baroness's guards who had been buried in the rubble.

It was only a matter of moments until the dragon was airborne, and then it would be Ellegon's turn to win or lose the only prize available. But this smaller dragon moved so fast—could it fly faster than Ellegon? With enough of a head start, Ellegon, still wheeling high in the sky, surely could get away, but did he have enough of a head start?

Thirien had kicked Kethol away, and was on his feet, running away. But he wasn't important now.

Ellegon. Go, Walter Slovotsky thought. *Run away. Fly, as fast and as high as you can.*

°It wouldn't do any good,° came back. °It's a crazy one, and it's younger and faster than me. On the ground, yes, I could outrun it. But not in the air. I can't outfly it, and I can't outfight it. I will try to draw it away from the rest of you—°

It was then that Walter Slovotsky heard Erenor muttering words that could only be heard and not remembered: harsh, almost inhumanly guttural sounds that vanished on the ear, like a fat snowflake hissing and dying on a hot frying pan.

While Kethol grabbed at his bow, Erenor stood his ground, alone, his tunic stripped off, leaving his powerfully muscled chest bare, his arms spread wide, obscene syllables spewing from his mouth in a vomitous torrent.

Walter had thought of Erenor as more comical than anything else, but the wizard seemed to grow in dignity as the syllables grew in speed and volume.

And then, in an eye-blink, Erenor was replaced by a dragon.

Yes, Walter Slovotsky's mind told him that it was only a seeming, but Slovotsky had seen seemings before, and this one was different. Better.

The false dragon stood easily half again Ellegon's size, huge and brown, each of its tens of thousands of rippling scales finely detailed, and Walter would have sworn that he could smell the sulfurous reek of its breath as it raised itself up on its tree-trunk hind legs and roared at the other dragon, a roar that was deafening in Walter's mind, not his ears, but nonetheless powerful for that.

It was all that Walter could do to keep control of his sphincter.

Its teeth were jagged yellow swords; its paws thundered against the ground as its wings spread wide, covering half the sky.

The smaller dragon leaped into the air, its wings beating so hard they blurred like a hummingbird's, almost vanishing from visibility as the dragon took flight and launched itself up the slope toward Erenor's seeming, only to be knocked from the air by a small sliver of an arrow launched from Kethol's bow.

It screamed, a horrible, high-pitched sound that rang in Walter's ears and his mind.

And it screamed again, and yet again as two other shafts sprouted from its hide, and it fell to the ground with a thump that almost shook Walter from his feet.

He had to cover his ears. But there was no way he could close his mind to the way the dragon's screams echoed in his mind, and the silent sobbing brought tears to his eyes that could not be washed away.

Please, it said.

And then its massive form shuddered into motionlessness, and its screams faded into a black silence.

What had it been asking for? Slovotsky shook his head. He would never know.

Kethol's face could have been carved from stone as he lowered his bow.

But a scream from a different direction spun him around, as it did Walter Slovotsky.

✧   ✧   ✧

There is a reason that wizards like to stay out of battles. It isn't cowardice, although certainly wizards can be cowards. A Wizard, Walter liked to explain to young soldiers, is like the man on the battlefield with a flamethrower—knowing full well that they would ask him what a flamethrower is.

It isn't that the flamethrower can kill you any more dead than a bullet or a sword or a bolt or an arrow—dead is dead, after all—but the thing about the flamethrower is that it draws attention to itself. Everybody on the other side immediately gets very interested in the future of the person operating the flamethrower.

Or the wizard operating the spell.

Now, Erenor wasn't much of a wizard. Walter had known some powerful ones in his time, and Erenor's tricks and slights and seemings were well done, certainly, but really trivial. After all, it wasn't as though he could have turned himself into a dragon, or called lightning bolts down from the sky, or caused the earth beneath their feet to turn to lava.

It had just been a seeming. Nothing more than that.

Yes, it had turned the tide of battle, it had lured the young dragon into range, leaving Ellegon safely sweeping through the skies above.

But it had just been a seeming.

Still, Erenor was a wizard on a battlefield, and perhaps Thirien didn't know or care that he wasn't much of a wizard, as the huge seeming of a dragon vanished, to leave Thirien standing behind the wizard, Erenor's hair in his hands, the not-much-of-a-wizard's throat quite literally slashed from ear to ear, dark red blood pouring out in a slow fountain.

Healing draughts in your saddlebags, a familiar voice sounded in Walter's head.

Ellegon came in fast and low, just a few feet above the ground, wings spread wide as it swept across the face of the hill, riding in ground effect until one clawed foot snatched Thirien up and away, the dragon's leathery wings now beating hard against the air, taking its prey up and into the sky, leaving little more than a scream behind.

"*Move* it, old man," Kethol shouted as he buried his hands in the wizard's blood.

I'm getting too fucking old for this, Slovotsky thought as he ran for his saddlebags. Everybody else seemed to have at least a half-step on him.

If you'll spend all your energy on running instead of feeling sorry for yourself, you might be able to get Erenor healed up before he bleeds out. Under the circumstances, that might be a nice thing.

Walter Slovotsky ran.

27

✠ Burials

Pirojil surveyed the battlefield. In the end, they were all the same: bodies stinking in the sun.

One of the beat-up old horses had been clawed by the small dragon, its hip slashed to white bone and yellow fat. It limped back and forth as it tried to escape the corral, a slow stream of dark blood pulsing rhythmically down its leg. Pirojil shrugged, and he pulled out his flintlock—the stupid thing might as well be of some use—cocked it, and tracked carefully before he shot the horse through the head.

It whinnied once, then died.

Ellegon loomed over him. *Remind me again why I like humans,* the dragon said.

Maybe it was talking to Pirojil. Or maybe not.

"There's a spade over there," Kethol said. "We can dig a grave for Durine."

"I'll start," Erenor said. If you didn't notice the tremor in his voice or the matching one in his fingers, you would have thought that he was his usual self.

Burying Durine was the right thing to think about. It was practical. It was good to think about practical things right now. And not about the woman cowering in that cave, hoping that they would forget about her.

Or, more likely, covering another spear in dragonbane, to make another try at Ellegon. Not that it would do her any good now, not without a fast young dragon to deliver it.

Ellegon pawed at the ground. °I'll dig his grave, if you'd like,° the dragon said.

Pirojil's jaw clenched so hard he thought his teeth might break. "We bury our own, dragon."

Erenor nodded; after a moment, so did Kethol.

°I thought you might.°

For a moment, Pirojil thought about their cached savings that were strapped to Durine, under the rags and the blood, and how they would need to recover it. He thought that he should be ashamed of himself for thinking such practical thoughts at a moment like this, then he gave a mental shrug.

Gold in the ground never did anybody any good. The ground was the place for dead bodies and growing plants.

And these other bodies?

Pirojil spat. Let them rot in the sun. Let their stink draw the vultures and crows to peck at their eyes.

Pirojil had left enough men lying in the sun to be eaten by carrion birds before.

But he and Kethol would bury Durine themselves.

No: it would be Pirojil, Kethol—and Erenor. The wizard was, for good or ill, one of them now. You bleed enough together and the blood and mind get mixed up as they get mixed together. Pirojil didn't have to like the wizard to recognize that Erenor had made himself Pirojil's companion in arms the moment he raised his arms and drew the attention of an attacking dragon to protect Pirojil and those Pirojil was sworn to protect.

Erenor. Pirojil didn't like having Erenor be one of them, but as usual it didn't much matter what Pirojil did or didn't like.

Erenor. As though Kethol's mindless heroics weren't enough of a problem, Pirojil was now saddled with Erenor. Erenor was no substitute for Durine, for huge, reliable, stolid Durine. Durine, who bore adversity without complaint, who in a fight was better protection for your back than a stone wall. Durine, who had tried so hard and so unsuccessfully not to like Erenor, so that he wouldn't be bothered when Erenor died.

Well, perhaps Durine wouldn't have seen it as a failure. After all, Durine wasn't bothered, because Durine was the one who was dead.

Pirojil smiled for just a moment, declining Walter Slovotsky's inclined-eyebrow request for an explanation with a shake of the head.

It wasn't that Walter Slovotsky wouldn't understand. It was that he *would* understand, he would understand all too easily, and all too well, but Pirojil didn't want him to. You were allowed to keep some things private, even if all you were was an ordinary soldier, and Pirojil was the most ordinary of soldiers.

Hmmm . . . what to do about the body of the small dragon? It looked peaceful lying there, stretched out on the ground. Of all the dead, it was the only one that hadn't voided itself in the dying, and while the air was filled with the shit-stink of death, none of it was from the dragon.

Well, that wasn't Pirojil's problem.

You are not the only one who can take care of his own, Ellegon said.

The massive head eyed the cave opening.

What would be the right punishment? Pirojil thought. As though there could be a proper punishment for what Elanee had done. For what they all had done.

Humans lived a short span of years; dwarves and elves more; but absent being killed—and dragons were notoriously hard to kill— dragons lived, well, they lived a long time . . .

The word you are looking for is "forever." Ellegon's words were coated in cold steel. *She—she and you—she and you and I robbed it of forever.*

The long saurian head ducked briefly, and a river of flame shot out into the cave mouth, quickly drowning out the screams inside.

Yes, the dragon could have made it hurt worse. It could have turned Elanee over to Pirojil, Kethol, and Erenor, and they would have obeyed its instructions, whether they involved a quick thrust of a sword or threading her, anus to mouth, on a stick in front of a fire.

But, in the end, would she have been any deader?

°Make sure she's dead,° Ellegon said as it lumbered toward the body of the fallen dragon, then stood astride it. °I'll count on you for that.°

Pirojil snorted. As though anyone could have survived that fire.

°I am not asking your opinion,° the dragon's mind said, its mental voice inhumanly even. °I am telling you to make certain that she is dead.°

Pirojil nodded. *Understood.*

The dragon had no desire to foul itself by touching the corpse, and Pirojil couldn't quite blame Ellegon for that. Pirojil could finish the baroness off, if it came to that; there was a death warrant in his pouch, signed by the emperor. Perhaps that was why Ellegon had chosen him.

°No. I chose you because you are here.°

It wasn't a warrant that had made Durine and the dragon and Elanee dead, but stone and steel and flame.

°As it always has been, eh?° Ellegon's claws and legs clamped tightly on the dead dragon's torso, dead eyes the size of dinner plates not complaining at all about the snapping and cracking as wing members gave way under the pressure of Ellegon's grip.

And then Ellegon's wings started to beat, hard, and harder, until Pirojil couldn't keep his eyes open and had to close and cover them with his hands to keep the dust out.

As the wind and dust began to ease, he opened his eyes to see Ellegon climbing slowly into the sky, clutching the dead dragon beneath its massive bulk.

Pirojil thought about trying to say something to Ellegon before the dragon got out of range, but instead he just shrugged, and turned away.

28

Uneasy Lies the Head, Part III

The emperor's dreams were light and gentle this night. He was out riding—as he had indeed been that very afternoon—and with this Lady Leria from Keranahan that there had been so much fuss over—as he had indeed been that very afternoon.

Of course, in the dream, he wasn't saddlesore the way he had been at the end of the real ride.

There was nothing at all wrong with that. Dreams were allowed to improve on life, after all. He would be sore enough in the morning, of a certainty—but that would be from his real ride of the afternoon, and not from his one.

Dreams were free.

"Do you get to do this often?" she asked, as she had that afternoon.

"No, not very often at all," he said, as he had said. "Until lately."

"Oh?" In a dream or in real life, it was polite to follow such an opening, particularly if the person leaving you the opening was the emperor. "And why might that be?"

"I think things have finally quieted down," the emperor said.

After all, if you couldn't lie to yourself or to a pretty young woman while you were dreaming, well, then, when could you?

Lady Leria smiled.